Good Sisters

Good Sisters

SINÉAD MORIARTY

SANDYCOVE

an imprint of

PENGUIN BOOKS

SANDYCOVE

UK | USA | Canada | Ireland | Australia
India | New Zealand | South Africa

Sandycove is part of the Penguin Random House group of companies
whose addresses can be found at global.penguinrandomhouse.com.

First published 2024

001

Copyright © Sinéad Moriarty, 2024

The moral right of the author has been asserted

Set in 13.5/16pt Garamond MT Std
Typeset by Jouve (UK), Milton Keynes
Printed and bound in Great Britain by Clays Ltd, Elcograf S.p.A.

The authorized representative in the EEA is Penguin Random House Ireland,
Morrison Chambers, 32 Nassau Street, Dublin D02 YH68

A CIP catalogue record for this book is available from the British Library

ISBN: 978–1–844–88634–0

For good sisters everywhere.
I am lucky to have one.

1. Julie

I sat on the edge of the bath, blocking out the chaos outside. I needed space. I was not ready for this. Then again, are you ever ready to bury your mother?

I dabbed my eyes with another lump of toilet paper, rubbing off the make-up I had applied five times.

My new funeral shoes were already pinching my toes. I should never have let Sophie talk me into buying them. They were too high. My younger sister was all about suffering for fashion, but at forty-nine years of age I craved comfort and lived in trainers or flats.

Louise had told me which of my black dresses was appropriate for our mother's funeral. As the eldest, Louise always seemed to know what to do in every circumstance, so we all just obeyed her. She was smarter than the rest of us put together and impossible to argue with, so we tended simply to follow her directions.

I could hear the triplets slagging each other and Harry shouting at them to 'bloody well behave today'.

Then Tom piped up. 'Come on, guys, it's a really sad day for Mum. She loved Granny.'

Even at just turned eleven years old, my 'baby', Tom, was still sweet and compliant. I knew his hormones would kick in soon and my mere existence would become mortifying to him, so I cherished him all the more.

To be fair, the triplets had tried to be sympathetic about Mum dying. Liam had hugged me for the first time in two years, which, at fifteen, was a big deal for him. Luke had made me a cup of coffee using unblended coffee beans that I'd almost choked on, but it was a sweet gesture. Leo had tried to distract me by telling me all of the messing they had got up to in school without getting caught, which only served to raise my anxiety levels through the roof: I'm permanently convinced they're going to be expelled from their posh school.

Harry was doing his best to be kind, of course, but his fussing about was getting on my nerves.

The only people who totally understood how I was feeling were my sisters and my brother. I just wanted to be with them and Dad. Only we five could understand the pain of losing Mum so quickly.

One minute she was fine, then she had a pain in her back, then she was having chemo, then she died. Seven weeks from the day she went to see her GP to the day she died. It felt like any minute we'd be called back to the hospital and told it was a crazy, stupid mistake and Mum would be standing there, smiling, herself again.

I pressed my hands against my eyes to steady my thoughts. I kept going off on these wild tangents, then having to come back to the awful truth. It hurt like hell every time. We were all reeling from shock as much as from grief. In fact, I wasn't even sure if the grief had arrived yet. I was cold and numb inside but I couldn't tell where shock ended and grief began.

My phone beeped. It was Sophie, posting on our siblings WhatsApp group.

Jack and Jess driving me nuts. How u all?

Gavin typed: *Struggling. Not sure I'll be able to read the prayer.*

Louise typed: *Get it together, we need to be strong for Dad and give Mum the funeral she deserves. I've finished my eulogy. See you all at Dad's in 20 mins. DO NOT BE LATE!!*

I knew that was aimed at me. Time-keeping was not my strong point and Louise was like a Swiss watch – always, without fail, on time.

See you there, I typed. It was important to keep her calm and not bring her wrath upon me. Not today, I couldn't handle it.

Harry knocked gently on the bathroom door. 'Julie, are you ready?'

I stood up and opened the door. There in front of me were Harry and the four boys all dressed in smart clothes. A lump formed in my throat and I welled up.

'You look so nice,' I sobbed.

'Dad!' Liam hissed. 'You said she'd be happy to see us dressed in these loser clothes.'

'I'm putting on my tracksuit.' Leo turned to go.

'No!' I cried out. 'I'm happy – these are happy tears. I love that you all dressed up smartly.'

'Jeez, Mum, it's hard to tell between happy and sad tears. How are we supposed to know which is which?' Luke wanted to know. 'Your eyes are all puffy and red, and you look sad.'

'I am sad, love, but I also appreciate you getting dressed up. I know you hate wearing shirts and chinos and lace-up shoes, but it's important to me.'

'Well, we did it for Granny too. She always said we dressed like hobos,' Leo reminded me.

Mum had been hard on the triplets. I wish they'd seen more of the sweet, loving side she'd shown to Jess, and especially to Clara. She hadn't really known how to connect with my boys. They'd never had the closeness their female cousins had enjoyed with my mother.

'Do I look nice, Mum?' Tom eagerly awaited approval.

'You always look like an angel,' I said.

The triplets made vomiting noises.

Harry put his arm around me. 'Let's go while they're still relatively calm. I'll drop you off at your dad's and take the boys straight to the church.'

I rested my head on his shoulder. 'Thanks.'

'Today will be exhausting. It's awful for you, Julie. I'm here for you, darling.'

'I just can't believe it, Harry.' I welled up again.

'It was very quick, which makes it even harder to take it in. Anne was such an integral part of the family. It'll be a big adjustment for you all.'

He was right. Mum was the glue that had held us all together. What were we going to do without her?

Gavin opened the door before I'd even rung the bell.

'Help!' he whispered.

'What's wrong?'

'Louise is doing my head in. She keeps bossing me and Dad around and snapping at Sophie.'

'It's just her way of processing grief. She's devastated too.'

He rolled his eyes. 'She's hiding it well.'

I stepped into the kitchen and took in the scene. Sophie was sitting down with her head back, holding a tissue against each eye to stop the tears ruining her make-up. Dad was leaning against the countertop, looking shattered. Louise was typing furiously into her phone.

'Hi.'

'You're late,' Louise informed me.

I glanced at the clock. I was two minutes late.

'Told you,' Gavin muttered.

Ignoring her, I turned to Dad and hugged him. 'How are you?'

'Ah, sure, as well as can be expected.'

'We're all here for you, Dad.' I kissed his cheek.

'Thanks, love.' He patted my shoulder.

Louise sighed impatiently and marched out to the front door. 'The undertakers should be here by now,' she huffed.

Dad shook his head. 'She has the poor undertakers tormented.'

I felt Louise was getting a hard time and it was, as it always has been, my job to defend her.

'Every family needs an organizer,' I said.

'Organizer?' Sophie looked up from reapplying her concealer. 'She's like a bloody sergeant major. She ripped my head off when I told her she had a ladder in her tights, even though I had a spare pair in my bag, which I gave her.'

'Just ignore her, she's upset.'

'So am I, Julie!' Sophie said. 'I was closer to Mum than she ever was. And poor Jess is distraught. She was really close to Mum too.'

It wasn't a very nice thing to say, but it was true. Sophie and Mum had always had a tight bond. But, then, in the last few years Mum and Louise had also formed a strong connection. Mum had been amazing with Clara. She was so patient and loving with her. She had become an expert on autism and had helped Louise so much with her young daughter. For the first time in her independent life, Louise had actually leaned on Mum and accepted help from her. It had been lovely to watch them find each other in that way.

I had been close to Mum too. She always called me her 'easy child'. But things had changed after the triplets were born. She stopped calling in to see me. She couldn't handle the boys: they were too boisterous for her. She wanted to sit down over a cup of tea and chat to me, but I could never take my eye off them because, if I did, mayhem would ensue. Mum made it clear that I was welcome to call in to see her on my own, or with Tom. She liked Tom because he was calm.

The triplets always broke and destroyed things when they were in their house, so Mum and Dad had stopped asking us to call in. It was hurtful at first, but as Louise pointed out, Mum had raised four kids and she was older now and just wasn't able for my crazy boys. 'No one is able for them, Julie. They're out of control,' my direct sister had told me.

That's why my nieces, Jess and Clara, were distraught but my boys weren't feeling it as deeply. They were a little upset, but they hadn't had a close relationship with their grandmother in the same way as Jess and Clara, so they weren't hit as hard by her death. I couldn't tell anyone, but it actually added to my own grief. I wished she'd known them better, I wished she'd tried harder with them. But, to be fair, she'd been busy helping out with Jess after Sophie and Jack broke up and then with Clara after her diagnosis. Sometimes, if I'm being honest, I resented it. Mum had invested so much time and effort into her relationships with the girls and very little into my boys. It stung.

I pushed the negative thoughts out of my head. She had been a great mother and a good granny.

'About time,' we heard Louise snap, as she led the undertakers into the living room where the coffin was laid out.

Dad said a final prayer over the closed coffin. Mum had told us to 'nail my coffin shut and put a gorgeous photo of me on top'.

We all placed a hand on the coffin while Dad prayed. His voice broke at the 'Amen' and we all wiped tears from our eyes.

'Goodbye, Anne, you were my one true love. We drove each other mad at times but we were as close as a couple could be and I loved you from the day I met you.'

'Goodbye, Mum,' Sophie sobbed.

'Send us a sign you're okay, if you can,' Gavin said.

Louise rolled her eyes at me and made a face, which made me smile and saved me from giving in to my grief and bawling all over the coffin.

My elder sister and I stood on either side of Dad, linking his arms, holding him up as he said his final farewell.

'At least you're out of pain now, Anne. See you on the other side,' he whispered.

My throat was raw from pressing down my emotions, but I had to be strong for Dad.

We stood in silence as the men, all dressed in black with suitably sombre expressions, carefully manoeuvred the coffin, my mother lying inside, out of the front door and into the hearse.

'The last time she'll ever be here,' Dad said softly.

I gave in and let the tears flow as my lovely mother left her home and her family for the last time.

Louise herded us all into the big black funeral car. I'd seen people driving by in these vehicles many times and wondered who had died and what their story was. Now here we were, our own diminished, grieving family.

Louise and Dad sat behind the driver, Sophie and I in the next row, and Gavin was squashed into the back seat.

'As usual, I get crushed down the back,' he grumbled. 'In the old days the only boy was treated with respect.'

'Thankfully, we've moved out of the dark ages. Now shut up and get in,' Louise ordered.

Sophie fixed my tear-streaked face yet again from her large make-up bag – she must have had fifty products in there. She never left home without it.

While my younger sister tried her best to make me look less awful, Louise ran through the running order of the mass for the hundredth time.

'I hope I don't blubber when I'm doing my reading,' Sophie whispered.

'Me too,' I whispered back.

'Julie!' Louise barked, from the front of the car.

'What?' I said, flinching at her tone.

'Do the boys know exactly what they're doing, when to go up and which bidding prayer they each have to read?'

'Yes, Louise.'

It was only a white lie. I wasn't sure who was supposed to read which. I'd given Liam the longest one because he was the most confident. Tom had the shortest because he was only eleven, and the other two got the rest. Harry had printed out Louise's detailed instructions and said he would make sure they went up at the right time. There was no way I could do it. Since Mum's death three days ago, I hadn't slept. My brain was addled and I was finding it hard to process information. I felt as if I was swimming underwater: sounds were muffled and loud noises made me jump out of my skin. It was a strange combination of being half deaf, but also hyper-alert. Harry had assured me it was a symptom of the shock of losing Mum so quickly.

Thank God Louise had taken the reins and arranged everything because neither Sophie nor Gavin nor I would have done a good job. Poor Dad just wandered around the house like a lost puppy, picking things up and putting them down. We all needed Louise, bossy or not. She was like a machine. While we were all reeling from shock and sobbing into tissues, my super-human older sister had organized the readings, music, priest, organist, undertakers, coffin, hearse, funeral cars, flowers and the funeral booklets. She'd chosen a photo of Mum to put on the front of the booklet that I didn't particularly like. Mum looked very serious in it. I would have preferred one of her smiling – she had a great smile – but I certainly wasn't going to mention that after all Louise's hard work. I also valued my life, and I was afraid I might end up in the coffin with Mum if I criticized anything.

'We're here,' Louise announced, as if we hadn't noticed the church, the hearse and the crowds of people streaming inside to pay their respects.

Sophie squeezed my hand. We climbed out and stood behind the coffin, waiting for the funeral singer to start. It was like a wedding – music, friends and family, good clothes and shoes on – but instead of a bride, we had a corpse.

My shoes were now causing me severe pain. My two little toes were being crushed into oblivion. I was trying to breathe through the throbbing when I felt a poke in the back. I turned to see Marion. 'Hey there.' I gave her a watery smile.

'Hey, yourself. You look like crap.' She hugged me tightly.

'Cheers, Marion.'

'I'm so sorry for your loss. I know your mum never liked me, but still, she liked you, which is what matters.'

'Thanks.' I grinned at my old neighbour and friend. Marion was never one to mince her words.

'Good luck. Funerals are a fucking nightmare. Throngs of old farts queuing up to tell you boring stories about your dead parent. All they really want is to be invited to the free lunch where they will criticize everything about the funeral and your family while stuffing their faces and throwing back the free wine.'

'That's just not true, we've heard some lovely stories about Mum from her friends,' Sophie hissed. Never a fan of Marion, she looked positively allergic to her right now.

Marion shrugged. 'I'll go in before I insult anyone else with my big mouth.'

9

'Probably for the best.' I urged her inside before she caused a scene.

The side door of the church opened and my stepdaughter, Christelle, came out with Clara, who rushed over to her mother.

'What's wrong, darling?' Louise's face melted on seeing her daughter.

'I want to be with you, Mummy. I know you're sad about Granny and I'm sad about Granny. I want to be beside you.'

Christelle put up her hands. 'I tried to get her to stay with me but she insisted and she was getting wound up – her breathing was getting heavy.'

We all knew that hand flapping or a change in Clara's breathing was the precursor to a meltdown. It was a warning sign that meant red alert. Christelle was so sweet with her.

'It's okay, Christelle, thanks. Clara can stay with me.' Louise held her daughter's hand, but Clara pulled it away.

'No, Mummy. Your hand's hot and wet.'

Louise let go immediately and placed her hand gently on her nine-year-old's shoulder. 'Is that okay?' she asked.

Clara nodded.

Christelle shuffled over to me. 'In other news, Leo has split his pants at the back so he can't do the bidding prayer, but don't worry, I'll do it instead.'

I loved my stepdaughter even more than usual at that moment. I mouthed, 'Thank you,' as she winked and disappeared back into the church.

'I'll walk with Dad and Clara, then you and Sophie, and Gavin at the back,' Louise barked.

'The loser on his own, again,' Gavin grumbled.

Once Louise's back was turned, Sophie and I linked arms with our younger brother and squashed him between us.

We all walked slowly up the aisle behind our mother's

coffin as a soloist sang 'The Soft Goodbye'. It was beautiful and haunting.

My heart broke as I finally accepted that Mum was gone, that there had been no terrible mistake, that this was goodbye. And I knew I'd never be quite the same again.

2. Louise

Clara pulled off her headphones. 'It's so loud, Mummy. I can hear the music through these,' she complained.

I was worried that the funeral would overwhelm her and lead to a meltdown. I had to keep her calm. Keeping my voice soft and low, I tried to reassure her. 'I know, darling, but there are only three more songs to go. I'll tell you when to put the headphones back on. Now do your breathing – in for four, hold for two and out for four.'

I breathed in and out with her and, as she followed my lead, I saw her fists begin to unclench. I couldn't manage a meltdown today – there was too much going on, too much to organize and oversee. I was hanging on by a thread and I needed to focus on my eulogy and do Mum proud.

The priest announced the bidding prayers. I nodded at Harry. He jumped up and led two of the triplets, Tom and then Christelle up to the altar. Why was Christelle going up? Why was Leo or Liam or Luke – I could never tell them apart – not going up? I had given Julie strict instructions. I had laid it all out in black and white. I had created a spreadsheet. All she had to do was get her sons to read a few lines, but somehow even that wasn't possible with this lot. Could they ever just bloody well do what they were told?

The triplet left behind tried to trip Tom as he shuffled out of the bench on his way to the altar. Tom almost landed on his face, but Christelle managed to catch him by the belt and lead him away. She truly was a wonder. Harry's teenage-holiday one-night stand had produced an incredible young woman we all loved. She was wonderful with Clara and had helped me enormously in those first few years after the diagnosis when she had minded Clara while I was at work.

I suddenly had a flashback to Mum and me sitting in the kitchen. Mum was leaning over her cup of Earl Grey – I could almost smell the distinct scent of her favourite tea, the memory was that vivid. In her usual blunt way Mum had told me she was very suspicious of Christelle. How did we know she was really Harry's long-lost daughter? Some random eighteen-year-old girl with multiple piercings turns up out of the blue and Julie and Harry don't even do a DNA test? It was utter lunacy . . .

'But that's your sister, always a soft touch, embracing this girl as if she's her own flesh and blood. I don't know, Louise. I just don't want to see my Julie taken advantage of. If it was you or me, we'd have every test available done to prove paternity.'

Mum had been slow to embrace Christelle, but once she saw how fantastic she was with the triplets and Tom, then with Clara, she had softened and fallen for her just like the rest of us. She always said, 'Christelle is lucky to have Julie as a stepmum. Julie is by far the most open and welcoming of all my children. She's not tough like you.'

I wasn't sure if that was meant as a compliment or an insult. But that was Mum: she had no filter and always gave you her opinion, whether it was asked for or not.

I forced my mind back to the church, to the here and now. Thankfully, the boys read their prayers well – their posh school was obviously rubbing off on them – and they spoke clearly and distinctly. Christelle read the last prayer and the boys managed to go back to their seats without wrestling each other.

A few minutes later, Jess and Sophie went up to read a

poem together. Jess's dress was ridiculously short – you could almost see the cheeks of her bum. Sophie really should have made her daughter wear something more appropriate. I don't know how Jess was able to see the text with the false eyelashes she was wearing either. Why did teenage girls make themselves up like drag queens? Jess was beautiful, but it was hard to see it under all the fake tan, make-up and fake eyelashes that you could have swept the floor with. Mum would have had a few words to say seeing Jess so 'dickied-up' as she called it. She liked her to look natural and didn't understand why her granddaughter plastered her lovely face with make-up and wore clothes that were 'only fit for a street-walker'.

Sophie's voice wobbled, but she got through it with Jess's help. Jess held her mother's hand as they walked back, crying, and sat down. I felt a small pang of envy. Clara would only hold my hand if it was the right temperature and completely dry, which was rare enough. Still, she allowed me to hug her, which I loved. Mum, Christelle, Gavin and I were the only people she'd allow to hug her. Now there were only three of us.

I glanced at Dad, who was staring straight ahead, still shell-shocked. It was our job to mind him now. I'd have to do up a rota of dinners and visits so he didn't feel alone.

I heard the first note of the organ and told Clara to put on her headphones.

From the front row we could see everyone coming up to take communion. Pippa walked up, holding Robert's hand. He was a gorgeous-looking little boy. Sophie bristled beside me. Pippa, Jack's ex-girlfriend and mother of Sophie's step-son Robert, was an enormous thorn in my sister's side.

'Who wears a skin-tight red dress to a funeral?' she whispered.

'It's burgundy, to be fair,' I said.

'Bit of a MILF,' Gavin said.

'Shut up,' Sophie grumbled.

'It was nice of her to come,' Julie said.

'She only came because she's dumping Robert on us today for two weeks while she goes away with her new boyfriend.'

'Again?' Julie whispered.

Sophie nodded.

'But you've had him for the last month,' Julie said.

'She's spent two days with him and now she's off again. She fought so hard for shared custody yet Robert is with us ninety per cent of the time. It's a joke, but Jack never says boo to her because she's so bloody volatile.' Sophie shook her head.

'Poor little kid. He's such a cutie, how could she not want to spend more time with him?' Julie wondered.

'Because she's a selfish, self-centred bitch,' Sophie muttered.

'That's ridiculous. Jack needs to sort that out. She has to adhere to the custody ruling,' I reminded her.

Sophie sighed. 'I know that, Louise, but Pippa is not some-one you can reason with.'

I bit back what I really wanted to say, which was: For good-ness' sake, could Jack not grow a pair of balls and stand up to his ex-girlfriend? It wasn't fair that Sophie was raising Pippa's child. What I did say was: 'Get your lawyer involved, then.'

'Jack wants to keep it as amicable and peaceful as possible for Robert.'

'Well, it's clearly not working.' I stated the obvious.

'Pippa is extremely difficult to manage, Louise. It's not black and white.'

'Guys, can we focus on Mum for now?' Gavin said, shoot-ing us a warning look.

The music ended and I told Clara she could take her head-phones off. It was time for my eulogy.

I had chaired conferences all over the world. I did pitches and presentations weekly. I had won all of the top debating prizes at university in England. I felt confident that I was the person best equipped to give this eulogy. We hadn't even needed to discuss it as a family – everyone had just immediately looked at me when the eulogy was mentioned. I wanted to do a good job for us all. I felt calm and composed as I strode towards the altar and stood behind the microphone.

'Good morning, everyone. We, the Devlin family, would like to thank you all for coming out today to pay your respects to Mum. She would have been delighted to see so many friends and family here to say goodbye and it is very comforting for us to see how loved she was.

'Mum was a no-nonsense woman who devoted herself to raising her four children, supporting her husband and creating a lovely home.

'Mum and Dad met fifty-three years ago at a dance and had been together ever since. We got to celebrate their fifty-second wedding anniversary with her in hospital, with cake and champagne. It was a very special day for all of us.

'They had a happy marriage. I won't lie and say there weren't any disagreements, but they were always resolved quickly and they were devoted to each other.

'Mum loved us four unconditionally, even when we were hard to love, but she was tough too. She never let us wallow when things went wrong, always told us to buck up and keep going. She said some days you just have to keep putting one foot in front of the other until you get through a difficult time. She was a very wise woman.

'But it was as a grandmother that Mum really excelled. She loved her grandchildren. She lit up when they were around her and was absolutely incredible with my daughter, Clara. Her patience and devotion to Clara were so . . .'

Oh, God. Keep it together, Louise, come on now. Control your voice. But I couldn't stop it.

I didn't stumble over my words, I didn't sniffle or sob. I completely lost it. Emotion bubbled up and exploded out of me.

Tears cascaded down my face as the memory of Mum holding me in the park that day, shortly after Clara was diagnosed as being on the autism spectrum, sprang into my mind. I saw her sitting patiently with Clara as she read her bird book over and over. I saw her hugging Clara – one of the few people Clara allowed to hug her. I saw her sitting outside the door of Clara's bedroom when Clara had a meltdown, crying silently as she felt her granddaughter's pain.

I couldn't catch my breath, but then I felt a hand on my shoulder. It was Julie. 'It's okay, I've got you,' she whispered. Handing me a tissue, Julie took my notes and finished my eulogy.

'Her patience and devotion to my daughter were humbling to see. I got to know her in a different way. I got to know my mother on a much deeper level and I truly saw how selfless and compassionate she was. Her loss has left a huge hole in all our lives and we are going to miss her so much.'

Julie finished by thanking everyone who needed to be thanked and inviting everyone back to the golf club for lunch.

She turned and hugged me.

'Thanks,' I said. I was furious and deeply disappointed in myself. I hadn't done my job. I hadn't honoured Mum properly. Grief had just hit me like a tsunami. I fought back the tears.

'You're welcome.' As if reading my mind Julie added, 'And don't you dare beat yourself up about this. You are human, Louise. You have feelings like everyone else and it's good to let them out occasionally.'

I sniffled into a handkerchief. 'What am I going to do without her, Julie? She was so good with Clara. Mum was one of the only people in the world who really understood her.'

'I know, but look at it this way. Clara had her granny for almost ten years. That's a lot. Mum's love is in her heart. She'll always have her precious memories.'

I began to cry again. 'Jesus, stop. I need to get a grip here. We have a lunch to host. We need to look after Dad.'

Julie put her hands on my shoulders. 'Louise, our mum died. We're sad. We're grieving. You hadn't cried until now, and it was freaking me out. This is normal, this is healthy. I'm delighted you broke down. You need to let it out.'

I smiled at her. The middle sister, the peacemaker, the one I was closest to. 'Well, don't get used to it. The emotions are going right back inside now, under lock and bloody key.' I dabbed my eyes and went to sit down as the priest said a final prayer. Clara reached over and patted my knee. I yearned to hold her hand but knew I mustn't.

We stood up and walked down the aisle to the heartbreaking sound of a soloist singing Mum's favourite song, Leonard Cohen's 'Hallelujah'. Clara was beside me with her headphones on. Dad was on my other side, head bowed as we followed the coffin out of the church.

I exhaled deeply, trying to prepare myself for the flow of mourners lining up to shake our hands and talk to us. Clara's small hand slipped into mine. I was so grateful. I needed her touch.

'I wish Granny wasn't gone,' Clara shouted, forgetting she had her headphones on.

'Me too, sweetheart.'

We stood outside the church on an overcast day and let the love, compassion and empathy of family and friends wash over us and carry us through as we said our final farewell to our lovely mum and began life without her.

3. Sophie

Pippa stood in the car park of the golf club and handed Jack a bag of clothes for Robert. I had no doubt that half of them would be dirty and need washing and ironing. She'd never been mother of the year, but over the past six months Pippa had really let things slide.

She crouched down and hugged her son goodbye.

'Be good for Daddy.'

'He always is. He's the best boy.' Jack's voice was cold.

'I'll see you in two weeks, Robert.' Pippa ignored Jack.

'Where are you going, Mummy?'

'On a little holiday, sweetie.'

'Again?' Robert's face fell.

'Don't make a fuss, sweetie, I'll be back soon. Doesn't Mummy deserve a break?'

'Yes, Mummy.' He looked crestfallen.

Little holiday, my arse. And holiday from what exactly? She barely seemed to be working, after being replaced by a younger presenter on her TV styling slot, and Robert spent most of his time with us. But apparently the poor thing was worn out and needed two weeks in Mallorca sitting on her backside drinking cocktails while Jack and I, once again, juggled work and having to leave early to pick up Robert from school. Adding a young child changed the whole routine of our house and it certainly wasn't easy.

I'd thought that when Pippa and Jack had agreed to shared custody, things would smooth over. I was happy to have Robert 50 per cent of the time: he was a sweet child and Jess doted on her little half-brother. But I had not bargained for raising my stepson almost full-time. I had a busy job and a tricky teenage daughter on my hands. Jack and I were still finding each other again after a four-year separation, and being a couple was much more difficult when there was a little boy in the next room who had regular nightmares and needed his dad's reassurance and attention. I didn't mind that Robert called for Jack, but we needed time and space to connect properly as well, and that had to take a back seat whenever Robert was there. It was hard for Jess too. She was getting used to her mum and dad being back together and now she had a little brother living in the house. I really wanted things to be calm at home for all of us, not unpredictable and messy.

'We'll have great fun, buddy,' Jack said. 'I'll take you to the Aqua Park on Saturday.'

'Yay!' Robert cheered.

I frowned. I was running a fashion show on Saturday. I'd told Jack I needed him there to keep an eye on Jess. I didn't like her being unsupervised at weekends. If she went to the park with the groups of teens I saw hanging about the place, she might start drinking, or vaping, or both. I wanted one of us always around to check up on her.

I'd deal with it later. I didn't have the headspace for it today. I needed to get back inside to the lunch and listen to stories about Mum, look after Dad and avoid Louise, who was driving everyone nuts. After her major wobble during the eulogy, she was now on a mission to show everyone how together she was, so she was bossing the poor golf-club staff around like an army general on manoeuvres.

'I'm off now,' Pippa said. 'By the way, can you make sure to check Robert's hair for nits? I got a message from the school that they're doing the rounds in his class.' She swished around, her cashmere camel coat floating behind her, climbed into her car and drove off without a backward glance.

I looked down at Robert who, sure enough, was scratching his head. I sighed. Could this day get any worse?

'I'm bored, Daddy,' Robert said. 'Can we go home now? Please?'

Jack glanced up at me. 'I'm so sorry, Sophie, but it's been a long day for him. Would you mind if I brought him home? Will you be okay without me?'

We hadn't even got as far as dessert. I wanted Jack to stay, to be at my side for the whole lunch. I wanted my husband with me and his heartbroken daughter on this awful day. I wanted Pippa to have the decency to look after her own son on the day of my mother's goddamn funeral. But none of that had happened. It had been a long day for the little boy, and I knew if he started acting up it would be a drag for everyone, so I said, 'It's fine, take him home.'

I walked them outside the restaurant and gave Robert a kiss and a hug so he knew I wasn't angry with him.

'Thanks, darling,' Jack said, squeezing my hand. 'I'll have a bath and a large gin and tonic waiting for you when you get home. Text me when you're on the way.'

'That sounds great, thanks.'

Jack kissed me and headed off with Robert, hand in hand. As I turned to go back into the lunch, I saw Gavin's girl-friend, Shania, sitting on a couch outside, cradling a cup of tea between her hands. 'Are you okay?' I asked.

'Yes, fine. Just a bit tired,' she said. 'The baby is kicking a lot and I needed to sit down for a minute. And if I'm, like, totally honest, I'm hiding from Gavin. He is determined to introduce me to every single cousin and relation in there. You guys have a crazy amount of relations. It's a lot.'

I sat down beside her. 'You poor thing. Our family can be

overwhelming. Jack found it hard in the beginning too. He could never remember all our uncles' and aunts' names. Seven siblings on Mum's side and eight on Dad's. It's definitely overwhelming.'

'Yeah, totally. I'm from a small family, so this is very different.'

'Are you feeling OK generally?'

She nodded. 'Just tired all the time. I'm hoping now I'm in the second trimester I'll get my energy back. Work is, like, super-busy so I need to be on my A-game. We've just signed a massive deal with the US to distribute my fake tan in all of the Walmart stores, so it's, like, a really big deal. I'll have to travel over as much as I can, before I get too big.'

I shook my head. This girl was unbelievable. When we'd first met her, we'd thought she was just another of Gavin's flings. Dad thought she was from America because of her mid-Atlantic drawl. Mum thought she was 'for the birds' and that she was 'too flighty for our Gavin'. Turns out we were all wrong, so wrong.

When she had set up her fake-tan brand four years ago, we all thought it was a 'little project', but she had turned it into a huge success in Europe and now she was planning to conquer the US. Shania had turned out to be a savvy and hard-working businesswoman.

'Seriously, Shania, that is incredible.'

'Well, having my whizz of an accountant dad helping me has been key in growing the business.'

'Let's not forget your fourteen-hour workdays and your great product. Gavin really landed on his feet with you. I hope my brother is being supportive.'

'OMG, he so is. He literally does everything for me. I couldn't do this without him. He's my personal assistant and my rock.'

'Good. You need support – you work so hard.'

'Yeah, but when you love what you do it doesn't feel like work.' She smiled.

I liked what I did, but did I love it? No. Did it feel like work? Yes. In the early days, dealing with the young models had been challenging, but I was up for it. I was good at encouraging them, boosting their bruised egos after rejection, getting them buzzed before fashion shows and shoots . . . I got it, I'd been there. I'd been a young, naïve, clueless model, so I knew what it felt like. But lately some of the girls coming in had seemed so entitled, needy and over-sensitive. They expected everything to be handed to them on a plate. If they were rejected for a brand deal, a campaign or a runway show, they'd have a full breakdown in my office, then need to take a few days off to 'recover from the hurtful rejection', to 'regroup', to 'meditate', to 'nurture my crushed self-esteem', to 'cleanse the negative energy from my personal space' . . . It was relentless and utterly irritating.

Models were rejected on a daily basis. It was part of the job. I was very upfront about that when I signed them. I always told them that being rebuffed was a large part of a model's life. If you can't handle it, don't sign the contract.

I'd stuck with the job because we needed the money. But even now that Jack was back in a well-paid job with his bankruptcy behind him, I would still never give up work. I would never again put myself in a position where I relied only on his salary. I'd learned the hard way how important it was for me to earn money too. I was absolutely determined that Jess would never make the mistakes I'd made by being completely dependent on her husband. She needed to earn her own money. She needed to have security in her life and never, ever end up on the floor, penniless, like I had.

'There you are, Shania!' Gavin's head appeared around the corner. 'I've been looking everywhere for you. Are you okay?'

Shania smiled up at him. 'I'm fine, babe, just needed a little break.'

He helped her up and kissed her. Turning to me he said, 'You have to come in, Soph. You have to see the way some of the women are flirting with Dad. They're shameless. At Mum's funeral!'

'What? You're kidding me?'

Who were these women, and did they have no respect? Mind you, Mum had always told us that when a wife died, which was rare as mostly the husbands died first, the widower was always mobbed. He was fair game and the numbers were in his favour. Seventy per cent of the golf-club members over the age of seventy-five were women. A freshly single man was manna from Heaven. It was every woman for herself. It was dog eat dog to see who could get their claws into a new widower first. Mum had chuckled and said it was like watching lionesses hunting an innocent antelope. It had been funny when it was about someone else, but now it was my dad and my mum and it wasn't remotely funny.

I marched in and headed straight towards Dad, who was backed up against a wall as some woman, with silver-grey hair blow-dried like a helmet, talked at him.

'I'll drop a casserole in to you tomorrow. You won't go hungry, George. We'll play golf next week. I'll book it all and let you know. Don't you worry, George. I'm here for you.'

I elbowed my way between them. 'Dad won't need any casseroles. We'll be looking after his meals.' I gave her my best fake smile.

'Oh, George, is this one of your beautiful daughters?' the silver vixen asked.

'Yes, this is my youngest, Sophie.'

'Lovely to meet you, Sophie. I'm Daphne, a great friend of your mother and father.'

Really? I wanted to ask. Then how come I've never heard of you?

What I said was, 'You must be devastated about Mum, then.'

'Oh, yes. Anne was a lovely woman.'

'Yes, she was. Herself and Dad had a wonderful marriage. We're all heartbroken.'

She made fake-sympathy noises and refused to move away.

I decided to opt for the blunt approach. 'I need to speak to my father alone.'

The shameless cow lunged at Dad, giving him a kiss on both cheeks, marking him with her awful pink lipstick.

I yanked him by the arm away from her.

'Who in the name of God is she?' I asked.

'I don't really know. I've met her a few times, but I didn't remember her name.'

'She certainly knows you. She was all over you.'

'Ah, she was only being nice.'

'Nice? Dad, she practically had her tongue down your throat, the pushy cow.'

'Jesus, Sophie, steady on.'

'There'll be lots more where she came from too. Single men are a target here and you're not bad-looking or too banjaxed for your age.'

'Don't hold back, Sophie, tell me what you really think.' Dad shook his head. 'You're overreacting, pet.'

'I'm not. Seriously, Dad, you'll be beating the women off with a stick. You're completely outnumbered.'

As if on cue, Dolores, Mum's choir friend, a busty woman a good ten years younger than Dad, came rushing over and threw her arms around him, 'George, my poor, poor George.'

'She might smother him with those breasts.' Gavin had sidled up beside me. 'They're huge, even bigger than Shania's, and hers are like watermelons since she got pregnant.'

We stifled a giggle. It was good to laugh. I felt some of the tension in my stomach recede. It had been such an awful time, watching Mum fade away into nothing, saying goodbye to her as she slowly died before our eyes. We were all completely drained, emotionally and physically.

'What are you laughing about? Please tell me. I need a laugh.' Julie nestled in beside us.

'Guys.' Louise's voice made us jump. 'You can't all stand together in a huddle. You need to mingle.'

'It's not a cocktail party, Louise,' I snapped. 'It's Mum's funeral lunch. We can talk to whoever we bloody want.' I'd had enough of her bossing us all around.

'Mum would want us to chat to her family and friends, Sophie.'

'She couldn't stand most of her family and, in case you hadn't noticed, a lot of her so-called friends are trying to throw the leg over Dad.'

'What? Are you serious?' Julie was clearly appalled.

'Yes, Julie, look over there right now.' I pointed to where Dad was trying to extricate himself from the vice-like grip of Dolores.

'How can she? How can they? Poor Mum. Have they no respect?' She welled up.

Louise drank deeply from her wine glass. 'A single, heterosexual man in a golf club is like the Hope Diamond.'

'Women of a certain age are scary.' Gavin watched in awe as Dolores clung to Dad's arm.

'She needs to back the hell away. I will not have my mother disrespected.' Louise's jaw was set. Uh-oh . . . She marched off towards Dad and the unsuspecting Dolores.

'We need popcorn for this,' Gavin said, and I thumped his arm.

Out of the corner of my eye I saw the triplets picking up a bottle of wine from one of the tables and sneaking to the back of the room to drink it. I spun around, looking for Jess. Thankfully, she was nowhere near them. She was sitting with Clara and Tom playing cards. She was so sweet with her younger cousins, it warmed my heart. As tricky as she was at the moment, pushing all the teenage boundaries, the sweet Jess was still in there. She had been a rock to me today.

I decided not to tell Julie about the wine. I'd go over and get it from them. Julie didn't need to be worried about her sons getting drunk at her mother's funeral.

Julie and Gavin were watching wide-eyed as Louise reached Dad and tapped Dolores firmly on the shoulder.

'Excuse me,' she said. 'My father needs to be with his family at this terrible time. He does not need to be harassed by women looking to replace my mother before she is even cold in her grave.'

'I beg your pardon?' Dolores spluttered.

'Back away, Dolores. Now is not your time. Mum was a very special woman and we miss her. We want her memory to be honoured and we need space to process our loss and grieve. So, back away and leave Dad alone. Have some respect. Mum is . . . Mum was . . . she . . .' Louise began to cry again. Before today, I hadn't seen her cry since Clara's diagnosis. And before that was when she was fifteen and came second in a national debating competition. She still claims it was a fix.

Julie rushed over, put her arm around Louise and led her away, mouthing, 'Sorry,' to Dolores. I didn't think Dolores deserved a sorry, but that was Julie, always nice to everyone.

I went over and linked Dad's arm. 'How are you holding up, Dad?'

'I just can't believe she's really gone,' he whispered. 'We drove each other mad at times but she was my Anne. I can't remember life without her. My lovely Anne.'

'Oh, Dad, I know.' I kissed his cheek.

Would I feel this level of grief if Jack died, I wondered. The thing was, I could remember life without him. I remembered life without him very well. I remembered our terrible break-up, then him meeting and shacking up with Pippa. I remembered all of the pain and heartache. It was still clear in my mind. Would I feel bereft if Jack passed away? I wasn't sure. I loved him, but there was a lot of hurt and mistrust in our past. And because of Robert, we were stuck with Pippa in our lives, a constant reminder of our years apart.

Mum and Dad had had fifty-three years of constancy. Ups and downs, to be sure, but consistent support, love and respect. It was true love in its raw and honest form.

We'd all have to rally around Dad to help him through. No doubt Louise would have an Excel spreadsheet drawn up for us, but we also needed to give him the space to grieve and feel, to sit and cry or stare at the wall.

I glanced at my watch. It was almost six o'clock. I hoped people would start heading home soon. I was exhausted and had nothing left to give. I prayed Jack would follow through on his promise of a hot bath and a gin and tonic.

4. Julie

I drove into the school car park and squeezed my electric car between two oversized brand-new Range Rovers. I got out, opened the boot and heaved out the boys' backpacks and sports kits. Plonking the bags on the ground, I looked around for the triplets. No sign of them.

I wrenched the back door of the car open. Heads bent together, they were looking at some TikTok video.

'GET OUT!' I roared. 'You lazy, ungrateful, useless lot.'

'Jeez, Mum, calm down,' Leo grumbled.

'Why are you going mental?' Luke asked.

'You're always narky these days,' Liam added.

'Leave Mum alone. She's sad about Granny,' Tom, my little pet, said.

'Still?' Liam seemed surprised.

Apparently there was a time limit to grief.

'In fairness, Mum, it's been a while. I know it's hard, but I'm just wondering how long you think you're going to be narky for,' Luke said.

'Are we talking days, weeks or months?' Leo was all about the details.

'I don't bloody know,' I hissed. 'But I'd be a lot less grumpy if you all helped a bit more. I'd be less irritated if you took your faces out of your bloody phones and got your own bags out of the boot.'

'No one asked you to do it,' Liam said.

'Yeah, like, if you'd waited ten seconds, we'd have done it.'

'It's not a big deal, Mum, chill.'

30

'Chill? *Chill?* My mother died five weeks ago and everyone seems to expect me to put it behind me and move on. I will not chill now, or probably for a long time, so get your lazy arses out of the car and go to school.'

'Jeez, okay.'

'No need to freak out.'

'No need to rip our heads off.'

The triplets picked up their backpacks and kitbags and headed into the senior school building. Tom picked up his bag and headed in the other direction, to the junior school. But then he turned and ran back towards me. He hugged me.

'I know you're still sad about Granny. I'm sorry, Mum. I'll try to help you more.'

I crouched down. 'Tom, you are always sweet and helpful. I love you.'

'I love you too,' he whispered quietly into my ear, making sure no one could hear him.

As he walked off, I began to cry again. I was like a tap. Once I started crying, I couldn't stop, and I cried a lot. I was still feeling hurt that the boys weren't more upset about Mum. Sophie and Louise kept saying how their daughters were heartbroken, whereas my lot were fine. I wished they'd known her better. I wished she'd spent more time with them, but it was too late now. She'd never know them and, although they drove me absolutely nuts, they were my pride and joy. They were growing into fine young men and she was missing it all.

I fumbled in my bag for my keys.

'Julie?'

Oh, for the love of Jesus, no. Not her. Not now. I ignored her.

'Julie.' She tapped me on the shoulder.

I roughly wiped my eyes with the sleeve of my hoodie and

turned to face an immaculately groomed Victoria Carter-Mills. Perfectly applied subtle make-up, glossy blow-dried hair and a beige cashmere coat that I wanted to wrap around me, like a soft hug.

'Yes?' I wasn't in the mood for small-talk or any of Victoria's usual digs about the triplets being rowdy hooligans who were unfit for this posh school. She was a poisonous snake and the last person I wanted to see right now.

'Have you heard anything about when the Junior Cup team is being picked? With three boys involved, I thought you might have some insight. Sebastian says he doesn't know and Mr Long isn't returning my calls or replying to my texts.'

Mr Long, the rugby coach, was like a brick wall. He gave nothing away. Even the formidable Victoria couldn't harass him into giving her any information. Go, Mr Long, I thought, mentally high-fiving him.

'No, I haven't.'

'Well, could you call him and see if you can get any insight?'

'No.'

'Excuse me?'

'No, I will not call him. He'll tell us when he's ready to tell us.'

Victoria tried to frown, but because of the Botox and fillers, her eyes just squinted a bit. 'There's no need to be so curt about it. It's just one phone call. Really and truly, I'm not asking you to climb Mount Everest.'

Unfortunately for Victoria, she was the straw that finally broke the camel's back. All the pushed-down rage and grief and exhaustion I'd been desperately trying to work around in order to be 'normal' rose up and spurted out of me.

'Let me put it this way, Victoria. First, I wouldn't call Mr Long if you paid me a million euro because he doesn't need pathetic, overambitious, delusional parents hounding him to find out if their kid is on the team. He will tell us when he's good and ready. Harassing him before then is only going to piss him off. Second, my mother died a few weeks ago and I'm still reeling. I'm barely holding it together. So can you please get the hell out of my face? I strongly suggest you step away or I may accidentally run you over.'

Victoria's face darkened. 'You are the rudest woman. No wonder your children are feral. I'm sorry about your mother, but that does not give you the right to be so uncouth.'

Ignoring her, I got into the car, slammed the door and hurtled out of the car-park space. Victoria had to jump sideways to avoid being run over. But instead of feeling victorious and delighted that I'd stood up to the viper, I was crying again. I felt lost, at sea and guilty. I was shouting at my kids because I was so sad and they weren't sad enough – it was completely unreasonable. I had barely cooked since Mum died and kept ordering in family dinners. I didn't work: being a mum was my job and I wasn't even doing that. I could barely drag myself out of bed in the mornings. All I wanted to do was stay in bed, look at old family photos and cry. I knew I should be moving on: five weeks was quite a long time. The sympathy cards had stopped arriving, the flowers had long since shrivelled up, but I seemed to be getting worse. My emotions were all over the place. How long did grief last? Was there a finite timeline? Was I just weak and overemotional?

I got home, crawled back into bed, watched videos of Mum last Christmas, in the full of her health, and sobbed.

That Sunday Louise had summoned us all to the house. She had decided that it was time to clear out Mum's things and not leave it to Dad.

I was sitting in my kitchen, at the marble counter, which

still made me feel slightly nauseous when I thought how much it had cost, drinking a strong coffee and trying to psych myself up for the day ahead. I was dreading going through Mum's things. I knew it would bring up so many emotions. Sophie, Gavin and I wanted to wait, but Louise was adamant that we do it this weekend. My big sister was channelling her grief via spreadsheets, rotas and clear-outs, and none of us had the energy to fight her.

Harry was reading *Winning!* by Clive Woodward. He was some English rugby coach who had won a rugby World Cup or something and Harry was obsessed with the book. He had a highlighter pen and kept underlining passages and reading them out to me, which made me want to poke my eyes out.

'Julie, listen to this.' Harry's eyes were shining. '"Concentrate on measuring performance and winning will take care of itself." The man is a genius.'

It seemed like a pretty obvious statement to me, but I just nodded. If I showed a modicum of interest, Harry would probably start reading out chapters and I couldn't take it. He was keen to learn as much technical detail as he could about rugby – playing, strategy, skills, training techniques – so he could chat to the other dads on the sidelines with confidence. In typical Harry fashion, he didn't just leaf through *The Idiot's Guide to Rugby*, he immersed himself in the entire subject. He had spent the past few months reading about the game, watching matches and, frankly, becoming a bit of a rugby bore.

At the matches, while Harry banged on about whatever statistic he'd just done a degree in, I usually tuned him out. When we went to watch the boys play, the only thing I cared about was the triplets' safety. I spent my time holding my breath in case they got injured. In the last twelve months alone, we'd had two broken arms, one fractured foot, three concussions and endless black eyes, cuts and bruises. I'd tried to persuade the triplets to play tennis instead, but they'd laughed at me and said tennis was for losers.

This was going to be a big year for them as they were all hoping to get onto the Junior Cup rugby team. So now, as well as praying they didn't get injured, I was also praying that they all got picked for the team. Leo was the one who was the least sure to get on as another guy played the same position and was as good as, if not better than, him. If the other two got picked and he didn't, he'd be crushed. I'd rather none of them were picked than just two. I felt sick thinking of poor Leo on the sideline while the others played.

As Harry was about to read out another golden nugget from his book, the kitchen door burst open. 'Water! I think I'm dying.' Marion stumbled in, hair all over the place and mascara streaks down her cheeks.

'You look rough.' I grinned.

'I got in at four. I'm too old for this shit. Dating is a fucking nightmare.'

'Morning, Marion, language, please,' Harry said, gesturing towards Tom, who was in the corner quietly finishing a huge bowl of Cheerios.

'Sorry, I can't help it. I've always sworn like a drunken sailor.'

'Try harder,' Harry said.

I handed her a large glass of water and two paracetamol.

'You're an angel. Honestly, I don't know what I'd do without you. You house me and you give me drugs.' Marion swallowed the tablets.

Marion had been staying with us one weekend a month, when her ex-husband, Greg, flew back from Dubai to see the kids. Harry wasn't particularly enthusiastic about this arrangement. Even when we used to live next door to her,

Harry had found Marion 'a lot to take'. But she had been there for me. When the boys were small and I was struggling, Marion had been a lifeline. With four kids of her own, she understood the long days and the feeling of being completely overwhelmed. We had been each other's support network and had become firm friends. I had insisted we help her out after her separation.

Besides, since we'd bought this huge house with the money Harry's aunt had left him, we'd converted the basement into a two-bedroom apartment for Christelle. She was happy for Marion to stay in the second bedroom once a month. Christelle thought Marion was nuts, but in a good way, and besides, Christelle was going travelling soon so the place would be empty.

'It was your daughter and Kelly who led me astray last night,' Marion told Harry.

'What?' Harry looked up from his book.

I saw Tom slip out of the room. Thank goodness: Marion's stories tended to be X-rated.

'Well, my date was a fucking disaster. Oops, sorry, a disaster. The guy did a runner when the bill came.'

'No!' Poor Marion.

'Yes. He went to the toilets and never came back. So I got lumped paying for everything and, let's be honest, it was pretty fucking humiliating. I waited for ages for the prick to reappear. Then I started to worry he'd had a heart attack or a stroke or something. So there I am, standing outside the door of the men's loo, shouting, "Jason . . . Jason, are you all right?" Next thing, the waiter appears behind me and says he thinks he saw the man I was with leaving the restaurant. I wanted to die. The poor young waiter was so embarrassed for me, he couldn't look me in the eye as I was paying for Jason, the fucking road-runner's, steak.

'So I'm leaving the restaurant, feeling like a piece of shit, and who do I bump into? Only Christelle and Kelly. I tell them my tale of woe and they insist I come out with them and not go home to either kill myself or track Jason down online and go and cut his knob off. So we go to this gay bar they like and, I swear to God, I had the best night ever. Gay women rock. I was propositioned twice and, I'm not gonna lie, I was tempted. I may forget men and just go for a woman. No snoring, no hairy arses, no blow-jobs, no dick poking you in the back in bed, no soggy condoms and no beard rash.'

'Jesus, Marion!' Harry shuffled in his stool. 'I'm still on my first coffee of the day. I'm not able for this.'

'I'm just being honest. Dating at fifty-one is a shit show. After last night, I think gay women have a better time. Your gay daughter has a fantastic girlfriend and their whole scene is amazing.'

'Well, I'm sure it's just as hard to meet the right person whether you're gay or straight,' I said, trying to steer the conversation towards safer territory before Marion gave Harry a coronary.

'Maybe, but there seem to be a lot of dickhead men out there. Look, I just had fun with them, and they and their friends were a tonic after I'd paid a hundred and fifty euros for a rubbish meal with Harry fucking Houdini. It's also nice to be with two people who are so in love. They're very cute together.'

'So loved up, aren't they? I'm so glad Christelle met Kelly. I love Kelly,' I gushed. I did. She was such a gorgeous girl and perfect for Christelle. While Christelle was all piercings and 'don't mess with me' on the outside, she was such a kind, generous and giving person. Kelly was soft and affectionate on the outside, but tough too. They complemented each other.

'Perhaps you're going on the wrong dating sites,' Harry said. 'You seem to be meeting awful men. Maybe you need to join a more reputable one.'

Marion opened the fridge and took out a yogurt. 'I've done Tinder, Bumble, Let's Do Lunch, Coffee Meet-up, Two's Company, 40s Dating, Match.com . . . You name it, I've joined it. Bottom line, men are just pricks.'

Harry cleared his throat. Uh-oh. What was he going to come out with? Harry had a habit of putting his foot in it. 'The thing is, Marion, now don't take this the wrong way, but you may be coming across a bit strongly, a bit too assertive for some of the men.'

Marion grinned. 'It's okay, Harry, I'm not a total muppet. I know I'm a fucked-up, loud-mouthed piece of work, but I believe there's a lid for every pot. Despite my bastard ex-husband cheating on me with "nice, kind Sally", I still believe in love. My mother shut down and spent forty years in a deep depression waiting for my dad to walk back in the door after he went AWOL. I'm not doing that. I would never do that to my kids. It was a nightmare. We didn't just lose our dad, we lost our mum too. I want my kids to see me as strong and capable. I also believe I deserve a second chance. I think everyone does.'

'Fair enough. I just think maybe you should consider toning down your strong personality a bit on the first date. Let the men get to know you before showing them the full force of your assertiveness,' Harry suggested.

'Why? Do guys tone it down on first dates? No. This is who I am. Like me or bog off.'

She had a point. Did men ever think they had to dampen themselves down to impress a woman? So, why should a woman have to do it? They'd find out soon enough who the real Marion was. Why waste time? I thought she was right:

show them who you are straight up and find out quickly if you're a good match or not.

Harry raised his hands. 'It was just a suggestion.' Changing the subject quickly, he asked, 'How's Greg, by the way?'

Marion scraped the last bit of yogurt out of the pot and licked her spoon. 'Happy as a pig in shite. All loved up with nice, kind Sally. Tells me he can't believe how peaceful his life in Dubai is. I'd say it is pretty fucking peaceful without four kids swinging out of him day and night. And he has the cheek to try to get out of having them for the next long weekend. Apparently nice, kind Sally isn't so keen on having four kids thumping about their luxury two-bed apartment. Greg tried to tell me the flights were too expensive, so I booked the flights and sent his lawyer the bill.'

'Good for you,' I said. Greg was always trying to get out of seeing his kids and, despite Marion's madness, she was a great mum. Having had no relationship with her own father, she was determined that her kids would have one with theirs.

'Anyway, enough about me and my failed love life. How are you?' she asked me.

'Dreading today,' I said.

'Oh, yeah, clearing out your mother's stuff is grim. Bring alcohol. Or weed. I have some really good stuff if you want some.'

'Christ almighty.' Harry groaned. 'Marion, I do not want any drugs in the house. What if the boys found it?'

'Don't worry. It's hidden in my tampon box. They'll never in a million years look in there.'

Harry turned to me for help. I was completely on board with him – if we discovered the boys had even looked at weed, they'd be grounded for life. I'd talk to Marion about it later. I didn't have time now. Besides, Christelle and Kelly smoked weed and, according to one of the school mums, so did a few of the boys in the triplets' year. If they wanted weed, they'd find it, but thankfully rugby had kept them on the straight and narrow and they were obsessed with fitness and health . . . so far.

I glanced at the clock. Damn, I was going to be late.

'Gotta fly.' I picked up my bag. 'I don't need another lecture from Louise on my inability to be punctual.' I kissed Harry.

'Good luck. Call me if you need me,' he said.

'Thanks.'

Marion handed me tissues. 'Hang in there.' She hugged me.

I climbed into the car and sat for a moment. I took a deep breath. It was going to be a long day.

5. Louise

Christ, they were crying again. We'd never get through Mum's things if Sophie and Julie didn't stop bawling every time they saw something that Mum used to wear. For God's sake, we were in Mum's bedroom: she wore everything in here – clothes, jewellery and shoes. Sophie sobbed over Mum's 'favourite' cardigan while I tried not to scream.

I hadn't been sleeping well since Mum died. I was worried about Clara. I could see she was trying to process Mum's death and it was overwhelming her. She'd had a huge meltdown last night and it had taken me ages to calm her. She had been exhausted this morning, so I'd left her in bed watching *Casablanca*, wrapped up in her favourite soft blanket with Luna cuddled up beside her, purring. *Casablanca* was Mum's favourite film and they'd watched it together a thousand times. Clara could quote every word. It was like a comfort blanket to her.

Christelle had called over to keep an eye on her, so I knew she was safe, but I was wiped out from lack of sleep and worrying about how Mum's death was affecting my daughter. She had been extra sensitive since the funeral. She'd had a lot of meltdowns, was finger-tapping a lot and had refused to go to school a few times. She desperately needed her routine and I needed to get her back on track. Work was full on and I had to deal with possibly the most annoying intern I'd ever had. My patience was frayed.

'Sophie! Do you want it or can it go in the charity pile?'

'I feel we're throwing Mum out of the house.' She sniffled.

'They're just clothes, Sophie.'

'I know that, Louise, but they're our mother's clothes. It's like we're getting rid of all traces of her.'

'Why don't we take a break?' Julie suggested. 'It's all a bit too much.'

'Yes, please.' Gavin jumped up. 'Can I go down and watch the footie with Dad? I don't want any of Mum's clothes or jewellery. The only things I want are some photos. You really don't need me here.'

'Okay, fine. Let's take fifteen minutes.' I needed to get out of the room before I lost my temper. Didn't they get it? We had to do hard and painful things, like clear out Mum's stuff, get her death certificate, organize her legal affairs, bank accounts . . . Yes, it was hard, but it had to be done and crying over everything was not helping.

We all headed down for a coffee break. Julie suggested we have Irish coffees to help us get through the rest of the afternoon.

'God, yes, I need alcohol,' Sophie said.

'I could do with a pick-me-up,' I agreed. My eyes were heavy from lack of rest.

I opened the fridge to see if Dad had enough food. It was crammed with two large casserole dishes and a plate of meringues.

'What's going on? We have a rota. There's too much food here – it'll go off.'

'We didn't make them, Dolores did.' Sophie rolled her eyes. 'She called over this morning to drop them in. She'd have plonked herself down for the day too, if I hadn't arrived and seen her off.'

'That's a lot of cooking. She's one determined woman.' I closed the fridge door.

Julie turned around holding the kettle. 'I've been thinking

about it. Maybe it's good for Dad to have some female attention. He's lonely in the house on his own. I called in last week and he was sitting in the dark drinking whiskey and crying. It was really sad. He's struggling without Mum, so I think any company is good for him.'

Sophie glared at her. 'Mum's barely gone six weeks. Dolores needs to back the hell away.'

'We're all busy with our lives,' Julie said. 'Dolores is just cooking him nice things and chatting to him. It's company, Sophie. She's not moving in.'

'How would you feel if Harry was having meringues with some younger woman when you were barely dead?' Sophie asked.

'As long as he wasn't putting all the photos of me into drawers and shagging her, I think I'd be okay with it.'

'Bullshit,' Sophie muttered.

Julie sighed and handed us hot Irish coffees. I took a long sip of mine. God, it tasted good. I let the whiskey warm my insides while the caffeine gave me a hit of energy. I felt myself begin to relax a little bit. We sat in silence for a few minutes.

'I just miss her,' Sophie said. 'She was my go-to person when everything went wrong with Jack and it was just me and Jess. She was really there for me, and she adored Jess and was so good to her.'

I remembered how good Mum and Dad had been to Sophie. They'd taken her in and let her live with them until I'd moved my tenants out and given her my apartment. Mum had been devastated when Jack and Sophie had broken up. She'd been so worried that Sophie would crumble, but my little sister had a lot more grit than any of us had given her credit for. Mum was thrilled when Sophie had got back together with Jack. She always said they were a good match. I was glad she'd lived to see that happen.

'She was amazing with Clara too,' I said. 'Poor Clara misses her granny so much.'

'Mum never showed any interest in my kids,' Julie said, an edge to her voice.

'Oh, come on now, that's not true,' Sophie defended Mum.

But Julie had a point. Mum couldn't handle the triplets – to be fair, no one could. They were much easier now that they were older, but when they were young they were absolutely wild.

Julie put down her coffee, her cheeks flushed. 'Yes, it is true, Sophie. While Mum was all over Jess, having her for sleepovers and taking her on shopping trips, she completely ignored the triplets. They were all born the same year and yet my boys had barely any relationship with Mum while your Jess was lavished with love and attention.'

'It wasn't that she didn't love them, just that the triplets were a lot. Mum wasn't able for them all at the same time,' Sophie said.

Julie's eyes flashed. 'I know that, but it was hard. While she was brilliant with Jess, and later with Clara, she really didn't show any interest in my boys and it hurt my bloody feelings. They're my kids. I love them. And it would have been nice if my mother had cared a bit more about them.'

Wow. I'd never known Julie felt so wounded by Mum's hands-off approach to the boys. It clearly bothered her. She'd mentioned once or twice how Mum and Dad sometimes pretended they had to be somewhere when they saw her arriving with the triplets, even one time that they hid behind the curtains and she pretended she didn't see them and went away. I suppose I didn't pay much attention to it. I was living in London then, working twelve-hour days, and I didn't have a child, so it kind of went over my head.

But looking at it now, from Julie's point of view, I would have felt very hurt if Mum hadn't embraced Clara. Mum's interest, love and affection for Clara had saved me at a time when I was really struggling with her diagnosis and panicking about her future. I still did panic about it, but Mum had helped hugely in bringing Clara on – encouraging her to communicate more, to look people in the eye, to reply to questions, to go to school. Plus it was Mum who had bought her Luna, our little white cat and the love of Clara's life. Mum had gently and ever so patiently helped Clara cope and manage in a world that confused and frightened her. That devotion was a lifeline to me and Clara, but also forged a very strong connection between me and Mum. I suddenly realized, for the first time, that Julie had missed out on that.

'I'm sorry, Julie, I never realized how hard that was for you,' I admitted.

'Me neither,' Sophie said.

Julie sighed. 'Look, she was a great mum to me, just not the amazing grandmother you both experienced. And it was hard, especially when the boys were young and I was struggling to get through the days. Thank God for Marion. She saved me. But at least Dad is finally showing some interest in the triplets now that they're good at rugby.'

'As is Jess, by the way. She keeps asking me if they've been picked to play. I think it'll give her big kudos with her friends that she has three cousins on the team. You know what teenage girls are like.' Sophie rolled her eyes.

'Well, now, I seem to remember you at fifteen, getting all tarted up and going to rugby matches to pick out the best-looking guy to target as your next boyfriend,' Julie reminded her.

Sophie laughed. 'God, yes, I did do that.'

'And you always got them because you were so bloody gorgeous,' Julie added.

'Were, being the operative word.' Sophie tugged at her face. 'Being surrounded every day by beautiful young models is not good for the ego.'

'You look much better without all that stuff in your face,' I said. Sophie had gone through a stage of doing far too much Botox and filler.

'Yes, well, thanks to you telling me I looked like a bloated puffer fish, I've stopped getting it. I'm sticking to light Botox.'

Sophie had relied on her looks to get her job as a model and to marry a rich man. Her life had been perfect – big house, designer clothes, luxury holidays – until it all came crashing down when Jack lost everything. I thought it was the best thing that could have happened to her, though. Sophie had become really vacuous, hanging around with awful women like Victoria Carter-Mills and other rich bitches who spent all day shopping and lunching. Julie and I had felt we were losing her, like she wasn't herself any more, but there was no way to tell her that. Losing everything had made her dig deep, get a job and begin living in the real world again. In my opinion she was a nicer, stronger and more rounded person now.

'You look great, Sophie,' Julie told her.

I finished my coffee and put down my cup. I needed to talk to my sisters about what had happened last night. I was still reeling from it, and it was the main reason I hadn't slept.

I cleared my throat. 'Clara came home from school yesterday and told me they were doing a project on their family tree. She said she drew hers, but it only had one side because

46

she has no dad. Her tree was lopsided, but everyone else had a proper round tree. She asked me, for the first time ever, about her dad and did she have other grandparents. She wanted to know did she have another granny now that Granny was dead.'

'What?' Julie's eyes widened.

'Oh, my God, Louise, what did you say?' Sophie asked.

'I said, "Your dad is Italian. I met him one night over ten years ago and I never saw him again."'

'What did she say?'

'She said, "Okay."'

'Really? That's it?' Julie said.

'Yes. But that's what Clara does. She'll process that now and probably come back with more questions.'

'What are you going to do if she does? How do you tell her you had a drunken one-night stand in a hotel in Italy and don't remember who her dad is?' Julie asked.

'I believe that with all kids, but especially kids on the autism spectrum, you have to be honest and tell the truth. Clara doesn't get nuance and won't accept vague answers.'

'But you can't tell her the actual truth,' Sophie said.

'I'll have to. I'll just say Mummy had too much wine and met a lovely man and had a romantic night and Clara is the result of it.'

'What will you do if she wants to find her dad?' Julie asked gently.

I shrugged. 'What can I do? I don't even remember his name. I think once I tell her he can't be found she'll accept it. Clara deals in absolutes. She's surrounded by love and family. I really don't feel she's missing out. How can you miss what you never had?'

Julie chewed her lip. 'I don't know, Louise. So many people who didn't have their dad in their life say they always missed

47

him, even when they didn't know him. Like a sort of ghost that haunts them. I'm not sure it's as simple as you're saying when it comes to parents and where you're from. I mean, that's a really core thing not to know.'

'Nonsense,' I said. 'People overcomplicate things. Clara is treasured by our family. That's all she needs.'

'Louise,' Julie said, laying a hand on my arm, 'I'm not trying to put pressure on you, but it is a big hole in Clara's life. Look at my friend Marion. She never really knew her dad and it's had a huge effect on her. Look at Christelle. She always yearned to find her father, and her relationship with Harry is so precious. All I'm saying is, don't under-estimate it.'

Sophie nodded. 'I know you can't change the past, but it's important to be aware that Clara could end up with feelings of rejection, even though she's never met her dad. It's import-ant that she doesn't feel he didn't love her enough to stick around, you know? I see it with Robert. When Pippa is away all the time, he really feels the loss.'

I sighed and put my head into my hands. These were some of the thoughts that had gnawed at my mind all night. 'I wanted you two to tell me it was fine and not to worry,' I said. 'It's really bothering me, but I do keep coming back to the fact that you can't miss what you don't know.'

'But she does know,' Julie pointed out, 'because all the other kids in her class have dads in their lives, or at least know who their dads are.'

My heart sank. She was right. 'I was hoping I'd be enough,' I said, 'that she wouldn't need to look for more. Clara was surrounded by love – she has you as her aunts, and Gavin and Christelle. Dad's quite good with her too and your hus-bands and kids are sweet to her.'

'We all adore her.' Sophie's eyes welled up again but this time it didn't annoy me, because I felt emotional too.

'Maybe if I just tell her the actual story, she'll accept it and move on,' I said.

Sophie and Julie looked at each other.

'Maybe,' Sophie said. 'But you do realize telling the story to Clara will mean questions and you'll probably end up explaining the birds and the bees to her. I don't mean the facts about the length of their wings, like in her bird book.'

'No, you'll be talking about the length of other parts of the anatomy.' Julie giggled.

I couldn't help laughing. 'Oh, God, that will be a mine-field. Clara's need for factual detail can be never-ending.'

'Well, you just try giving that talk to three boys,' Julie said, rolling her eyes. 'You two have it easy compared to me. That was some fun, I can tell you. Harry ran and left me to it. I even did a demonstration of putting a condom on a banana except I didn't have a condom, so I used cling film which just didn't work. It kept getting tangled and knotted. Even-tually I just hissed, "Keep your penises in your pants," and walked off.'

We all burst out laughing. It felt good. I couldn't help thinking that if Mum had been there, she'd have been laugh-ing with us. She had a great sense of humour.

'For now,' I said, 'I'm going to say nothing. You never know with Clara. Maybe, with a bit of luck, she might just accept what I've said and leave it at that.'

I knew I was being over-optimistic. But, on the other hand, Clara was surrounded by love, support and kindness. She had men – uncles and a granddad – in her life, who loved her, and she knew she was the centre of my world: I told her so every day. She didn't need a father and, besides,

I genuinely had no idea who he was. I'd just have to deal with her queries, if they came up, and put the whole issue to bed as quickly and efficiently as possible. It had always been the two of us, and it always would be. We'd be fine on our own.

6. Sophie

I clenched my hands together as Robyn talked at me about what she needed, wanted and deserved. She was wearing leggings and an oversized jumper with the arms pulled down over her hands. Her hair was unwashed and tied up, she had no make-up on, but she still managed to look stunning. She had so much potential, but her attitude was appalling. She sat back in the chair opposite me, pouting like a grumpy toddler.

'The thing is, Robyn, you turned up two hours late to the shoot. The company had to pay studio costs and the photographer and the stylist for their time.'

She shrugged. No sign of remorse. 'I woke up feeling uncomfortable in my skin. I needed to get into the right headspace so I went to a yoga class and had some me-time. There was no point in turning up when I was feeling all, like, negative and down on myself. When I arrived, I was in a good place and feeling up for it.'

It was always about how she was, her feelings, her aura, her headspace . . . I was sick and tired of listening to Robyn's bullshit.

'They said that after arriving two hours late you complained about the water not being room temperature and the snacks not being vegan.'

Robyn looked affronted. 'I mean, yeah! Everyone knows I'm vegan, and who drinks cold water? Like, hello, are we living in the olden days?'

'You cannot arrive two hours late and complain. The only

thing you should have done was apologize profusely and do an amazing job.'

Robyn frowned. 'Listen, Sophie, back in the old days when you modelled, women let themselves be treated badly, but my generation,' she thumped her chest, 'is not letting anyone walk over us. We know our rights. We know our worth and our value. Hashtag MeToo.'

Hashtag You're An Entitled, Spoiled, Bad-mannered Pain In My Arse.

I kept my voice steady. 'Back in the old days, as you put it, we turned up on time because it's called being professional. As for the temperature of our water, we didn't cause a fuss about it because it was, and still is, considered rude to complain when someone offers you a free beverage. The client is furious and is insisting that the agency covers the cost of the two lost hours. Quentin and I will not be covering the cost of you being late. It's coming out of your commission. So the total remuneration for you on this campaign is a hundred and eighty-nine euros.'

Robyn's eyebrows flew up. 'Are you joking right now? My commission is eight thousand.'

'It was, but after costs it's now a hundred and eighty-nine.'

She stood up. 'That's illegal!'

'No, it isn't. It's called wasting client's time and money, and on top of that your behaviour reflected badly on this agency.'

'I don't give a flying fuck about this agency. I want my money. My dad's a lawyer. I'll sue you.'

'Go ahead, Robyn, you haven't got a leg to stand on.'

'I've two legs actually, two great legs. I will not be treated like this. I will not be bullied by some old, washed-up model, who's jealous of me.'

Ouch. Talk about hitting my Achilles heel. This girl was a piece of work and I'd had enough.

Using my 'Ice Voice', as Jack called it, I said, 'I think it's time for you to leave.'

Robyn grabbed her oversized bag and headed towards the door. 'I quit,' she screamed. 'Your top model is leaving this dump of an agency. Good luck trying to survive without me.' She strode out of my office and down the corridor, then disappeared into the lift.

Quentin came out of his office and stood in the doorway to mine. 'What in the name of God is going on?'

'Robyn just quit.'

'Because we're charging her for the client's bill?'

'Yes, and because she's an overindulged pain in the arse.'

'Agreed, but she was a good earner.'

'Don't worry. I've just signed a knock-out – Angelika, who will easily fill Robyn's shoes. She's from Lithuania, actually appreciates working and is happy to drink water, no matter what the temperature.'

Quentin grinned. 'Robyn was a royal pain the arse. What a drama queen. Show me the new girl.' He came into my office, where I had Angelika's photos laid out on the table. He oohed and aahed. 'Well done, Sophie. She'll make herself and us a fortune.'

'And no more dealing with Robyn and her dramas.'

'Praise Jesus.' Quentin laughed. He put down Angelika's photos and pushed his designer tortoiseshell glasses up his nose. 'How are things with you? Is Louise still ordering you all about? Has Daddy popped his cherry with delicious Dolores?'

I swatted his arm. 'Stop it! Dad is heartbroken. I found him looking at his wedding album last night when I called in. He's lost without Mum. She always organized everything and made plans and invited friends over, but now she's gone and he doesn't seem to know what to do with himself. Julie thinks

Dolores is a nice bit of company for him, but I think she's a predator. As for Louise, she's calmed down a bit. She's working on some big project in work and she has some young intern who's driving her nuts, so thankfully she's distracted with that, which is a relief to us all.'

'And dare I mention Pippa?'

My stomach clenched at the sound of her name. Pippa was a big fat thorn in my side. Quentin knew all about her. I could trust him with my life. Quentin had saved me when Jack lost everything by hiring me as a model booker. He'd seen me in all stages of my life – as one of his agency's top models, as a rich housewife and then as a penniless basket case. This job had paid the bills and kept us afloat while Jack had struggled to rebuild his life. Not only was Quentin my fairy godfather, but he also disliked Pippa every bit as much as I did.

I sighed. 'It's the usual Pippa story. She was supposed to have Robert this weekend but *something came up* so we now have him . . . yet again.'

'Jack is lucky that you're so fond of his son. Other women would really not be so tolerant. You've been amazing and I hope Jack is busy thinking up ways to thank you.'

I loved that Quentin always had my back. Jack was lucky: I was very patient about having Robert so much. He was a sweet kid but, at the end of the day, he wasn't mine. I had one daughter, whom I was finding difficult to manage; an ex who was now not an ex, who I loved, but we had our issues; and a very busy job. I didn't want to be a full-time stand-in mother for Robert. I was sorry that he had a selfish, feckless mother, but I was beginning to resent all the time he spent with us because Jack and I never got time alone any more. Robert was very clingy to his dad because of his unreliable mother and wouldn't let Jack out of his sight. I was worried about the future: would Robert be damaged because Pippa preferred partying to being with him? Would he act out and cause chaos when he was a teenager? He was already taking a lot of Jack's attention away from Jess and me. I worried about helping to raise a boy. I didn't know boys. Julie's boys were a handful. Was I up to the task?

'You know,' Quentin said leaning closer, 'rumour has it that Pippa is sleeping around and has grown very fond of the white powder.'

'I knew it,' I said. 'I actually thought Pippa was high the last time I saw her because her eyes were glassy. I was right! I said so to Jack at the time, but he said I was being ridiculous, that Pippa would never do drugs, that she was too into her health. What is she thinking, though?'

'She's probably feeling pretty low,' Quentin said. 'I mean, her career is on a downward slide. She has that one little make-over slot on the morning show, but it's a five-minute piece of fluff. All of her UK work has dried up, given to younger, prettier girls. She has to be feeling the pressure. It's daunting for women like her – they forget they're ten-a-penny until it's too late. And I don't think she has many other talents to offer the world.'

I knew I should feel sorry for a fellow woman with a declining career at such a young age, but she had been so mean to Jess that I wasn't capable of feeling sympathy for her. Poor Jess had adored Pippa – to the point of driving me crazy and making me pathetically jealous – but she had been chucked aside the minute Robert was born. Since then, Pippa had barely given Jess the time of day and, thankfully, after licking her wounds, Jess had seen Pippa for the bitch she was.

'Who's Pippa sleeping with?' I loved that Quentin always had the latest gossip.

'Jackson Flinch, and I also heard she's been shagging Paul Howarth – you know, the millionaire tech guy?'

'No surprise she's sleeping with rich men. I hope she moves in with one and starts looking after her son.'

Quentin pursed his lips. 'Unlikely, I'm afraid. None of the men are sticking around. She's got a bit of a reputation about town. She's not as young or gorgeous as she once was and apparently she gets messy when she's out.'

'Oh, God, I really want her to be in a stable relationship so she can be a better mother. It's not fair on Robert, Jack or me. Why did Jack have to bloody well have a child with her? It would be so much easier if there was no Robert, because Pippa would be out of our lives. Instead she's plonked in the middle of them . . . for ever.'

'It'll get easier as Robert gets older and needs less minding. And there's always boarding school.' Quentin grinned at me.

I laughed. 'Not a bad idea, but Jack would never send his precious son to boarding school. And I don't think boys get easier to parent, or any teenagers for that matter. I'd send Jess to a boarding school in the morning. She's driving me insane.'

'I won't have a bad word said about my beautiful Jess.'

'I love that you love Jess, but she is being a very bolshie teenager right now.'

'Yes, but she's dealing with raging hormones and she's missing her grandmother,' he reminded me. 'Go easy on her.'

'I'll try, but I'm struggling too. I miss Mum so much. It'd be nice if Jess wasn't so rude to me. I'd like a bit of comfort and kindness too.'

Quentin put his short, chubby arms around me and kissed my cheek. 'I know you're heartbroken and I'm here for you. Now, come on, wait until I tell you the model gossip I heard earlier. It's *so* good it'll make you forget all your woes, I promise.'

When I got home, Jess was in her bedroom as usual, screeching on the phone to her friends. Had I been that loud and shrill when I was fifteen? I didn't think so. At Jess's age I had already started modelling part-time and making my own money. I had a boyfriend called Henry I'd met on a shoot. He was very handsome and hot and, truth be told, not the sharpest knife in the drawer, but then again, neither was I. Louise called him 'Henry the Halfwit'. He was terrified of her, as were the rest of us. We only lasted about six months, but he was nice to me and I'd liked him.

Even Mum was a bit intimidated by Louise because she was impossible to argue with, even when she was a kid. From the age of about ten, Louise's vocabulary was off the charts because she ate books. She read all day and almost all night too. She would debate and question everything. I mean every single thing. If Mum asked her to hang up the washing, Louise would go off on a tangent, using all these long words, as to why she shouldn't and wouldn't do it. Eventually Mum would shove her out of the kitchen and do it herself, muttering, 'Bloody know-it-all.' Teenage Louise didn't have conversations with you, she gave lectures. Julie was the only one she talked to like an actual person. With Julie, Louise had always been nicer and less dismissive. Gavin and I had got the you're-young-stupid-and-irrelevant Louise. Mum always tried to excuse her to us by saying, 'It's just that Louise's brain works so fast she gets frustrated,' but it had hurt at the time. No one wants to be told they're thick. Thankfully, she was mellowing as she got older.

Although it was still a huge surprise when Mum and Louise had got so close after Clara was diagnosed. It was nice to see a softer side to Louise, and Mum had been brilliant. Louise had let Mum into her life and leaned on her – for the first time, really. It was lovely to see. Mum adored Clara and would have taken a bullet for her. She felt the same about Jess too. God, I missed her.

I shook my head, as if I could dislodge the memories. Some days it was so hard to keep my brain on track – I kept wandering off into the past, remembering moments with Mum, us lot as kids and teenagers, how she took care of us and parented us. Ever since she'd died, it was like I was living half in the past. Julie said she felt the exact same. It was weird to me how grief worked and how the flashbacks kept coming. In a way the memories were a comfort because it meant I wasn't forgetting Mum. I was actually remembering more about her than I ever had before. But right now I had to pull myself out of my memories and deal with my own tricky teen. I genuinely don't know how Mum had survived this with four of us.

I knocked gently on Jess's bedroom door.

'What?'

She was at that 'charming' stage where everything she said sounded aggressively defensive.

I opened the door.

She was sprawled on her bed, holding her phone up to her face. 'What? I'm on the phone to Grace.'

'Hi, Grace.' I waved at the phone screen. 'I need to talk to Jess now.'

'OMG, you're so annoying. We were having a really good chat,' Jess muttered. 'I'll deal with this and call you back, okay?' She hung up.

'Did you get your report card?' I ignored her rudeness.

Jess's face dropped. 'Yeah.'

'Can I see it?'

She sat up and pulled her backpack onto her lap. 'Okay, but you're not to go mad.'

I tensed. 'Why would I?'

'Because I didn't do great in all my tests this week.'

'Why not?' I tried to keep my cool, but Jess doing badly in school was a big trigger for me. I hadn't worked in school: I'd foolishly relied on modelling for a career and my looks to get me a rich husband. It had worked, temporarily, until it had shattered into a thousand pieces.

'Because they were hard, Mum. Maths was, like, impossible. Everyone did badly in it, and science was, like, insane. Mr Frederick asked us really hard stuff that we haven't even studied.'

'So you're telling me that your science teacher asked you questions in a test that you had never studied in school?'

'Yeah.'

'Well, I'll have to call him and tell him it's not fair.'

Jess avoided eye contact. 'Well, I mean he'd gone over a few bits, but it was really hard. I told you, everyone got bad results.'

'How did Lisa do?' I asked. Lisa was my benchmark: she was the kid you wanted yours to be best mates with. She was smart, sweet, studious, polite, always smiling, class captain, head of the science club . . . Lisa was the dream child.

Jess's cheeks reddened. 'You always do this. You always compare me to bloody Lisa, who is, like, a genius and has no actual life except studying. All she does, all day long, is work. Her life is hell.'

'Really, Jess? Because she looks happy to me. Every time I see her, she's smiling.'

Jess rolled her eyes. 'She's a total nerd. She has never even been to a disco.'

'Wow, poor Lisa. I bet when she's running some billion-euro company she'll really regret that.'

'When she's living in her big mansion, alone with no friends and just, like, loads of books for company, she might actually,' Jess snapped back.

'I doubt she'll be alone with her books if she's that successful. Hand it over, Jess.' I put out my hand for the report card that she reluctantly gave me.

It was not good: 53 per cent in science and 48 per cent in maths.

I glared at her. 'What the hell, Jess? These are way down on last week. You obviously did no work. You need to spend less time on your bloody phone and more time studying.'

The front door opened. Jess jumped off her bed, raced past me and ran to her dad. 'Help! Mum's attacking me. It's not fair, Dad, she's being really hard on me.'

I went out to the hall, where Jess was standing beside Jack, hanging out of his arm.

'What's going on?' Jack put down his laptop bag and took off his jacket. He turned around and there was Robert behind him, in his school uniform, his bag dangling from his hand, looking like he'd been crying. 'In you come, Robert,' Jack said, taking his bag.

'Oh, hi, Robert,' I said, shooting Jack a look. 'I wasn't expecting you. It's lovely to see you.' I reached down to hug him as Jack mouthed, 'Sorry,' at me.

I really didn't need Robert here right now. I wanted Jack to talk to Jess with me about studying and knuckling down.

I pulled out of my hug and said, 'Sweetie, I need to talk to your dad and Jess. Would you go inside and put on the TV? We'll be with you in five minutes. Would that be okay?'

Robert nodded and went off without saying anything. As soon as the door shut behind him, I looked at Jack. 'Why is he here? We have him this weekend, not for the weekdays.'

'I'm so sorry,' Jack said, loosening his tie and making his

way into the kitchen. 'Pippa showed up at the office and dumped him with the receptionist. I was in a meeting. The poor child had to sit waiting for two hours before I came and got him. Now his bloody mother isn't answering her phone, so I guess that means he's staying with us.'

I stared at the ceiling and took a very deep breath. 'This is not a good week for the extra pick-ups and minding. I've so much on.'

'I'm up to my neck too,' he said. 'We'll have to text his friend Max's mum and see if we can sort some lifts out.'

'Fine,' I said, wishing Pippa would walk through the door so I could wring her skinny neck. She seriously needed to reset her life and step up as a mother.

'So what is going on here?' Jack said. 'What are you two arguing about now?'

I filled him in on Jess's poor results.

'It was the teachers, Dad. They made the tests super-hard to freak us out.' Jess leaned even closer to her protector.

'Don't worry, princess, they're only Mickey Mouse weekly tests. Let's just have a family dinner and relax. It's been a long day for everyone.'

'Jack.' My voice was sharp. 'Jess's results have been getting worse for the last month. It is *not* okay.'

Jack looked over his daughter's shoulder at me. 'Come on, Sophie, it's not that big of a deal. Don't overreact.'

I clenched my fists. 'It is a big deal. I am not overreacting, I'm pointing out the fact that our daughter's results are getting worse. I think we need to curb her phone use.'

'No way!' Jess's plaintive little Daddy-save-me-from-psycho-Mum voice was gone and her growl was back. She glared at me.

As usual, Jack took her side. 'Kids need their phones, Sophie. It's how they communicate with each other and keep up with what's going on.'

'I am well aware of that, Jack, but she doesn't need it beside her at every hour of every day. She needs to leave it downstairs from seven to ten every evening and then have it for half an hour before she goes to bed.'

'WHAT? Have you lost your mind?' Jess exploded. 'My homework usually takes an hour max. What am I supposed to do for the other two hours?'

'I dunno, Jess – study, read, talk to me and your dad, play with Robert.'

She rolled her eyes. 'Seriously? Dad? Come on.'

Jack clicked on the kettle. 'I don't think depriving Jess of her phone is fair. Why don't we just see how she does in next week's tests?'

Typical Jack. Kick everything down the line and deal with it later.

'No, Jack. We are not going to stick our heads in the sand on this. Jess has to do well in school. She needs to get a good degree and be self-sufficient in life.'

'Oh, God, not the never-rely-on-anyone-else-to-support-you speech.' Jess groaned as Jack stifled a smile.

I felt anger simmering. 'Well, Jess, when I found myself homeless and penniless, I realized that I'd been a complete idiot not to keep working and earning my own money. It was a complete nightmare and I do not want that to happen to you.'

'I've heard this a zillion times. I know. I get it.'

'Well, if you get it, Jess, go up to your room and start studying.' I held out my hand for her phone.

'Dad?' She looked to Jack.

Jack shrugged. 'Give your phone to your mum and go up and do your homework. I'll be up to you later.'

Jess smacked her phone into the palm of my hand and flounced off, muttering under her breath about what a psycho mother she had.

'To hell with coffee,' Jack said. He clicked the kettle off, opened the fridge and poured himself a glass of wine.

'I'll have one, thanks.'

He poured it for me and handed it to me in silence.

'What, Jack? Spit it out.'

He took a long swig of wine and sat down opposite me. 'Sophie, it's been nine years since I lost everything and we had to move in with your parents. It was a horrible time in all our lives and one I prefer not to think about or dwell on. I've worked my bollocks off to rebuild my life and my career. I'm in a really good place, we're back together, and life is great again.'

'I know that.'

'Well, why do you insist on bringing up the past all the time? It happened, Sophie. It was hell, but we survived it and we're happy now. Can you please stop harking back to it? It drives me nuts.'

I bristled. 'I'm not harking back to it. I just need Jess to know that life can be tough and she has to be able to rely on herself.'

'And not a useless man who will let her down?' Jack drank deeply.

'That's not what I said, Jack. I completely respect you for turning everything around, but I was stupid, naïve and lazy. I don't want that for Jess. If I hadn't sat back and let you earn all the money, we could have used my salary when things went belly-up. But I was an idiot, and I will not let my daughter make the same mistakes I did.' I felt myself begin to get emotional. It still stung that I had been so foolish. The memories of having lost everything overnight still woke me up at night in a cold sweat. Mum used to say to me, 'When you've fully settled back into your relationship with Jack, the past won't haunt you any more.' But it did. The fear never fully went away.

'You weren't stupid or selfish. You were a great wife and mother, through everything.'

'Were?'

Jack smiled. 'Are. But I do think you're hard on Jess. She's a good kid.'

'I know that, but if I don't stay on her, she'll fall behind. Believe it or not, Jess, your perfect princess, can be lazy. I want the best for her and we both know that takes work. I want her to understand that effort equals reward and you get nothing from life if you don't invest in yourself.'

Jack reached over and squeezed my hand. 'I know. Just go easy on her, please. We want a happy home life as well as a hard-working daughter. There has to be balance.' He stood up and kissed the top of my head. 'I'll go and check on Robert.'

I nodded at him to keep the peace, but I had no intention of going easy on Jess. Over my dead body was she going to fail in school. She would not make the stupid mistakes I had. Absolutely no way.

7. Julie

Harry thundered up the stairs, shouting, 'Ju*lieeeeeee*!' He burst into the bedroom. My heart leaped in my chest.

'Is it Dad? Is he dead too?' I cried.

Harry came to an abrupt halt. 'What? No. No, nothing like that, darling. It's good news.'

'Jesus, you nearly gave me a heart attack.'

'Sorry. No, it's the boys. They've all been picked for the Junior Cup rugby team. All three of them, Julie!' Harry's face was a picture of pure, radiant happiness.

'Oh, great. That's a relief.'

'Great? Julie! This is momentous. This is a huge deal. This is historic. The school has never had three brothers on the team at the same time.'

I was about to say that was because they'd probably never had triplets in the school before, but I decided not to ruin Harry's buzz, and I was delighted for the boys.

'Brilliant!' I tried to ramp up my enthusiasm.

Harry paced the room. 'It's incredible. I was worried about Leo. He was the one I felt was on the edge of the squad, but he's on. The three brothers, together, representing Castle Academy.'

I was thrilled for the boys, and for Harry, but I also knew that our lives would now be completely ruled by rugby. Harry was already obsessing about it, but this would bring him to a whole new level.

'It's a good thing I've been studying the game. I'll be ready for those rugby dads now. I've a proper handle on it.'

Poor Harry. Having gone to a very ordinary school that barely had a patch of concrete to kick a football around, he was overawed by Castle Academy and its rolling rugby pitches, swimming pool, gym, squash courts, tennis courts and basketball court. He was also intimidated by the confident fathers, most of them former pupils of the school, who strode about as if they owned the place, talking about rugby like experts.

Personally, I thought the school was a bit over the top, but when Harry had inherited the money from his aunt, he'd wanted the boys to go to the best school, and he'd heard good things about this one. Mum said Harry was right to invest money in the boys' education, that it was the best money he'd ever spend. To be fair she had a point, and the pupils did get very good results in their final exams.

I found a lot of the school parents intimidating, though, especially the mothers. Glossy, groomed, assertive women who were forces to be reckoned with. Castle Academy seemed to breed Tiger Mums. 'Don't mind their air of confidence, Julie,' Mum said. 'Sure everyone has troubles in life. No one has it easy all the time.' She might have been right, but they hid their problems well and always seemed on top of everything, unlike me: I was a last-minute kind of person.

'Please tell me Sebastian Carter-Mills isn't on the team?' I said to Harry.

'Sorry, Julie, he's a sub. You'll have to suffer Victoria on the sidelines and I'll have to listen to Gerry lecturing me on the finer points of rugby.'

I put my pillow over my face. '*Nooooo*. She's insufferable.'

'Just ignore her,' Harry said. Not even the Carter-Millses were going to ruin his buzz.

Harry came over and pulled the pillow off my face. 'And

the best news is . . . Are you ready for this? Brace yourself, Julie.'

Oh, God, what now? Harry's idea of brilliant news and mine were poles apart. He considered a hole-in-one on a golf course to be the Second Coming of Christ. I thought an afternoon in bed watching *The Real Housewives of Beverly Hills* while eating a family pack of Maltesers was a slice of pure Heaven.

'Go on.'

'The triplets have been made joint captains, or whatever the collective noun for three people sharing one job is. They're going to be leading the team on and off the pitch. It's a huge responsibility and you and I, as parents of the captains, will be setting up the WhatsApp group and sending out all the communications to the parents, arranging group meetings, activities and acting as go-betweens and buffers between the coaches and the parents.'

I gasped. *What?* Was he serious? 'Jesus Christ, Harry, that's a nightmare. I don't want to be involved in the bloody team WhatsApp group, never mind run it.'

Harry grinned. 'It'll be great, Julie! We'll be in the thick of it all. Don't worry, I'll do most of it. You'll just have to organize hosting the party.'

I sat bolt upright. Did he just say party?

'What party? What hosting?'

'It's tradition, every year the captain's parents host a party for the team, the other parents and the coaches before the season kicks off.'

'Please tell me you're winding me up right now.'

'I'm afraid not.'

'So, you're telling me, super-casually, that I have to organize a party in our house for a bunch of random parents I barely know and the coaches?'

'Yes, and the boys.'

I wanted to cry. 'When?'

'In about a month's time.'

'How many people?'

'Probably about ninety, maybe more.'

I lay back and put the pillow over my head again. As happy as I was for my boys, I did not want to be involved in any WhatsApp group. I hated them. And now I was going to have to host events in my house! I had kept away from the school as much as I could – the boys had got into a bit of mischief when they'd first started and we'd been called in to see the headmaster a few times. But once they'd settled, I'd kept my head firmly down. I dropped the boys to school, picked them up and watched their matches, if it wasn't too cold or raining. That was it.

I was very deliberately not involved in any other aspect of their school life. I avoided committees and parents' associations like the plague. I even hated the school information meetings. I found it all far too intense. You always had one or two parents who took over and tried to bend everyone, including the teachers and headmaster, to their will. Then you had the parents who asked questions just so they could boast about their kids: 'Excuse me, Headmaster, but Johnny has cello master-class/worldwide debating champion club/European tennis training/Olympic rowing coaching five nights a week so he can't attend the chess lesson on Tuesdays and lead the chess team to victory in the national finals, as he would do if he didn't have cello masterclass/worldwide debating champion club/European tennis training/Olympic rowing coaching, blah blah blah . . .' I just felt out of my comfort zone, so I avoided the school and it had worked perfectly for me – up to now.

I groaned into the pillow. This was going to be a long, long year.

*

Christelle sat at the counter, cutting up strawberries for the pavlova. She was so helpful and wonderful. I was glad that after four boys I'd got to have this bonus stepdaughter. I'd never have had Harry down for a one-night-stand kind of guy, and I'd never have thought I'd be grateful for it, but here we were: his college summer fling had produced this gorgeous young woman, and I was so happy to have her in our lives.

'That smells good,' Christelle said, as I plonked the large casserole dish down on the counter.

'Beef bourguignon, Dad's favourite. Mum's special recipe.' I paused as a wave of grief hit me. It was like a punch in the gut. It winded me.

Christelle patted my hand. 'It's hard for you, Julie. It must still be very raw.'

I wiped my eyes with the bottom of my apron. 'It still hurts like hell, to be honest.'

She gave me a hug. 'Anne was a unique person. It's only natural she would leave a big hole in your life.'

I nodded. 'That's exactly it. She was so special, so good to all of us.'

Christelle grinned. 'Well, I thought she didn't like me at first. She sort of, like, held me at arm's length, like, who is this person? What does she want?'

I laughed. 'I can't deny it,' I said. 'She was wary of you, this gorgeous French-American young woman suddenly turning up and saying you were Harry's daughter.'

'I can understand it,' Christelle said, with one of her magnificent Parisian shrugs. She was such a brilliant mix of her American mother and her childhood in Paris. 'Anne was looking out for her son-in-law. She really liked Harry.'

'She did,' I said, feeling another gut-punch. 'They were great friends from the very start. The first time I brought

69

him home, he ended up helping her fix a shelf in the hot-press. Then they had a whiskey to toast each other and talked for about two hours straight. I didn't get a look-in.'

Christelle threw back her head and laughed. 'I can so see that.'

'She loved you too. Once Mum got to know you, she thought the world of you. She was always telling me how lucky I was to have you, as if I didn't know.'

'That's lovely,' Christelle said softly. 'I had so much respect for the way Anne was with Clara, and I think she respected how I was able to connect so well with Clara too. And she always said I was the only person who could keep the triplets under control. "I don't know how you do it," she'd say. "Those boys never listen to me."'

'She was right. Oh, God, what am I going to do without you?' I hugged my stepdaughter tightly.

'I'm only going for a few months. You and Dad should come and visit me and Kelly in South America.'

'If I survive this rugby palaver, I might!' I chuckled.

'It's just a game. Don't get stressed. Enjoy watching the boys being happy playing their beloved rugby. It's good that they can get all of their energy out on the pitch. Dad prom-ised to send me videos of the games.'

'I'll try to get him to send just the highlights. He's obsessed.'

'One of the reasons I'm going to a different continent is so that I don't have to listen to any more quotes from Clive Woodwork, or whatever his name is.'

We fell about laughing. I was really going to miss having Christelle around, Kelly too. My laughing tears turned to sad ones . . . again.

Luke strolled in and, seeing me wiping my cheeks, stopped dead in his tracks. 'Are you okay, Mum?' he asked.

'I'm fine, pet.'

'No, you're not,' Christelle said. 'Luke, your mum is sad about your granny, also about me leaving, and she's stressed about all the rugby stuff too. Give her a hug,' she ordered her brother.

'What?' Luke's eyes widened.

'Go on, she needs a hug.'

Luke put his arms around my shoulders and tapped them awkwardly.

I kissed his cheek. 'Thanks, love.'

Liam walked in. 'Dude, are you hugging Mum?'

'Christelle made me.'

'It's called affection and being kind to your mother,' Christelle said.

'Do I have to give her one too?' Liam asked. 'No offence, Mum, it's just embarrassing.'

I tried not to let his horror upset me. 'You can set the table instead,' I said.

Looking relieved, he took the plates from the counter and began placing them on the table.

'Smells good.' Leo came into the kitchen.

'Boeuf bourguignon,' Christelle told him.

'Is there lots of beef in it? I need to load up on protein,' Leo reminded me. 'Mr Long said I need to bulk up for the season.'

'Yeah, me too. We need chicken for breakfast from now on, Mum,' Liam added.

'And five meals a day, not three. You need to give us extra lunches, Mum,' Luke said.

'We need to load up on six-egg omelettes too.'

'And tuna and oats and veggies and brown rice and bananas as well,' Leo told me.

I stared at my sons, open-mouthed. 'Brown rice and tuna and vegetables? Are you serious? I've been trying to get you

71

to eat those foods for years but all you'd bloody eat was white pasta, toast and cereal.'

Luke, who was doing some kind of push-ups against the countertop, said, 'It's different now. We have a reason to eat better.'

'Yeah, and no offence, Mum, but our lunches are crap. We need proper meals. No more manky ham and cheese rolls.'

'The other lads have serious lunches in these, like, massive Thermos flasks and loads of healthy snacks too.'

'Seriously, Mum, you need to up your game this year. We have to bulk up,' Luke said.

'Especially you, Leo.' Liam pinched his brother's arm. 'Toothpick.'

'Piss off, you're not much bigger.' Leo shoved him away.

'You're the smallest on the team,' Luke told him.

'Not for long, I'm gonna eat four hundred grams of protein a day from now on,' Leo shouted.

'How much is that?' I asked.

'Forty grams is half a chicken,' Leo said.

What? If forty grams was half a chicken . . . Maths wasn't my strong point but that meant four hundred was, like, ten times that, which was . . . five whole chickens!

'Leo, you cannot eat five chickens a day. That's insane and completely unhealthy.'

'Relax, Mum, Leo's exaggerating. The coach said we only need two hundred and fifty to three hundred grams of protein a day,' Liam reassured me.

'That's still three or four chickens per kid! I am not buying and cooking twelve chickens a day for you lot. There'll be no feckin' chickens left in the entire country if I do that.'

I imagined my shopping trolley. My weekly shop would be . . . eighty-four chickens . . . and about a thousand euro.

'Jeez, relax, it doesn't have to be all chicken. You can do eggs instead, or turkey, or, like, lean meat.'

'Yeah, chill out, Mum, it's not that big of a deal.'

Christelle rapped the countertop loudly with her spoon. 'Hey! It is a big deal. There are three of you, so it's three times the organizing, shopping and cooking. If you want to put on muscle, get off your lazy bottoms, do the shopping and make your own lunches. Your mum is still grieving and she does so much for you. Give her a break.' Pointing at the triplets, she added, 'This Saturday, before I go, I'm going to take you shopping. We'll buy all the food you need for one week's meals and then I'll teach you how to make great omelettes. French people make the best omelettes. My American mother was a terrible cook, but my French nanny was fantastic. I won't be around to help you for the next while, so you need to be more independent. Now, leave your mother alone and help finish setting the table.'

I threw my arms around Christelle and held her tight. 'I love you.'

She laughed.

'Oi, hands off my bird.' Kelly strolled into the room.

'She's a diamond,' I said.

'Don't I know it.' Kelly grinned at Christelle and they kissed passionately.

'Hello.' Harry announced his presence loudly, looking everywhere except at his daughter and her girlfriend. He was delighted that Christelle was happy, but struggled with her and Kelly's displays of affection. 'It's not the fact that she's gay,' he regularly said to me. 'I don't care if she's with a boy or a girl, I just don't need to see her with her tongue down someone's throat. Why can't they save it for when they're alone?'

To be fair to him, they were very demonstrative. I think it

was Christelle's French upbringing that made her very at home with being physical with her partner in front of others. Harry barely held my hand in public, never mind shoved his tongue down my throat.

'Dad, catch.' Liam threw a rugby ball across the kitchen at Harry who, despite his best efforts, completely fumbled the catch. I watched as the ball hit a bottle of wine, which toppled over and smashed on the floor.

'I told you! No balls in the kitchen!' I roared.

Christelle and Kelly finally stopped snogging and jumped up to help clean up the mess.

The doorbell rang. I could hear Tom running to open the door.

Dad, Gavin and a very pregnant Shania walked in. Dad looked exhausted and his shirt was crumpled. It needed a good iron. I made a mental note to take his shirts next time I called in.

'How are you, Dad?' I asked quietly.

'Ah, sure, getting on with it. What else can I do?'

'Are you sleeping? You look tired.'

He patted me on the shoulder. 'Not much. It's strange to be in a bed by yourself after decades of sharing. But don't worry, pet, I'll get used to it.'

'I presume Julie told you the great news, George?' Harry asked.

Dad beamed at the boys. 'She certainly did, and I'm so proud of you all. What an achievement, the three of you together playing for your school. Incredible! I want a try from each of you.' He ruffled the triplets' hair one by one, which they absolutely hated.

'Granddad, you're ruining my trim,' Luke grumbled.

Leo looked at his reflection in the window and tried to fix his hair.

'Are you coming to our first game? It's only a friendly but

it's against our main rivals, King's College.' Liam had cut his hair as short as possible so there was nothing to ruffle.

'I wouldn't miss it for the world. When is it?' Dad asked.

'Wednesday at three o'clock,' Harry said.

Dad's brow creased. 'Oh, I think I might be tied up.'

'By . . . I mean, with Dolores?' Gavin winked at his father.

What? Was Dolores still sniffing around Dad like a dog in heat? He hadn't mentioned her to me in weeks and I hadn't seen any casserole dishes in the house. I thought she'd moved on to another unsuspecting widower.

Dad hung his jacket on the back of one of the chairs and ignored Gavin.

'What are you tied up with?' I wanted to know.

'Ah, I think I have a golf thing on.' Dad was vague and avoided eye contact.

'Who are you playing with? Paddy and the boys?'

'I'm not sure yet,' he fudged.

Gavin picked up the rugby ball and threw it at Luke, who thankfully caught it. 'Dad's playing in a mixed day out with Dolores,' he said.

'No balls in the kitchen,' I said automatically. Then I looked at Dad, who was a bit red in the face. 'Are you?'

'Oh, yes, that's it,' he said, faking a bad memory. 'I'm giving Dolores a dig-out. She was stuck for a partner.'

'She's looking for you to dig into her,' Gavin muttered. The triplets sniggered and Tom asked what was so funny.

'Nothing, Tom. There is nothing funny about any of this.' I glared at Gavin.

'It's only sex, Julie, not an emotional attachment. It's nothing like with your mother,' Christelle said.

'Sex?' I gasped.

'Go, Granddad!' Luke whooped.

'Still got it,' Liam said.

75

'Lady-killer.' Leo grinned.

'Do old people have sex?' Tom asked.

Dad spluttered. 'Jesus, Mary and Joseph, there is none of that going on. I am not doing anything of the sort with anyone, thank you very much, Christelle.'

She shrugged in her nonchalant way. 'Okay, if you say so.'

'I do say so,' Dad said. 'I find that very offensive.'

'Kinda defensive there, Dad,' Gavin said under his breath.

'Drink, George?' Harry cut across and poured Dad a large glass of wine.

We sat down. I put Gavin at the opposite end of the table to Dad, to avoid an argument, and served everyone large plates of bourguignon.

'What are these?' Tom held a mushroom up with his fork.

'Mushrooms, Tom. You know it's a mushroom.'

'I'm allergic.'

'No, you're not.'

'Yes, I am, they make me want to puke.'

'Just eat the beef and the carrots.'

'Yuk.' Tom shoved his plate away.

'I'll eat it.' Liam grabbed Tom's plate and piled the food onto his.

'Tom, you have to eat something,' I said. He was small and slight for his age and, unlike his brothers, never seemed to be very hungry.

'I'll have toast.'

'Harry?' I looked over for some support.

'Let him be. I only ate toast and bananas when I was his age.'

'Gavin's going to do all the cooking for our baby,' Shania said. 'I'm hopeless.'

'I'm going to give them organic food and make sure they love healthy food from a young age,' my delusional younger brother announced.

'Good luck with that,' I murmured.

'It's all about nurturing their palate, Julie,' Gavin, the not-yet-a-parent, lectured me, the mother of four children. 'If your children only know fresh fruit and vegetables from a young age, they'll want to eat them for their whole lives. They'll crave healthy food.'

I resisted the urge to tell him that I'd tried mashed broccoli, carrots and cauliflower but when your kids kept spitting it back at you, the veggie-loving-kid dreams dry up and you end up raising them on pasta.

'Your bump is massive, Shania. When is the baby coming?' Liam asked.

'It's not massive, it's a very neat bump,' I lied. Shania had a small frame and her bump was huge. She looked like she was going to topple over, but no woman wanted the word 'massive' associated with her.

'I've still got a couple of months to go, but I feel like a whale. Gavin is being so great. I come home from work to a hot bath, a foot massage and a healthy dinner every night.' She looked adoringly at him.

'Just like me.' Harry snorted.

I bristled. 'You get dinner, Harry.'

He raised his eyebrows. 'I've had yogurt, cereal and toast for dinner three days this week.'

'Well, it's not my bloody fault the boys hoover up all the food in the house. Anyway, your "office" is in the attic so it's not like you can't come down and cook your own dinner.'

'A bath would be nice, and I like the sound of a foot massage.'

'After giving birth to four boys – including triplets – cooking, cleaning and chasing after them for fifteen years, I'm the one who needs my feet massaged. You can massage your own crusty feet.'

77

'I take it that's a no, then?'

'Gavin needs less massaging of feet and more working.' Dad huffed.

'Gavin can't take up a job now, George. I need him to look after our baby. I don't want some stranger raising our child. Work is crazy right now and getting busier by the second. I want Gavin to be at home.'

Dad snorted. 'Being a kept man isn't right. Being a house-wife is no job for a man.'

'But it's all right for a woman?' Christelle asked.

Dad was on dangerous ground here. Mum was always quick to put him back in his box when he was being an old fogey, as she called it, and smooth things over, especially with Gavin, her pet. I felt a pang of missing her. She was the only one who could properly manage Dad.

'Women have always been housewives. Some work, but the majority still stay at home and raise their families. Kids need their mothers,' Dad announced.

Part of me wanted to save him, but another part wanted to sit back and watch.

'They need their fathers too,' Shania said evenly.

'They need their mothers more.'

'Why?'

'Because women are nurturers.'

'Are they, George? Or is that something men made up because we're the ones who get pregnant and give birth?' Shania was no walkover.

'It's in your nature.'

'I disagree. I'm not particularly maternal. Gavin is way better with kids than I am. He's amazing with Clara. I want to work and grow my business, not be at home all day with a baby. Gavin is happy to do that. It makes perfect sense for us to play to our strengths and desires, so what's the big deal?'

'It's just not good for a man to be at home and not earning his own money,' Dad said stubbornly.

'What about Kelly and me?' Christelle asked. 'Do we both have to stay at home with our baby because we're both women?'

'Are you having a baby?' Harry was shocked.

'No, but we've talked about it and we hope to, down the line.'

'How can you have a baby with no sperm?' Tom asked. He'd just had the birds and bees talk in school and thought he knew it all now.

'We can buy it.'

'You can buy sperm? Like in a shop?' Tom was blown away. 'Mrs Kelleher never told us that.'

'No, dork, in a sperm bank,' Leo said.

How did Leo know so much about obtaining sperm?

'Or you just get a guy friend to jerk off in a cup and then you use a turkey baster,' Luke added.

'Luke!' I choked on my wine.

'What? That's what people do.' He shrugged.

Were they teaching this in school now? Did they show you how to put a condom on a banana and then how to put sperm in a turkey baster?

'What's a turkey basher?' Tom was all about the sperm info.

'Baster, you dork. It's like a – a thingy.' Luke clearly didn't have a clue either.

'It's the long plastic tube thing with the red squidgy blob at the top that I use to pour gravy over meat,' I explained.

Tom looked appalled. 'What do you do with it? Do you squirt sperm over the woman with it?'

'Jesus, no!' This conversation had taken a crazy turn.

'Mother of God.' Dad was stunned, and I couldn't blame him. 'Is this what passes for table talk, these days? And with children?'

'They don't actually use a baster, Tom. The medical term is ICI, Intracervical Insemination. You use a syringe to inject sperm near the cervix.' Christelle never minced her words.

'Isn't it sore?' Tom looked traumatized.

'That's gross,' Leo said.

'I'm never having kids,' Liam said.

'Harry,' I hissed, 'this is not nice dinner conversation. Do something.'

'I am well aware of that,' he whispered. 'Give me a minute. I'm trying to get my head around Christelle and Kelly having a baby.'

'How do you get the sperm into the syringe? It's, like, really narrow.' Leo was all about the detail.

'Sweet Jesus,' Dad muttered.

I stood up and shouted, 'Who'd like dessert? It's pavlova.'

The triplets jumped up and raced to the counter to fight over who got the biggest slice, followed closely by Tom.

Dad came over to me. 'I think I'll head off before I get accused of being a bigot, a misogynist or just outdated. I'm not able for any of this.'

'Come on, Dad, stay for dessert. I'll make sure the conversation stays light. It's so great to have you here.'

'No, sweetheart, honestly, I'll head off. I'm tired.'

I walked him to the door. 'Are you okay? I know you miss Mum. It's so hard.'

He put on his coat. 'I do miss her. I even miss her nagging.'

I smiled at him. 'Me too. I keep expecting her to call in and give out to me because the house is a mess or I'm in a baggy tracksuit or the garden needs weeding.'

'It's mad the things you miss.' Dad smiled sadly.

I gave him a hug and opened the front door. His phone

pinged. It was a text message. Dad's eyes were bad, so his text size was huge – you could read his messages from space.

I've a hot whiskey waiting for you, D xx

D? Oh, my God, was that Dolores? And two kisses? What the hell?

'Is that Dolores? Are you leaving my dinner early to meet up with her?'

Dad looked sheepish. 'No, that is . . . She just said to pop in on my way home, for a casual drink.'

'Are you seeing her regularly?'

'No, we're just friends. The days are long, Julie, and you're all so busy with your own lives. She's a nice woman and I enjoy her company, that's all.'

Rage rose inside me. What about Mum? I wanted to shout. Yes, we were all busy, but right now I was bloody well feeding him his dinner and he was leaving early to meet another woman. It was so soon. I mean, Christ, it was way too soon. And I had been the one who had defended him, told my sisters it was just a little company, no harm done. What a fool I'd been. What was he doing, replacing our mother already? Had he lost his mind? I could feel the blood pulsing through my head and I felt physically ill.

'Well, don't let me keep you from your *date*, Dad.' I slammed the door behind him.

8. Louise

Clara was wearing her soft gloves with no seams, so I was allowed to hold her hand. I loved holding her hand and her hugs. I wondered how long they would last. Would she push me away during puberty, like most kids? There were no rules with kids, each one was different, and it was the same with children who had autism spectrum disorder. It made me think about Colin because that was the first thing he had taught me when I went to see him about Clara: every child is different. He was the best child psychologist in the country and had been hugely helpful to me and Clara.

Falling for him had not been part of my plan, but I had. We'd had three wonderful years together, but then he got an offer he couldn't refuse to do a PhD at Harvard. He was hesitant to go, but I made him. I would never stop someone taking up a dream opportunity. The long-distance thing just didn't work, as I knew it wouldn't, no matter what he said. We fizzled out. No drama, no histrionics, it just slowly fizzled. He had since met someone and seemed happy. We remained friends and I knew I could call him anytime for advice about Clara, which was a pretty good outcome.

I had always been practical about relationships, I'd never believed I'd fall madly in love and spend the rest of my life with someone. It wasn't what I wanted. I liked my own company. I liked my own space. I liked having control over my life. Sure, I liked having someone to have sex with, go to the theatre with, walks, drinks, dinner . . . but I didn't need it. Julie could never be on her own and Sophie, although she had been alone for a few years, had hated it. They needed love and partnership – Mum had been the same – but I didn't. Even after two years of dating I had said no when Colin had suggested moving in together. It would be far too messy if we broke up and I didn't want Clara getting used to someone, only for them one day to leave. As it turned out, I had made the right decision.

'Mummy?'

'Yes, sweetheart.'

'Why do people say that dead people go to Heaven and live on clouds and become angels and all that when it's not true?'

'I think they just want to think happy thoughts about the people who have died.'

'But why don't they just say the truth? I saw the coffin go into the ground, so I know that's where Granny is.'

She had a point. The whole Heaven, afterlife, angel thing was just to make us, the left behind, feel better. But the cold fact that my mother was lying in a coffin underground was hard to think about.

'Yes, Clara, you're right. That is where Granny is. Do you miss her?'

Clara hadn't talked much about Mum and I was worried she was internalizing her grief. She barely mentioned her and hadn't cried, which I knew was not unusual for a child with her disorder. But she'd had a few momentous meltdowns that I knew were related to her trying to cope with the loss. I wanted to try to get her to talk about how she was feeling.

Clara said nothing and we walked on.

'I liked watching movies with her. I liked reading my bird books with her. I liked her egg-and-soldiers teas. I liked her hugs. I liked her laugh. I liked her being around.'

I squeezed her hand gently. 'Me too. Mum did the best egg-and-soldiers.'

Clara pulled her hand away and tucked it into her cardigan pocket.

'What happens if you die?' she asked. 'Who will mind me?'

I stopped walking. 'Oh, Clara, I'm not going to die.'

'Everyone dies, Mummy.'

'Well, yes, they do, but I won't die for a very long time. Please don't worry about that. I'm super-healthy.'

'Healthy people die too,' she said, looking at her feet. 'Billy's dad was healthy, but he got hit by a truck on his bicycle.'

Billy was a boy who lived three doors down from us. His poor dad had been killed cycling home from work last year.

'That's true, but I don't cycle because I think it's dangerous. I promise you, Clara, Mummy is not going to die.'

'You can't promise that.' She stopped walking. Crossing her hands over her chest, she announced, 'I don't want to go to school. I want to go home.'

Oh, no. I had a meeting at nine that I could not be late for. She had refused to go to school on two days last week and I'd had to get Gavin to help me. But once his baby arrived, he wouldn't be available for last-minute SOS calls. I wished for the umpteenth time that Christelle hadn't gone travelling. Still, I had to manage this, now and going forward. Clara needed to go to school, have structure in her life and get used to being with other people. It was a small school and they were so kind to her, very accommodating of her needs. I had to get her into class. I kept my voice soft but firm.

'Clara, Miss Rogers is waiting for you. I have to go to work. There is no one to mind you at home. Gavin will pick you up at two forty-five p.m. We talked about this, and you promised you'd go to school every day this week.'

'I want to go home. It's too noisy in school.'

'I'll talk to Miss Rogers and see if you can go to the library

84

for a bit. You can read your bird book until you feel ready for class.'

'As long as I want?'

'Yes,' I lied.

Miss Rogers would have to work on getting her out of the library. If I didn't go soon, I'd be late, and this meeting had taken ages to set up. I'd been schmoozing the potential client for months. If they signed with us, it would be worth millions to the firm. I needed to bring home this deal. Since Mum's death, I hadn't been on my A-game. My concentration was awful. Where I used to read a document and be able almost to quote it back verbatim, I was now struggling to find basic words for things. It could be grief, could be perimenopause, but whatever it was, it was driving me crazy.

I managed to get Clara to the door of the school and handed her over to Miss Rogers, who agreed that she could go to the library for 'a bit'.

'How long is a bit?' Clara asked.

Not waiting to hear the answer, I backed out of the school as fast as my legs could carry me and hopped into a taxi.

The meeting went well. I was flying along, firing on all cylinders until the client, R. B. James, was signing the documents. Ronald James pulled out a silver Montblanc pen. It was the same model I had bought Mum for her birthday years ago and the one she proudly used to do the crossword every day. Whenever I called into the house it would be sitting on the little side table beside her favourite chair. I could see her getting Clara to write the letters down on the crossword. It was something they'd enjoyed doing together. Emotion welled up. Jesus, not now. I squashed it back down. Focus, Louise.

'We're delighted to welcome you to Price Jackson and I can promise you that our structured finance and . . . and . . .'

I could not for the life of me remember the word for securitization, which, considering I was head of the securitization department at Price Jackson, was not a good look. Oh, my God, what was wrong with me? Mum's face swam before my eyes. I began to sweat. Ronald James was frowning at me. I could feel sweat pooling under my arms and I was wearing a dove-grey silk blouse. I clamped my arms to my sides as I floundered around. This was not me. Louise Devlin did not forget words. Louise Devlin was a boss bitch. Louise Devlin did not forget the name of her own bloody department. But, right now, Louise Devlin was about to bawl her eyes out.

'What I mean to say is that . . . the team here . . . has enjoyed a pre-eminent reputation in arranging . . . uhm, in arranging . . .'

'Structured finance transactions,' Ian, my right-hand man, jumped in.

'Yes, exactly.'

'Are you all right?' Ronald looked at me.

'Absolutely,' I said, as confidently as I could. 'Right then, let's have a glass of champagne to celebrate.'

'I'll get that sorted,' Ian offered.

'Not at all, I have a special bottle in my office for the occasion.'

I left the boardroom as quickly as I could and rushed to my office.

Jenny looked up as I sprinted past her. She followed me in and closed the door.

'What's up?'

'I'm . . . I'm . . . it's just . . . my mum . . .' I began to sob.

'Aww, Louise, you had a memory about her, didn't you? They catch you when you least expect it.'

Jenny was one of those rare people who knew what you

wanted, needed and were feeling before you did. I'd never had a secretary like her. She was incredible and I paid her over the odds to keep her.

She handed me a tissue.

'I just miss her, and so does Clara, but she can't express it and . . . uh, uh, Mum was so good with Clara. It's a big gap in her life and she's all confused and I don't know how to help her. I think Mum would have known what to do, but I can't ask her because she's gone. I'm so worried about Clara, and the one person who loved her as much as I do is gone.'

Jenny rubbed my back. 'Don't forget that your mum was there to help you and Clara when you most needed it. Her bond with Clara helped her so much. That will always stand to Clara. You're doing your best, Louise. Don't be so hard on yourself. You never give yourself a break.'

Jenny handed me a glass of water. I took a sip, wiped my eyes and stood up. I had to get it together. Ronald was waiting for me upstairs.

'Help me, Jenny. I have to go back up with a bottle of champagne and celebrate the deal. I have to show him I'm on top of my game and not a bloody mess.'

Jenny grabbed her make-up bag and began to patch up my face. Then she looked at my blouse. 'Right, take that off and put mine on.' She whipped her shirt off and handed it to me. She then gave me deodorant from her own bag.

'Okay, you look better now. A bit red around the eyes, but if you put your glasses on, they'll hide it.'

'Now I need to find a bottle of champagne.'

'I'll ask Aisling. I know she bought a case for Ivan last week.'

Jenny was back within seconds with a bottle of champagne. 'You're a life-saver.'

'You're welcome. And, Louise, it's normal to grieve. You have to let it out or it'll drown you.'

But how could I let it out? I had a daughter to look after, a very busy job that paid the bills, and a widowed father to mind. I didn't have time for grief. I had to keep the show on the road. I was all Clara had. She needed me to be a good mother, provider and supporter. Falling apart was just not an option.

When I got home at seven, Gavin met me at the front door. 'I wanted to tell you something before Clara sees you,' he whispered.

'What?'

'She came home from school, and when we were having our snack, she asked me about her dad, who he was, if I knew his name. She's never asked me anything like that before.'

Damnit. 'This is only the second time it's come up,' I told him. 'She asked me a little while ago. I was hoping she'd forget about it. What did you say?'

'I said she had to talk to you.'

'Okay, thanks, Gavin.'

'I've got to fly. Shania wants a hot red curry tonight. She's got mad cravings for spicy food.'

'Go and look after her. Thanks for helping me out.'

I put my bag down on the hall table and went to Clara's room. Her door was closed and I could hear 'Fernando' playing. Mum had introduced her to ABBA and Clara had become obsessed. 'Fernando' was Mum's favourite ABBA song. I swallowed the lump forming in my throat and knocked gently. 'It's Mummy.' I opened the door.

Clara was sitting on her bed, wrapped in her favourite blanket, Luna asleep beside her. Clara had her lights turned down low, the way she liked them. She looked younger than her almost ten years, young and fragile. She was humming to the song. I sat on the edge of her bed and let the song finish.

88

'How was school?'

Looking down, she rubbed the corner of the blanket. 'Why don't I have a daddy?' she asked. 'Everyone else does, except Billy, whose daddy died.'

'Well, you do have a daddy. We just don't know where he is.'

'I know you said you don't know him, but how can you not know him? Jude said everyone knows who their daddy is.'

To hell with Jude. I'd had a long day and I didn't need this.

'I told you, sweetheart. I met your daddy in Italy and we had one lovely, romantic night together and then I came back to Ireland. I had no idea that you would be conceived that night. It was a total surprise, an amazing and incredible surprise.'

'I said that, and Jude said you must be a slut to be with my daddy for only one night and not know where he is. What's a slut? What does it mean?'

The little prick. I'd be having a word with Miss Rogers first thing in the morning.

'First of all, "slut" is a really horrible word and Jude should never have used it. Second, you mustn't worry about what other people say. The important thing is that you have a mummy who adores you and aunties and uncles and cousins and a granddad who all love you so much.'

Clara looked up at me. 'I know that, Mummy, but I want to find my daddy. He's my daddy and he might want to find me too because I'm his little girl. And I think we could find him because Christelle found Uncle Harry after a long time. It's the same.'

'No, it's not the same,' I said gently. 'Christelle's mummy knew Uncle Harry's name. I'm so sorry, sweetheart, but I don't know your daddy's name.'

'I bet if you tried really hard, you could remember. You're so clever and you always fix problems. I bet my daddy would be happy to know about the incredible surprise that happened.'

How was I going to get out of this? It was a drunken one-night stand and I could barely remember the sex, never mind his name. I was not proud of myself. It was a very out-of-character mistake, but I'd got my precious Clara from it, so I had no regrets.

'Darling, there are some things even I can't fix, but I love you more than enough for ten mummies and daddies. Now, will we watch *Casablanca*?'

Clara pushed me away. 'I want you to find my daddy.' She pressed play on her phone as 'Fernando' filled the air and she closed her eyes. 'Go away, Mummy. I want to be on my own.'

I left her room, locked myself into the bathroom, buried my face in a towel and wept. I cried for my lost mother, my confused child and because I knew Clara would not let go of this request . . . ever.

9. Sophie

I answered the door in my pyjamas. Who was calling at seven in the morning? Rubbing sleep out of my eyes, I opened the door.

Pippa, dressed to the nines and perfectly made-up, stood in front of me with Robert. Hang on, this was not planned. Why was she dropping him over today?

'It's well for some lounging around in their pyjamas,' she said.

'It's seven o'clock in the morning. What are you doing here?'

'A last-minute work thing cropped up so I need you to drop Robert to school and get Jack to collect him. I'll pick him up from school tomorrow.'

'Jack's got clients over from the UK. He can't swan off at two o'clock to pick up Robert and neither can I.'

Pippa spun on her heel and hurried down the path. 'You'll figure it out.'

'PIPPA!' I roared after her, as she climbed into a waiting taxi. 'You can't keep doing this!'

The taxi sped away and all I saw was the back of her glossy blow-dried head.

'Can nobody collect me from school?' Robert's lip wobbled.

I bent down. 'Sorry, pet, of course we can. I'll sort something out. Don't worry at all.' I gave him what I hoped was a reassuring hug. 'Come on inside. Are you hungry?'

'Yes, very. Mummy didn't have time to give me breakfast and I only haded crackers for my dinner.'

Jesus, Pippa, what was going on? This was getting out of control. The poor little mite was clearly starving.

Jack came down to find Robert sitting up at the counter, stuffing himself with slices of toast and a mountain of scrambled eggs. 'Hey, buddy, this is a nice surprise.' He kissed his son's head, then looked at me.

'Pippa had a last-minute work thing, so Robert is staying with us for the night.' I tried to sound breezy in front of Robert and not boiling with rage.

Jack's jaw set. 'Another one. Wow, she's busy.'

'Mmm, she sure is.' I left the kitchen and signalled for Jack to follow me into the hallway.

'She didn't feed him last night or this morning. The poor kid is starving. She's getting worse, Jack.'

'Jesus Christ.' Jack looked really upset.

'I'm sorry, but I can't pick Robert up today,' I said. 'I have a fashion show at two.'

'I have clients over from the UK and we have a big lunch, so I can't either.'

'She can't keep doing this, Jack. You have to put your foot down.'

'What can I do? She never tells me she's dropping him in. He's my son. He's five years old.' Jack rubbed his eyes. 'Could Gavin pick him up?'

'No. He's helping Shania with her online orders. She's overwhelmed with work.'

'Your dad?'

'He's looking after Clara because Gavin can't. Besides, why is it always my family who have to dig your selfish, self-centred ex out of a hole?'

'I'll do it,' Jess said.

We spun around. We hadn't realized she was behind us, listening.

'Thank you, but you can't because you don't finish school until three thirty,' I said.

'My last class is only stupid religion. I can skip it and pick him up.'

'That would be great, Jess. You're a star.' Jack hugged her.

I was not happy about Jess skipping any school, religion or not. Why was my daughter now having to leave school early to look after Pippa's child? This was all getting way out of hand. I loved Jack and I was happy we were back together, but I had not counted on raising his son. Pippa was doing less and less parenting, and I was shouldering the fallout. Besides, I had a strong suspicion that Pippa was not going to a work thing but off on a jolly with whoever she was shagging these days. This whole custody situation was just not working – she was treating us like a drop-off centre. But for today, we had no choice.

'Okay, Jess, but just this once. I'll write you a note.' I gave in, knowing it was the only solution. If Mum was still alive, I could have asked her. She would have been brilliant with Robert and I know her heart would have melted for him. She'd have had a few choice words to say to Pippa too. Mum would have helped me to navigate the car-crash this custody agreement was becoming. God, I missed her support and advice.

Jess went in to talk to her little brother.

I glared at Jack. 'This has to stop.'

He threw his hands into the air. 'If I cross her, she'll take me to court and ask for full custody and you know courts usually side with the mothers.'

'I don't think she will, Jack, because I don't think she wants more custody. In fact, I think she'd gladly hand over full custody to you. She just threatens to do that because she wants the maintenance money.'

93

'I can't risk it, Sophie. I can't risk losing joint custody.'

I understood he was nervous about a court leaning towards the mother, but surely if the judge saw we were the ones who looked after Robert most of the time anyway, they'd never rule for Pippa. That was if she took Jack to court, which I didn't think she would. She was just using it as a threat so Jack wouldn't challenge her. She was controlling all of us, and I was thoroughly sick of it.

I held Robert's hand as we walked to school.

'I can't wait for Jess to pick me up. It's gonna be so cool. She said we can go to the playground on the way home.' He skipped along beside me.

'That sounds like fun.'

'Jess is the best sister in the whole big world.' He smiled up at me.

He was a very sweet kid, despite his deadbeat mother's DNA.

'Yes, she is, and you're a wonderful little brother, and she loves you so much.'

He beamed. 'And she said we can get sweeties too.'

'Not too many, though. We have to mind our teeth, don't we?'

'Yes, Sophie, we do. But a few is okay.'

I winked. 'Yes, they are.'

'Mummy's friend Vincent gives me lots of sweeties.'

'Does he?' My ears pricked up. 'Is he nice?'

'I only know him a tiny bit.'

'Is he a new friend?'

'Yep. Mummy says I need to be super-good when he comes over cos he's a zillionaire.'

Wow, she was some operator, using her kid to reel in a man with money.

'He has his own plane. Mummy says it's a*maaaaaaa*zing and one day, if I'm really nice to Vincent and show him what a good boy I am, I can go on the plane too.'

'That sounds like fun.'

Vincent who? I'd have to ask Quentin. He'd definitely know.

'Does Vincent have any kids?'

'Two, but they're not kids, they're all growed up.'

So, an older guy, then.

'I hope he's nice to you because you're a very special boy.'

Robert grinned up at me. 'You're special too, Sophie. Mummy says you can be grumpy, but I think you're super-nice.'

I kissed the top of his head. 'Thank you, sweetie.'

How dare that bitch give out about me? The cheek of her! Grumpy, my arse. I was practically raising her son – and doing a much better job of it than she was.

We arrived at the school where Robert ran into the classroom and over to his friends. I explained to the teacher that Jess was picking him up, filled out a permission form, waved him goodbye, then rushed into work to talk to Quentin and figure out who Vincent with the private plane was.

Julianne tapped my shoulder. 'I can't fit into this stupid dress. It's shrunk,' she whined.

I tried to pull up the zip, but it refused to go past her hips.

Quentin glared at her. 'Darling, that dress hasn't shrunk, you just need to eat a few salads or tape your mouth shut after five p.m.'

She gasped. 'You can't say that to me. That is not a body positive comment.'

'Don't give me that crap. You're a model, you have to be thin. It's your job.' Quentin put his hands on his hips. 'If you want to eat burgers, go and work in McDonald's.'

'How dare you?' she said. 'You're just a stupid . . . old . . .'

'What? Spit it out, honey. I'm just a stupid old fag? Well, this stupid old fag runs a very successful modelling agency and clients don't want girls with fat arses modelling their clothes. Find yourself another career.'

Julianne yanked the dress off and pulled on her tracksuit. 'You're a nasty old prick. I'm going to hashtag MeToo you on my socials.'

'Go ahead, darling. I grew up as a gay man in Ireland in the seventies. It was pure hell. I can take a little social-media bitching. Knock yourself out. Hashtag the hell out of me.'

Julianne stormed out while the other models – some looking shocked, some giggling – carried on getting ready for the show. I pulled Quentin aside.

'Quentin, please be careful with your words. You have to be so mindful, these days. If clients hear rumours that you're body-shaming models, they may pull out.'

'Body-shaming? Give me a break. She wants to be a model, so she has to be thin. If I want to be a sumo wrestler and all I eat are salads and I'm eight stone wringing wet, is my coach going to clap me on the back and say, "Well done, we'll put you on the Olympic team"? No, he bloody isn't. He's going to scream at me to eat more food. If you choose to be a model, fitting into designer clothes is part of the job. I'm sick of people telling me I can't say this or that. You can't have a goddamn opinion on anything any more.'

I understood what he meant. The world, and people, had got very precious. While it was positive in the main that people were being more mindful, sometimes it felt like walking through a minefield, trying to make sure you didn't say anything that could be deemed offensive by anyone, anywhere.

'Okay, I know what you're saying, but just make sure you don't stray into outright insults. We definitely don't need that reputation.'

Now that we were one model down, I had to rearrange the running order of the fashion show. I managed to get all of the outfits into the show by rejigging the line-up and helping to dress and undress the models myself.

'You're a wonder, Sophie.' Quentin praised me as we sat in his office and he enjoyed a post-workday glass of wine. Donatella and Miuccia snored in their fluffy beds at our feet. I wasn't a fan of pugs, but they were Quentin's fur babies and came to work with him every day. Quentin's dogs, and there had been quite a few over the years, were part of the package.

'Thanks, boss.' I winked at him.

'By the way, while you were putting out fires, I was grilling my sources. I found out who Pippa's new lover is, the mysterious Vincent.'

'Yes! Come on, fill me in.'

'So, my friend Paul, an ex but awful in bed, has a brother –'

'Quentin, get to the point!' I was dying to know who Pippa's new man was and Quentin had a habit of taking ages to tell stories.

'Don't be so impatient. Anyway, Paul's brother works for Vincent – his name is Vincent Hughes. He's a multi-millionaire property developer who indeed has a private jet. According to Paul's brother, Vincent is known to be a bit shady in his dealings. But here's the real kicker . . .' Quentin paused for maximum effect. 'He's married.'

I almost spilled my wine. 'What? Are you sure?'

'Paul is one hundred per cent sure. His brother was at a

party in Vincent's house last week to celebrate the thirtieth wedding anniversary of Vincent and his charming wife, Hazel!'

Oh, my God. Pippa was having a full-blown affair. This was serious gossip. What would happen if Hazel found out? Dublin was tiny when it came to scandal – there was no way they could keep it under wraps for ever. Would Vincent leave Hazel for Pippa? Did Pippa know he was married? Did she care? Was Vincent promising Pippa he would leave his wife just to string her along?

Whatever about him being married, which was bad enough, I didn't like that he was shady. I didn't want Robert around anyone who was a bad influence or was involved with any dodgy people. Should I tell Jack? He was already pretty anxious about Robert and how the whole toxic situation with Pippa might be damaging him. I knew Jack felt guilty that Robert didn't have a stable family life like Jess. On balance, I decided it might be best to say nothing for now. Why worry him unnecessarily? I could keep an eye on things, and the affair would probably fizzle out quickly anyway. Pippa's relationships never seemed to last long, although I'd say she'd be keen to hang on to this multi-millionaire and his private plane.

'I bet you her last-minute "work thing" today is actually a dirty night away with Vincent,' Quentin said.

'I was thinking the exact same thi—'

My phone rang. JESS flashed up on the screen. I grabbed it. 'Hi, love, is everything –'

'MUUUUUUUUUUM! Help!' she screamed.

My heart skipped a beat. 'Jess, what's wrong? What is it?'

'It's Robert. He fell off the swing and I think he's broken his arm. Help me, Mum.' She sobbed.

I could hear Robert bawling in the background. 'Where are you?'

98

'In the playground down the road from his school.'

'Stay there and don't move. Cover Robert with a coat. He's in shock. Keep talking to him. I'm on my way.'

Quentin had my bag and coat ready for me by the time I hung up. 'Go and look after the kids. I'll finish up here.'

I thanked him and sprinted out of the door to my car.

By the time I reached the park, a group had formed around Jess and Robert. Everyone was being kind and offering help. Jess was sitting on a bench holding Robert on her knee. Both of them had tear-stained faces and red eyes. They were covered with coats and scarves.

I ran over to them.

'I'm so sorry, Mum. He kept asking me to push him higher and I did and then he just slipped off.'

Hiding my shock, I switched into Mum mode. 'It's okay, Jess. We'll get Robert to a doctor now.'

A woman tapped my arm and whispered, 'I'm a nurse. I had a look and I think it's definitely broken.'

'Thanks, I'll take him to A and E.'

I picked Robert up gently and held him to me. 'You poor boy, what a shock. We're going to find a doctor to look at your arm and make you all better.'

He buried his face into my shoulder and sobbed. 'It hurts really bad, Sophie.'

'I know, pet, we'll get you some medicine now to stop the pain.'

Jess followed behind us, tugging at my coat. 'I never thought he'd fall . . . It all happened so quickly . . . I feel so bad.'

I settled Robert in the back seat of the car and turned to Jess. I put my hands on her shoulders. 'It's not your fault, Jess. Kids have accidents all the time.'

'But I feel so responsible,' she said, starting to cry again.

'Jess, I need you to be strong now. If Robert sees you crying, he'll get upset too. I need you to sit beside him in the back and try to distract him. Okay?'

She nodded. I hugged her, jumped into the front seat and got us to the hospital in record time.

I stayed with Robert while he was being triaged, X-rayed and having his arm put in a plaster cast. Jess, meanwhile, got in touch with Jack and filled him in.

A little later, from behind our curtain in A and E, I could hear my husband shouting my name. I stuck my head out and waved him over.

'Is he okay?' Jack's face was pale.

'He's fine. He broke his arm and they've just finished putting it in plaster. They said it's a straight break and will heal just fine. Don't worry.'

Jack stifled a sob and fell on his young son. 'Hey, buddy. How's my superman? You poor soldier, that's bad luck. Is it very sore?'

'It was s*uuuu*per-sore, Daddy, but it's okay now.'

Jack kissed his wet cheek. 'You're such a brave boy. You'll have to get all the kids in school to sign your plaster. You'll be the king of the class with that. Now, you can have anything you want for dinner – you can have pizza or McDonald's or just a big plate of sweets if you want.'

'Can I? For real?' Robert's eyes widened.

'Absolutely.'

I nudged Jack and pointed to Jess, who was sitting quietly in the corner.

'I'm sorry, Dad,' she said, as Jack went over to her. 'I'm so sorry.'

Jack wrapped her in his arms. 'Oh, Jess, love, it's not your fault. You're the best big sister for collecting him from school and taking him to the park. Falling is part of growing up. You broke your arm once, remember? On my watch too, and I felt awful. And your triplet cousins were forever breaking bones.'

Jess nodded. 'That's true, but I feel it was kind of my fault for pushing him so high on the swing.'

'I wanted to go higher,' Robert said.

'I know, but I should have said no.' Jess sniffed. 'I'm your big sister. I should have known it was too high.'

'Don't be sad, Jess. I'm okay now,' Robert told her.

'I'm so sorry, Robert.' She was sobbing again.

'Don't cry, Jess, I love you.' Robert hated seeing Jess so upset.

'It's no one's fault, it was just an unfortunate accident. They happen every day,' Jack tried to reassure Jess.

Before Jess could answer, the curtain was ripped back.

'What the hell is going on here?' Pippa shrieked. 'I'm in work and I get a call from a school mum to say she saw Robert falling to his almost death in the playground and I needed to come quickly. She said some child was looking after Robert. I leave my son with you for one day and he ends up in hospital. What kind of a father are you?'

I was standing closest to Pippa and I could smell alcohol on her breath. Work, my arse. Also, if she'd been so worried about Robert's fall, how had it taken her three hours to get to the hospital to see her 'almost dead' son?

'Calm down, Pippa,' I said briskly. 'It was an accident. He fell off a swing. Robert's fine. He's just got a broken arm.'

'Just a broken arm.' Pippa sneered. 'He could have been dead if he'd hit his head. And who was looking after him?'

'I was.' Jess raised her hand.

'You?' Pippa's eyes flashed. 'You're a teenager obsessed with TikTok and lip-gloss. Who the hell thought it was a good idea to have you look after Robert?' Turning to Jack she hissed, 'How could you leave Robert with her?'

Jess sobbed. 'I'm sorry, Pippa, it was –'

Jack held up his hand to stop Jess speaking. His face was red. Grabbing Pippa by the arm he pulled her out of the cubicle to one side. I followed them. I wasn't going to miss this.

'Don't you ever criticize my daughter again. She stood up and collected her brother from school because you, mother-of-the-year, dumped him on our doorstep again this morning. I'm sick and tired of you dropping him over whenever it suits you. You expect me or Sophie to leave work to pick up the pieces when you couldn't be arsed to look after your own child. And don't insult my intelligence with your "working" bullshit. You stink of alcohol and, judging by your bloodshot eyes, you've been on the sauce all day.'

'How dare you speak to me like that? I'll take you to court, Jack, and I'll get full custody.'

'Really, Pippa? Which judge in the land is going to give Robert to a mother who is more interested in partying than looking after him? I've kept an account of every single time you've left Robert on our doorstep and, believe me, they add up and they do not reflect well on you. Now go home, sober up and pick up our son tomorrow.'

I punched the air. Finally! Finally, Jack had stood up to her.

Her eyes narrowed. 'Don't you dare threaten me! I'd be very careful if I was you, Jack. I have a very rich friend who'll pay for the best lawyers in town to take Robert away from you. Everyone knows that kids are better off with their mothers.'

'That very much depends on the mother.' Jack was not backing down. 'I don't think feeding your son crackers

102

because you forgot to buy him any food shows you in a very good light.'

'Don't push me, Jack, or you'll regret it. How do you think Robert would feel if he only got to see you once every few months? Do you want to hurt your son? Do you want to lose joint custody? I could make life very hard for you after this negligent accident, Jack. Robert has never had a potentially fatal accident on my watch.'

The conniving bitch would use this accident against us.

Jack said nothing but I could see his hands clench into fists. 'Let's focus on Robert's best interests, shall we?' he hissed.

'Fine by me,' Pippa said.

'I'm taking him home to look after him. I think we need to keep him off school tomorrow,' Jack said.

'Fine. I'll be over at about eleven.'

'Could you make it nine so I can get to my ten o'clock meeting?' Jack asked tersely.

Pippa reapplied her lip-gloss. 'No. Eleven is the time that suits me.' Glancing round the curtain at her son, she waved. 'Bye-bye, sweetie-pie. Mummy's going now but I'll see you tomorrow. Okay?'

Robert nodded. 'Okay, Mummy. I love you,' he called, but her back was turned and she was already halfway down the corridor.

Jack clutched my hand very tightly. 'How did I ever get involved with that woman?'

'There was a time when you loved her,' I reminded him.

He shook his head. 'That was seriously bad judgement on my part. I honestly don't know what I was thinking. I was a bloody idiot.'

'I agree completely.' I smiled at him.

'Thank God I saw sense and won you back.'

I put my arm around him. 'I'm very glad you did. Now, come on, let's get our kids home, order take-out, open some wine and put this day behind us.'

'Can we open lots of wine?' He grinned.

'Absolutely.'

Jack held Robert and Jess slipped her arm into mine as our little family unit walked out to the car to go home.

10. Julie

I was brushing my teeth and watching my phone screen light up and ping over and over and over again. This bloody WhatsApp group was out of control.

I could see Harry sitting on the edge of the bed, furiously typing into his phone. He was taking the whole parents-of-the-captains thing far too seriously. It was a rugby team, not the G7 summit.

He wasn't the only one, either. Some of the parents were total nut jobs. Every message sent out garnered at least thirty responses. Some were passive-aggressive, others just plain aggressive. Some of the parents whose boys were on the fringes of the team, subs or worried about being dropped, were like Rottweilers and, of course, 'luckily' for me, Victoria was one of them. Why, oh, why did her stupid son Sebastian have to be a sub? I would honestly have preferred it if he was the star of the bloody team. At least then Victoria might not be such a wagon towards Harry and me.

I read Harry's latest message. It said that the coaches were asking parents to give fifty euros per player to pay for a talk from a sports psychologist.

I put down my toothbrush and stood at the bathroom door glaring at him. 'Is this a joke?'

He looked up and took off his glasses, 'What?'

'Are you seriously telling me that the coaches have booked a sports psychologist to speak to a bunch of spotty fifteen-year-olds?'

'That's what Coach Long told me. I'm just passing on the message. Don't shoot the messenger.'

'But it's ridiculous, Harry.'

'Actually, Julie, it's a great opportunity for the boys to learn life lessons on how to succeed as top-level sportsmen.'

'It's a schools rugby tournament, not the sodding Olympics. This is completely over the top. Why can't Mr Long bloody well talk to them himself? Read a book on how to motivate a team and regurgitate a few good lines? Save us all having to fork out more money to the school.'

'It's fifty quid, Julie, not five hundred.'

'It's a hundred and fifty quid, Harry, given we have three players to pay for, and that's a hundred and fifty on top of all the other extra costs. Not everyone is like us and has the money to spend. The rugby kit alone costs two hundred euros each, and that's before you buy the boots. It's just a massive amount of money – and most especially for us when we have to multiply it all by three.'

Harry pulled a jumper over his head. 'I can promise you this. Every parent is only delighted to pay for their kid's gear. They're all bursting with pride that their sons have been picked for the squad.'

'I know that, but it's non-stop money for this and that, and some of the boys will never even get a minute on the pitch.'

'That's sport, Julie. It's tough.'

'Who is this sports psychologist anyway? Is he any good?'

Harry pulled on the boots he'd bought especially for watching rugby matches on wet, muddy days. They were waterproof and had a cashmere lining. He thought they were the bomb. I thought they looked absolutely ridiculous, like he was about to climb Mount Everest, not stroll across manicured grounds to stand on the side of a 4G synthetic grass pitch in deepest suburbia.

Harry wrestled with the complex laces on his boots. 'His name is Dr Ulrich Haddington and he's supposed to be great. Coach Long told me that –'

'Harry, can you please just call him Bob? Coach Long sounds ridiculous, like we're in some cheesy American high-school football movie.'

Harry had a tendency to be impressed by certain people. When he'd first received the inheritance from his aunt, it was investment 'legend' Donald McGreegan he'd been obsessed with. Now it was Coach Long.

'Fine. *Bob* said this guy, Ulrich Haddington, has spoken to the actual Irish rugby team and really helped them.'

For the love of God, they were just kids.

'Bob reckons Ulrich can give our boys a psychological edge over all their competitors.'

'Sure. Why doesn't he fly in Barack Obama to talk to them about leadership? Dream big, you know.'

Harry grinned. 'Someone suggested trying to get Richard Branson. Even I thought that was a bit much.'

I'd get eye strain from rolling my eyes if people kept on being so insane about all this.

As if on cue, our phones lit up with a message from Victoria: *Ulrich is a close family friend. He has spoken to Sebastian many times. I think the other boys will benefit from his wise words. I've hired a nutritionist to make Sebastian's meals for the duration of the campaign. I'm happy to pass on his number to anyone who wants their son to have an elite diet for success.*

I almost gagged. What total arse-ology.

Harry looked up from his phone. 'Maybe we should look into the nutritionist for the triplets.'

I stared at my normally sensible, down-to-earth husband. What the hell had got into him? 'Have you lost your mind? This is bullshit, Harry. This is over-the-top, overprivileged, more-money-than-sense bullshit. I cannot believe you're even thinking of it.'

'I know it's a lot, Julie, but our boys are competing with the sons of these high-intensity parents for places on the team and I just want them to get picked for every game. I'd hate any of them to be sidelined.'

'I know that, Harry, but can you please remember they're teenage boys and it's a game?'

'You're right.' He finished lacing up his mountain boots. 'It's easy to get caught up in the whole circus. But I can look into a good nutrition plan for the boys myself. Clive Wood-ward is a fan of good nutrition.'

I sighed. 'Knock yourself out, but leave me out of it. If you want to cook them special meals, that's on you.'

As Harry left the room, he said, 'Fine. By the way, I'm leaving in fifteen minutes so hurry up and get dressed.'

'But it's just a friendly warm-up game, right?'

'Yes, but it's the last one before the cup begins and it's against St Fintan's, one of their biggest rivals. It's important, Julie.'

'I'll follow you down.'

Harry laughed. 'I'll see you after the match, then.'

I pointed to the black winter clouds outside our bedroom window. 'It's cold and looks like rain. I'll be down later.'

'You should invest in weatherproof boots like mine,' Harry told me.

Over my dead body was I wearing those ugly yokes. 'Should I go?'

'As mother of the captains, I kind of think you should, yes, and you'll enjoy it. Watching the boys playing for their school is my favourite thing in the world. I know it sounds a bit silly, but it makes me so proud.'

'It's not silly, it's lovely. You're a great dad. I promise to come to the second half.'

'Great.' Harry beamed at me as he hurried out of the room.

I listened to the sounds of them all scrambling about downstairs, shouting at each other, losing things, finding things, then, at long last, the front door slammed. Silence. That moment of silent bliss never ever got old.

I went downstairs, ignored the mess they'd made and switched on Harry's fancy coffee machine. I heard the first spatters of raindrops against the windows and smiled to myself. Good choice, Julie! It was only a friendly, they didn't really need me there, and I'd get a blow-by-blow replay of the match later anyway.

I was lolling about drinking coffee when my phone rang. It was Sophie.

'Hi, are you going to the boys' match?'

'Of course I am,' I lied.

'Jess is mad keen to go. She's all dressed up and has asked me to bring her – which she never does as I'm an embarrassment to her in general. Can we go together? I need you beside me to face that bitch Victoria.'

Victoria had been a friend of Sophie's when she was in the wealthy social scene but had dropped her like a stone when Jack lost all his money. I'd always thought she was a vacuous cow, but Sophie had been dazzled by Victoria's wealth, designer clothes and lavish lifestyle. Losing everything had taught Sophie to cop on, come back down to earth and choose nicer friends. That's why she didn't go anywhere near Victoria now.

'Okay, but I was only planning to go to the second half,' I admitted.

'Julie! Jess says this is the last pre-cup game.'

'I know, but it's raining and I'll be going to all the cup games.'

'I'll pick you up in fifteen minutes. We'll only be ten minutes late. Besides, you have that Antarctic Goose coat Harry bought you. It'll keep you warm.'

I hated the stupid thing. According to Harry, it was a coat people wore in the Antarctic in minus forty degrees. It was big, black, bulky and looked ridiculous. Despite the eye-watering cost of this high-end, Antarctic-proof coat, I still felt cold even when it was six degrees on the sideline. I was clearly a very cold-blooded soul.

Victoria had an Antarctic Goose coat too, but hers was red with a big fur collar and it wasn't faux-fur either. Animals had died for that collar. I thought she looked silly in hers and she was tall and stick thin. I was short and chubby, so I looked like a Teletubby in mine. I didn't want to wear it, but it was warmer than any other coat I had, so I reluctantly pulled it on.

Jess stood between Sophie and me in low-slung jeans and a cropped faux-fur jacket that was hanging off one shoulder.

'Are you not freezing?' I asked her. 'I'm cold looking at you.'

'No, I'm ff-fff-fine.' She shivered, as she applied more lip-gloss. Her lips were turning a light shade of blue.

She didn't need any more lip-gloss or make-up. She looked like she was heading out to a party. She was a mini-Sophie, all blonde hair and long, slim limbs. I'd noticed a few of the boys who'd come to support their classmates ogling her. The boys on the subs bench, which was directly to our left, were checking her out too.

'Who's that?' Jess asked, pointing at Sebastian.

'Never mind. Stay away from him,' I said.

Sophie looked over. 'Oh, God, is that Sebastian?'

'The one and only.'

'He used to be a scrawny little kid.'

He was now five foot ten, muscly and broad-chested – probably from the gym and the pool he had at his house, as well as the private nutritionist.

'Sebastian Carter-Mills?' Jess wasn't letting go.

'Yes,' Sophie said.

'Didn't I used to know him when I was younger?'

'Yes, before we lost our money and Victoria completely dumped me.' Sophie's mouth set in a hard line.

'He's fit.'

'No, he's not, he's a dickhead.' I put my niece right.

'Stay away from him,' Sophie warned her daughter.

Jess completely ignored us both and I saw her smile at him. He smiled back. To be fair, he was a good-looking kid, but he had been horrible to the triplets when they'd first arrived in the school. Unfortunately for Sebastian, the triplets had grown taller than him and shone on the rugby pitch, so he'd changed his tune and decided he actually wanted to be friends with them. The triplets had the measure of him, though: they tolerated him but that was all. They hadn't forgotten how vile he had been to them when they'd first arrived in Castle Academy. The great thing about being a triplet is that you don't need to be friends with anyone you don't want to because you already have two best mates. My boys were as thick as thieves. Although they fought morning, noon and night, they always had each other's backs and I loved seeing them support each other.

'Have you been talking to Louise?' I asked.

'Not this week,' Sophie said. 'The Robert saga continues with Pippa doing her dump-and-run act at the most inconvenient moments, so I've just been running from work to school to home with no time for anything else. I'll call Louise tonight, maybe, see how she's doing. I think she's been having a tough time with Clara not wanting to go to school. And what about Dad? Have you seen him this week? I feel bad that I haven't.'

'Yeah, I popped in yesterday.'

'How do you think he is?'

'He was sitting in the TV room, in the cold, watching football with a plate of toast on his lap. He said there was no point putting the heat on for just him. It kind of broke my heart. I never realized how much he depended on Mum for everything – social life, food, a warm, welcoming home, company . . . all of it.'

Sophie's eyes filled with tears. 'I'll call over tonight.'

Seeing Dad sitting in the cold had made my heart ache. We all dropped in as much as we could, but as the weeks had passed and we'd all got busier, it had gone from someone calling in every night to every second or third night.

'I was so angry at him for leaving my house the last time to call into Dolores, but seeing him yesterday, I went back to thinking that maybe having Dolores for a bit of company wasn't the worst thing after all. At least she gets him out and about and up to the golf club,' I said.

Sophie sighed. 'I can't stand her, but I suppose it's better than him being alone in a cold house.'

'I miss Mum,' I said quietly.

'Me too.' Sophie reached for my gloved hand and squeezed it.

'I just thought it would get easier, but it hasn't. Life around you has moved on, but you're standing still. It's like, okay, that's over now, you've cried, been sad, and now it's time to crack on with life. But I'm still really struggling.'

'Me too,' Sophie said.

We gave each other watery smiles. I knew she understood.

She inhaled deeply. 'Right, come on. Let's focus on your superstar sons. This is a proud day for all of us and I know Mum is cheering them on.'

The match ended with a winning try by Luke. It was hard to see who'd scored because there was a big pile-on, but Luke was the one holding the ball when they all peeled off him. Liam and Leo ran over to him and hugged him. I fought back tears, happy ones this time.

Sophie whooped and cheered. Harry, standing on the opposite side of the pitch with the other parents, including Victoria, clapped Luke on the back as he ran past.

I was delighted for Luke, he trained so hard and was so dedicated to the team. It was lovely to see him shine.

As the players left the pitch, Sophie and I were catching up on Shania's pregnancy, when we heard a voice.

'Oh, God, no!' Sophie mouthed.

'Is that you, Sophie?' Victoria drawled.

Sophie turned to face her. 'Yes, it is.'

'I thought it was, but I wasn't sure. You look exhausted.'

The bitch. Sophie's face reddened.

'What are you doing at Castle Academy?'

'I've come to watch my amazing nephews playing for the school team. Wasn't Luke's winning try incredible?'

Victoria struggled to mutter, 'Yes, they finished strongly.'

'What are you doing here? Is Sebastian on the team?' Sophie feigned innocence.

'Oh, yes, he's a key player.'

'Really? I didn't see him on the pitch?'

'Well, he's carrying a slight injury,' Victoria blatantly lied. Then turning to me she said, 'You and Henry really need to improve the communication on the WhatsApp group. There should be far more information from the coaches coming through.'

'It's Harry, not Henry, and the coaches were very clear that they do not want to bombard parents with information.'

'I'd be happy to take over. Communication is my forte. I'm up to my eyes as usual but I'm an excellent multi-tasker.'

'No, thanks. As the captains' parents, it's our role.' I shut her down.

'Why are you so busy? Are you working now?' Sophie poked the bear.

Victoria's eyes narrowed. 'I don't have time to work. I'm run ragged looking after Sebastian and Gerry and decorating our new apartment in London.'

'I thought you had interior designers and staff to do all that.' Sophie wasn't letting go. The same Sophie who, nine years ago, had spent her days with Victoria doing yoga and shopping.

'Staff need to be managed, Sophie. Are you still working in that modelling place?' Victoria waved her hand dismissively.

'I'm a partner at the Beauty Spot, yes.'

'Did I hear you got back with Jack?'

'Correct.'

'Didn't he have a child with that much younger woman?'

'Yes, he did. Robert is a lovely boy.'

'Must be difficult to trust Jack, though. I mean, he let you down a lot, financially, and then shacking up with someone young enough to be your daughter.'

'Jack and I are great, thanks. Speaking of daughters, that's my Jess.' Sophie pointed to Jess, who was standing a few feet away, talking into her phone. 'You probably remember her from when she was much younger.'

Victoria looked Jess up and down. 'Here to try to find an elite boyfriend, I suppose?'

'No, she's here to support her cousins, the three stars of the team.'

Thankfully, before a full cat fight broke out, the triplets trundled over to say hi to their cousin.

'What are you doing here? Are you lost?' Liam slagged her.

Jess put her phone down and grinned. 'I was bored, so I thought I'd come down and see if you're actually any good.'

'And?' Leo asked.

'Not bad.'

'Not bad? I scored the winning try!' Luke playfully hit her on the arm.

'I kicked most of the points,' Liam said.

'Did you see my pass to Barry for his try?' Leo asked.

'Okay, okay, you were all great.' Jess laughed.

They walked over to us and Sophie congratulated them loudly and effusively.

Sebastian came up behind them.

'Hello, darling,' Victoria gushed, trying to hug him as he swatted her away.

He locked eyes with Jess. 'Hi.'

'Hi.' Jess blushed.

'I'm Sebastian,' he said.

'This is our cousin, Jess.' Leo introduced her.

'How come you guys never told me you had a supermodel cousin?' Sebastian drawled.

The triplets made vomit noises. I felt like joining them. Smarmy, overconfident little git.

'Could you be any lamer?' Luke asked Sebastian.

'Dude, you're so cheesy,' Leo said.

'Step away,' Liam warned.

I watched Jess's face. Her eyes were on Sebastian and she was lapping up his attention.

'Jess!' Sophie said sharply. 'We need to go.'

'Yes, so do we, Sebastian.' Victoria tugged at her son's arm.

'Really nice to meet you, Jess,' Sebastian said, not taking his eyes off her.

'You too.' She fluttered her eyelashes at him.

'Will I see you at the next game?'

'Definitely.'

Victoria pulled Sebastian away as he looked back over his shoulder.

'Don't go there, he's a jerk,' Liam said to Jess.

'Tosser,' Luke agreed.

'Wanker,' Leo said.

Judging by the way Jess was looking at Sebastian, it was clear she was not listening to a single word her cousins were saying.

11. Louise

I pressed play, grabbed the shampoo bottle, and as quickly as possible washed Clara's hair. I had exactly two minutes and twenty-one seconds before the song ended.

Clara hummed along with her eyes squeezed tightly shut. Just as the song ended, I rinsed the last suds from her hair.

'Towel, Mummy,' Clara shouted.

I grabbed a warm, fluffy towel and wrapped my daughter in it, drying all the water from her body, then quickly tied up her hair in a soft towel on her head.

The whole bath, hair-washing and drying had to happen before the song ended. I had tried to get Clara to agree to a longer song – I had pushed for 'Bohemian Rhapsody' – but it had to be Dolly Parton's 'Love Is Like A Butterfly', which Mum had introduced her to when she was a baby.

I handed Clara her soft dressing-gown with no seams, then sat down to catch my breath. Clara hugged the dressing-gown to her.

I was hanging up the wet towels when she said, 'It was Hannah's birthday today.'

'Oh, that's nice. Did she bring in a cake? Did you all sing "Happy Birthday"?'

Clara fiddled with the belt on her dressing-gown. 'She brought in a cake, but it wasn't nice at all. It was disgusting. I said I didn't like it.'

Oh, no.

'And Hannah got really angry and said I was mean to say

her cake tasted horrible, but it did. It was a carrot cake and there were bits of carrot sticking out of it. Yuk.'

'Clara, we've talked about this. It's not nice to say negative things about other people's clothes or body shape or food or anything about them.'

'I *know*, Mummy, I didn't say anything, but she asked me. She said, "Why are you making a weird face? Do you not like my cake? I think it's the best cake ever," and I said, "No, I don't, it's horrible," because it was horrible.'

'I understand, sweetheart, but nobody wants to hear that their birthday cake is horrible.'

'Well, why did she ask me? If you don't want to know the truth, don't ask.'

She had a point. The weird face was probably enough information for Hannah to go on. Still, Clara had to learn how to manage people and situations.

'Anyway, she said I'm not invited to her party. She said she only invited me because her mummy said she had to invite everyone in the class, even the people she doesn't like. But because I said her cake is horrible, I'm disinvited.'

Little bitch.

'Why don't I ring her mum and explain that you were just being honest?'

Clara looked up at me. 'I don't think that's a good idea. Her mummy made the cake.'

Oh, for goodness' sake, why didn't the woman buy a bloody shop cake that all the kids liked and make all of our lives easier? What kind of a clown makes a poxy carrot cake for a ten-year-old's birthday anyway?

'Okay. Well, why don't you talk to Hannah and just say you didn't mean to criticize the cake? You just don't like carrots.'

'But I do like carrots.'

'Okay, but not in a cake. Look, just talk to her. It'll be nice to go to her party and have fun.'

'I don't want to go to her party. It'll be too noisy and her mum will probably make more disgusting cakes.'

'Clara, you have to get used to going to parties and having fun with your classmates. I know it's hard sometimes and parties can be noisy, but it's part of life. Remember what Granny always said? "The more you try, the easier it'll get."'

'Well, Granny's dead now.'

That hit me like a punch.

Clara continued, seemingly unaffected by her reference to her grandmother's passing while I struggled to control my emotions. 'Anyway, Mummy, I've been disinvited and I don't want to go. Hannah and her friends don't like me. They think I'm weird.'

My heart sank. My beautiful girl was always going to be an outsider, the kid who didn't fit in. I wanted her to have friends and fun, but as Colin had told me, Clara's idea of a good time was not the same as most kids'. Clara's idea of a perfect day was being in her bedroom with the lights dimmed, snuggled up in her blanket with Luna, reading or watching a movie of her choice with the volume down low.

'Okay. You and I can do something fun on Saturday afternoon instead. What would you like to do? We could go for a walk in the forest and have a picnic, or –'

'We could try and find my daddy.' Clara cut across me. 'You're so clever, Mummy. Gavin and Sophie and Julie are always saying how clever you are. I bet you could find him. I want to find him. Everyone has a daddy except me. William said I have no daddy because when he saw how weird I am he ran away.'

I felt my heart shatter. I'd thought my love would be enough. I'd thought my family and the village I'd surrounded

Clara with was enough, but it wasn't. My sisters had warned me this would happen. They'd said Clara would get to an age where she'd want to know more. But how could I help my beautiful daughter, when I had no clue who her father was?

'I'll tell you what, I'll try really hard, but I may not be able to find him. You understand that, right?'

She put her arms around me. 'Thank you, Mummy.'

I held her gently, enjoying the hug, and tried to figure out what the hell to do next.

Dad came to visit us on Saturday. I was in the kitchen making lunch, listening to him and Clara talking while they sat on the couch, Dad with his arm lightly around Clara. I could hear her telling him a very long story about birds and he was doing a good job of sounding interested. He had always been sweet to Clara, but he was a little nervous of her, wary of saying or doing the wrong thing and setting her off. He'd always taken the lead from Mum and followed what she did with Clara.

Clara finally finished her story and Dad said, 'Well, now, I've learned a lot today. You are a very clever girl. I don't know how you remember all those facts.'

'I'm clever like my mummy.'

'That's true. Your mother was always the smartest of my children.'

'Is she your favourite?' Clara asked.

I smiled to myself. If Sophie and Julie were here, they'd be straining their ears too.

'Ah, now, fathers don't have favourites. I love all my kids equally.'

'What about your grandchildren?'

'The same. I love you all equally.'

'Granny always said I was her favourite.'

'Yes, pet, I think you were. Sure, she was mad about you.'

'I miss Granny.'

'I do too.'

'I wish she didn't die.'

'I do too.'

'Are you lonely, Granddad?'

'I am, pet, but I have a lovely family, so I'm lucky.'

I stopped stirring the soup and tried not to cry. Dad sounded so sad.

'If you only had one child, then they'd be your favourite,' Clara said.

'That's true. You are your mum's favourite and Jess is Sophie's favourite.'

'But Jack loves Jess and Robert the same.'

'I think so, yes.'

'I wish I had a daddy.'

Silence. I froze and held my breath.

'I wish my mummy could find my daddy. I'd be his favourite then too.'

'Well, now . . . I suppose . . . it's a bit like . . . Well, not everyone has a mummy and a daddy. Some people only have a mummy and some only a daddy and some have great parents and some have not-so-great parents. But you have the best mummy in the world, so that's lucky for you, isn't it?'

'I know, Granddad, but I would like to meet my daddy and see what he's like. If I like him, he can be my daddy. If I don't like him, he won't be.'

'It's a little more complicated than that, sweetheart, and I suppose if your mother said she can't find him, then . . . well . . . that's it.'

I needed to get in there and save Dad.

'Lunch is ready,' I called.

We chatted about everything and nothing over lunch, and

while Dad and I were having coffee, Clara went to her room to snuggle with Luna.

'Did you hear what she was asking me?' Dad asked quietly. I nodded.

'She seems set on it, Louise. Have you no way of finding him?'

'No. I looked up the hotel online, but it's not a hotel any more. It's a block of apartments.'

'And you remember nothing?'

'Not really, no. I was so excited about the promotion to partner that I got very drunk, which is unlike me, and I . . . well, I ended up in bed with a man.' It felt very strange to be having this conversation with my father.

Dad sipped his coffee. 'It's the most un-Louise thing I've ever known you to do.'

I smiled. 'I know, and what were the chances that I'd get bloody pregnant? But, then again, look at what I have now.'

'She's a little dote. You wouldn't be without her.'

'Clara's my world.'

Dad looked down. 'Anne was mine.'

I reached across and put my hand over his. 'Oh, Dad, I'm sorry you're lonely. Is there anything I can do?'

'Nothing at all. Sure you've all been so good to me. It's life. I'll get used to it, in time. It's just very quiet in the house without her.'

'I'm so glad I got closer to her in the last few years.'

'So was she. It made her so happy.'

'Are you still seeing Dolores?'

'I am, but we're just pals. She's a bit of company. We play golf and have lunch in the golf club.'

'Be careful, Dad, she's looking for more than friendship.'

'Ah, no, she knows the score.'

Dad was delusional if he thought Dolores was going to be

happy with the odd lunch going forward. She was on a mission to hook him in.

'How's work?' Dad asked, sticking to safer ground.

'Busy as ever, but I'm struggling with this snowflake intern, Zoë. She got dumped on me by Walter, the managing partner. She's his goddaughter and honestly, Dad, she is the most self-obsessed, lazy, unprofessional employee I've ever had to deal with.'

'Did you talk to Walter about it?'

'I did, but he asked me to hang on to her for a year as a personal favour.'

'And you can't say no to the managing partner.'

'Exactly.'

'I had a few employees in my day that were difficult. You have to learn to manage them. Try to find a way to keep her busy but away from you, so you only have to deal with her occasionally.'

'Good advice, I'll do that. We're a small team, but I definitely need to see less of her. And, to be fair, I'm not sleeping well with the Clara-wanting-to-meet-her-dad thing hanging over me, so I'm probably less tolerant than usual.'

Dad burst out laughing. 'Because you're so tolerant normally.'

I chuckled. 'Fair point.'

It felt nice to laugh with Dad. We hadn't done it in a long time. I was so lucky to have such a brilliant dad. I ached for Clara's loss, but what could I do? I would just have to be the best mother and father for her.

12. Sophie

Louise plonked a big box on Julie's kitchen counter, followed by Harry with two more. She had asked us all to meet up in Julie's because she had found more of Mum's stuff. What we had already gone through had been divvied up between us or donated to the charity shop, and we thought it was all done – until Dad had asked Louise to check the attic.

'Most of it is old coats and shoes that Mum no longer wore and some bags and hats,' Louise said, as she pulled back the lids of the boxes. 'I've no idea why she stuck it up in the attic instead of just getting rid of it, but I thought you'd like to see it before I give it all to the charity shop.'

I poked about, but I had enough coats, shoes and hats and, besides, most of it was old-fashioned, and not in a cool vintage way, but in a decidedly uncool seventies and eighties way. But then I spied something tucked away at the bottom. There was no mistaking that it was a designer bag.

'Oooh, can I have this?' I asked, holding up the silver leather clutch bag. 'It's gorgeous. Not very Mum, but I love it.'

'Fine by me,' Julie said.

'Hang on.' Louise took it from my hand. 'That's my Prada clutch bag. I lent this to Mum years ago. I totally forgot about it.'

'Oh. Do you want it back?'

'No, you can have it,' she said, handing it to me.

'Really?'

'Sure. It's too small, barely holds anything.'

I was delighted. I'd sold all of my designer clothes and

accessories to pay the rent when Jack lost his business, and designer items were no longer in my budget, so this was a treat.

'Coffee, anyone?' Harry asked.

'Yes, please,' I said, and Louise accepted gratefully.

Harry had bought a brasserie-style machine that made the nicest coffee.

While Harry frothed milk I turned to my sisters. 'Brace yourselves for who Jess is chatting to online.'

'Who?'

I looked at Julie.

'No,' she said. 'Please no.'

'Yes.'

'For God's sake, who?' Louise's patience ran out – it never lasted long.

'Sebastian Carter-Mills.'

'Is he that awful woman's son?'

'Yes,' Julie and I answered at once.

'Are you absolutely sure? How did you find out?' Julie asked.

I told them how I'd suspected Jess was flirting with some-one on the phone, so I'd checked her Instagram DMs and had just found out it was Sebastian. 'Why?' I said, putting my head in my hands. 'Of all the hundreds of boys out there, thousands, why does she have to be attracted to him? What am I going to do? How do I stop this? There is no way in hell my Jess can go out with Victoria's son.'

'No way,' Julie agreed.

'Well, you can't order her not to see him,' Louise said, 'because that will only make her even more determined.'

'True.'

'All you can do is watch her like a hawk.'

'Remember when Mum told you to stay away from Freddy Finlay?' Julie reminded me.

'Who's Freddy Finlay?' Harry said. 'Was he a bad boy?'

I laughed. 'I suppose he was. Freddy was a stoner and known for it. It was all very brief and I wasn't really that into him, but then Mum went nuts and forbade me to see him. I was about to break up with him because he was always stoned and really boring, but when Mum ordered me to dump him, I refused and went out with him for longer than I actually wanted to just to defy her. Mum ordering me to break up with him totally backfired,' I told Harry.

'Could we ask the triplets to suss it out from their end?' Julie suggested. 'Maybe they could casually ask Sebastian if he's seeing anyone or has his eye on anyone or whatever.'

Harry shook his head. 'That won't work. Boys don't chat the way girls do.'

'True,' Julie said, sighing. 'All they seem to talk about is food, weight training and rugby. But, look, I'll ask them. They might be able to find out something.'

'Okay,' I said – anything that might help was worth trying. 'But tell them to be super-casual about it. If it gets back to Jess, I'm dead.'

'Don't worry,' Julie said. 'I want him as far away from Jess as you do.'

Harry handed us perfectly made lattes.

'I know Victoria is a pain, but maybe Sebastian isn't so bad,' he said. 'You know, don't judge the child for the sins of the parents.'

'He's got her DNA, Harry. He has no hope,' I said.

'And he was awful to our boys when they first went to Castle Academy,' Julie reminded him.

'I know, but he was young and stupid then. We all are at that age.'

'Sorry, Harry, it's just not happening. I don't want my Jess near that family.'

'To be honest, Sophie, the boys on the squad are on such a tight schedule, he won't have much time to see her. They're going all-in for the cup this year.' Harry tried to reassure me.

'Good.'

'And what about you, Louise?' Harry asked, offering her a biscuit. 'Is Clara still asking about her dad?'

Louise nodded. 'She will not let it go. I don't know what to do. If there was a way to track him down, I'd do it for her sake.'

'I have to say the day Christelle contacted me was a shock. A huge shock. I didn't know she existed. But it was the best thing that ever happened to me.'

'Excuse me!'

Harry rubbed Julie's back. 'The sixth best thing, after Julie and the boys.'

She smiled at him.

'Anyway, the point is that she's enriched my life and all our lives beyond measure. I wish for your sake and Clara's that you could find him. I think it would be a good thing.'

'But then again, he might be a deadbeat,' I said. 'Christelle happens to be fantastic, but Clara's dad might not be.'

'That's possible,' Harry acknowledged, 'but if he turned out to be a great guy, it would be lovely for Clara to know him.'

Louise put down her coffee. 'I tend to agree, but I have no way of finding him and she has a loving family, so she'll be fine.'

'Of course she will.' Julie smiled at Louise.

I reached for my jacket. 'I've got to fly. I have a pile of things to get for Robert's sixth birthday party.'

'You are a saint,' Julie said.

'Where's his mother?' Louise asked.

'Oh, you know Pippa, busy, busy, busy . . .'

'Doing what?' Louise frowned.

'That's the million-dollar question. According to Quentin, she's shagging some married multi-millionaire.'

'Oh dear. That won't end well,' Harry said.

'Would you like some help on the day?' Julie said. 'Tom and I could come over.'

'That would be great, thanks.' It would be fantastic to have the back-up. I was not looking forward to a houseful of sugar-crazed six-year-olds.

'I'd offer to bring Clara, but she hates parties,' Louise said.

I patted Louise's shoulder. 'No worries – and thanks again for the cool bag.'

When I got home, I could hear Jess giggling on the phone. It was a high giggle, a flirty giggle. I knew that giggle well: I'd used it myself a lot as a teenager. She'd been using it a lot in the last few weeks and was spending hours on her phone. Whoever was at the other end, and I was pretty sure it was bloody Sebastian, she liked them a lot.

I knocked gently on her door.

'We have to leave now or you'll be late for your hockey match,' I said, peeking in.

She waved me away and said to the screen, 'It's just my naggy mum. Oh, my God, she's always on my back. Like, seriously, she's such a pain.'

I knew all teenage girls went through phases of finding their mothers annoying, but it still stung. After her brief obsession with Pippa, Jess had come back to me and we'd been so close. But then she'd turned thirteen and for the last two years I had become a nag, a pain, the worst mum in the world, a psycho mum and, my personal favourite, a bore. *What would you know? You're so boring. I bet you never even went out when you were my age.*

128

If only she knew. I'd partied very hard at her age, sneaking out of the window when Mum and Dad were asleep, getting Julie to let me in when I got home in the early hours of the morning. Louise was the boring one: all she did was study. Julie always had a steady boyfriend, but I liked to party. I'd tap on Julie's bedroom window and she'd let me in whatever time it was and never say anything.

I rapped on the door again, louder. She was slating me anyway so I might as well play my part.

'Hurry up, Jess, we need to go.'

She huffed, said goodbye and glared at me. 'Oh, my God, you are so rude. I was on a call.'

'With who?'

'No one.'

'It was someone.'

'You don't know them,' she said, blushing.

'A boy?'

'Mum, go away.'

I smiled. 'I was a teenager once too, Jess. I know it's hard for you to believe, but I also dated boys and had crushes. You can talk to me.'

She looked up, her eyes wide. 'Are you for real right now? Talk to you about boys? I'd rather die. You're so weird.'

I let it go. I didn't want to push her, because it was important for me to keep communication with Jess open, however small the window was. But I did want to shout, I'm not weird, I'm just lonely. I miss you. I miss our closeness. I miss you coming to me with your problems and your hugs and your love. I miss us being a team, Sophie and Jess against the world. Snuggling up on rainy days watching movies, going for walks, having hot chocolate in cosy cafés, baking together . . . I miss it all. And I'm worried about you, worried about boys and sex and drink and vaping and drugs. These days I felt like I was losing her and it hurt. It was a grief all of its own – very different from mine for Mum, but a deep grief all the same. I mourned the loss of my girl, even though she was right there in front of me.

What I actually said was, 'Come on, let's go.'

In the car I asked her what she thought Robert would like for his birthday.

Barely looking up from her phone, she muttered, 'I dunno. Just get him a truck or something.'

'Jess, put your phone down. I'm trying to talk to you.'

'I'm just texting Lauren. Relax.'

'I am relaxed,' I said, through gritted teeth.

'Yeah, right.'

'So do you think I should get him a truck?'

'Who?'

Jesus Christ. 'Robert.'

'Oh, yeah, whatever.'

'Okay. Thanks for your help.'

'What? He's six. He'll like anything you give him. God, chill out.'

I gripped the steering wheel and counted to ten, but I still wanted to shout at her. Thankfully, we reached the school before I lost my temper and she hopped out without so much as a backward glance or a 'Thanks for the lift.'

When I got home Jack was packing his suitcase, carefully folding his shirts into the small carry-on. He was travelling more, these days, and while it was good for his job as a business consultant, it meant he was away a lot and left me to manage Jess and Robert on my own.

'Promise you'll be back before Robert's party?'

'I promise.'

'Swear, Jack?'

'Sophie, I'm not going to miss my son's birthday and, by the way, thank you for organizing it. Pippa's brief mother-of-the-year show after Robert's fall hasn't lasted long.'

It had lasted exactly one week. She'd fawned all over Robert, gleefully accused us of neglect, but then got bored of 'mothering' and handed him back.

'I'll send a text out to the WhatsApp class group this morning to get an idea of numbers, book the magician and sort out the food.'

Jack pulled me to him. 'You're an angel, Sophie. Thanks for being such a brilliant stepmum. I know it's not easy.'

I nuzzled into the crook of his neck. 'Thank you for appreciating what I do, unlike our grumpy teen.'

'Ah, Jess is great. You're hard on her.'

I tensed. In Jack's eyes, Jess could do no wrong. When she shouted at me, she was just tired. When she was rude, I'd 'obviously' wound her up. Since the moment he'd laid eyes on her in the delivery room, Jack had been head over heels in love with his daughter. While I loved that he was so crazy about her, it bothered me that he never said no to her. I had spoiled her too when she was younger, but I'd come to realize that spoiling kids did them no favours. Life was tough and you needed resilience to get through it.

I pulled back from Jack's embrace. 'I know she's great, but she was rude to me this morning and that's not okay. By the way, she's been chatting to someone a lot lately.'

'Really? Who?'

'I'm pretty sure it's Sebastian Carter-Mills.'

Jack zipped up his suitcase. 'Hopefully he's not as much of a dick as his father. He'd better be nice to Jess or I'll be having serious words with him.'

'Relax, Rambo. I think it's just flirting and chatting so far. Maybe it'll fizzle out soon. He's very tied up with the rugby,

so he hardly has any time to be socializing. Julie says the triplets barely have time to breathe.'

Jack shuddered. 'I can't stand the thought of some hormonal fifteen-year-old all over Jess.'

I grinned. 'You were a hormonal fifteen-year-old once.'

'Exactly. I know what was on my mind, and it wasn't
chatting.'

'Stop!'

Jack laughed, kissed me and left to catch his flight.

13. Julie

'What? Is Daddy not going to be here on my special day?'
Robert's face fell. 'So . . . is it just you here? No Mummy or
Daddy or Jess?' His big brown eyes blinked.

'Daddy is trying hard to get back in time, but his plane is
delayed. Hopefully your mummy will make it in time for the
cake.'

Jess crouched down. 'Hey, of course I'll stay. I'll just tell
the girls I'll see them later. We'll have great fun, okay?'

Her little brother beamed up at Jess and I saw Sophie
mouthing, 'Thank you,' to her. Jess had just finished piling
on her make-up when Sophie had the text from Jack to say
he was stuck at Heathrow. Poor Robert. My heart went out
to him.

The doorbell rang. Sophie held Robert's hand and they
went to open it. Kids started to flow in.

Sophie made sure Robert had a great day and Jess was
wonderful and endlessly patient with the kids. Tom helped
her organize Pass the Parcel, then relay races and sack races
in the garden to tire them out. Sophie held off cutting the
cake as long as she could, but it was clear Jack wasn't going
to make it.

'Jack is so upset and poor Robert is going to be gutted,'
she said. 'Pippa promised to be here.'

'It's not your fault, Sophie. You've done everything to
make the day special. You are an unbelievable stepmother.
But the parents will be here to pick the kids up very soon, so
you have to do the cake now,' I said.

'Hurry up, Mum. I want to go out.' Jess was hovering beside us.

'Where are you off to?' I asked.

'Just out with some of my mates.'

'Girl mates or boy mates?'

'Girl mates, Julie.'

'You're very dressed up for the girls. Is there not one boy among these mates? A gorgeous girl like yourself must have fellas chasing you around.'

I could feel Sophie listening, but she just kept putting candles on the cake.

'Oh, my God, Julie, stop. This is so embarrassing. Do you interrogate the triplets when they go out?'

'Yes, but sure they're only interested in chasing a ball. So?'

'So nothing, Julie. I'm meeting some mates.'

'Jeepers, Jess, you should apply to the secret service. Talk about giving nothing away,' I teased, but she didn't laugh. 'Well, be careful, some boys are dickheads.'

'Okay, thanks for the tip.' I could tell she was surprised by my harsh choice of words, but she needed to be warned and Sebastian was a jerk.

'She's right, Jess,' Sophie said. 'A lot of boys are only after one thing and they can be very persuasive and charming to get what they want.'

'Especially boys who've been spoiled by their parents. They're the worst,' I said.

'Yes, they're completely self-centred and only care about themselves,' Sophie said, hammering home the point.

'OMG, can you both please stop? This is so embarrassing. Mum, can I go now?' Jess begged.

'After the cake,' Sophie said.

'*Muuuuum*,' Jess pleaded. 'I've done everything to help you today. I've waited for hours to go out.'

'Okay,' Sophie said, but I could see she didn't want to let her go. The teenage years were so bloody difficult. 'But keep your phone on and don't turn off phone locator.'

'And don't waste your time on boys who are not nice and kind,' I shouted after my niece, as a parting shot. Jess acted so sassy and strong, but she was actually quite fragile. Her parents' separation had really affected her. Then Pippa had come along and Robert was born. She'd had a tough time being shunned by Pippa and seeing her dad all over his new baby son. For a while she had felt rejected and sidelined. I had watched her struggle with it. She was a fantastic girl, but I worried that the wrong guy could play on that fragility and her need for attention and affection.

'Did you get any info from the triplets?' Sophie said, the moment the front door slammed.

'None,' I said. 'Sorry. They'll keep an ear open, though. They can't stand Sebastian, so they don't hang out with him, but they have a couple of friends in common. I'll let you know if I hear anything.'

The doorbell went – it was finally almost pick-up time. I was exhausted. As parents began to arrive to pick up their kids, we called Robert over and told him it was time for the cake and candles.

Robert frowned. 'But Mummy and Daddy aren't here yet. We can't.'

'I know, sweetie,' Sophie said gently, 'but everyone is going home now. Julie is going to video it so your dad can watch it when he gets home and we'll send it to your mummy too.'

'Oh, okay.' He looked forlorn and I had to block the urge to grab him into my arms and wrap him up tight. The poor little thing.

'Hey, Robert, let's see if you can blow all the candles out in one go,' Tom said. I smiled at my kind, sweet boy. 'I tried on my last birthday, when I was eleven, but I could only blow out five at once. Can you blow out six?' he asked.

'I can, I can!' Robert was up for the challenge.

We gathered everyone around the table and sang 'Happy Birthday' as Robert blew out his candles in one go, using a fair amount of spit but achieving his goal.

Tom high-fived him.

Just as Sophie was picking the candles out of the cake, the door flew open and Pippa swooshed in, dressed to the nines in a long black velvet coat. She brushed past everyone, stood on my foot as she nudged me out of the way, and enveloped her son in a big hug.

'Hello, darling, did you make a wish for me? Here I am!'

'Mummy.' He hugged her, thrilled she was there.

'Nice of her to show up,' I muttered to Sophie.

'Now, who would like a slice?' Pippa grabbed the knife from Sophie's hand and completely took over. She handed out slices of cake like the bloody Queen of Sheba and 'graciously' accepted the other parents' thanks for the 'lovely party'. I stood back, trying not to explode with rage. The absolute neck of her was unbelievable.

'Oh, you're so welcome. It was my pleasure,' Pippa gushed. 'It's a big day for Robert.'

I looked around and saw Sophie standing in the corner of the kitchen, watching Pippa soaking up the praise for the party that she had organized and paid for. Sophie looked exhausted and drained. There was no way I was standing by and watching Pippa take credit for all the work my sister had done. No bloody way.

'I think we all need to give Sophie a big round of applause,' I shouted, over the noise of the kids munching and the parents chatting. 'After all, Sophie was the one who organized this whole party for Robert on her own, so she deserves a big thank-you.' I began to clap and everyone joined in.

Pippa glared at me, but I was far beyond caring what a selfish cow like her thought or felt about anything.

I smiled widely at her. 'I know you'd like to thank Sophie yourself for hosting your son's birthday party, Pippa. It's pretty great for you that Robert's stepmother happens to be such a thoughtful, generous and kind person. You must be so grateful.'

There was a deep, awkward silence as everyone looked from me to Pippa to Sophie, and I could see some of the other mothers suppressing smiles. I reckoned they had the measure of Pippa and her haphazard approach to mother-hood. I didn't speak or move, just stared at Pippa, daring her to say one single thing against my sister.

She gave me the filthiest look imaginable, then said, through a clenched jaw, 'Thank you, Sophie.'

Sophie nodded at Pippa, then winked at me. Mission accomplished. Devlin sisters 1 – Pippa 0.

Back home that evening, I was wishing I had Sophie there to help me. I deleted the draft message for the tenth time. Come on, Julie, it's just a bloody WhatsApp message, I told myself. Get a grip. I typed it again, but as my finger hovered over the send button, I hesitated.

Why did I have to organize the stupid scarves and hats anyway? Who thought it was necessary for the team and their parents to wear matching scarves and hats? We'd all look like total dorks.

'Boys?' I tried to get the triplets' attention, but they were arguing over how much protein powder to put into their smoothies.

'Four big scoops,' Liam said.

'No way! That's too much. Two is the right amount,' Luke said.

'For God's sake, Liam, you've used up all the bananas,' Leo shouted.

Luke punched Liam's arm. 'You're always doing that. I'm sick of having no bananas for my shakes.'

'Piss off. You finished off the strawberries yesterday.' Liam punched him back, harder.

'And the blueberries,' Leo added.

'BOYS!' I shouted.

They turned to me.

'No need to shout,' Luke said.

'Do you think we could just forget about the stupid team hats and scarves this year and let everyone wear whatever they want?'

The all stared at me open-mouthed.

'What?'

'Are you mental?'

'No way.'

I was not expecting that reaction. The boys wore whatever was on the floor of their bedroom, whether it was filthy or not. Sartorial elegance was not at the top of their priority list. I'd presumed they'd immediately agree with me.

'The squad hats and scarves are a school tradition,' Liam said.

'Every team has had them. No way are we not having them,' Luke added.

'Mum, do not try to change anything. Do it the same as every year,' Leo warned me.

'I like the hats,' Liam said.

'Yeah, they're handy for training when it's freezing,' Luke said.

'I want a hat,' Tom piped up. 'I want to wear it into school so everyone knows my bros are on the team.'

'Yeah, Tom wants one, and all the siblings get them. Seriously, Mum, just follow the rules,' Liam lectured me.

I threw up my hands. 'Okay, okay, I'll get the hats. I didn't think you'd feel so strongly about it. I've looked around and the cheapest dark red ones I can find are in Penneys.'

'Grand, yeah, get those.' They all nodded and went back to arguing about their smoothies while I composed my text.

Dear parents, Re the hats and scarves. I have found red ones that are close to the school colours in Penneys. €3 a hat and €4 for the scarf. If you would let me know how many each family would like to order, I'll sort it out.

I pressed send and went to try to wrestle the boys away from the fridge, so I could take out some meat for dinner.

As I pulled the steaks from the drawer, my phone began to hop.

Ping. Ping. Ping. Ping. Ping. Ping . . .

Penneys? Are they wool? They need to be warm.

Can you send a photo please? The red needs to be a burgundy and not a cherry or a wine.

WTF?

I think we can do better than Penneys. Have you tried Zara?

Penneys? Please! We need to be warm and not have some cheap polyester around our necks. Go to Atelier de Cashmere and order from them.

That was from Victoria, of course. The stupid, snobby cow.

Oh yes, cashmere would be lovely.

So snug.

So cosy.

Much more appropriate for Castle Academy than Penneys.

I think Penneys sounds fine.

Yes! A kindred spirit.

Atelier de Cashmere in London has a beautiful shade of deep burgundy – a perfect match for the jerseys. We want quality, not tat.

Victoria again.
I felt my cheeks burning. Over my dead body was I buying cashmere from some poncy shop in London.

If we order from London we'll have to pay tax. Surely we can source something locally.

That was Catherine, a sensible mum.

A soft wool would work, it doesn't have to be cashmere.

Agreed, cashmere might be a bit pricey.

We want quality, though, not scratchy wool that the boys won't wear.

Stick to merino, cashmere, alpaca or lamb's wool.

I find lamb's wool can be a bit itchy. Julian has very sensitive skin and is prone to eczema, I'd be happier with cashmere.

As I said, it has to be cashmere. [Victoria again.] I will happily take on the sourcing of appropriate accessories for the team.

No need. I'll have a look around and see what I can source locally.

'And fuck off, you snobby, condescending bitch,' I hissed at the phone.

'Who are you shouting at?' Liam asked.

'Stupid parents banging on about different types of wool. Seriously, a hat is a hat.'

'Don't fight with the parents, Mum. Just chill,' Luke said.

'It's just some hats and scarves. There's no need to lose it, Mum.' Leo put a huge scoop of protein powder into the Nutribullet.

That was the sodding point. It should be just hats and scarves but it wasn't because of a few ridiculous parents. It was a bloody minefield of skin sensitivity, school image, exact colour-matching, snobbery and general fuck-wittery.

I was definitely going to ring Sophie for help. Over my dead body was I ordering expensive cashmere from London to wear at the side of a rainy rugby pitch in Dublin.

When Harry came home from his business dinner, I was already in bed searching woolly hat websites. As he sat down to take off his shoes, he was subjected to me ranting and raging about Cashmere-gate. I presumed he'd have seen the messages and be firmly on my side.

'We need to be careful, Julie. We can't rock the boat. We don't want to bring any negativity on us because it might affect the boys.'

I sat up. 'Do you honestly think that the coach is going to penalize the boys because their sensible mother decided not to bankrupt the parents by getting expensive hats and scarves?'

Harry pulled off his socks. 'No, but parents can cause trouble and we need to keep the peace for the boys. Please run any future texts by me before sending them out on the WhatsApp group.'

What? Was he for real? Was I five years old?

'For God's sake, Harry, I don't need you to read my texts. I need you to support me.'

'Julie, we have about three months of a campaign left, if the team does well. Can you please just stay calm and do not wind up any of the parents. If they want stupid cashmere hats, get them. I'll happily subsidize the cost if that makes you feel better.'

'Well, brace yourself because cashmere is very expensive.'

'How expensive?'

'Eighty quid a hat. Sterling, not euros.'

'That's extortion!'

'Told you.'

'See if you can find a compromise, something everyone is happy with,' he suggested, as he pulled on his pyjama bottoms. 'On the subject of the team, how are the plans for Saturday coming along?'

I had totted up the guest list and it came to ninety-four people.

'I'm going to say again that I totally disagree with this,' I said. 'It's a massive undertaking for any captain's parents for no real reason and no gain. It's okay for us because we have a big house and we can afford it, but what if it was the old us, Harry? In our small house with no extra money?'

'The boys wouldn't be going to Castle Academy if we were in the old house. We had no money for school fees.'

'Okay, but some people are making huge sacrifices to pay the fees and don't have spare cash to host big parties. Why does all this tradition have to be followed? Why can't we break the cycle and make it fairer and more equitable?'

'Julie, we've had this conversation. I understand what you want to do and the reasoning behind it, but we have to put the boys first and that means rowing in with tradition.'

Harry had almost had a full-on heart attack when I'd suggested sending out a text asking everyone to put thirty euros into a kitty to help pay for the party. It wasn't because we needed it, but because I wanted to stop this ridiculous pressure being put on the captain's parents in the future.

Needless to say, I was not allowed to send that text. I'd say people probably went bankrupt rather than refuse to host the sacred party.

'Fine, you're right. I'll try to stop giving out. I've ordered wine, prosecco and beer, and Marion is going to help me cook the food.'

'It's a lot of food, Julie. Why don't you just get it catered?'

'Because I can throw together a chicken curry and a few salads and I don't want it to be over the top. I want it to be a down-to-earth party, a more casual get-together.'

Harry pulled off his shirt and pulled on the AC/DC T-shirt he slept in. It was so old it had holes in the shoulder, but he loved it and refused to throw it out. I think it reminded him of when he was young and fun, not middle-aged and exhausted.

'Julie, I love that you're practical and thinking of others but, honestly, you're going to wear yourself out.'

'I refuse to have caterers. I'm determined to keep this as low-key as possible.'

Harry held up his hand. 'Okay, do it your way.'

He went to brush his teeth as I continued to search 'cheap

cashmere'. When he got into bed, I closed my computer and turned out the light. Harry opened his laptop.

'What are you doing?'

'I want to answer an email from Christelle. They arrived in São Paulo today. Then I need to work on my speech for the party on Saturday.'

'What speech?'

'Obviously as father of the captains I have to make a speech. It's –'

'Don't tell me – tradition?'

'Well, yes.' He grinned.

I winced. Harry had a tendency to be a bit long-winded when he had a captive audience, which was incredibly rare as no one at home ever listened to him. I was worried he might not know when to stop talking. I knew he'd be nervous, too, as he was still the 'not-posh dad who had never played rugby' and didn't quite fit in.

'Keep it short, Harry.'

'It will be the length it needs to be, Julie.'

'Short, Harry.'

'Go to sleep.'

'Three minutes max.'

'Goodnight, Julie.'

14. Louise

The door opened and Zoë strutted in holding a freshly made green smoothie. She sat down and shrugged off her coat.

Silence.

Was she seriously not going to apologize for turning up twenty-five minutes late to our weekly meeting?

'You're late, Zoë.' I glared at her.

'Oh, right, yeah, sorry. I had a splitting migraine. I didn't think I'd make it in, but I meditated and I felt just about well enough to come but I'll probably have to leave early.'

She sipped her smoothie as I resisted the urge to pour it down her silk blouse. She was so self-centred and entitled, it was beyond belief.

Clasping my hands together, I said, 'I really need all hands on deck this week. As you may remember, Zoë, we're in the middle of closing the largest MBS deal this company has ever handled.'

Zoë's eyebrows rose. 'What's an MBS again?'

Was she joking? How the hell could she not know what an MBS was? I wasn't sure I could take much more of Zoë. The joke of it was that this irritating, spoiled girl wasn't even studying law. She had dropped out of her Social Science course and was 'thinking about law'. Our managing partner, Walter, had dumped her on me, probably because I was the only female partner in the firm and was supposed to be some kind of 'role model' for this completely disinterested snowflake. I usually hired all of my own interns and they were fantastic, hard-working, bright, keen-to-learn young people. Zoë was an anomaly and a big fat pain in my arse.

'An MBS, Zoë, is a mortgage-backed security, a phrase that should be as familiar to you by this stage as your own name.'

Mike leaned in and whispered, 'You know, it's when you get a load of mortgages and sell them on from the bank, who lent the people the money, to another financial institution and they combine all the mortgages and loans into one unit that the public can invest in.'

'Right, okay, gotcha,' Zoë drawled.

'So, as I was saying before Zoë interrupted us, this is a big week for our department and I need everyone to be punctual and to be aware that there will probably be some late nights. Thursday could be an all-nighter.'

Zoë looked up. 'Late nights? That could be a problem for me, I have plans pretty much every night. And Thursday is a definite no.'

I stared at her. Her cavalier attitude to work drove me to distraction. I had worked so bloody hard to get where I was – no one had pulled any favours to give me a leg-up – and this piece of work had swanned into a fantastic internship opportunity and announced that she's not even sure if she's interested in a career in law.

Swallowing my rage, I said, 'I recommend you cancel your plans ASAP. This is your chance to show commitment to the department and to the firm, Zoë, and I suggest you take it. We are a team, and we all pull together when things get busy, is that understood?'

Zoë stifled a yawn. 'Did you not know it's Walter's sixtieth birthday on Thursday? I thought you guys were close. Anyway, I've invited a small group to a surprise dinner for him in Xavier de la Tour's new restaurant. Bernard is going too. I'll be leaving at five to get ready. Pre-dinner drinks are at six. In fact, I'll probably have to leave at four – I'll need to fit in a blow-dry.'

I gripped the side of my chair and willed myself not to slap her face. The little bitch had invited the other senior partner, Bernard, and not me? I felt humiliated and sidelined.

Using all the willpower I had, I kept my face as impassive as possible. 'Okay, then. I'll need you in at six a.m. on Thursday. Walter knows how important this deal is, and I'm sure if you end up having to work overtime, he'll understand.'

'I don't think so. As his only godchild and surrogate daughter, I'm giving a pre-dinner speech, so being late is not an option. As I said, it's a surprise for Walter, so I'd appreciate it if you kept quiet about it.'

In a strangled voice I managed to say, 'Fine. Then you can come in at six a.m. on Wednesday too.'

'I won't be much use to you if I've had no sleep. I'm not really a morning person.'

'Well, maybe we can change that.' I gave her my frostiest smile and carried on with the meeting.

Sophie had booked a local Italian restaurant for a 'last supper' with Gavin before the baby arrived and he disappeared into parenthood. Gavin had told me he was really struggling with the fact that Mum wouldn't meet his baby. I'd told Julie and Sophie, and Julie had immediately started crying. Sophie had decided we had to do something and make a fuss of him. So here we all were on the dot of seven p.m. – well, everyone except Julie, who was always late. She'd give Zoë a run for her money. It was only Tuesday but I had loads of work to do when I got home, so I was hoping for a quick dinner. Besides, Shania had generously offered to babysit Clara and I wanted her to get home to bed early.

Dad looked well. He'd put on a nice shirt and seemed less exhausted than last time I'd seen him, which, I realized with a sharp stab of guilt, had been about ten days ago. Work had completely taken over my life these past few weeks.

Gavin was wearing a branded *Tantastic by Shania* hoodie.

'Nice of you to dress up,' I said to him.

'It's called marketing, Louise.'

'It's called a hoodie, Gavin.' I grinned at him.

'It's a great name for a brand,' Sophie said.

'I came up with it,' Gavin said proudly. 'And I designed the logo and the fashion merchandise.'

'Hoodies, beanies and T-shirts don't exactly make you the Miuccia Prada of fashion.' Sophie laughed.

'They're selling like hot cakes,' Gavin told her.

Sophie punched him playfully on the arm. 'They're great and I'm just slagging you. I gave beanies to all our models and told them to post about them.'

'Cool, thanks.'

'I think a shirt when you're going out for dinner is more appropriate,' Dad noted. Gavin's relaxed attitude to life had always been a bugbear to him. He couldn't understand how his son didn't have a 'proper' nine-to-five job with a pension. He'd always worried about Gavin's future.

'Speaking of Prada,' I jumped in before Gavin got a lecture on employment, 'I see you're wearing the bag.'

Sophie patted the Prada bag I'd given her. 'Yes. It's the first chance I've had to use it – it's too good for work. I absolutely love it.' She beamed.

We ordered food, I ordered for Julie, and Dad poured us all wine.

'None for me, thanks.' Gavin put his hand over the wine glass.

'How come?' Sophie asked.

'It's not fair to Shania.'

'What's not fair to Shania?' Julie plonked herself down beside him. 'Sorry I'm late.'

'Drinking,' Gavin replied.

'Why?' I asked. Gavin loved his wine and beer.

'Because she can't, so I've decided not to either.'

'I ate for two and Harry drank for two when I was pregnant.' Julie laughed.

'Jack was the same,' Sophie said.

'Well, I'm supporting my girlfriend on our pregnancy.'

'Oh, God, can you please not do the we're-pregnant-our-pregnancy thing?' I said. 'It makes me want to throw up. Like, seriously, you're not pregnant. Shania is.'

'Agreed.' Sophie backed me up. 'Her body is being put through the wringer and stretched in every direction and her vagina will never be the same again, while you're just watching from the sidelines.'

'You will not have saggy boobs, stretch marks and a scar across your body after the birth,' Julie added.

'Mother of God, can we change the subject?' Dad groaned. 'Every time I have dinner with you lot the conversation ends up in the nether regions. It's enough to put a man off his food.'

'Sorry, Dad,' Julie said, giggling. 'Have you decided on any names yet, Gavin?'

'Yeah, but we're not telling anyone because we know everyone will start giving us their opinions and we want to make up our own minds.'

'Just make sure you give the child a sensible name,' Dad said.

I doubted very much that Gavin and Shania were going to name their child John or Mary. Chances are it would be something a little left-field.

'I see Shania's got into even more stores in the US. She's

really killing it with her tan,' Sophie said. 'You must be so proud of her.'

Gavin smiled. 'I so am. She's a rock star.'

'I have to say she's surprised me. She's a very good business head on her,' Dad said.

'And she'll be a great mum,' I added. 'She's always been fantastic with Clara.'

'I just wish that Mum would get to meet our baby,' Gavin said quietly. 'My baby will never know their granny.'

'That sucks,' Sophie said.

Dad fiddled with his napkin, twisting it around his hand. 'I'm very sorry, son. Your mother would have been so excited to meet your baby. She was so good with the grandchildren. I'm not a patch on her and I know that. I suppose I don't really know what to say to Jess now she's a teenager, and I'm trying to get to know the boys through rugby, and sure Clara is a dote but I do worry about saying or doing the wrong thing and upsetting her. I wish I was more useful to you all. I can see the hole Anne has left in all of your lives. I never realized just how much I relied on her, especially since I retired. She organized everything – family get-togethers, holidays, days out, dinners with friends, birthday gifts, birthday cakes, trips to the cinema and the theatre . . . I got lazy and just let her do it all. I'm a bit lost, to be honest. I don't know what to be doing with myself. Anne always had jobs for me, or an outing for us or a plan for the day. Now . . . well, now I wake up and I . . . well, I . . .'

'Oh, Dad.' Julie reached out and held his hand. 'It's awful for you.'

'No, pet, it's awful for all of us.'

'Yes, but hardest on you,' Sophie said.

'Well, I think it's pretty tough on me that my baby will never know Mum.' Gavin was not to be outdone on the loss front.

'I'm sorry, Gavin,' Julie said. 'Mum would have been all over your baby, her favourite child's child.'

'I wasn't her favourite.'

'Yes, you were,' we three sisters all said.

'Apple of her eye,' Dad agreed.

'Only son.'

'Little prince.'

'Youngest and finest.'

'Sod off.' Gavin smiled sadly. 'She loved us all.'

'Not me so much until Clara came along,' I noted.

'You were hard to love,' Gavin said.

'Thanks a lot.'

'Well . . .' Sophie said, '. . . you were a bit dismissive of everyone except Dad and Julie.'

She had a point. I had been hard on Mum, Sophie and Gavin. Julie had always got a pass because she was so nice and Dad was smart so I had related to him.

'Clara has brought out your softer side,' Julie said.

'Your mother doted on Clara,' Dad said. 'She worried about her all the time, the little pet.'

'So do I,' I admitted. 'She really misses Mum.' My voice broke.

'Oh, Louise.' Julie hugged me.

'I really miss her advice with Jess. She'd raised three teen-age girls and she knew what to do and say, and she always had my back with Pippa.' Sophie welled up.

'She was our biggest cheerleader and our harshest critic,' Julie said.

'She was a woman who spoke her mind,' Dad agreed.

'And never sugar-coated things.' I grinned.

'Or backed down if she felt she was in the right,' Julie added.

'Which was all the time.' Gavin laughed.

'She was one in a million. That saying "You don't know what you've got till it's gone" is very true,' Dad said.

'Do you want to move into Christelle's room for a few months, Dad? It'd be less lonely for you?' Julie suggested.

'You'd only have to put up with Marion once a month,' Sophie added.

'You certainly wouldn't be lonely in Julie's house,' I noted. I reckoned after a week in Julie's madhouse Dad would be sprinting home.

Dad patted Julie's hand. 'Not at all, pet, but thanks. I have to get used to this new normal. I'm just feeling a bit sorry for myself and a bit useless. I'll get there. I'll do my best to be a better granddad and try to fill the gap Anne left a little bit.'

'You're doing great, Dad. We love you and we're here for you.' Sophie sniffed.

'You are a good granddad.' I tried to reassure him.

Beside me, Sophie fished around in her bag for a tissue. She pulled one out and a piece of paper fluttered to the floor. She reached down to pick it up.

She looked at it and frowned. 'Hotel Dolce Vita in Rome.' Then she gasped. 'Oh, my God, Louise!'

Everyone turned to look at her.

'What?'

Sophie handed me the piece of paper. It was headed paper – *Hotel Dolce Vita*. On the paper was the name Marco and a phone number.

I stared at the piece of paper and then my heart skipped a beat.

'What is it?' Julie asked.

'Louise, you've gone as white as a ghost,' Dad said.

My heart was pounding. The bag. The Prada bag. I'd bought it in Italy on that work trip. I'd gone into the Prada shop and treated myself to it. I'd had it with me that night . . . the night I'd been made partner . . . the night I'd drunk way too much . . . the night I'd had unprotected sex with a stranger. Turns out the stranger's name was Marco.

'Is it him?' Sophie asked.

Julie grabbed the paper from my hand. 'Oh, my God, is this the hotel?'

I nodded, unable to speak.

'What the hell is going on?' Gavin asked. 'What hotel, who is "him"?'

Sophie turned to them. 'This Marco guy is Clara's dad and there's a phone number.'

'Oh, my God, this is huge.' Gavin's eyes widened. 'You can find him now.'

'Unless he's changed his number,' Julie said.

'I'm sure you can track it back or find an address or, I don't know, get an investigator to do it for you,' Sophie said. 'Quentin once hired a private investigator to find out if his boyfriend was cheating on him. He was very good. I can get his name, if you like?'

Julie leaned over. 'Hey, Louise, are you okay? This is a lot.'

I was in complete shock. I didn't know how to feel. On the one hand, it was easier not having had any way of finding Clara's dad, but Clara was so insistent and so obsessed with finding him, I owed it to her to try. And now I could find him, but did I want to? Would it be wise? Would he be a bonus in Clara's delicate life, or a hindrance?

'I . . . I don't know. I have to protect Clara but . . . but I should . . . I . . . ' I stuttered.

'Louise,' Dad said gently, 'Clara has asked me several times recently about her dad. Why don't you find this Marco fellow, meet him and then decide? We'll all help you. We're all here for you. I'll be with you every step of the way.'

'If he's a douche bag, we'll see him off. But if he's a good bloke, it could be great for Clara,' Gavin pointed out.

But did I really want to open this huge can of worms? I knew my family would support me, but at the end of the day it was me and Clara. The others all had their own families to look after. Clara and I had always been two peas in a pod. How would this affect my fragile daughter? Then again, Clara was obsessed with finding her dad and she did deserve to know him – *if* he was nice and accepted her and loved her. Oh, God, it was so complicated. My head throbbed.

'Take some time to process it all,' Julie told me. 'You can't work it all through here and now.'

Sophie chewed her lip. 'I'm not trying to be hippie-dippy here, but it kind of feels like a sign.'

'What do you mean?' Julie asked.

'Louise lends Mum her bag years ago and forgets about it. It's in the attic and in the charity pile. I take it because I love Prada. And here we are at dinner together and I'm using the bag for the first time. I go to get a tissue when we're all talking about how much we miss Mum, and the piece of paper falls out.'

'Jeez, you're right, it is a sign,' Gavin whispered. 'It's totally a sign from Mum.'

'It's certainly a big coincidence,' Julie admitted.

Dad looked at me. 'To be honest, your mum always wanted you to find Clara's father. We talked about it a lot, especially close to her death. She felt that Clara could really benefit from having a father and knowing where that side of her came from. Obviously, that always depended on whether he was a good man or not. Your mum also felt that finding him could take some of the pressure off you. It's not easy being mother and father to a child. You've done a wonderful job, but your mother knew that, when she died, her loss would leave a big void in Clara's life. Maybe it's time to see if Clara's father can fill it. If not, at least you'll know you tried.'

I looked at them. Everyone was in tears. My logical brain said it was a mere coincidence, but my heart said Mum had sent me a message.

I raised my glass. 'Well, it looks like Mum might get her wish.'

We clinked. I drank deeply and tried to stop my heart jumping out of my chest with nerves, anxiety and fear.

15. Sophie

When I got home Jess was hovering at the front door. She was usually in her bedroom with the door closed, on her phone, so I was surprised to see her.

'Mum, Pippa's here with Robert. I think . . . I think she's drunk.' Jess looked upset.

'What?'

Jess flapped her arms around nervously. 'She arrived ten minutes ago to drop him off and she looked kind of weird. She's been locked in the bathroom since. She won't answer me.'

First, it was not our day to have Robert, and second, what the hell was Pippa doing turning up drunk to the house? Had she driven him over? Had she put him at risk? My head was spinning.

I took charge. I needed to keep Jess calm.

'Okay. You take Robert up to his bedroom. I need to speak to Pippa. I've had enough of her bullshit.'

Jess went to get Robert from the TV room and brought him upstairs.

I marched to the bathroom and knocked loudly on the door. 'Pippa, it's Sophie. What's going on?'

Silence.

'Pippa! Open the door.'

The door unlocked.

'What the hell?' she slurred. 'Can I not use the bathroom without you being on my case? God, you're such a control freak. How does Jack stand it?'

She tried to push past me, but I blocked her.

'Have you been drinking, Pippa?'

'That's none of your business.'

'Did you drive over here with your son in the car?'

She laughed. 'No, Sergeant Major Sophie. I got a taxi.'

'Why is Robert here? It's your week.'

'Because I have to go to London.'

'Right now?'

'Yeah. I'm heading to the airport.'

'What's in London?'

'What is this interrogation? Who the hell do you think you are? I don't have to answer to you.'

'Who I am is your son's stepmother and, frankly, the person who's looked after him eighty per cent of the time lately. This has got to stop, Pippa. You can't keep dropping him off unannounced. It's not fair on him or us.'

Her unfocused eyes narrowed. 'Jack's his father and he's always banging on about how he wants to spend more time with him. He wanted full custody, remember.'

'Jack's not here. He's in Germany for work.'

She shrugged. 'You took him back. You knew he had a kid, so suck it up.'

The bitch. 'You need to take Robert home.'

She laughed. 'Not happening. I'm going now.'

Her pupils were dilated, and I suspected she'd taken more than drink. It looked like Quentin's gossip about her was spot-on. I tried to keep my voice calm, but my blood was at boiling point. 'Regardless of the fact that you don't give a toss about me or Jack or our work and demands, at least think about Robert. He needs a stable environment and a proper routine. All of this chopping and changing of plans is very unsettling for him.'

Her face darkened. 'Don't you dare tell me how to raise

my son. What the hell would you know about parenting anyway? I saw a boy sneaking out of your house as I was coming in. Tall, handsome guy in rugby gear. Gorgeous blue eyes. A confident swagger. Jess is clearly a lot more fun than you are.'

What? What boy? Did Jess have Sebastian over while I was at work? I couldn't process the thoughts fast enough.

Pippa grinned at me. 'Surprised, are you? Didn't know your precious Jessica was entertaining boys,' she sneered. 'You're not exactly great mother material yourself, are you, Sophie?'

I was so tempted to punch her in the middle of her smug face. Using every single bit of self-control I had, I said, 'This isn't about Jess, this is about Robert, and it's about you not sticking to the joint custody arrangement.'

Pippa shoved me out of the way. 'I'm late. Move.'

'Pippa, come on, be reasonable. Robert needs you.'

She stopped and spun around. 'I need a life, Sophie. I deserve to have fun. I'm not old and miserable like you.'

'Oh, I can see you're having fun, Pippa. Lots of it. But you seem to be forgetting that you have a son who needs his mother. Any idea when you'll be back to pick Robert up?'

'A couple of days. I'll text Jack. I don't have to deal with you.' She swept out of the house, slamming the front door and leaving the smell of perfume and booze in her wake.

Using buckets of willpower, I managed somehow to wait until Robert was in bed to talk to Jess. I willed myself not to scream, *What the hell do you think you're doing? You are grounded for life. You will never leave this house again.*

I took three deep breaths and knocked on her bedroom door. She was lying on her bed in leggings and a crop top, on the phone as usual.

'What?'

'I need to talk to you.'

'Can it wait?'

'Absolutely not. Not even for one second.'

She frowned. 'Is this about Pippa? What happened? Is she coming back for Robert?'

'Hang up the phone, Jess.'

She held it up and waved into it. 'Gotta go, family drama.'

'Okay, later,' a boy's voice said.

She put her phone down and sat up. 'What's going on?'

I leaned against her chest of drawers.

'You tell me, Jess. What's going on in your life?' I stared at her.

I could tell by her face that she was wary of my tone and body language. 'Nothing.'

'We both know that's a lie. How long have you been dating Sebastian?'

She rolled her eyes. 'I'm not dating him, we're just chatting. It's no big deal.'

'Just chatting.'

'Yeah.' She crossed her arms over her chest.

'So, he wasn't here this afternoon before I got home from work? He didn't sneak out of the house before I came through the front door?'

Her face dropped as she realized Pippa had told me. 'He just called in for ten minutes.'

'Really?'

'Yeah. We're, like, friends. It's no big deal.'

'Well, then, why did you fail to mention it?'

'Because I knew you'd overreact, like you always do.'

'So you think it's okay to have boys here when you're home alone?'

'OMG, it was one time and it was one boy.'

I counted to five.

'Jess, you knew perfectly well that your dad and I would be furious if we found out you had a boy here when we were at work.'

'Nothing happened. We just hung out.'

'Swear on your grandmother's grave that you didn't do anything more than kiss.'

Jess's eyes flashed. 'I swear on Granny's grave, but that's a horrible thing to ask me to do.'

She was right, but I was desperate. Desperate that she didn't do something stupid with bloody Sebastian of all people.

'So nothing else happened? You didn't go upstairs and take any of your clothes off? Teenage boys will always push for sex, Jess.'

'OMG, Mum!' She put her hands over her face. 'Nothing happened. I'm not stupid. Sebastian's not like that.'

God, she was clueless. 'Sebastian's mother, as you well know, is a very nasty person. I'm not saying he's the same, but he certainly grew up around toxic people. I would prefer you to stay away from him.'

Jess threw her hands into the air. 'You're the one who always says not to judge people until you get to know them. And that's exactly what you're doing. I know Sebastian's mother was a bitch to you and, yes, she seems like a total idiot, but he is a nice guy.'

'The triplets don't think so.' I played my trump card. Jess loved her cousins and would value their opinion far higher than mine.

'Well, Sebastian told me that now he's got to know the triplets properly through rugby he really likes them and that the whole team are bonding this year.'

'He was horrible to them when they first arrived in Castle Academy.'

'He was only nine or ten then. He's grown up.'

Wow, Sebastian had clearly got under her skin. Damnit. If she was defending him against her cousins, she must really like him.

'I just want you to be careful, Jess. You are a beautiful, amazing girl and you deserve to be with a really great guy. I'm not sure Sebastian is that person.'

'OMG, Mum, we're not getting married, just hanging out. Chill.'

I knew, from all the podcasts I'd listened to on 'how to connect with your teen', that it was vital Jess didn't shut me out. I had to keep the communication lines open. If I grounded her, she'd possibly never speak to me again, but I couldn't let the incident go unpunished.

'Jess, I'm going to give you the benefit of the doubt because I think you're being honest and I have to trust you, but if you ever sneak any boy into this house behind our backs again, I will ground you for a very, very long time. Are we clear?'

She nodded.

'I know you don't believe me, but teenage boys only have one thing on their minds – at all times.'

She blushed. 'Please stop talking.'

'Sex. Remember that. If Sebastian wants to call in, he will only do so when a parent is present. Is that clear?'

'Yes.'

'I want to be able to trust you, Jess. I've a lot going on with Pippa and Robert and work, so please behave and don't make stupid decisions.'

'I won't.'

'Okay. I'm going to bed now. I'm taking your phone. You can read a book.'

'*Muuuum*, it's only ten.'

'Jess, you're on very thin ice here. You're extremely lucky I'm not grounding you.'

'Okay, fine.'

I kissed her head. 'I love you and I know you think I'm hard on you, but it's my job to protect you.'

'I know, but you're way stricter than most parents.'

'Well, you're stuck with me and I'm not that awful. Would you prefer Pippa as your mother?'

'Obviously not. I feel sorry for Robert. He's lucky he has Dad and you.'

I folded Jess's school jumper and placed it on her desk. 'I keep hoping Pippa will turn a corner and become more maternal, but she seems to be getting worse.'

'Even when she was with Dad, he did everything for Robert. She's just not a mother type,' Jess said.

'I've never met anyone like her. She just doesn't seem to care about Robert. Louise wasn't maternal at first either, but pretty soon she fell head over heels for Clara and she's turned out to be an incredible mother. Pippa seems to be less interested in Robert than ever. It's really sad.'

'We'll just have to love him extra hard.'

I smiled at her. 'Yes, we will. Goodnight, love.'

'Night, Mum.' She turned her back to me.

I tapped her on the shoulder. 'Jess, hand it over.'

'Okay.' She reluctantly gave me her phone.

I left her room and made my way to bed. It might only be ten o'clock but I was shattered. It had been a long day and I was now freaking out about Pippa and Sebastian. I doubted I'd get much sleep. I'd have to try to tackle Jack again about Pippa, and I'd have to watch Jess like a hawk.

16. Julie

On Saturday, Marion, my sisters and I were in the kitchen preparing food for the ninety-four people coming to our pre-cup rugby party. I had roped them in to help me, and to stop me freaking out.

Marion checked the oven. 'Looking good, Julie. I reckon we can take the curry out in ten minutes and leave it in the warming drawer.'

'Thanks so much for coming early to help. I could never have done this without you all.'

I had completely underestimated how much prepping and chopping and cooking I'd have to do to feed so many people, thirty-six of whom were ravenous boys who ate families of chickens every day.

Marion had been with me since nine a.m. It was her weekend to stay with us, thankfully, and she had been a life-saver. Louise and Sophie had come early as well, to help with the salads and desserts.

Sophie put her Prada clutch carefully to one side, away from any food. She chopped cucumber while Louise filled pavlova bases with cream and strawberries.

'I just don't get it,' Louise said. 'Are we living in the dark ages that people presume mothers have time to host huge parties for teams? That's what venues and caterers are for.'

'I agree with you, Louise,' Marion said, 'and the posh fuckers in this school are loaded. They could well afford a restaurant.'

'It's part of the whole ra-ra team-bonding, I get it,' Sophie said. 'Tradition is a good thing. It's a community coming together to celebrate their sons. It's lovely.'

I wiped my sweaty brow. 'Look, I agree it should be out-sourced to the local pub, but the triplets are so excited to be on the team and part of the whole hoopla around it that I'm doing it for them.'

'You are a bit of a martyr, though,' Louise said bluntly. 'You didn't have to do it all yourself. You could have ordered the food in.'

'I know, but I want to show that it can be done without breaking the bank. I'm trying to keep it low-key.'

Marion snorted. 'Low-key would be chicken nuggets and a swiss roll.'

'Mid-key, then.' I laughed.

'Did you contact that shop?' Sophie asked.

She had given me the name of a shop in Kerry that sold wool hats and scarves made by local women with wool sourced from Irish sheep. They weren't cashmere but they were lovely Irish wool and they'd assured me they could dye the wool to match the special burgundy colour of the rugby jerseys.

'Yes, they were so nice and a quarter of the price of the ones from Atelier de stupid Cashmere.'

'What a load of bolloxology. For Oscar's football team we all packed bags in the local supermarket to make money to pay for their jerseys.'

Sophie ignored Marion. 'I'm glad it worked out. What did Victoria say?'

I grinned. 'I haven't told her. I just went ahead and ordered them. I've already paid for them. I'll hand them out next week before the first game and then tell everyone to let me have the money.'

'Good for you. No point in getting into a whole

WhatsApp pile-on about it. I'll be dying to hear how Victoria reacts.' Sophie chuckled.

'I'll keep you posted.' I grinned.

'How was Dad yesterday?' Louise asked Sophie. 'He was so emotional at dinner the other night. Was he all right?'

'He was better, actually. I think being honest about how he was feeling was good for him. He seems less down in the dumps. Besides, he had plans. He was going to some golf dinner, so I only saw him for a few minutes.'

'Was he going with that Dolores one?' Marion asked. 'Are they having sex yet?'

I elbowed Marion.

'What? You should be happy for him. A man who is having sex is a happy man.'

'Marion, please do not talk about our father like that,' Sophie snapped.

'No wonder Harry's so grumpy.' I giggled.

'I need sex badly,' Louise said. 'It's been ages.'

'Me too. Vibrators are just not the same,' Marion agreed.

'Handy, though,' Louise said.

'Yeah, but I like the weight of a man on top of me banging away.' Marion grinned.

Sophie bristled. 'Can we please change the subject?'

'I'd say Jack's good in the sack,' Marion said to her.

'Excuse me?'

'He's fit. I'd say he's a good ride.'

'Do you mind not making comments about my husband?'

'Ex-husband-now-partner, you haven't remarried,' Louise said, always one for the technical detail.

'Jesus, Louise, that's not the point,' Sophie hissed.

'Relax,' Marion said. '*I* don't want to shag Jack, he's not my type. Too pretty-boy for me. I like my fellas a bit rough around the edges.'

'A bit like yourself.' I chuckled and Marion cracked up.

Sophie slammed the knife down on the cucumber, muttering, 'Really and truly,' under her breath.

Thankfully, Harry came in before Sophie could aim her chopping knife at Marion.

'There he is, the man himself. How's the speech coming along, Harry? It'd better be good because it's taken you long enough.'

'Hello, Marion. The speech is finished, thank you.'

'Harry, did you move the couches back?' I asked.

'Yes, Julie, and the bar is set up and the boys are dressed.'

'Good.'

'Oh, and Jess is here,' Harry said.

'What?' Sophie looked up.

'She said she came to see if you needed any help.'

'She's supposed to be at home with Jack, working on her history project.' Sophie frowned. 'And staying the hell away from Sebastian,' she muttered.

Harry left to check the ice supplies as the boys and Jess came in. The boys headed straight for the pavlovas. As Liam was about to try to pick out some strawberries, Louise smacked his hand with the back of her spoon.

'Ouch,' Liam squealed.

'No need to injure us, Louise,' Leo said. 'These hands are precious. I need them to score tries with.'

'You'd better keep them out of the desserts, then. These are for the guests.' She was firm, like Christelle. And, just like it did with Christelle, it worked. The boys backed off.

'Hi, Jess,' I said, taking in her short skirt, halter-neck top and face full of make-up. She was dressed to kill.

'Hi, Julie, can I help with anything?'

'You're supposed to be at home,' Sophie said sharply.

'I finished my project, so Dad said I could come down.' Her smile was angelic.

'With that skirt and at least thirty hormonal teenage boys in the room, you'll need your mother's knife to keep the lads away,' Marion said, grinning at her.

'We're actually finishing up now,' Sophie said.

'Can I stay, Mum, please?' Jess pleaded.

'Yeah, we want Jess to stay.' The triplets put their arms around their cousin.

'Why don't you all stay for a drink?' I suggested. 'You've been so helpful, you deserve one. You can slip off when everyone arrives.'

'No, I want Jess to –'

Before Sophie had time to argue, the boys hustled Jess out of the kitchen.

'Fuck one drink, I'm staying for the whole night. I want to meet these cashmere-obsessed freaks.' Marion pulled off her apron and pulled her glittery top even lower so her cleavage was fully on show. 'And you never know, there might be a divorced dad with a big bank account who's looking for a woman with saggy boobs, back fat, no money, four kids and a shedload of baggage. I'm a serious fucking catch.'

'You are a good catch! You're the best friend.' I side-hugged her. 'But just so we're clear, you will not have sex with any single dads, or any of the coaches. Harry will literally have a heart attack and I need him alive to get through this rugby campaign.'

'I'll be on my best behaviour.'

'I'll stay for a quick drink, then head home,' Louise said. 'Dad's looking after Clara and I know he's a bit nervous about her bedtime routine. I promised I'd be back by eight thirty.'

'Aww, it's great that he's trying to help out more,' I said. Good for Dad, he really was making an effort.

'Me too, and then I'll drag Jess out of here,' Sophie said.

I took off my apron. She came over to adjust my belt and fix my lipstick. 'Now you look perfect. The gorgeous mother of three captains.'

'Thanks, sis. I'm glad you're all staying for a bit. I could use the moral support.'

Sophie applied blusher to her cheeks. 'To be honest, I'm dying to see what Victoria and the other mums are wearing,' she admitted. 'I may not be able to afford designer clothes any more, but I still love looking at them.'

I headed for the fridge and the bottles of prosecco. 'Right, let's open a bottle of fizz!'

My sisters and Marion gathered with me in our big hallway and watched as a stream of Range Rovers, Lexuses, Audis and BMWs blocked up our entire road. The parents and players all made a beeline for our front door. The triplets took their coats as they entered and Jess pitched in to guide them to the living room and the drinks table. Every time the bell rang, Jess jumped to open the door.

Victoria was the last to arrive, gliding through the door in a floor-length fur coat.

'How many rabbits died to keep you warm?' Marion asked, as Victoria wriggled out of it.

She stared at her. 'I'm sorry, who are you?'

'Marion, my good friend,' I introduced them.

'Be careful with my coat,' Victoria ordered, as Leo held it casually, the bottom trailing on the hall floor. 'It's chinchilla, actually,' she said to Marion.

Behind her, I saw Leo stamp on the hem of her coat.

'Aren't they rodents?' Marion said. 'Like the poor cousins of squirrels or something?'

Louise snorted while Sophie tried not to laugh.

'They most certainly are not,' Victoria glared at her.

'Actually, they are. Chinchillas are crepuscular rodents of the parvorder Caviomorpha,' Louise said.

'What?' Victoria glared at Louise.

'You could have saved a right few quid and skinned a few squirrels. There are loads in my local park.' Marion was enjoying herself.

Sophie giggled.

Before Victoria could think of a nasty retort, Sebastian rushed in behind her. She stalked off in her designer outfit to find her husband.

'Hi, sorry we're so late,' Sebastian said to Jess, not to me, his hostess.

'That's okay.' Jess's face lit up like a Christmas tree. They stood grinning at each other, gazing into each other's eyes, completely oblivious to everyone around them.

'I think you're in trouble, Sophie,' Louise murmured.

'She is smitten,' I mumbled.

Sophie groaned. 'Of all the bloody boys. I warned her to back off.'

'It's gone way beyond that,' I whispered. 'They're mad about each other, I'm sorry to tell you. I remember those looks – it's serious.'

'The lads are all in the den,' Luke told Sebastian and the teenagers headed downstairs.

'Jess,' Sophie called. Her daughter turned. 'We're leaving soon.'

Jess's face fell. 'Can I stay, please, Mum?'

'No.'

'Please.' Jess looked to me for help.

'Come on, Sophie, let her hang out with us,' the triplets pleaded.

'Maybe she could stay for a bit and I'll drop her home later?' I said to Sophie.

'Can I, Mum?' Jess's face was flushed.

'She'll be safe here with the boys and Julie,' Louise said quietly to Sophie. 'If you drag her home now, she'll kick up hell.'

Sophie caved. 'Okay, but I want you home before eleven at the very, very latest.'

'Thanks, Mum.' Jess and the triplets raced downstairs.

I put my arm around Sophie. 'I know it's hard. I'll try to keep an eye on her. If you made her leave with you, she'd hate you and it would make her want to be with Sebastian even more. It's a teen romance. They're usually intense but brief.'

'I hope so,' Sophie said.

'If he's anything like the mother, she'll run a mile in no time,' Marion assured her.

'Julie!' Harry came into the hall looking flushed. 'Everyone's here, and it's time for my speech.'

'It's short, right?' Louise asked me.

'I told him to keep it short.'

'Have you heard it?' Sophie asked.

'No.'

My sisters looked at each other in panic.

'That's dangerous,' Marion said. 'No offence, but Harry can be very fucking long-winded.'

My heart sank. Please, God, may he have listened to me for once.

'The greatest leader is not necessarily the one who does the greatest things. He is the one who gets people to do the

170

greatest things. That's what this campaign is about: great leaders. We have a fantastic coaching team, and the most wonderful group of boys. I am the proud father of three boys on that team, the joint captains. They will not let you down. They will fight with everything they have. They will lead and inspire . . .'

At the back of the room I saw Luke sticking two breadsticks up his nose while Leo put ice cubes down the back of Liam's top. Sebastian and Jess were holding hands.

Harry droned on: 'It's an honour to be part of this journey, to be part of this Castle Academy tradition. We as parents must . . .'

'Jesus, Julie, do something,' Louise muttered.

'They should send Harry to torture people. This is worse than waterboarding or having your nails pulled out.' Marion drained her glass of wine.

'I have to go.' Sophie backed out of the room.

'. . . and it's important that the boys feel our full support. We need them to know that whatever the day or the hour, they can come to us. We are –'

'WELL SAID,' I cut across him, and began to clap. Louise and Marion joined in.

The other parents enthusiastically clapped too, stopping Harry turning to yet another page of his notes. One of the other parents rushed over to shake his hand, and that signalled the end of the speech. The conversations swelled around the room again.

Harry made his way across to us, looking disappointed.

'You came in too early there, Julie,' he said. 'I had an excellent ending coming up. Some really inspirational quotes.'

'Harry, you put everyone into an induced coma. If you'd stripped bollock naked and done the samba, they wouldn't have noticed.' Marion refilled her glass.

'What?' Harry spluttered.

'It was too long, Harry, way too long.' Louise was her usual blunt self.

'It was really good, darling, but that was the perfect time to end it.' I tried to soften the blows. 'Well done. Here, let me get you a drink.'

The party went on, and while some parents took it easy, others tried to drink us out of house and home, including one father who knocked over a table of glasses and collapsed like a whale on the ground. His mortified wife dragged him away while Marion and I swept up the broken glass.

The time flew by and I only realized it was eleven when Tom came over and asked me if he could sleep in our room because there was someone in his bedroom and the door was locked.

'What do you mean, the door is locked?'

'I can't get in,' Tom said. 'I keep knocking, and I know someone's in there, but they won't open the door. I'm really tired, Mum. Can I just climb into your bed?'

I felt a cold dread seep through me. Who the hell was locked into Tom's bedroom? I didn't wait to ask any more questions.

I raced upstairs, with Tom hot on my heels. I tried the door and, sure enough, it was locked. I knocked. I could just make out voices.

'Who's in there? This is Julie, the triplets' mother. Open the door immediately.'

Silence.

I banged on the door. 'You are not permitted in our bedrooms. If you do not open this bloody door, I'm going to kick it down. Five . . . four . . .'

'Hold on, I'm coming,' a boy's voice called.

The door swung open and Sebastian stood before us, with no top on, his jeans unbuttoned.

172

I gasped. 'What the hell is going on?'

'Nothing, I just wanted some privacy,' he slurred, cool as you like. Apparently, he wasn't remotely bothered by being found half naked, locked into my eleven-year-old's bedroom.

'Mum, look, it's Jess.' Tom pointed to the figure lying on his bed.

Oh, no. No no no no no. Not Jess. Not my niece.

I forced myself to speak calmly. 'Tom, go to my room and close the door, please.'

Tom, sensing danger, scurried off.

Shoving past Sebastian, I rushed to Tom's bed where Jess was lying topless and very drunk. She still had her skirt and knickers on, and I prayed that meant she hadn't had sex.

'Jess, Jess, are you okay?' I shook her.

She looked at me bleary-eyed. 'I don't feel well,' she said. I sat her up, she retched and then threw up all over me and Tom's bed.

'Oops.' Sebastian cracked up laughing and stumbled sideways.

'What did you do to her?' I shouted at him. 'What the hell was going on in here? If you touched her, I swear to God . . .'

'We weren't doing anything,' Sebastian said.

I looked from his naked torso to hers.

'Nothing? Really? You expect me to believe that? Shall we get your parents up here and ask them if this looks like nothing?'

'Jesus, it's all right,' Sebastian said, finally a little glint of fear in his eyes. 'I would never hurt Jess. We weren't doing anything bad, I promise.'

'Did you have sex?'

'No!' Sebastian shook his head vehemently.

Jess groaned. 'I'm okay, Julie. I'm sorry . . . We didn't do anything.'

I was aware of the guests downstairs. I needed to keep this

quiet. I wanted to protect Jess. I needed to shut this down. I wanted the little prick out of my house.

'Get out of my sight before I kill you, you little shit,' I hissed at him. 'Right now!'

'What's going on?' Luke arrived at the door, out of breath.

'Tom told us Jess was locked in here.' Leo was right behind him.

They stopped dead when they saw the scene in front of them.

'What the fuck are you doing?' Liam asked Sebastian.

I managed to pull Jess's top on.

'Help me get Jess into the bathroom,' I told Leo. 'Luke, go down and get me a bottle of water and a cup of coffee.'

'Liam, show Sebastian to the front door and don't say a word to anyone. We need to contain this, for Jess's sake.'

I watched as Liam grabbed Sebastian and shoved him roughly out of the door.

Leo helped me get Jess into the bathroom. I told him to leave us then – I had to clean her and myself up. Vomiting had sobered her a little.

'I'm so sorry, Julie. I had too much prosecco.'

'You're fifteen. You're not supposed to be drinking. And as for going into a bedroom with a boy and locking the door, what were you thinking, Jess? That is just so dangerous. Anything could have happened. You might have said no and he might not have stopped.'

'It's okay, Julie. Sebastian is really nice. We like each other. We just wanted to hang out on our own.'

'Jess, you were doing a lot more than hanging out. You're drunk and half naked. If I hadn't come in, God knows how far you'd have gone.'

She swayed. 'Julie, it wasn't like that. He just wanted to mess around a bit. I really like him.'

I wiped vomit off her chin with a wet facecloth. 'Jess, listen to me. I have to ask you – and you *must* be honest. Did you have sex with Sebastian?'

'What? My God, Julie, no. Of course not. Just a bit of, like, kissing and stuff. I wouldn't be that stupid.'

'Swear?'

'I swear.'

I dried her face with a towel. 'Are you absolutely sure? Think for a moment. You're pretty drunk, pet, so are you really sure?'

'Julie, are you mad! We did not have sex. I would never do that. I know I'm too young and I also know that Mum would actually kill me.'

'Thank Christ for that,' I said, and hugged her. 'I was so worried. Now you need to listen to me, okay? Sebastian is a nasty piece of work. Please stay away from him. He is trouble. He should never, ever have brought you up here so drunk and locked the door. The fact that he did says a lot about him. And you should not have come up here with him. You need to take care of yourself, Jess. I'm asking you to stay away from him and do not drink. Alcohol leads to bad decisions. Do you hear me?'

Jess's eyes filled with tears. 'But I really like him, Julie. Just . . . please, please, please don't tell my mum. She'll kill me if she finds out and she'll ground me for ever.'

She'll kill me first, I thought. I was supposed to be looking out for Jess, but I'd got distracted with the guests. I had never in my wildest dreams imagined she'd sneak upstairs with Sebastian. Sophie would lose her mind if she knew what had happened. I was not looking forward to telling her. She might never forgive me for not looking after Jess properly. But, then, Jess had just been a bit silly and nothing had actually happened. We didn't need the morning-after pill or anything like that, so maybe it was best if Sophie didn't know.

I could see Jess watching me intently as I went back and forth in my mind, trying to figure out the best course of action. I was completely conflicted. If I told Sophie, she would probably never let Jess out or trust her again, and she would be disgusted with me and would probably never trust me again either. Did I want to hurt my niece, fall out with my sister and really upset her? Or should I just contain this, let Jess learn from the experience and not involve her parents? I mean, we all made mistakes when were young and the most important thing was that Jess didn't seem to be traumatized or hurt in any way. Plus, Jess could talk to me about it at any time. She knew I had her back.

I nodded to myself, thinking that was the best thing to do. I wouldn't tell my sister. It would only upset her and she already had so much stress in her life, with Pippa and Robert. She'd have a breakdown if I loaded more on her plate.

'Jess, I'm not going to tell on you this time – you get one free pass, but that's it. Your actions have put me in a really difficult position. I hope you understand that. You did this in my house, on my watch, and I'm furious with you. As for that cocky little shit Sebastian, he doesn't deserve to be any-where near you. I want you to look me in the eye and tell me you'll break all contact with him.'

Jess bit her lip. 'Do I have to, Julie?' she said quietly.

'One hundred per cent, Jess, or I'll drive you home now and we can both face your mother with the truth.'

She held up her hands. 'God, no, please. I promise I'll do it.'

'Okay. Now you're going to have a shower, drink lots of water and coffee and get yourself sorted. I'll call Sophie and tell her I'll drop you home in an hour. You need to be ready by then.'

I hated the idea of lying to Sophie. I couldn't think of a

time when I'd lied to my sisters about something big. This wasn't exactly lying, though. I was just omitting to share information. But it still didn't sit well with me. I just had to focus on what was best for Sophie, and right now she didn't need another major situation on her hands. It didn't feel good, but it was for the best. What Sophie didn't know couldn't hurt her. Right?

17. Louise

I sat in front of Ross Moore, the company HR manager, and tried very hard not to lose my temper.

Ross pulled up a file on his computer and began to read: 'Zoë said, and I quote, "I feel that Louise has no empathy. She is very cold and difficult to communicate with. She doesn't show any compassion for my social anxiety. She dismisses my issues as if they're not real."'

I remained silent.

'Louise, this is the second serious complaint we've had from Zoë.'

I exhaled deeply in an attempt to control my rage. Thankfully, this could be quickly cleared up with some honest facts.

'Zoë has taken eight days off in the last two months for "mental-health" issues,' I said. 'The other – hard-working and uncomplaining – young interns have to pick up the slack when she decides not to come to work, which is unfair on them. When she does bother to show up, she is usually late, hung-over and unapologetic. It's total and utter bullshit, not to put too fine a point on it.'

Ross took off his glasses. 'I understand your frustration, Louise, but we have to be very careful around our employees and the area of mental health.'

'What about my mental health? She's wrecking my head and wasting my precious time with her never-ending bullshit and her made-up migraines that she only ever seems to get on a Monday morning after going on a bender all weekend. She's too stupid to make her Instagram account private, so everyone can see her partying on Sunday night and pulling the migraine excuse on Monday.'

'Look, she's Walter's goddaughter and he's asked me to keep an eye on her and make sure that she's happy here. I know it's not easy and she doesn't seem particularly cut out for the law, but we need to tread very carefully. Perhaps if she felt that you were a little more sympathetic and encouraging, she might be more productive in work.'

I was so sick of Zoë and her crap – and of my colleagues trying to put the ball in my court constantly, as if my behaviour were the problem and not hers.

'I am well aware of her relationship with Walter, which she uses constantly as her get-out-of-jail-free card. For someone with self-diagnosed social anxiety she never misses Friday-night drinks, client lunches or any excuse to have fun. Her anxiety only seems to kick in when she's late delivering notes, files or contracts.'

Ross chose his words carefully. 'We're living in different times from when we started our careers, Louise. Young people now are more open and in tune with their issues and anxieties and, in the main, that's a good thing. You, me and all the senior employees here must adjust and be more conscious of the emotional wellbeing of all our employees.'

I had real issues and anxieties, lots of them. I knew what it was like to lie awake at night panicking about life. I worried constantly about Clara and her future. I barely slept for months after her diagnosis, but I still gave my all at work. I was struggling with the grief of losing my mother, the person who cared most about Clara after me; I was sleep-deprived because I was lying awake at night worrying about Clara's father – going back and forth over the pros and cons of looking for him and finding him, what it would mean, how I would control it . . . My head was melted, but

I still got up every day, went to work and behaved like a professional.

I had sympathy for people with actual mental-health problems, but Zoë was an overindulged, spoiled princess who chose her mental-health days strategically. I couldn't stand that kind of deception.

I stood up. 'Ross, I have a daughter with additional needs. She suffers from real anxiety, off-the-charts anxiety, yet she gets up every day and does her best to try to fit into a world that makes no sense to her. I cannot deal with Zoë's bullshit. You need to move her to another department before I throw something at her.'

Ross laughed. 'I must advise very strongly against any violence. That would be impossible for me to defend. But seriously, Louise, for your own sake, go easy on her. Walter is very fond of his goddaughter. In the meantime, I'll see if we can get her moved to Conveyancing.'

'Please do.'

I left and went outside to get a coffee and cool off. I was on my way back to the office when my phone rang. It was the private investigator, Benedict Tyrell. I'd hired him to find Clara's dad. He was an English colleague of the guy Quentin had hired to spy on his cheating boyfriend. Apparently, the European private-investigation world was relatively small and most of them knew each other. Benedict was based in Italy, so I'd hired him to help me.

'Hello?'

'Louise, it's Benedict.'

'Well?'

'I've found him.'

My heart stopped.

'Alive?'

'Alive and kicking.'

'Where?'

'In Italy, in a little village not too far from Rome.'

'Married?'

'No.'

'Kids?'

'No.'

'Gay?'

'No.'

'Oh, God, he's not a priest, is he?'

Benedict snorted 'No. He's just a middle-aged bloke who runs a small olive farm and lives with his mother.'

A middle-aged man who lived with his mother? It sounded a bit odd.

'His mother? Is he . . . I mean, does he seem normal?'

'Yes. I did a bit of digging and there don't seem to be any red flags. Marco is just a simple bloke who lives a simple life and seems very happy. He was married briefly years ago but it didn't work out. He goes to the local bar for a few beers on a Friday night, likes football and runs his olive farm in a lovely place called Pico. About an hour's drive from the airport in Rome. It's a beautiful little town.'

My mind was racing. He was alive. Clara's dad was alive and we had found him.

'Are you sure it's him?'

'Positive. I did a DNA test from a glass he drank out of in his local bar and he's a ninety-nine point nine per cent match for Clara.'

I felt faint. I reached out to the wall to steady myself. I'd found Marco, but now what? What did I do next? I couldn't think straight. I told Benedict to email me all the information. I needed to think, figure out my next move. I needed my sisters. I took out my phone and sent a message to our WhatsApp: *Crisis meeting, 8 p.m. Nina's wine bar.*

I arrived at the wine bar first, as usual, and was already one glass of wine down before Sophie and Julie arrived. Julie plonked herself beside me as Sophie sat on my other side. Her hair was tied back and looked greasy, which was so unlike her.

'Stop,' she said, patting her hair down. 'I know it's awful, but Robert has bloody nits again. I've just spent an hour combing eggs out of his hair – it's so gross. Jess never had them. I almost gagged. I'm so paranoid he might have given them to me that I put the anti-nit product in my hair too.'

'I spent half my life combing nits out of the triplets' hair,' Julie said. 'There was one kid in the class whose parents just would not deal with his nits. The teacher had told them over and over that he had nits and his hair needed to be treated, but they refused to believe it or do anything. How they couldn't see the full nit clan having a party in this kid's hair is beyond me. Anyway, the teacher reached the end of her tether and caught one of the many nits in his hair on a piece of Sellotape and taped it into his homework notebook.'

'No!' Sophie giggled.

'Yes. And she wrote, "This came from your son's head. Please deal with the problem."'

We all cracked up laughing.

'That's my kind of woman,' I said.

'What did the parents do?' Sophie asked.

Julie rolled her eyes. 'They tried to have the teacher sacked for shaming their child, emotional abuse, trauma, blah blah blah, but the headmistress stuck by her.'

'Good for her,' I said.

Sophie and Julie ordered drinks and I ordered a second glass of wine.

'So what's going on?' Julie cut to the chase.

'I've found him.'

'Who?' Sophie asked.

'You've met someone.' Julie beamed. 'I'm so happy for you, Louise, you deserve it.'

'No. I've found Clara's dad.'

They gasped.

'What . . . when . . . I mean . . .' Julie spluttered.

'Tell us everything,' Sophie said.

I filled them in on what I knew about Marco.

Julie held my hand. 'Oh, my God, Louise, this is huge.'

I nodded. 'I know.'

'So what are you going to do next?' Sophie asked. 'Have you decided?'

'You have to meet him before you say anything to Clara,' Julie said.

'Obviously. I guess I'll have to visit him. Check out if he's normal, nice, worth it, whatever.'

'This is a lot to take in,' Julie said gently.

'Yeah, it is.' I felt my voice quiver. The emotion I'd held back all day was now surfacing. It was huge. It was potentially life-changing. If he was open to knowing Clara, it would change everything. If he wasn't . . . well, I'd have to pretend he was dead and hope to God that Clara accepted it. I'd probably have to buy a plot and get a fake headstone erected. Was that even possible? My head throbbed.

'First of all, are you a hundred per cent sure it's him?' Sophie asked.

'The DNA match is ninety-nine point nine per cent and then I saw his photo. She has his nose.'

Clara had an upturned nose. It was very cute but no one in

183

our family had one. It was unusual and distinctive. After talking to Benedict, I still had a sliver of doubt in my mind, but when I saw Marco's photo, I knew he was Clara's dad.

'Can we see him?' Julie asked.

I pulled up the photos of him on my phone and showed my sisters. They leaned in eagerly.

Silence.

'He's very . . . Italian-looking,' Julie said.

'I see the nose,' Sophie added.

'He . . . he's . . . he's got kind eyes,' Julie stuttered.

'Yes, and . . . and . . . he looks robust,' Sophie said.

'I'd say he enjoys his pasta.' Julie started to giggle.

'And tiramisu.' Sophie snorted.

'And cheese.'

'And cream.'

They cracked up.

'Piss off.'

Marco was, let's just say, on the chubby side.

Julie wiped tears from her eyes. 'And a lovely shiny head.'

Sophie creased over.

'You're the worst sisters ever.' I tried to be annoyed, but their laughter was infectious and it was a welcome release from all the tension I'd been holding.

'Sorry, Louise, but I had an image of some tall, muscly Italian hunk,' Sophie said, 'but he's small, round and bald. It's a bit of a surprise.'

'I thought a hot Italian stallion had swept you off your feet for that one night of passion,' Julie said, through her giggles, 'but it was the Italian Danny DeVito.'

'Danny DeVito!' Sophie whooped.

We laughed until our stomachs hurt.

'Sorry,' Sophie said, when she'd caught her breath, 'it's just

184

that you always go for really good-looking, well-groomed, successful men and Marco is . . . different.'

'I'm not going to lie, I was surprised myself. But I guess in my wine haze I found him attractive.'

'Hang on,' Julie said. 'I know I've just been slagging you, but he's probably really charming and he does have kind eyes and it doesn't matter what he looks like as long as he's a good person.'

'And, on a shallow note, Clara looks like you – apart from the nose, which is his nicest feature.' Sophie grinned.

Julie drained her wine and ordered another. 'I'm coming with you,' she said. 'I want to be there when you meet Marco. You should not be alone.'

'Yes! Me too. I'm coming. No way you two are leaving me out of this,' Sophie said.

'Don't be mad, you're all busy.'

Julie snorted. 'Busy sourcing stupid bloody scarves and hats.'

'Busy dealing with delusional young women who all think they're going to be the next Gigi Hadid. I'd welcome a break.'

'Let's do it, Louise, come on,' Julie said. 'Let's go and find Marco together. Remember how supportive you were when I thought Harry was having an affair and it turned out he was just going to Paris to meet Christelle for the first time? Well, I want to be there for you, like you were for me.'

'And you let me live in your apartment rent-free when we lost everything. I want to support you in any way I can,' Sophie added.

I cleared my throat to push down the emotion rising inside me. 'Thank you. I'd love you both to come along. I can tackle anything with you two by my side.'

Julie took my hand in hers. 'We're your sisters, we'll always be here for you, and I know how hard it's been since Mum died, for you and for Clara.'

'Yeah, it really has been,' I admitted.

We raised our glasses in a clinking toast and drank deeply.

Julie put her glass down. 'Now, can we talk about Italian Danny DeVito again?'

We ordered another round of drinks and planned our trip to Italy to meet Clara's father. I was dreading it: Clara was my everything, and it was my job to protect her. She wanted to meet her dad so I had to facilitate that, but I was terrified of how all this change would affect her. She was so fragile. I was very glad my sisters were coming with me. Having them there would make this awful experience easier to bear.

'I have a suggestion to make,' Sophie said. 'Will we bring Dad?'

'To Italy?' Julie frowned.

'Yes. He's lonely, he's lost, he's mad about Clara and Louise, and you said he's been making a big effort to be more involved with her. Maybe we should include him.'

'I don't know. It's going to be really emotional and delicate and I can't be worrying about Dad when I'm trying to figure out this massive decision.'

'Julie and I will look after him. You wouldn't have to do anything,' Sophie added.

'I actually think it's a good idea. I feel a bit guilty that we aren't spending more time with him. Dad could be helpful. It might not be a bad thing to have a man with us. Just in case Marco turns out to be a tricky character,' Julie pointed out.

I wasn't sure. I didn't want Dad putting his foot in it or trying to control the situation or give me advice. I knew what I had to do. I needed quiet background support, nothing else.

'I think he'd love to be involved and he's good at advice.

He was amazing when Jack lost everything. He gave me brilliant advice,' Sophie reminded us.

'We'll make sure he doesn't do or say anything to interfere, although to be fair, Dad is pretty subtle, unlike Mum.' Julie laughed.

'She'd certainly have had something to say about everything and everyone,' I agreed.

'Dad will be easy. He'll just be in the background, quietly supporting you,' Sophie said.

I needed to think about it. My head was spinning with everything that was happening.

'Leave it with me. I'm not saying no, but I'm not saying yes either. I need to process everything for a few days.'

'As soon as you've decided, let us know and I'll book our flights,' Sophie said.

Julie reached over and hugged me. 'It'll be okay. We're all here for you.'

I knew they were, but at the end of the day it was my daughter's life and happiness that hung in the balance.

18. Sophie

Balancing a casserole dish on my left arm, I pulled out my keys and let myself into the house.

'Dad?' I called.

I could hear music coming from the kitchen. Mozart, Dad's favourite. It reminded me of being a kid, sitting at the table while Dad cooked us breakfast on a Sunday. Sunday morning was Mum's time off. She would lie in bed reading novels. The music brought me right back. Happy memories.

I'd been lucky. I'd had a lovely childhood with two parents who loved each other and stayed together through thick and thin. I'd wanted that for Jess, and I felt so guilty that I hadn't provided it. Instead, she'd weathered lots of upheaval with me and Jack falling apart and separating, then getting back together, and Jack bringing a half-brother for Jess into the mix. It was messy and I felt bad about it. Some days I felt I was a decent enough parent, others that I was failing miserably and Jess would pay the price.

At least the Sebastian fling appeared to have cooled off. Jess was being really moody and grumpy lately, and she wouldn't talk to me about it, but she was on her phone much less and hadn't asked to go out since the rugby party. I was hoping that meant they had broken up. Julie had told me she'd had a word with Jess after Sebastian had been obnoxious to some people at the party, and Jess had told her she was done with him. Hallelujah! I knew he'd eventually reveal himself to be as nasty as his mother. Thank God it had happened sooner rather than later. I was so grateful to Julie for pointing it out and getting through to Jess. I owed my sister, big-time.

As I pushed open the kitchen door, I heard Dad laughing and then a very female giggle. I walked in and stopped dead. The kitchen lights were on low and the table was set with candles and Mum's best china – the set she used only on Christmas Day. Sitting opposite Dad was Dolores, in Mum's chair.

Dad jumped up when he saw me. 'Sophie . . . I didn't . . . I . . .' he stuttered.

'I called, but obviously you couldn't hear with the music and the giggling.' I tried to keep my voice calm, but I felt shocked to my core.

'Hello, Sophie, nice to see you again,' the shameless Dolores said, as composed as you like.

I hated that her fat arse was in my mum's chair. I wanted to push her off it. One part of my brain knew I was reacting too intensely, but this was my mum's home, her house, her kitchen, and I was struggling with the feelings that were crowding around me.

'I brought you dinner, Dad, but it looks like you don't need it.'

Looking sheepish Dad said, 'You're so good, thanks, pet. Dolores just popped over with a stew.'

'Beef bourguignon, George.'

'Yes, yes, a beef bourguignon.'

'I know it's your dad's favourite.' She grinned like a Cheshire cat.

Her wrap dress was too low at the front and revealed far too much cleavage. Wrinkly old cleavage that shouldn't be on show. Her helmet hair was welded into place with cans of hairspray and her lipstick was a bright pink that clashed with her purple dress.

'Actually, Dolores, Dad's favourite meal is my mum's steak

with Béarnaise sauce. Isn't it, Dad?' I dared him to disagree with me.

He looked panic-stricken. 'Will you have a glass of wine?' He dodged the question and I felt even more furious.

'Oh, I'm sure Sophie's far too busy for that,' Dolores said. She could go to Hell.

I took my coat off, hung it on the back of a chair and sat down. 'I'd love one. I've all the time in the world.' I beamed at Dolores, who smiled sourly at me.

'This music reminds me of old times, Dad,' I said, as I sipped my wine. 'Happy times as a family here. You and Mum were such a brilliant match. Peas in a pod. Soul-mates.'

Dad took a gulp of wine.

'Wasn't the charity golf day out great fun, George?' Dolores interrupted.

I talked over her. 'A love like you and Mum had is a once-in-a-lifetime thing. We all aspire to have a relationship like yours. I was just thinking as I came through the door that I wished I'd provided Jess with as solid, loving and stable a home as you and Mum created here, together. I think Julie and Harry are probably closest to achieving it, but even they're not in your league.'

Dad looked at me and I eyeballed him right back. I was only speaking the truth.

'Life goes on, though,' Dolores said briskly. 'When my David passed I was heartbroken, but I picked myself up and got on with things. We have to keep living and having fun. People are not made to be alone. We all crave company and I believe in second chances, don't you, George?'

According to Mum, David had died of exhaustion from trying to keep Dolores happy. Mum always said she was a 'piece of work' and, boy, was I witnessing it now. I felt it would be monumentally disloyal to Mum not to run this woman out of her house. I was going to make damn sure that Louise agreed to bring Dad to Italy. We had to get him away from Dolores and talk to him about making good choices.

'True love can never be replicated,' I said firmly.

'Love comes in different forms,' Dolores shot back. 'Just because we're older doesn't mean we're not capable or deserving of love and happiness.'

'Yes, but –' I was about to deliver Dolores a death-blow when my phone buzzed, then Dad's.

I looked at the screen. Message from Gavin: *D-day. Shania in labour. On way to hospital. Come quickly!!!!!!*

Dad and I looked at each other.

'Gavin's panicking,' I said. 'He needs us.'

'Oh, George, another grandchild and your son's heir. How exciting.'

'We'd better go.' Dad stood up, his attention firmly on our family again. Good.

'No need to panic, George.' Dolores laughed. 'She'll probably be in labour for hours, or even days. They'll be tripping over you. Sure there's nothing you can do anyway.'

'I suppose I am a bit useless,' Dad said. 'You're right, I'd probably only be in the way.' He sat down again.

'No, you wouldn't,' I said. 'You're our dad. We want you there at big moments. Gavin needs you. He doesn't have Mum so he needs us all to rally. Come on, Dad. Family is everything and we must support each other.'

'Why don't you go ahead, Sophie, and call George when she's in full labour?' Dolores was not letting go.

I stood up, walked over to the coat rack, grabbed Dolores's coat, marched over and handed it to her. 'We are going to the hospital, to be with our family on this big day. Goodnight, Dolores.'

She turned to Dad, who looked at the floor and muttered, 'Sorry.' While he went to get his wallet and his keys, I walked Dolores to the door and slammed it behind her.

Dad came back down the stairs, ready to go.

'Seriously, Dad? Why her? She's awful,' I said.

'Ah, now, Dolores is a nice person when you get to know her.'

'No, she is not. And does she have to sit in Mum's chair?' I'd promised myself I wouldn't mention it, but I couldn't help it. It just felt like a betrayal.

Dad sighed. 'I know what you mean, love, but it's just a chair.'

'No, it isn't. It's Mum's chair.' I knew I sounded half crazy, but everything still felt so raw. This was Mum's house, her home. 'She's only gone a matter of months, Dad! What are you doing with that dreadful woman?'

Dad leaned against the front door, looking old and weary. 'I'm lonely, Sophie. I miss your mum every minute of every day. I find the days and nights very long. You're all great kids and are very good to me, but you're busy with your own lives and children. I like having company. Dolores is easy to be around. She gets me out of my head and out of the house. Most days I don't know what to do with myself. You have to remember, love, you lost a mother, but I lost a wife – it's a different kind of loss.'

I bit my lip. I had been too quick to judge. Poor Dad. My anger melted away. 'I'm sorry, Dad. I'm sorry you feel lonely. I know you miss Mum. So do I. I miss her so much. But it's much harder for you, I get that. I just . . . well, it's just that . . .'

Dad took my hand in his. 'Sophie, I'm not running off into the sunset with Dolores. We're just having dinner. She could never replace my Anne. That's not what this is about.'

Yes, but it was dinner on Mum's best china, used once a year, and Dolores was sitting in Mum's chair, and she was pushy and brash and I hated her.

My phone rang.

'Damn, it's Gavin,' I said. 'Hi, Gavin, we're just –'

'What the actual? Where are you? I need support here. My girlfriend is having a baby and Mum's not here to help me!' he roared.

'Jesus, let's get to him before he combusts,' Dad said, as he hurried me out of the door and locked it behind us.

'We're on the way right now. Relax, she'll be in labour for a while. I'm bringing Dad. We're coming.'

We walked into the hospital and saw Louise and Julie at the desk. The receptionist gave us directions.

'Has the baby arrived?' I asked.

'Not yet,' Julie said. 'But Gavin keeps calling. He sounds manic.'

'He's hyperventilating down the phone.' Louise pressed the button on the lift. 'You'd swear he was the one in labour.'

'God, I hope this doesn't go on all night.' I stepped into the lift.

'I brought snacks and drinks in case it does.' Julie indicated a big holdall.

Dad hesitated at the lift doors. 'Maybe I should go home. I'm a bit of a spare tool here. He has all of you girls. I don't want to be in the way.'

I silently cursed Dolores for feeding his self-doubt. We'd have to work on reassuring him and making him feel wanted in every situation.

'No way.' Julie linked his arm. 'We're all suffering this labour together.'

Gavin was pacing up and down outside the delivery room

shouting into his phone, 'Dad! Where are you? I've left three messages. Shania is in labour. I need you here.'

We waved at him and he hung up.

'Answer your phone, will you?' Gavin immediately launched at Dad.

'He was busy,' I muttered.

'It's all right, son. Take a breath. I'm here,' Dad said, wrapping him in a hug. Gavin looked instantly calmer. They clashed a lot and had lost Mum as their glue, but their bond went deep all the same.

Dad walked Gavin over to the window, talking calmly to him all the while, his arm firmly around his shoulders.

'What was Dad busy with?' Louise asked.

'Dinner with Dolores,' I said.

'What?' Julie looked upset. 'In our house?'

'Yes. She was sitting in Mum's chair and he had the Christmas china on the table.' The words were out before I could stop them.

'No!' Julie looked as shocked as I'd felt. 'Jesus, the Christmas china? Mum would give him a real piece of her mind for that. She loved that set.'

'Definitely trying to impress her,' Louise noted.

'I'm being a bit of a bitch,' I said. 'I was shocked, but then Dad told me how lonely he feels and how no one could replace Mum. He's not forgetting her, he's just trying to get on with life without her, I suppose.'

Julie and Louise looked at me, then at Dad.

'I really should get over to him more often,' Louise said. 'The days just slip by, work is a nightmare, and suddenly I realize I haven't seen him for ages.'

'Well, actually,' I said, 'on that note, I think we have to bring him to Italy. We need to spend time with him, make

him feel useful and valued, and get him away from Dolores.'
I stared at Louise.

'I agree. Come on, Louise,' Julie urged her.

She sighed. 'Okay, fine, but you two are in charge of him.'

'Deal,' Julie and I answered.

I was thrilled. It was just what Dad needed.

'Stop yapping – come on,' Gavin called. 'Shania's in here.'

We followed him into the birthing room where Shania was sitting on a big ball. She was in a hospital gown looking very serene. There was a big bath in the corner.

'Hey!' She smiled.

Dad was standing at the door, looking uncomfortable again.

'How are you doing, Shania?' I asked.

'Getting closer, I think.' She glanced at the midwife, who nodded.

'Wow, this is nice,' Julie said, looking around. 'I had the triplets in a small, windowless room. This is seriously fancy. I'd move in here myself.'

'What is that godawful noise?' Louise asked.

'Monks chanting,' Shania said. 'It's these monks who live in, like, this tiny village in some country, I can't remember the name, but they're like super-holy and their chant is supposed to put you in a Zen-like trance. Close your eyes and go with it, Louise.'

I tried not to look at Louise's face – I knew I'd laugh. Julie fake-coughed to hide her giggles.

'Trance?' Louise said. 'Shania, that wailing will give you and your baby a migraine.'

'She likes it,' Gavin said firmly.

'I have no words,' Dad muttered.

'I gave birth to Jess to Take That's "Rule The World". Oh, it was gorgeous.' I could see it all. Jack holding my hand and

Jess's kitten-like cry as she came into the world with the song playing in the background. I'd thought, Yes, my beautiful baby girl will rule the world.

'I had no music and Harry and I cried the whole way through, half because of joy but also because we had no money and we knew that looking after triplets was going to be a nightmare. Then Tom, our accident, came along, and we were even more freaked out.'

'Oh, Julie, I feel so bad for you.' Shania made a sad face.

Julie laughed. 'It's fine, it all worked out, and Tom was an angel baby.'

'I don't remember much about Clara's birth. I felt numb. It took me a while to bond with her, but then . . . well . . .' Louise smiled.

Julie, Mum and I had been worried about Louise's complete lack of maternal instinct. She had no reaction when Clara was born. It was like one of her work transactions – 'Right, baby is born, I need her in a crèche, and how soon can I get back to work?'

Thankfully, after a while she'd fallen hook, line and sinker for Clara and it had made her a nicer person. She'd been a bit hard and intimidating before motherhood had softened her edges. Mum always said it was the making of her.

'Well, our baby is going to be born to chanting and a calm, peaceful environment,' Shania said.

'Dad,' I asked, 'what are your memories of our births?'

'Well, now, they were different times, the men stayed out of the room and waited. The midwife came and told me the good news and then I came in and Anne was holding you . . . It was . . . well, it was . . . a miracle each time.' He stopped and gathered himself. 'Anyway, I think I'll step out now. Shania doesn't need me in here taking up space and, to be honest, the chanting is doing my head in.'

'We all need earplugs,' Louise muttered.

'Can I have a bath while I'm waiting?' Julie joked.

'Shania's having a water birth. It's going to be so cool,' Gavin told us.

'What happens when the bathwater goes cold? Do you just keep emptying it out and refilling it?' Julie asked.

'It's at thirty-seven degrees Celsius, which is the same as Shania's body temperature. It's much better to have babies this way because Shania will feel counter-pressure on her back, her sacrum, her legs and vulva.'

'Gavin, did you actually just say "vulva"?' Julie snorted.

'Sweet divine Jesus, I'm gone.' Dad hurriedly exited the room to wait outside.

'Yes, Julie, I did. I'm not fifteen, I can talk about women's body parts. Water births are supposed to be better because they reduce the risk of tearing or an episiotomy.'

'Okay, okay, I get it, you're a modern man.' Julie covered her ears with her hands.

'Gavin is super-supportive of the water birth and I really don't want to tear. I want my vagina intact. I don't want to end up with, like, a big tunnel down there,' Shania said.

'I lost count of how many stitches I had after Tom,' Julie said. 'I'd say it's the feckin' Eurotunnel down there.'

Louise and I cracked up.

'Thanks, Julie, that's really helpful,' Gavin said sarcastically. 'We want the birthing room to be a calm and positive space, please.'

Louise picked up her bag. 'I can't take the wailing monks. I'm going to wait outside with Dad.'

'Me too,' I said. 'Good luck, Shania.'

'Me three.' Julie followed us out.

We sat in the waiting room, laughing and eating snacks. Two hours later the baby got into distress and Shania was

rushed into surgery for an emergency C-section. No chanting, no water, no calm or peaceful arrival.

I knocked gently on the door.

'Come in.'

We three and Dad walked in. Gavin was holding his newborn baby in his arms.

'Congratulations!' Louise said.

'Well done.' Dad patted Gavin on the back and gave Shania
the thumbs-up.

Shania was lying back on the bed looking exhausted and
happy.

'So?' Julie asked.

'A girl.' Gavin showed us his baby proudly.

'Awwwww,' we all cooed.

'What are you calling her?' Dad asked.

'Lemon.' Shania said the name as if it was a prayer.

We all froze.

Dad laughed. 'Good one! What's her middle name? Kiwi?
So what are you calling her?'

I tried to catch his eye, but he was looking at Gavin.

'It's Lemon, Dad.'

'What?'

'Her name is Lemon.'

'How do you spell it?' Dad asked.

'L-E-M-O-N,' Shania said. 'Isn't it beautiful? It's nature,
sunshine yellow and light all rolled into one name.'

'So, just like the fruit?' Dad was incredulous.

'Yes.' Gavin's jaw set just as it did when Dad said men
should go out to work.

'You're calling your child a lemon?'

'No, Dad, not a lemon, Lemon.'

'You're a lemon if you do that,' Dad said. 'Pure cruel that is. The child has no hope in life with a name like that.'

Gavin looked like he was about to throw a punch.

'Dad, it's Shania and Gavin's baby and they like the name, so let's go with it,' said Julie.

'Lemon is a fruit, not a name.' Dad was just as stubborn as Gavin.

'It's certainly unique. She'll be the only Lemon in the country.' Julie tried to smooth things over.

'Exactly.' Shania beamed. 'I'm the only Shania I know and I love it.'

'Well, if it's unique you were going for, you've definitely achieved that goal,' Louise said.

'I think it's lovely.' I wanted to paper over Dad's disapproval. 'Can I hold her?'

Gavin passed Lemon to me and I inhaled her milky scent. Oh, I missed this. I missed Jess's sweet scent and holding her close, feeling like her protector.

Dad shuffled about beside me. You could have cut the air with a knife.

'In case you're interested, Dad, her full name is Lemon Anne Devlin,' Gavin said.

'Oh,' Dad said quietly. 'Well, that's lovely, son. Your mother would be very pleased.'

I held out the baby. Dad took her in his arms.

'Well, hello there, little Lem— little one. I'm your granddad and your granny is smiling down at you, I can promise you that. She'd have surely loved to meet you.'

I swallowed back tears and saw that my siblings were all doing the same. Gavin wiped one away. Mum loved babies. She would have been so happy to see Gavin, her only son and the apple of her eye, become a father.

Dad rocked the baby and gazed into her sweet little face. 'Mind you, she would have struggled with the fruit-naming side of things.'

'DAD!' all four of us said at once. Thankfully, Shania started laughing.

19. Julie

I ripped open the box and pulled out the scarves and hats. They were almost an identical match to the colour of the school jerseys. A tiny bit brighter, maybe, but close enough. There was a letter inside thanking me for supporting the local business and wishing the team all the best for the season. I bet I wouldn't have had that personal touch from Atelier de Cashmere.

I wrapped a scarf around my neck. If I was being totally honest, the scarf did feel a bit itchy, but it was warm and it looked good.

Marion came in. 'Ah, they arrived.'

'Yes, what do you think?'

'They look great, really cosy.'

She put one on. 'Oh, *helloooooooo*, my name is Jemima Stockport Aitken and Jones, and my son is the *staaar* of the team.'

We burst out laughing.

'Do you think Victoria will be happy?' I asked.

'Fuck, no. These are proper woolly sheep scarves, not soft baby's arse scarves. She'll hate them.'

She was right, but I no longer cared. I pulled out my 'Rugby' notebook and ran through all the orders. Marion helped me package them up and wrote the family name on each individual bag. Honestly, it was like running a business.

'Who are the McAndrews? They've ordered ten scarves and hats. How many kids do they have?'

I grinned. 'Six kids and they want one each for the granddads. They're a lovely family. No airs and graces.'

Marion shook her head. 'It's all a bit mad, but in another way I kind of envy you. I know it's over the top, but there is a real sense of community and coming together about it all. You're in a kind of bubble and there's an in-it-all-together kind of vibe.'

She was right in a way. Aside from some of the nonsense and a few annoying parents, most people were really nice and there was camaraderie and team spirit among the boys.

'I just think because Harry and I didn't go to private schools and aren't used to all this hot-housing, fuss and hoopla, we find it a bit uncomfortable. But I do see how much the boys are getting out of it and for that reason I'm going to try to embrace their first cup match today.'

'You should. The boys will remember this time in their lives for ever.' Marion stood up. 'Right, I'd better go. I've to bring Molly to the dentist to get a letter from him saying she desperately needs braces. Her prick of a father is saying her teeth are fine because he doesn't want to pay for them. She looks like Bugs fucking Bunny. I wish he'd just be a decent father and not fight me on every penny. I never overspend, buy nothing for myself, just want our daughter to have some hope of finding a lad and not end up living alone gnawing on fucking carrots.'

'It's awful for you to have to go through all this hassle. You know I'd be happy to —'

Marion held up her hand. 'Stop. I know you'd pay for the braces in a second, but our friendship is not going to be you looking after me financially. I really appreciate that you let me stay here once a month. I will never let you pay for anything else. But thanks for the offer.'

Marion had been adamant since the day we inherited all the money that I never give her a penny. She wanted our friendship to stay as it was and I admired her and loved her for it.

'Right, go to the match and good luck to the lads.'

'Thanks.' I headed off with a boot full of woolly goods.

Victoria sat in the centre of the parents' section of the stand, dressed immaculately. The woolly hat and scarf rested on her lap. She had turned up her nose when she'd taken them out of the bag.

The other parents duly put theirs on, although I did see a few mums scratching their necks.

I sat surrounded by Harry, Sophie, Louise, Dad, Jack, Jess, Robert and Clara. Tom was on the sideline with his classmates, proudly wearing his hat and scarf.

When the team ran onto the pitch and I saw my three boys all kitted out in the school colours, slapping each other on the back, I felt a huge surge of pride.

I looked at Harry. His eyes were shining with tears. I grabbed his hand. 'Wow,' I said.

'Unreal,' Harry croaked.

'Big day.' Dad beamed. 'Three grandsons playing. This is a momentous day.'

'At least it got him away from Dolores,' Louise whispered.

'Sorry I'm late.' Gavin plonked himself down beside us.

'What is that?' Louise pointed to the bright multi-coloured wrap Gavin had around his body.

'It's a traditional African papoose.'

'Is the baby in there?' Clara said, peering in.

'Yes, she's snuggled up.' Gavin pulled down the side of the papoose so Clara could see her.

'Christ almighty.' Dad groaned.

'Can she breathe?' Sophie asked.

Lemon's head did look a bit squashed against Gavin's chest.

'Duh, like, obviously. It's the most natural way to carry a

baby. African mothers have been doing it this way for, like, millions of years.'

'How's fatherhood going?' Jack asked.

'It's awesome. I just want to be with her all the time. Shania, Lemon and me are a love bubble, a little unit. I can't believe how amazing it is. She's such a good baby. She never cries and she sleeps a lot.'

'That won't last,' I muttered.

'Definitely not,' Harry muttered back.

Jack held Robert up so he could see Lemon.

'She's teeny tiny, Daddy,' Robert said.

'She's not actually. She's the normal size for a three-week-old baby,' Clara corrected him.

'She's perfect,' Sophie said.

'I see you got your cast off, Robert,' Dad said, nodding at his arm.

'Yes, I did, and I have to do lots of exercises to make it strong again. Jess is helping me. Look.' Robert flexed his skinny arm.

'My goodness, you're nearly as strong as your cousins.' Dad ruffled Robert's hair.

'How's Shania?' I asked Gavin.

Gavin gently stroked Lemon's head. 'Crazy busy. The US sales of her tan have gone nuts. She's on Zoom calls all day, trying to sort out production to meet the demand.'

'Good for her,' Sophie said. 'But I hope she's minding herself too. A C-section is a big procedure.'

'I'm looking after her, don't you worry.'

'You're a lucky man,' Jack noted. 'A gorgeous and success-ful wife. Happy days.'

Louise nudged me. I knew what she was thinking: did Jack have a death wish?

Sophie glared at him. 'What do you mean?'

'What? I just mean it's great for Gavin.'

'I work my butt off, Jack, and I look bloody good for my age.'

'I know you do.'

'So do you consider yourself lucky too?'

'But you don't, Sophie. You still have a big bottom,' Clara said.

Oh, dear God.

'Yes, I am lucky, very lucky.' Jack pulled back from the brink.

'It's just an expression, darling,' Louise told her daughter. 'To work your butt off means to work very hard. You don't actually get rid of your bottom.'

'Do I have a big butt?' Sophie looked affronted.

'No, you have a perfect one,' Jack said.

I made vomit noises.

'Are you going to vomit, Julie?' Clara asked.

'No, sweetie. Jack is just being smarmy so I'm making fun.'

'Is vomiting fun for you?'

Gavin stepped in. 'Julie is just being silly, Clara.'

'Yes, she is.'

Louise and Sophie started laughing.

'She's been silly all her life,' Jack said, grinning at me.

'*Touché,*' I said, sticking out my tongue at him.

We heard loud singing from the school supporters beside us.

Louise held out Clara's earphones. 'Put these on, sweetie. The cheering is going to get very noisy.'

Clara put them on.

Sophie leaned in to me and said, 'Is my bum big?'

'No, it isn't. It's half the size of mine,' I told her.

'For the love of God, will you all pipe down? The match is about to start.' Dad was getting wound up. He always got uptight when there was a sports match to be watched. We had spent most Saturdays of our childhood being shouted out of the TV room for 'ruining the game'.

At half-time Castle Academy were six points ahead. I thought the triplets were playing brilliantly. But Dad had quite a bit to say about Leo.

'He needs to work on his upper-body strength. He's missed a few key tackles.'

'I thought he was great.' I defended my son.

'He's the weakest link. He'll have to up his game or he'll get dropped. Liam's kicking is off too. Luke is the only one playing well.'

'Do you really think so, George?' Harry looked panic-stricken.

'Dad,' I eyeballed him, 'I only want to hear positive comments, okay? Keep your negative thoughts to yourself. I think they're all playing fantastically well and I'm very proud.'

He huffed, 'I'm only saying I've seen them play better. Sure all I want is for them to shine like the stars they are. Besides, you've barely watched the game, between cooing at the baby and chatting to your sisters.'

'I agree with Julie. I think they're doing really well,' Sophie said. Considering she'd spent most of the match watching Jess and checking Instagram, I wasn't that confident in her opinion.

'Jack?' I asked my brother-in-law, who had actually played rugby.

'Look, there are always things players can work on, but they're a solid team and the triplets are a key part of it.'

'Thank you.'

'I wanna be like the big boys,' Robert said.

'You will, buddy. We'll send you to Castle Academy too.'

'Really?' Sophie seemed surprised.

'Definitely.'

'Aw, it'll be lovely for him to be with his cousins,' I said. 'Is Pippa keen too?'

Jack sighed. 'If I make it seem like it was her decision, we'll be okay. Otherwise, she'll just disagree for the sake of it.'

'Mummy, how long more?' Clara asked.

Louise, who had spent most of the game typing into her phone, looked up. 'Actually, I have to go now. There's a problem in work, another Zoë balls-up. God, I'm so sick of that girl. Clara, do you want to stay with Gavin and Granddad or come to the office with me?'

'Quiet office, please.' Clara was delighted to be going. 'I don't understand rugby. Why do boys want to hurt each other and fall down chasing a ball that isn't even round?'

'You have a point there,' Louise said.

'For the love of God!' Dad was at breaking point.

We waved them goodbye.

The second half went well, I thought. Dad, however, continued to give out and curse and mutter throughout. When it was over, with a comfortable win for our team, he turned around beaming and said, 'I'm a very proud grandfather today.'

'You hid it well,' I grumbled.

'Ah, that was just me wanting them to do their best and stand out, Julie.'

'Well, you can sit beside someone else at the next match. You totally stressed me out.'

Gavin rearranged his papoose. 'Dad never praised me. He always told me what I did wrong in my football matches.'

'I just wanted you to get better, and you did.'

'A bit of praise wouldn't have gone amiss.'

Dad pulled his gloves off. 'I stood on the sidelines of every match you played, hail, rain or snow. Don't give me that boo-hoo my-dad-wasn't-there-for-me crap. I was there every single Saturday without fail.'

'I know you were, Dad, and I appreciate it, but you were short on compliments.'

'I was balancing out your mother, who told you the sun shone out of your arse every day of your life.'

Sophie and I giggled. 'So true. You could do no wrong in Mum's eyes,' Sophie said.

'Well, me and Shania are going to tell Lemon she's brilliant every day of her life.'

'You'll need to build her confidence with that name,' Jack muttered. Sophie stifled a laugh.

'We all parent differently. There's no right or wrong way,' I said, wanting to shut the conversation down.

We went over to congratulate the team. The triplets all hugged me, which was a miracle. They were clearly on a high from the win. Dad clapped them on the back enthusiastically and congratulated them, keeping his criticism to himself.

Harry put his arm around me and we beamed at each other – we were bursting with pride but trying to be cool.

'They were just . . .' He couldn't finish his sentence.

'I know . . .'

'It's all just so incredible . . .'

'I want to jump up and down and scream, "They are my beautiful sons."'

'Me too.' He laughed and we hugged, ridiculously proud parents.

Over Harry's shoulder I saw Sebastian approach Jess, whose face went bright red. He said something to her and she half smiled, but thankfully Sophie made a beeline for her and pulled her away. I still felt rage every time I looked at him. All I could see was him at the bedroom door, all swagger, and Jess on the bed behind him. I shuddered. I sincerely hoped she'd kept up her part of the agreement and broken all ties with him.

Harry went off to chat to the other dads and I was feeling all warm and fuzzy from the glow of the match when I heard, 'She's incapable of ordering anything. These scarves are appalling. They'll give us all rashes. I'm ordering a set from Atelier de Cashmere tonight. These are going straight in the bin.' Of course, it was Victoria.

I felt Sophie's hand on my arm. 'Ignore her. She's a bitch.' Then, loudly, she said, 'These scarves are so cosy. It's wonderful to support local Irish businesses. I don't understand people who order from abroad when what we have here is such good quality. We need to support local to help businesses survive and thrive. Well done, Julie, for sourcing these home-grown and home-made products.'

A few of the parents murmured their approval. Sophie winked at me and walked off, her arm protectively around Jess.

20. Louise

Clara was curled up on the couch petting Luna while she hummed 'Fernando'. She was small for her age. Small and pale because she hated sports and only liked being outside if we were bird-watching or in a quiet park or forest.

I sat down beside her. 'Well done on your tests, sweetie. All As, you clever girl.'

Clara stopped humming. 'I only ever want to get As. Never, ever Bs.'

I stroked Luna. 'I know, but it's okay if you do get a B sometimes.'

'No, Mummy, it's not okay. I want As. I want to be as clever as you.'

'You're cleverer than I was at your age.'

'Am I?'

Probably not, but Clara was very bright and had a photographic memory, like I did. Still, I didn't want her putting too much pressure on herself because if she did get a B, it would lead to a meltdown.

'I think so. I got Bs sometimes,' I lied.

'Julie said you were the cleverest in the whole school.'

'It wasn't that hard, our school wasn't a particularly good school, to be honest.'

It hadn't been. It was the local secondary school, the teachers were very average and only about thirty per cent of the girls went on to third-level education, so the bar was not set particularly high. I hadn't enjoyed school. It had been something I'd needed to get through to achieve my goal, which was to study law at Cambridge. Julie had loved it and was in the thick of everything, sports, musicals, social life. Sophie was modelling part-time from the age of fifteen, so she had to deal with a fair bit of jealousy. She hadn't liked school much either.

'How are you getting on with the other kids? Is Jarlath being nicer to you?'

Clara picked Luna up and held her close. 'No. He says I'm weird and useless at games, so he never asks me to play. I don't mind, Mummy, I hate playing dodgeball. Why do people want to be hit by a ball? It's so stupid.'

I laughed. 'I agree. I always thought dodgeball was a ridiculous game.'

She smiled and I took the opportunity to tell her I was going away.

'So, this weekend, Julie, Sophie, Granddad and I are going away for two days.'

Clara squeezed Luna tighter. I was on thin ice.

'I'll only be gone Friday, Saturday and back on Sunday. I'll be back to tuck you into bed on Sunday night.'

'Where are you going?'

'Italy.'

'Why?'

'For a little family trip away.'

'What time will you leave and come back?'

'I'll bring you to school on Friday, then pick up your aunties and go to the airport for a ten-fifty flight. I'll be back on Sunday. My flight lands at six twenty so I'll be home before you go to sleep at eight. Gavin will pick you up from school on Friday and bring you back to his apartment for two days, okay? You'll be sleeping in his spare bedroom. I'll drop off your blanket and your bedside lamp, your pyjamas, iPad and your headphones. Luna is going with you too.'

Clara was quiet.

'Maybe you could help Gavin look after Lemon.'

'I only like Lemon when she's asleep.'

I laughed. 'That's how most people feel about babies.'

'But I suppose I could help push the buggy.'

'That would be great.'

'And maybe sing "Fernando" to her?'

'She'd love that. So are you okay about staying with Gavin and Shania?'

She nodded. 'As long as I have Luna and all my things, it's okay. But only two nights, Mummy, right?'

'Yes, pet. Maybe you and I can go to Italy together some time.'

She shook her head. 'No, Mummy, I don't like airports. They're too noisy and crowded. I don't want to go to Italy.'

I needed to keep her calm and feeling secure. I was so wound up about the trip and meeting Marco that I wasn't sure I could handle a meltdown.

I kissed her head gently. 'Okay, sweetheart, we won't go. Would you like a snack?'

'Yes.'

'Yogurt?'

'Yes, strawberry.'

Clara ate her snack and asked a few more questions about her weekend schedule, then seemed quiet and relatively content. I thanked my lucky stars that she loved and trusted Gavin and was used to being minded by him. I thought the addition of Lemon would throw her off, but she seemed open to the idea of helping Gavin mind the baby. It gave me hope that she could manage life in the future.

And what would her future hold? I felt almost sick at the idea of opening a can of worms with Marco. I had to control this situation from the very first moment, to suss him out and then, if we got as far as talking, to ensure he couldn't mess up our lives in any way. There was no way some random man was going to undo all the hard work I had put in, with Mum, to make Clara as able for the world as possible. I had prepared airtight legal documents that set out the parameters of any future contact. If he didn't agree to all my conditions, he was out. There was nothing I wouldn't do to protect Clara.

'Wish me luck, Mum,' I whispered.

Dad was standing at the gate with a small, neat suitcase beside him. He popped it into the boot and climbed into the passenger seat.

'Thanks for being ready.'

'I've been up all night, worried the alarm wouldn't go off. I wanted to be sure to be on time for you.'

'I appreciate it. I'm nervous, Dad.'

'Of course you are, pet. It's a serious business, but I'll be right behind you and if this fella steps out of line or seems a bit fishy, we'll just walk away.'

I exhaled deeply. 'I hope I'm doing the right thing.'

'You're doing the best for Clara. That's all you can do. I'm glad you asked me along, I'm happy to help in any way I can.'

'Thanks, Dad.' I was glad we'd asked him. He had been really touched and chuffed when I'd said it to him. It had been the right thing to do. Sophie had been right to push me. It felt nice having my dad by my side.

We arrived at Julie's. I pressed the doorbell and banged on the door with my fist. I couldn't handle Julie's tardiness today. Like Dad, Sophie had been standing at her garden gate, immaculately dressed and made-up with a small, neat suitcase packed and ready to go when we'd arrived at her place. Here, there was no sign of Julie.

Finally, Julie yanked open the door. She was in a tracksuit and her hair was soaking wet.

'Jesus, Julie! You swore you'd be ready!'

'I was all set to be ready and then Tom forgot his project, so I had to whizz back to the school. I'll be with you in two minutes.'

I was not letting her wander off. I followed her up to her bedroom. Her suitcase was open and there were clothes all over the bed. My blood pressure spiked.

'You're not even packed?'

'I wasn't sure what to wear to meet my niece's biological father in a village outside Rome.'

Sophie came up the stairs behind us. 'You left the front door open.' Seeing the mess and my clenched fists, she took charge.

Glancing over Julie's mound of clothes, Sophie pulled out a dress, a pair of jeans, a skirt, one T-shirt, two blouses, two pairs of shoes, a cardigan, a light jacket and two scarves. She rolled them up and packed them neatly into the case. She handed Julie a pair of cargo pants, a long-sleeved T-shirt, a light wool jumper and a pair of trainers to wear. While Julie got dressed, Sophie went into the bathroom and packed her make-up and beauty products.

'Passport?' I barked.

Julie said it was in her bedside locker. I opened the locker drawer. It was crammed with junk. I rifled through it and found her passport.

Within five minutes we were in the car.

'I have to say, Sophie, that was impressive,' I said.

'Thanks. Neat packing is a tip I got from my heyday as a guest on luxury yachts where you can only bring small bags on board.'

'Are you sure I have everything I need?' Julie asked. 'I usually bring a massive case when I go away.'

'Julie, it's a two-day trip. You probably won't even wear everything I packed for you.'

I slammed on the brakes just before I hit the car in front of me.

'Steady on, Louise, do you want me to drive?' Dad asked.

'I'm fine, just a bit tense.'

'Do the Clara breathing thing, in and out for four,' Julie suggested.

'Maybe we should all do it,' Sophie suggested, as I narrowly missed taking the side mirror off a car in the next lane. Dad clung to the grab handle and cursed under his breath.

We made it to the airport and onto our flight, despite Julie wandering off in Duty Free and Sophie having to find her and drag her to the boarding gate.

Even though it was only ten thirty a.m., I ordered a gin and tonic to calm my nerves. Julie ordered one to keep me company, Dad ordered a whiskey, but Sophie had water.

'I don't want to dehydrate,' she explained.

'After that car ride, I need this.' Dad knocked back his drink.

'So what's the plan?' Sophie asked me, turning to look through the gap in the seats so she could see me and Dad in the row behind.

I fished three folders out of my bag and handed them to my family.

'I should have known there'd be a folder.' Julie grinned.

'It's good to be organized, Julie. You could do with a bit more of it,' Dad noted.

'Thanks a lot. You try raising four boys.'

Sophie jumped in. 'So we're going straight to Pico, having dinner in the hotel and drinks in the local bar.'

'Yes, the hotel is small and sweet, not luxurious, but it looks clean and has good reviews. The bar is where Marco drinks every Friday.'

'It's a medieval village with only 2,776 inhabitants,' Julie read her notes. 'It sounds gorgeous.'

'I looked it up. It's lovely all right, stone walls and cobbled streets. It's a hundred and ninety-two metres above sea level,' Dad told us.

'In English, please,' Sophie asked.

'It means it's up in the hills,' Dad said.

'It's an hour's drive from Rome,' Julie read.

'Correct.'

'Can Sophie drive?' Julie asked.

'No! I'm taking over the driving. I'm sorry, Louise, but you nearly killed us on the motorway in Dublin so we'd definitely die on winding roads up to this medieval village.'

'Fine.' I was happy for Dad to drive. I trusted him. He had always been a good driver, unlike Mum who was the most distracted driver in the world. She'd had quite a lot of 'bumps' in her day. Mostly because she liked to do her make-up while driving.

'Fine with me too,' Sophie said.

We settled into a comfortable silence. Sophie took out her iPad and watched a movie. Julie fell asleep. Beside me, Dad drank his whiskey and studied his folder, underlining key points. It was reassuring having someone on the trip who was as invested in detail as I was.

I sipped my drink and read the research notes I had asked Zoë to write up on a prospective client. She had lasted exactly one week in Conveyancing before being bounced back to me because Brendan, the snake, told Walter that his department was overstaffed and 'poor Zoë will be bored'.

The notes that Zoë had clearly thrown together were the laziest, most half-arsed thing I had ever read. She had blatantly copied and pasted the company's home page and thrown in a few other random facts. No effort had been made to do a deep dive, as I'd requested, and there were several glaring spelling mistakes. I closed my laptop. This was not good for my already sky-high blood pressure. I took out my phone and watched videos of Clara to calm myself down.

Dad drove us carefully and skilfully up to Pico. I sat in the front beside him, navigating, while Julie and Sophie sat in the back oohing and aahing at the incredible scenery. Julie kept shouting, '*Bellissima*,' which got a bit irritating after a while.

We pulled up outside the hotel, which I was relieved to see looked exactly as it did online. No trick photography here. Julie said it was *bellissima*, Sophie thought it looked 'utterly charming' and Dad said it looked 'clean and functional'. I'd booked a three-bedroom apartment on the first floor. One bedroom for me, one for Dad and one for my sisters to share, with a small communal space for the four of us to hang out. The rooms were simply decorated, white linen, plain wooden furniture. I liked that they weren't cluttered. The two bathrooms were compact but had large modern-looking showers squeezed in. I had an en-suite, while Dad and my sisters were sharing the main bathroom

Despite all our objections, Dad insisted on trying to lug the four suitcases up the narrow stairs, but ended up dropping two of them.

A young Italian employee rushed out when he heard the clatter. 'Let me 'elp you,' he said.

'Not at all. I have it under control, thank you,' Dad said.

'For goodness' sake, Dad, you can't carry four cases on your own. Let the guy help. I don't need you having a bloody heart attack in Italy, thank you. That would not be helpful in any way.' The last thing I needed was my father collapsing on this trip.

'No need to bite my head off,' Dad said.

'Let him help, Dad. It's his job,' Sophie said.

'*Grazie mille.*' Julie was determined to use her few words of Italian.

'*Grazie,*' I said, tipping the young man.

'Steady now, Louise.' Julie winked at me. 'He's a bit young for you.'

'We know how much you like one-night stands in Italy,' Sophie giggled.

'One half-Italian child is probably enough.' Dad chuckled.

'Sod off.' I threw a cushion at them as they all cracked up.

'What time is dinner?' Julie asked.

'Seven sharp. I want to be in the bar by nine. Benedict said Marco goes to the bar in the main square every Friday at about eight thirty and stays until ten thirty, eleven.'

'What's your plan?' Dad asked. 'How are you going to approach him?'

I'd thought about this a lot and decided that I first needed to figure out who Marco was before I even mentioned who I was, let alone Clara. I might leave Pico without ever telling Marco about his daughter.

'The plan is to engage him casually in conversation and just see what he's like. Hopefully he speaks some English.'

'Send Julie over. Sure she's almost bilingual.'

'Can you be serious for a minute?' I asked.

'I think Dad should try to initiate a conversation with him and you two can join in. I want to stay in the background and see what sort of vibe I get from him.'

'Good idea, Louise. I'll approach him first, man to man,' Dad said.

'Yes, but not man to man in a threatening way,' Julie said.

'In a friendly how's-it-going way,' Sophie told Dad.

'I know how to chat casually to a man in a bar.' Dad shook his head.

'We'd better be careful, though. We know, even though he looks like an Italian Danny DeVito, Marco is so charming that he charmed Louise's knickers off.' Julie giggled.

'We promise to do our best not to fall into bed with him.' Sophie snorted.

'Stop that now. Louise is uptight enough,' Dad said.

'I'm not uptight. I'm just focused.'

'Right, yes, whatever you say.' Dad raised an eyebrow.

'We know, Dad, we're just trying to distract her,' Julie explained.

Dad rolled his suitcase towards the door of his bedroom. 'It's not working. She looks even more uptight, sorry, focused than she was earlier.'

My sisters were trying to distract me, but I was too on edge to join in their banter. I was completely addled and sick with nerves. I headed off to have a shower and try to calm down before going out and doing something that might change my life for ever.

21. Sophie

We three sisters and Dad stood outside the bar in a medieval town in Italy – Louise and Dad both in a shirt and trousers, Julie in a flowing dress, and me in white denims and a silk shirt.

Julie squeezed Louise's hand. 'Ready?'

'No.'

'You're as ready as you can be. Remember, you have the power here. You can pull the plug on this at any time. Just give me the word and we'll be out of here.' Dad patted Louise on the back.

'Dad's right. You can always tell Clara he's dead,' I said. 'Marco knows nothing, so you hold all the cards.'

Louise nodded.

'Okay, let's do it.' Julie pushed open the door and led us into the small local bar.

Every head turned and all conversation stopped. Three middle-aged foreign women and an older man coming into the bar in March was clearly an anomaly.

Julie marched purposefully towards a table for four, and I scanned the room. I spotted him. Italy's Danny DeVito was leaning up against the bar, chatting to two other men. They were all dressed in scruffy jeans. Two of the men were in T-shirts but Marco had a nice blue shirt on.

The other clientele consisted of three couples sitting around a table playing cards, two old men sitting up at the bar, the barman and a dog.

'He's at the bar, blue shirt,' I said, out of the side of my mouth, like some undercover cop.

'I see him,' Dad said.

'Act casual,' Julie hissed.

We took our seats and the barman came straight over. We ordered three large gin and tonics and a beer for Dad.

'No denying he's her father,' Dad said, which was what we were all thinking.

You could see Clara in his nose and charming lopsided smile.

'He's better-looking in the flesh, to be fair,' Julie said.

'Nice smiley face,' I added.

'Louise?' Julie shook her arm gently.

'Are you okay?' Dad asked.

Louise finally found her voice. 'I just need a minute, and a drink.'

The barman came back with our drinks.

'What bring you loffely ladeez to Pico?' he asked.

'We're just . . .'

'Uhm, we thought . . .'

'A private matter.' Dad cut him dead.

Looking affronted, he backed away.

'Jesus, Dad, we're trying to get to know the locals, not frighten the hell out of them,' I said.

'You might need to work on your small-talk, Dad.' Julie handed Louise her drink and told her to take a good gulp of it.

We took turns spying on Marco, who was chatting animatedly with his friends.

'He looks very relaxed and he has kind eyes,' Julie said.

'You think everyone has kind eyes,' Louise replied.

'Not everyone. Victoria has snake eyes.'

'He smiles a lot, which is always a good sign,' I said.

'Stupid people smile a lot,' Louise said.

'He seems popular,' Julie said.

'He's talking to two people. He's not exactly being mobbed.'

Julie looked at me, raised her eyebrows and sipped her drink.

'Okay, Dad,' Louise barked suddenly, making us jump. 'Go over and chat to him. Sophie, go with him so he doesn't insult anyone. You're good at all that boring small-talk.'

Louise had a knack of insulting you and paying you a compliment at the same time.

Dad and I rose from the table and walked over to where the three men were standing.

I waited for Dad to say something, but he seemed to have frozen.

'Good evening, do you speak English?' I said.

'A leetle bit,' the tall friend said.

The other two just stared at him.

'Okay, so, we were wondering if . . . uhm . . . if you could recommend any special things to do in the area?'

'Do you like walking?' the middle-sized one asked.

'I guess so, yes.'

'Many beautiful walks 'ere. But maybe your 'usband is too old for long walking?'

'Mother of God, she's my daughter, not my wife.' Dad finally found his voice.

'I was thinking you were a very lucky man.' The two men laughed.

'Are they you seesters?' Marco asked, nodding to Julie and Louise, who were doing a very bad job of pretending not to look over.

I looked at him directly for the first time. Julie was right, he did have kind eyes. Lovely soft, kind brown eyes unlike my eldest sister's steely blue ones.

'Yes, we are.'

'Why are you 'ere?' the tall one asked.

'You bringing Papa on 'oliday?' the middle one asked.

'Kind of,' I fudged.

'Where are you from?' the tall one asked.

'Ireland,' I answered.

'Ah, Irlanda.' They all smiled.

I smiled back. Silence. I looked at Dad, still frozen. Right, small-talk, my alleged forte.

'So what do you do?' I asked.

'We farm the olives,' Marco said.

'Oh, you have olive farms? How fantastic. I love olives. Well, I like green ones, not the black ones so much. Actually, do they grow on different trees?' I sounded like a total idiot but I ploughed on. Queen of small-talk.

The three men laughed.

Marco said, 'No, eet ees the same tree but the green olives are the first ones you are picking and then if you want black ones you are waiting until later to pick.'

'Oh, I see, so the black ones are riper?'

'What is riper?' the tall one asked.

God, this was painful, I really didn't give a toss about olives.

'Dad,' I glared at him, 'feel free to jump in.'

Dad cleared his throat and started babbling. 'I don't like olives. My wife used to love them. She tried for years, decades actually, to persuade me they were nice, but I just can't stomach them. She'd try to hide them in casseroles, but I always found them and picked them out. The black ones have a very strong taste in my opinion . . .'

He was worse than me. I had to stop his crazy rambling.

This was not working. Sod it, it was time to get my sisters involved.

'Why don't I introduce you to my sisters and they can explain what "riper" means?'

I invited the men to join our table, which they willingly did.

I introduced my sisters. They told us their names. Tall man was Lorenzo and middle-sized man was Tommaso.

'Louise, could you please explain what "riper" means?' I asked.

'What are you talking about?' She scowled at me.

I was getting fed up with being dismissed, especially as I had succeeded in doing what I had been ordered to do – make small-talk and bring them over – while Dad had failed. Glaring at my sister, I said, 'We were chatting, as you do, about these men's olive farms and they were saying they pick the black olives later in the season. I said, "So the black ones are riper," and they didn't understand the word. I thought with you being in Mensa and all, you could explain it. You know, get involved in the conversation that I started.'

Julie, sensing the tension, jumped in. '"Riper" means that you wait until the fruit – actually, hang on, is an olive a fruit?'

'Yes,' Louise hissed.

'Oh, that's funny, I always thought of it as a veggie. Anyway, "ripe" means it's ready to pick, and the fruit you pick later on in the season is riper.'

'Yes, yes.' Lorenzo nodded. 'The black olive is riper.'

We all smiled and nodded, except Louise, who looked like she wanted to kill someone.

'Louisa, why you look so angry?' Tommaso asked.

Louise frowned, making her look even crosser. 'I'm not. I'm perfectly relaxed.'

The men all cracked up, laughing.

'You Irish, you supposed to be smiling, happy, drinking Guinness . . .' Lorenzo said.

'We're not all drunk leprechauns,' Louise huffed.

'Jesus, Louise, chill,' Julie said, under her breath. To the group she said, 'We are very happy to be here in your beautiful town.'

I noticed Marco studying Louise. A crease formed between his brows. He was staring at her intently. Slowly his eyes opened wider and then . . .

'You!' he said suddenly, pointing at her. 'You . . . you are the woman . . . Rome . . . long times ago.'

'Hold on a minute now, Mister.' Dad jumped up, blocking Marco from Louise.

Louise flinched, then regained her composure and looked directly at him. 'Yes, it's me.'

We all gasped. Tommaso and Lorenzo looked from one face to the next, perplexed.

This was not going according to Louise's plan, not at all, and I had no clue what to do next.

22. Julie

I thought I was going to have a heart attack. In all the scenarios we'd imagined, we hadn't thought that Marco would recognize Louise. It was a decade ago and I suppose we'd presumed he'd been as blind drunk as her. We didn't think for a moment that he'd suddenly cop on to who she was. The man must have a memory like an elephant – or maybe Louise was the night of his life.

I slipped my hand into Sophie's and the two of us held our breath, while Dad eyeballed Marco, and Marco's friends stood there looking the picture of confusion. Louise was perfectly still. Marco spoke in rapid-fire Italian to Lorenzo and Tommaso, clearly filling them in on his one-night stand and her sudden appearance ten years later. They looked as shocked as the rest of us.

'Okay, that's enough Italian. In English, please.' Dad had found his voice and was trying to take charge of the crazy situation.

'*Perché è qui?*' Tommaso asked.

Marco shrugged and then asked Louise, 'You come 'ere to find me?'

'Yes, I did.' Louise was calm now. Icy calm.

You could see Marco trying to work it all out. 'So long ago. Why?' he asked, suspiciously.

'Are you a good person?' Louise, queen of no small-talk, asked.

'Am I good person?' Marco was completely thrown.

I felt thrown too – I mean, how would anyone answer that

226

question? Of course you're going to say you're good. No one is going to say they're awful. But Marco saying he was good meant nothing. It didn't mean he was. I looked at Sophie and she gave a little shrug as if to say, I don't know what she's at either, but we'd better keep our mouths shut. I felt Louise was just rushing it, trying to tick boxes as fast as possible to give herself a sense of control. All I could do was pray she didn't end up regretting it.

'You heard my daughter. Answer the question,' Dad said gruffly, trying to establish his position as head of the family, when we all knew Louise was.

'I thinking so.' Marco directed his answer to Louise.

'Is he?' Louise asked his friends. 'Is Marco a good man?'

They looked completely confused again.

'We want the truth now,' Dad told them. Obviously, Dad had decided to row in with Louise's strange approach. My sister and father were clearly at sea, just jumping in with random questions. Sophie gripped my hand. What was going on?

'Yes, he is very good man.'

'Best man,' Tommaso added, nodding.

'Is he kind?' Louise asked.

'Yes.'

'Is he a solid man?' Dad continued with the senseless questions.

'What is solid?' Lorenzo asked.

'It means strong, reliable.' Sophie was working hard as a live thesaurus.

'Very solid,' Tommaso said. 'Marco look after his mother.'

'That's a good sign,' Dad acknowledged.

'Why are you asking all this? What do you wanting?' Marco was beginning to look alarmed.

'You want 'usband?' Lorenzo asked.

'You want to marry Marco?' Tommaso exclaimed.

'She most certainly does not. Louise doesn't need any man. She's by far the most independent of all my children,' Dad informed them.

'I'm pretty independent too,' Sophie muttered. I smiled. Sophie had always been competitive – if any of us got any snippet of praise, she was on it, looking for her share. It annoyed her when Mum or Dad praised the rest of us, although I always felt it was because, deep down, she didn't feel good enough.

'I need to speak to you,' Louise said to Marco.

'You speaking to me now.'

'It's a delicate matter.'

'What is delicate?' Lorenzo asked.

'It means . . . uhm . . . well . . . Julie, feel free to help me out,' Sophie said.

'In this case,' I said, 'delicate means sensitive.'

'*Sensibile*?' Tommaso looked at Marco.

Marco looked at Louise.

'Yes. I think we should talk in private.'

Marco folded his arms and shook his head. 'No private. You speak 'ere. I want friends to listen. I not know what you saying or doing.' Marco was clearly suspicious of Louise's intentions.

Dad slapped his hand on the table. 'Hold on a minute, sonny. If my daughter asks you to speak to her in private, you will speak in private.'

'Why is Dad behaving like some kind of gangster boss?' Sophie whispered.

I stifled a laugh. 'He's watched too much *Sopranos*.'

Marco folded his arms. 'My friends is my family. I staying 'ere.'

It looked like Danny DeVito was no pushover.

Dad stood up straighter. Mum called this look his 'argument face' – you knew he was about to let you have it with both barrels. 'It's okay, Dad.' Louise stopped him responding. She pulled her briefcase onto her lap. Tommaso and Lorenzo looked alarmed.

Louise pulled out the DNA test results and a DNA kit.

'This is a DNA test. Test *del* DNA.'

'DNA?' the three men said in unison.

Marco went white.

Louise went into lawyer mode. 'If you remember me, you will remember that we had unprotected sex. The result of that is my daughter, Clara. She is nine years old. She will be ten later this year. You are her father.'

'*Che cosa?*' Lorenzo gasped.

'*Una Figlia?*' Tommaso spluttered.

Marco's voice was calm. 'You say you have DNA test. How you have mine DNA?'

'A few weeks ago an English detective I hired to find you came here and took a glass that you had drunk from. But if you don't believe it, and I understand that, I have brought a DNA kit with me. I have Clara's hair and we can do another test.'

Sometimes my sister astonished me. Louise was now in crisis-control mode and she was incredible. She was all practicality and zero emotion.

'All the proof is right here.' Dad tapped the folder.

Marco's voice wavered as he spoke to his friends. There was a lot of hand movement and raised voices. Finally, Marco nodded. They all turned to look at Louise.

Lorenzo asked, 'Do you have photo?'

'Of course.' Louise pulled out a folder. She handed it to Marco. It had six A4-size photos of Clara.

The three men bent over to look at them. Marco's hands shook.

229

'*Dio mio.*'

'*Incredibile.*'

While his friends exclaimed, Marco was quiet. He stared at a photo of Clara where she was smiling. We all watched as he recognized himself in her.

Finally, he looked up. There were tears in his eyes. 'No DNA. She is my mother.'

'*È identica a tua madre!*' Lorenzo agreed.

'*Il naso!*' Tommaso pointed to her nose and shook his head in awe.

'Yes, the nose is what proved it to me, more than any DNA test,' Louise said.

'The nose did it for all of us.' Dad doubled down.

'*Mia figlia.*' Marco's voice was full of raw emotion.

Sophie wiped her eyes and I worked hard to swallow the lump in my throat. The whole situation was completely bonkers. We were in the middle of nowhere, telling a stranger that Clara was his daughter, yet it was also beautiful and moving and heart-warming.

'Well, to be clear, she's *my* daughter and you are her biological father.' Louise cut through the emotion.

'Louise is the boss here,' Dad said.

'Why are you coming now?' Lorenzo asked.

'It's not my choice, believe me, but Clara wants to know who her father is. I have a very hazy memory of the night I met Marco, so I had to hire a private investigator to find him.'

I winced. She could have made it sound a little less clinical.

'Is Clara 'ere?' Marco asked.

'Absolutely not. I had to see if you were suitable first. I had to see if you were someone I could introduce her to. Clara is the most important thing in my life. She is a very special girl. She's unique and fragile and . . .'

There it was, the emotion buried inside my elder sister finally welled up. I loved that Clara had brought out such a tender side to Louise. Clara had knocked down her mother's thick walls and melted her heart.

Louise let out a sob and Sophie and I instantly reached out to put a hand on her shoulder.

'Clara is the most important person in our family. We're all mad about her. My wife was crazy about her. She loved that child more than anything,' Dad croaked, choking up too.

'*Mia figlia*,' Marco said again, shaking his head in disbelief.

Turning to him, I explained, 'Clara is a very sensitive child. She has autism spectrum disorder. She is very intelligent, like her mother, and sweet and lovely and talented and gifted and we all adore her. She is lucky to have an incredible mother. Because of Louise, Clara is living her best life.' I began to choke up then.

'We all feel very protective of Clara.' Sophie stepped in. 'We would never let anyone into her life who is not going to enhance it.'

'Enhance?' Marco asked.

'Make it better,' Sophie explained.

'She can talk?' Lorenzo asked. 'My cousin child is autism and he no talk.'

'Oh, yes, Clara can talk better than any of us,' Sophie said.

'She's full of facts and information,' Dad added proudly.

With trembling hands, Louise opened her laptop and pressed play. Clara's sweet face filled the screen. She was reading a poem she had written about living with ASD.

Marco and his two friends watched intently. Marco's chin wobbled, his eyes filled with tears, and as Clara read the last line, 'I know I'm different, but different can be good', he completely crumpled and began to sob.

I bent down to grab my handbag, rooted out a pack of tissues and handed one to him.

'*Mia preziosa figlia,*' he cried.

I nodded, yes, she was precious.

By now, the whole bar knew something big was happening and they had all been peering over, but when Marco began to sob loudly, they gathered around us.

Marco pointed to the screen and cried out, '*Mia figlia!*' a few more times.

Everyone oohed and aahed and stared at us and at Clara and shook their heads in amazement. Marco was patted on the back and there were a lot of loud Italian exclamations. This was not how I had pictured it going down.

Drinks appeared and toasts were made, and we just nodded along, smiling.

'*Sono padre!*' Marco sobbed over and over.

I watched Louise flinch every time he said it. After the fifth or sixth time, when the cheers were getting bigger, Louise stood up and shouted, 'STOP.'

The place hushed. 'Yes, Marco is a father. He is my daughter's biological father, but I will decide if and when he meets her. We have a lot more to discuss and it will not be done in front of a crowd. Marco, I want you to come to the hotel tomorrow morning to talk properly. I'm exhausted. It's been a very long day. Nothing has been decided. This is just an initial conversation. I need to sleep now. Goodnight.'

'I come in morning. *Grazie*, Louisa.' Marco was full of emotion.

'Come alone,' Dad said.

'My name is Louise and don't thank me yet.' I could see Louise was worried now that the news had been broken. She had to deal with the logistics of it all. She looked completely spent. She packed up her laptop and her emotions, and indicated that we were all leaving. We waved goodbye to the men and followed her. Once outside, we threw our arms around her.

'Louise, that was crazy and incredible,' Sophie said.

'Are you okay?' I asked.

'How are you feeling?' Sophie said, trying to take her hand.

Louise shrugged us off. 'Please, not now, I can't. It's been a lot. I need peace and quiet. I need to think. I can't take any more questions or drama. I'm drained. I'll talk to you in the morning.'

'Give her space, girls. It's been a very emotional evening.' Dad put his arm around Louise's shoulders. 'I am so proud of you for the way you handled that. Your mother would be too. Sleep on it. We'll talk to Marco tomorrow and figure out the next step. Come on, pet, I'll walk you back to your room. I'm exhausted myself after all that.'

'Did I do the right thing, Dad?' Louise asked.

'Yes, pet. It was all a bit haywire, but at the end of the day you have found Clara's dad and he seems like a decent man. Now we all need to get some sleep. With clear heads, we'll get a real sense of him tomorrow. You did well tonight. I'm very proud of you.'

'Us too,' I said.

'So proud,' Sophie agreed.

'You need to rest, pet. You look exhausted.' Dad and Louise disappeared inside the hotel.

'Well, I for one need a drink.' Sophie let out a long exhale.

'Me too. Let's go in and order a bottle of wine. I'm high on adrenaline after that.' My heart was pounding with excitement and nerves.

'That was the maddest and most amazing thing I have ever witnessed, and I've seen some mad things with Pippa.' Sophie shook her head.

'Do you think he's a good man?'

'Yes, I do. He seems very genuine, but . . . we need to see where he lives and if he is truly someone Louise can allow into Clara's life.'

'Agreed. You can tell a lot by someone's home and Louise needs to have a calm and very direct conversation with him about boundaries and access to Clara and all of that.'

'I know a lot about access to children and it is not, in any way, shape, manner or form, straightforward.' Sophie sighed. 'Louise needs to be very careful.'

'It's Louise,' I reminded her. 'She was emotional tonight, but tomorrow she'll have Marco wrapped up in so many legal documents that he won't know what hit him.'

'I hope it works out. I think Clara could really benefit from having a second parent, as long as he's not a nightmare like Pippa.'

I nodded. 'Now, let's get that wine.'

Sophie and I sat up all night in our bedroom talking, high on emotion, until the sun came up and we finally drifted off to sleep.

23. Louise

I slept badly. Seeing Marco in the flesh had floored me. It wasn't just that he had Clara's nose, he had her smile – her beautiful crooked smile that she didn't give away easily, but when she did, it was as if the sun was shining on you. Obviously I was glad Marco seemed like a good, steady man, but now I had to deal with the reality of introducing a stranger – albeit her biological father – into Clara's life. His English was poor, he'd have to work on that, and Clara and I would have to learn Italian.

I also had to be very careful about Marco's expectations. He needed to understand that I would be controlling access, and that if Clara did not warm to him, he would be out of her life again. Her happiness was the only thing that mattered. My head throbbed from lack of sleep and stress. I had worked so hard to give Clara the best life and to get her to the best place. I was terrified of Marco messing things up. I'd really have to assess his suitability today. I wished for the millionth time that Mum was still alive. She would give me the best advice and help calm my nerves about this whole palaver. It was nice having Dad there, but he had behaved very oddly in the bar, like some kind of Mafia boss. I don't know what got into him, but I needed him to calm down and let me do the talking today.

I gave up on sleeping and got up early to go for a run. As I ran up the narrow, cobbled lane away from the hotel, the sun rose from behind the distant Apennine mountains. The golden light spread across the surrounding hills, which were covered with olive trees and grape vines. It was utterly breathtaking. I stopped and took it all in. I breathed deeply and began to feel less anxious. I could do this. I could make it work. I had no choice now. I had done what Clara had begged me to do. I had taken the note as a sign from Mum and I had found Marco. I'd told him about his daughter and now I had to make him comply with my terms.

By the time I got back from my run, showered, dressed and headed down for breakfast, it was almost nine. Dad was sitting at the table looking like he hadn't slept much either, but there was no sign of my sisters. I drank the rich dark coffee, embracing the kick it gave me, and ate the warm, freshly baked bread slathered in butter.

'How are you feeling this morning, pet?' Dad asked.

'Shattered and apprehensive about meeting Marco. I've been texting back and forth with him this morning and we've agreed that I'll go over to his farm at ten to meet his mother, see the olive farm and have a private chat with him. He's desperate for me to meet his mother and show her the photos.'

Dad stirred sugar into his coffee. 'I reckon it's a good sign that he's close to her and wants her to be involved in the discovery of his daughter. It shows that he respects her. Sure, look at Gavin and your mother. They were very close.'

'I suppose so, but is it not a bit strange that he lives with her? He must be fifty-plus.'

'It's different with farms. In rural Ireland lots of different generations of families live together on farms. They all help run them.'

He had a point. This wasn't suburban Dublin: it was a small village in the hills.

'I'd forgotten how spectacular Italy is. I came here with your mum before you were born. We spent a few days in Rome and then we came to a village like this one, but not as far out, for two nights. Great memories. We always said we'd come back, but sure, life got in the way and it won't happen now.'

Dad and I were not touchy-feely, but I reached out and held his hand. 'I feel her close to me,' I admitted. 'I feel her here, cheering me on. Does that sound mad?'

'Not at all. I talk to her all the time.' He smiled sadly.

'I'm glad you're here, Dad.'

'Me too, pet, and from the little I saw of Marco, he seems like a decent enough fellow. We'll know more today when we see how he reacts to your terms.'

I rubbed my eyes.

'You look worn out. You need to get some rest. Could you take a few days off when you get back?'

I shook my head. 'No chance. I've a crazy few weeks coming up in work and I'm still trying to manage Zoë, the worst intern in the history of interns.' I turned a sachet of sugar between my fingers. 'I dunno, Dad, I'm beginning to wonder, what's it all about?'

'What do you mean?'

'I'm working long hours, trying to juggle single-parenting, putting money aside for Clara, because who knows what kind of job or career she'll have? But am I missing out on life? Should I be spending more quality time with her? I have no life outside work and Clara. I don't have time for anything else. Do I want to work in a firm where I'm beholden to the managing partner and have to babysit his wretched god-daughter? Is this what I want to do for the next fifteen years?'

Dad poured more coffee into my cup. 'When something big happens in your life it throws up all of these questions. Losing your mum and now finding Marco has turned your life upside-down. It's normal to question things. And you're also at a stage in your career where you've achieved great things. Now you have to think about the future and what you really want from life. Maybe you need a better work-life balance. Could you go to a four-day week?'

'I don't think so. I could work from home, but that's still working.'

'Don't make any rash decisions. Take time to let everything that's happened sink in. When I retired, I was lost. Work was such a huge part of my life. It took a while to adjust. I should have cut back slowly instead of working full-time and retiring overnight. I drove your poor mother mad at first because I didn't know what to be doing with myself all day. She found me jobs, got me into the golf and helped me navigate retirement. My advice to you is to take your time. Deal with the Marco situation first and then, when your head is clearer, think about what you really want for the future.'

'Thanks, Dad. It helps to talk about it. My head is scrambled at the moment.' I glanced at my watch. It was nine thirty and my sisters still hadn't come down. 'Speaking of Marco, we're going to be late if Sophie and Julie don't hurry up.'

Dad laughed. 'They were the same getting up for school. They never wanted to get out of bed. You were always up and dressed before they'd even opened their eyes.'

Dad and I went up to knock on their door. We had a lot to do and no time to waste.

Sophie answered the door in pink silk pyjamas with her matching sleep mask pushed up on her forehead.

'It's nine thirty, come on. Get up. Louise has a big day ahead.' Dad clapped his hands together.

'Sorry, we stayed up for ages chatting,' Sophie croaked.

Julie was lying in the bed with the duvet over her head.

'I just need a little more sleep.' She groaned.

'Julie! Your sister needs to get going, she has important matters to attend to,' Dad said sharply.

'Okay, keep your hair on.'

Julie scrambled out of bed. Her hair was all over the place and she was wearing an oversized T-shirt. 'How are you feeling?' she asked me.

'Tired and stressed, but I went for a run and had some coffee and a chat with Dad and I feel a little calmer now.'

'God, Louise, you're amazing. When I'm tired and stressed I stay in bed, eat junk food and feel worse,' Julie said.

'I can't drink coffee when I'm stressed. It makes me too jumpy,' Sophie said.

I could feel my overstretched patience wearing very thin. 'As much as I'd love to stand here and analyse what you do and don't do when you're stressed, I need you to get your arses downstairs ASAP. We're going to Marco's farm.'

'He's so lovely, Louise. You can just tell he's a good man,' Julie gushed.

'Such kind eyes, and his smile!' Sophie said.

I fiddled with my necklace. 'We'll see. It's baby steps for now.'

'I'm so happy for you.'

Oh, no, Julie was getting emotional.

'For the love of God, Julie, we haven't time for tears. Get dressed,' Dad said firmly. 'Less talking, more moving. Hurry up.' He left the room.

Julie threw on a crumpled top and jeans from the bottom of her suitcase. 'I need coffee and food,' she said.

'The kitchen is about to close.'

Julie rushed out the door.

Sophie asked if she had time to iron her dress. I stared at her.

'Okay, that's a no. I'll have the quickest shower ever and meet you downstairs in ten minutes.'

'Fine.'

'Can you order me a skinny cappuccino?'

'I'll order you a cappuccino. They don't do skinny milk here.'

'Then I'll have an Americano with hot milk on the side and a plain yogurt if they have it. If not, maybe just some fruit but only berries and maybe some muesli.'

I couldn't listen to Sophie's irritating breakfast order. Ignoring her I left the room as she said, 'Actually, an egg-white omelette would be good.'

I sat opposite Julie, having my third coffee of the morning.

'I'm very proud of you, Louise. Mum would be too. This was such a selfless act. You could have told Clara that Marco was dead. But you took the hard road and did the right thing for her. You're amazing.'

'Thanks. I just hope it's not a huge mistake.'

'Mum would love it here. She loved Italy and this village would be right up her street. "Authentic Italy," she'd say.' Julie laughed.

'That's what Dad said. Apparently they came to Italy years ago. It's mad, I never imagined I'd miss Mum as much as I do,' I admitted.

'That's because you got so close to her in the last few years.'

'True. I'm so glad I had Clara. She was the glue between me and Mum.'

'I think Clara brought us all closer. I loved working at the Clara Devlin Foundation with Dad and Gavin, and doing fundraisers, with Sophie and Mum pitching in. It was an amazing time.'

I smiled. 'It was, but we were right to let it be subsumed into Supporting Autism Ireland. All the same, it was hard to let it go.'

'I know, but you're right. It was the best thing to do. It

grew so fast we couldn't handle it on our own. I have really fond memories of that time. Sophie and Jack getting back together, Dad and Gavin getting along, you and Colin . . . Do you ever miss him?'

I put my coffee down. 'In the beginning I did, more than I'd care to admit, but after about six months the hole he left filled with work and Clara. I'm glad we're still friends, though.'

'What about Marco? Any sparks when you saw him last night?'

I rolled my eyes. 'None. He is so completely the opposite of my type.'

'To be fair, he's more attractive in the flesh and seems lovely.'

'We'll see how lovely he is when I show him the contracts.'

Dad and Sophie walked in, Sophie looking fresh and rosy.

'How the hell do you look so good?' Julie asked.

'Make-up.'

'Will you do mine, please?'

'We don't have time for that, Julie.'

'Did you order my breakfast?' Sophie asked.

'No, Sophie, it's not the Hilton. I ordered you coffee and there is bread if you want a quick slice.'

'I don't eat carbs,' she muttered, as she drank her coffee.

'You could do with a few bread rolls. You're too thin,' Dad grumbled.

'Do you think so?' Sophie was thrilled.

Ping ping ping. Julie's phone had been pinging non-stop since we left Dublin. It was doing my head in.

'Julie, turn off your bloody notifications before I throw your phone into my coffee. It's infuriating.'

'I need to keep on top of it. If I turn them off, I'll have hundreds to deal with when I get back to it.'

'It's a stupid, pointless WhatsApp group. Who cares?' I had no patience for the WhatsApp nonsense.

Julie bristled. 'It is actually important. Harry and I have to give out all the information the coaches give us about the games and all that.'

'To be fair, you do need to keep on top of these school WhatsApp groups,' Sophie said. 'They're incredibly annoying, but they keep you in the loop. Besides, Julie is the captains' mum. It's a big job.'

I snorted. 'Come on, it's a few messages about match times, not press officer to the White House. Julie, you said yourself a lot of it is people complaining or pontificating.'

'True, but I don't want to let the triplets down so I have to make sure everyone feels included and involved. I know what an outsider I felt at first in the school, so I want everyone, even the parents of boys who will never get to play, to feel part of the experience.'

'Fine, but the constant pinging of your phone is too much.'

'I agree with Louise. The notifications are relentless,' Sophie said.

'It's ridiculous,' Dad said. 'You're like a prisoner to that phone and Harry's worse. He's never off his.'

'I know, Dad, and it drives me nuts too, but it's only for a few more weeks.'

'Fine, but for the rest of today I need you to put it on silent. My nerves are frayed enough,' Dad said. 'And Louise does not need it distracting her.'

Julie pulled out her phone as it pinged again and put it on silent. 'Fine.'

'Can we please go?' I stood up. 'Dad, you're driving, I'll navigate.'

'What can I do?' Julie asked.

'Ideally, keep quiet,' I snapped. I was feeling more and

more anxious, and all this prattling was starting to grate on me.

Julie did not look happy. 'I'm giving you a pass because you're stressed, Louise, but I suggest that you smile, not snarl, at Marco's poor mother.'

Ignoring her, I headed out to the car.

Marco had texted me directions and thank God he had because we would never have found the farm otherwise. It was down the end of several winding and narrow old roads.

'It's certainly remote anyway,' Dad said, as we turned the final corner and were met with a large farmhouse. The stone was a pale grey and the shutters on every window were painted sky blue, which gave the house a warm and welcoming feel. Acres of olive groves surrounded it.

'It's so pretty,' Sophie said.

'Gorgeous,' Julie agreed.

'I have to be honest, it's much nicer than I imagined,' Dad said.

The front door was open, and before we had come to a halt, Marco was rushing out, followed by his mother, who was a tiny woman with a head of snow-white hair. '*Benvenuti!*' she cried, waving her arms.

'Aww, she's lovely,' Julie said.

'Julie!' I snapped.

'Jesus! Okay, fine, I'll say nothing.'

We climbed out of the car and were all swept up in big hugs. When she got to me – 'Louisa', as she called me – she clung on. It was awkward as her head was squashed against my boobs and I'm not a big hugger, especially not with strangers.

Thankfully, Marco peeled his mother off me and showed us into the house. Despite my earlier threats to silence Julie, I was so glad that she, Sophie and Dad were there to keep the conversation flowing and try to make this crazy situation seem normal.

'Anna.' Marco's mum pointed to her chest.

'Julie.'

'Sophie.'

'George.'

'Louise.'

'Our mother was called Anne,' Sophie said.

'My wife,' Dad explained.

Marco translated.

'Is she also coming to Italy?' Marco asked.

'No, she's dead,' I said.

'*Morta*,' Marco said to his mother.

'*Le mie condoglianze*,' Anna said, her eyes filling with tears.

'Thank you,' I said.

She looked at Dad and tilted her head to one side. '*Mi dispiace per la tua perdita.*'

'I think that means "I'm sorry for your loss,"' Sophie said.

Dad put his hand to his heart and said slowly and loudly, 'Thank. You. Very. Much.'

'She's Italian, not deaf,' Julie whispered.

Anna said something. Marco translated. 'My mother say she know how you feels. My father die ten years ago. Her heart was breaking.'

Dad tried to fight back tears while Anna patted his hand.

It was all too much. I could feel my own emotions welling up. I felt Julie's hand on my back.

'Breathe.'

I did as she said, and regained some control.

We sat down at their big kitchen table on wooden chairs covered with checked blue and white cushions. The house was bright, airy, clean and uncluttered. Clara would like that.

Marco made us coffee while Anna produced a freshly baked lemon ricotta cake from the oven.

When we were all sitting down, Anna, who had perched beside me, looked over at Marco and said something in Italian.

'My mother would like to see photo of Clara.'

I pulled up my briefcase and handed her the photos.

'*Dio mio*,' she exclaimed. She looked up at Marco. '*Tua zia*.'

He nodded. 'She say Clara look like my aunt.'

Anna wept as she looked through the photos. She kissed Clara's picture and stroked her head. I could feel pain shooting through my heart. Here was a grandmother seeing her grandchild for the first time. It reminded me of when Mum first held Clara. I felt a wave of emotion crash over me. I gripped the table to steady myself. I had to stay focused for the conversation ahead.

Around me everyone was crying. Julie and Sophie were wiping their eyes while Marco dabbed his and rubbed his mother's back. Even Dad was looking misty.

'*Mia nipoté*,' Anna sobbed. Looking up at me she said, '*Grazie, mia cara*.'

I nodded, unable to speak for the raw emotion on her face.

I drank my fourth cup of coffee and then, clearing my throat, said, 'Marco, we need to talk about logistics.'

'Logistics?' He looked confused.

'Plans, details,' Dad said. 'Louise has documents for you to look over.'

'*Ah, sì*.'

I opened my briefcase and handed him a folder.

'In there is a return ticket to Dublin dated for three weeks' time. I need that time to prepare Clara to meet you. I'll take photos now and videos to show her where you live and for her to see you and your mother. I will organize a FaceTime in one week when you can talk to Clara. You will need to improve your English. Clara and I will take Italian lessons. I have a tutor lined up. I have written a list of things Clara likes and dislikes. I have also explained that she is different and needs to be handled with care. The documents are in English but I also had them translated into Italian so there is no language barrier. You must understand Clara before you meet her. She is the most precious thing in my life. I will not have her upset. If she decides she doesn't want to meet you, then this is over. Clara is the one who will decide, not you or me. Is that clear?'

'I only see Clara if Clara want?'

'Yes. She has to want to meet you. She's very . . . she's . . .'

'I understand. Clara ees fragile.'

'Yes, she is fragile. But also incredible.'

'*Sì, sì*, incredible. Be calm, Louisa. I only do what Clara want. I want her to be happy. No stress.'

'I will need you to sign some documents.'

'Why?'

'Because she needs to protect her daughter and herself,' Dad said firmly.

'Louisa, no need for documents. I do what you say. I do what Clara want. I only want to make my daughter happy. I can see you are good mother, protective mother. I understand, but no need for documents.'

'I'm afraid it's non-negotiable. You have to sign, Marco. I'm giving you rights to visit and be in her life as long as Clara is happy. It's a very fair deal that protects Clara.'

'Okay, okay, I sign.'

Anna tugged Marco's sleeve and asked him something.

'Do you 'ave the video of Clara with you?'

'Yes, lots of videos. I've put a few on this USB stick for you, but I can show you some now on my phone.'

I brought up the file of videos I had chosen to show Marco and pressed play. Clara's face filled the screen. She was singing along to 'Fernando'.

Anna held her hands to her mouth and shook her head as she cried, '*Mia sorella Maria.*'

Marco explained. 'Clara is looking like my mother's sister, Maria.'

'Can we meet her?' Julie asked.

He shook his head. 'She die when she twenty-two, in a car accident.'

'Oh, that's desperate,' Dad said softly. 'I'm very sorry,' he said to Anna.

She smiled sadly at him, then touched the screen with her hand. 'Maria.'

She turned to me and there was so much pain mixed with joy in her eyes that it floored me. '*Grazie,*' she said, holding my hand.

'You're welcome,' I croaked, as tears welled in my eyes.

Anna stroked my cheek and patted my hand. I sobbed with relief, fear of the future, happiness that Clara had a lovely dad and grandmother, worry about how it would all work out, sadness that Mum was missing it, and also from pure emotional exhaustion.

My sisters and father gathered around me and we watched as Clara finished her song and her beautiful crooked smile lit up the screen.

24. Sophie

I lay on the couch sipping a glass of cold white wine and wriggling my sore toes. I knew I should give up wearing high heels every day to work, but I felt better when I had them on. I felt empowered and they elongated my legs. Still, my toes were throbbing so I'd have to wear trainers tomorrow.

Italy had been amazing but also exhausting. Julie and I had barely slept and poor Louise had come home completely shattered. She'd been keeping a low profile, getting Clara used to the idea of Marco and Anna, and keeping things as calm as possible. She really was amazing, a single parent who had a huge kick-ass job and a daughter who needed a lot of care. I could barely manage my own life and I had Jack to help with Jess and a job I could do in my sleep.

Jack came in and threw his phone onto the chair opposite me. He sat beside me on the couch and put his arms around me.

'What happened?'

'Can I not hug my wife for no reason?'

'Technically, I'm still your ex-wife. Go on, spill the beans.'

'I just feel so lucky that I have you in my life. You are kind, reliable, considerate and sane.'

'Bad call with Pippa?'

He sighed. 'Is there ever a good one? She's such a selfish bitch. She's not coming to Robert's school play. She's going on a last-minute trip to Paris. Obviously her married shag has snapped his fingers and she's letting Robert down – again.'

'Oh, poor Robert.' He was so excited about the play. He had

248

the lead role: he was the Gruffalo. He'd been practising his lines for ages. Pippa, who was supposed to get him a costume, had failed to do so, so I'd got one of my contacts in the fashion industry to make him one. He looked utterly adorable in it.

'I'm just so hurt for the little man. You want your parents to cheer you on. You remember them being there. I still remember my dad not coming to my rugby final because he had some medical conference. It hurt like hell. At least he had an excuse – he was actually working. Pippa is too busy being someone's mistress to witness her son's big moment.'

I stroked Jack's hair. 'Hey, I know it's awful, but at least Robert has a great dad. You make up for Pippa.'

'And a brilliant stepmother.' He kissed me. 'I really hope this Marco guy is a good man. I hope Louise has him tied up in an airtight custody agreement because it's not easy.'

Louise had made Marco sign lots of documents when we were in Pico. Julie thought it was a bit cold to do it the day after he'd discovered he was a dad, but I understood Louise's reasoning. I'd seen the reality of co-parenting first-hand. She was dead right.

'I think Marco is going to be a great addition to Clara's life. I always think you can tell a lot about a man by the way he treats his mother and he's so lovely to her.'

'Maybe he'll rekindle his love with Louise, like you and I did.' Jack chuckled.

'I somehow doubt it. I didn't see any spark there. Not even a teeny tiny hint of one, on either side.'

'And definitely no girlfriend hiding in the wings?'

Julie and I had wondered that too, but when Louise had asked Marco, in her direct way, if there was anyone in his life, he had said he got divorced five years ago and had been so badly burned that he never wanted to be with another woman. They had no children. Louise was delighted. She didn't want another woman or children complicating things. Marco's broken heart and lack of offspring was a win for her.

'Nope.'

'Do you think Clara will take to him?'

'I do. He's really calm and gentle. I think he'll be very careful with her and, to be fair, Louise has drilled him on what to do and what not to do. You know, though, when we were over there, I looked at Marco's life, simple, quiet and peaceful, and found myself thinking that maybe we should move to the country.'

'And do what exactly?'

'I dunno . . . grow vegetables and meditate, go for long walks and read more books.'

Jack cracked up. 'Sophie! You'd hate it. You're a city girl through and through. Imagine no shops, restaurants, cafés, cinemas, nail bars . . . You wouldn't last a week.'

I giggled. He had a point. I did like city living. But when I saw how calm Marco's life was, it had made me think.

'Okay, I agree, but think of how much less stress we'd have. No commuting, no wondering where Jess is because there's only one bar in town and nowhere else to go to get into trouble. Robert could walk to the local school and play football in the village square. No phones ringing all the time, no commitments, no family dramas, just us and nature.'

'You hate spiders, bugs, flies, mud, dust and most animals. You love your comforts. You like having places to go and people to see. You'd be bored rigid.'

I snuggled into his chest. 'You're right, I wouldn't last a week.'

'It would be nice to know where Jess was at all times, though. I worry about randy teenage boys. Is it still off with Sebastian?'

'As far as I know it is. Why? Has she said anything to you?'

'No.'

'Good. Even Julie, who tries to see the good in everyone, said he's awful and the triplets can't stand him either.'

'To be fair, the triplets together are a force. Maybe Sebastian finds them hard to deal with, and you can't tar the kid because you don't like his parents.'

'I know, but I just get a bad vibe from him.' If Jack knew that Sebastian had been in the house alone with Jess, he'd have freaked. I'd never told him because Jess had begged me not to and I didn't want to add to his worries. He had enough on his plate with his rotten ex.

'Well, she dodged a bullet by breaking up with him.'

'Definitely. She seemed upset at first but she's in better form now, thank God.'

I snuggled into Jack's chest again and was luxuriating in this rare one-on-one time with him before Jess came back from basketball training and Robert needed to be picked up from football, when my phone rang. It was Gavin.

'Ignore it.' Jack held me tighter.

I'd call him back later. I closed my eyes. The phone buzzed. Text message from Gavin: *CALL ME ASAP. URGENT!*

I sat bolt upright. 'Oh, no, it must be Dad. Something must have happened.'

My fingers shook as I called his number.

'Is it Dad?'

'What?'

'The emergency! Is it Dad? Is he okay?'

'I dunno, I presume so. He was fine yesterday.'

'What's wrong, then?'

'It's Lemon.'

'What?' For a second I forgot his baby was called Lemon and thought he was talking about the fruit.

'She's gone mental, Sophie. She won't sleep. She's screaming all the time. She's turned into a monster.'

251

'It's probably colic,' Jack, who was listening in, said. 'Robert had it. Tell him to walk her around in one of those baby-carrier things when she's bad.'

'Jack says she's probably just got colic. Have you tried carrying her around when she's grizzly?'

'Yeah, I have her in the papoose all the time.'

'Well, she looked like she was smothering in that thing. Get her a proper BabyBjörn carrier and she'll probably be much happier.'

'I have one. Shania's friend gave it to us as a present. I've tried her in that and in the car seat and in the electric swing and in the bouncy chair and in the bath and in the buggy but absolutely nothing works. She won't stop roaring.'

'Where's Shania?'

'She had to go to New York two days ago and suddenly Lemon's gone mental. I'm on my own here, Sophie. I think there's something wrong with her.'

I could hear Lemon wailing in the background. It sounded like colic to me.

'I tried calling Julie, but she's out at some stupid rugby thing, so I called you.'

'Gee, thanks. Nice to know I'm not your first choice.'

'Can you come over?' His voice was strained.

'I'll be there in ten.'

'Thanks. And could you pick up a few vital things on your way? I haven't been able to leave the house. I'll text you a list.'

'Bloody hell, Gavin. We all had kids we had to look after on our own. You're not incapacitated, just put her into the buggy and go to the shops. Who cares if she's roaring?'

'Can you save the lecture for later? I'm dying here. The only thing I've eaten all day is toast and I've barely slept in the last two nights.'

'Welcome to parenthood. Forget about sleep because when they're teenagers you don't sleep either – you're worried about where they are and what they're up to.'

'Yeah, okay, just hurry up.'

My phone pinged with Gavin's list of vital things:

Paracetamol
Bread
Bacon
HP Brown Sauce
Crisps – prawn cocktail flavour
3 Fulfil bars – the orange ones, the dark orange ones not the light ones
3 bottles of Vit-Hit – the green one

Jack laughed when he saw the list. 'He's like a teenager in a man's body. Thank God he met a successful woman.'

'Aren't you both lucky you met amazing women?'

'Yes, we are.' Jack pulled me close and kissed me. 'How about I drop you off at Gavin's, pick up the kids and collect you on the way back?' he offered.

I peeled myself off the couch, pulled on my trainers and headed out to 'save' my brother.

Gavin answered the door unshaven and, frankly, unclean.

'Thank God.' He pulled me in, along the apartment hallway and into the TV room, which looked like a bomb had exploded in it.

Jack followed. 'Mate, you need to sort this out.'

There were nappies, baby clothes, towels, muslin squares, bibs and bottles everywhere. In the middle of the room Lemon was swaying back and forth on a complicated-looking swing, red-faced and roaring.

'I just can't seem to find the time.'

'Sophie, you sort out some food for Gavin,' Jack said, 'and I'll try to calm Lemon down.'

Jack went over and took my niece out of the swing. He held her to his shoulder and made cooing sounds as he walked her around the room, making circles on her back with his hand in a gentle rhythm.

Gavin followed me into the kitchen, where I unpacked the groceries. 'Load the washing-machine with all these clothes and towels,' I ordered.

'I want you to help me stop her crying, not do laundry,' Gavin said.

'Just do it,' I barked.

'Fine. God, you're so bossy,' he grumbled, as he scooped up a mound of washing.

I was tidying up the dirty dishes in the kitchen when Jack came in with a still-crying Lemon. He took her into the small laundry area where Gavin was loading the machine. Jack placed Lemon in the buggy and put her in front of it as Gavin popped in some powder and turned it on.

'This is a trick that worked with Robert,' Jack said, to a bemused Gavin.

Within ten seconds Lemon stopped crying, mesmerized by the hum of the machine and the spin of the clothes.

'Oh, my God,' Gavin whispered. 'It's a miracle.'

'She should fall asleep soon,' Jack whispered back. 'I've got to go. Good luck, mate, and call me if you need any tips. Robert had colic. It's not easy.'

I fell in love with my ex-husband a little bit more.

'You're a legend.' Gavin hugged Jack.

Jack pulled out of the hug. 'Oooh, you need a very long hot shower,' he said.

'I know I stink.'

Jack left and I told Gavin to go and have a shower while I

put the kettle on and made him some food. He didn't need to be told twice. He raced out of the room.

Twenty minutes later we sat opposite each other in their small kitchen. Lemon had fallen asleep to the hum of the washing-machine, just as Jack had predicted.

'I never thought I'd love silence so much.' Gavin ate his bacon sandwich hungrily.

'It's just a phase. She'll grow out of it.'

'That's what the paediatrician said, but it's hard going. I'm knackered. How the hell did Julie do this with three at the same time?'

I sipped my tea. 'I have no idea. She's a saint.'

'I wanted two kids. Now I think I'll stick with one.'

'Give it a few months. She'll start sleeping and interacting more and you'll forget this hard part.'

'I hope so. I want to be the best dad. I thought I'd be brilliant at it. I'm good with Clara and the boys and Jess, but . . . I dunno, babies are hard.'

'They can be, but it's only temporary. You just have to keep telling yourself that.'

Gavin looked around at the now tidy kitchen. 'I'm supposed to be the house-husband. Shania is working her arse off and being super-successful, so I'm the one who runs the house. I'm fine with it. I know Dad thinks it's emasculating, but I don't care. I live in the now, not the olden days. Shania and I have our thing and it works. But I'm failing. When Shania comes home the place is a tip and Lemon is wailing and I want to throw Lemon at her and head out. She's wrecked from her day's work and doesn't want a screaming kid handed to her and a messy kitchen to clean up.'

I smiled. That was exactly how so many women had felt for so long. I remembered Jack coming home from work and expecting the house to be calm and warm and peaceful, his dinner on the table and Jess to be either asleep or at least freshly bathed and ready for bed. When she woke up at night, it was just expected that I'd get up, Jack had work . . . That was the unspoken deal. Then he had a baptism of fire when he met Pippa and they had Robert. She had done almost nothing, so Jack had had to step up and do almost everything.

'Look, all you can do is your best. Every new parent struggles in the beginning.'

'You made it look easy.'

'In fairness, I had help and . . .' I paused. I had never admitted this to my family, only Jack, and I'd told him years afterwards, but it might help Gavin to know. 'I did struggle. I actually had post-natal depression. I ended up on anti-depressants for a year.'

'What?' He was shocked. 'I had no idea. You always seemed so together.'

I shrugged. 'I'm good at faking it.'

'Wow. That must have been tough. Can men get post-natal depression?'

I grinned. 'I don't know. But I don't think you have it. You're just overwhelmed. This is all completely normal. Newborn babies are a shock to the system and turn your life upside-down. And when you're on your own all day with no help or partner to hand the baby over to, even for half an hour, it's really, really hard.'

'Yeah. I can't wait for Shania to come back. The days are *loooooong*. I never knew how much I need my sleep.'

'Get used to surviving on a few hours.'

'I wish Mum was here. She'd help me.'

'Yeah, she'd probably have moved in and helped you full-time.'

'God, that would have been brilliant.'

'Are Shania's parents involved?'

'They have three other grandkids so they're spread thin. Besides, I don't want them to know I'm struggling. Their daughter is the one paying the bills, so I can't be failing at my job. I really miss Mum at the moment. I keep going to call her and then . . . you know . . .'

I reached over and held his hand. 'I know. It's hard.'

'I called Dad yesterday just to come and take Lemon out for a walk, but he was busy playing golf or something with Dolores. I haven't seen him in over a week.'

'To be fair to him, Dad never babysat alone. He's nervous around babies – he's never changed a nappy. He only ever babysat with Mum. And Julie will tell you they didn't help her much at all because Mum and Dad found the triplets so challenging.'

'I know but, like, he said he wanted to be more helpful yet he's all caught up with Dolores.'

'He's struggling, Gavin. He opened up in Italy. He's finding it really hard to figure out life without Mum. I know Dolores is a royal pain in the arse, but at least she's good to him and she gets him out of the house. Do you know what? We should all go out together and catch up. I think I'll organize a coffee and invite Dolores too.'

'What?'

'If she's being nice to Dad, we need to be nice to her.'

Gavin wiped HP sauce from his chin with a square of kitchen roll. 'You can fill me in properly on the details of the Italian trip you all went on without me.'

'Get over it. You wouldn't have been able to come anyway. You have Lemon to look after.'

'I know that, but it would have been nice to be asked. Like, the whole family went except me.'

Sometimes we forgot that Gavin felt a bit left out. When

Mum was alive, she'd always fuss over him and make sure he felt included, but now that she was gone, we needed to be more sensitive.

I stood up. 'Right, let's get this place cleaned up, so Shania can come home to a nice, tidy house tomorrow.'

Gavin threw his arms around me. 'Thanks, sis. Honestly, I was about to crack up. And thanks to Jack for his awesome tip.'

I kissed his cheek. 'Hey, it's okay. All new parents feel like this. Call us anytime.'

We cleaned up and later, as I closed the front door behind me, I breathed a sigh of relief. I'd forgotten how difficult the early days could be. As tricky as Jess's moods were, at least she wasn't a screaming baby.

25. Julie

Marion sat opposite me in her fleecy pyjamas, drinking coffee with a large splash of brandy in it. Leaning her chin on her hand, she sighed. 'I'm lonely, Julie. I'm fed up of being on my own. That prick is away in Dubai with nice kind Sally and I'm here raising the kids on a shoestring and going to bed alone every night, having spent all day earning money on my sex line encouraging lonely farmers to jerk off. And when I go online to date, all I meet are dickheads. Are there no nice single, separated or divorced dads in that posh school?'

There were a few, but I didn't think they'd be Marion's type or, let's be honest, vice versa.

'Maybe you need to change your online dating profile. Let's jazz it up a bit. We'll go out, get your hair and make-up done, take a new photo, and FaceTime Christelle and Kelly to help with the wording.'

Marion put down her cup. 'They don't want me bothering them on their big trip. Besides, that's the problem right there. People getting all dressed up and made-up, and pretending they look better than they do and that they're into opera when they actually like Dolly Parton. Saying they love to travel when the furthest they've been is bloody Blackpool. Saying they like going to cultural events when that means watching football in the local pub over a rake of pints. Saying they're forty-five when they're on a zimmer frame, and that they're six feet tall when they're fucking Oompa Loompas. I'm just so over it. In fact, you know what? I'm going to put up the only honest profile online.'

Before I could stop her, she had taken a selfie – and, in truth, it was not a good look. She looked like she'd just rolled out of bed, which she had. She had no make-up on and hadn't even brushed her hair. She began to type furiously. I peered over her shoulder.

Honest profile – I'm fifty-one. I have a shit load of baggage: I'm divorced, with four kids. I'm fed-up spending every night sleeping alone. I'm lonely as hell. I want a companion. I want occasional, undemanding sex. I want a laugh, a few beers, and someone to hold my hand when it all gets too much. I fucking hate opera and posh dinners. I like pubs, cheesy eighties pop music and reading romance novels. I like mindless TV. I hate subtitled films or TV shows – if I want to read, I'll get a book. This is what I actually look like, no filter, no make-up, no bull- shit. I am five foot four and about a stone overweight. I have bags under my eyes and my boobs sag a bit, but I'm funny and I know how to have a good time. If you're a short, fat, ugly bloke, be honest about it. If you make me laugh, I'll give you a chance anyway. Life's too hard to spend it on your own. I've had lots of shit dates, one when the guy legged it and left me paying the dinner bill. If you want to meet me, be honest and don't be a fucking wanker. PS No dick pics. If I want to see your penis, I'll let you know.

Wow, I didn't know whether to laugh or cry. It was so raw and honest.

'I'm sorry you're lonely. I wish I could help more.'

Marion put down her phone. 'Julie, you house me every month. You listen to me moaning and you're always boosting my ego and telling me I'm great. You are a brilliant friend. No one can fix loneliness, except maybe your man, that actor fella, the big strong one, The Rock. He'd definitely help.'

Before I could respond, Marion's phone began to ping and ping and ping. It was worse than my WhatsApp group.

She picked it up and began to laugh. 'Well, well, well. It seems I've hit a nerve. I'm being inundated.'

'Let me see.'

She turned her phone around and we checked out the replies. To be fair, there were a lot of frogs, but a few decent-looking men too.

Marion flicked through them. We finally agreed on one for a coffee date. He was medium height and looked a bit nerdy, but his reply was so enthusiastic and effusive that I thought she should give him a try. She replied to him and the coffee date was set up.

Marion peered at her watch. 'That took twenty minutes. From now on I'm only going to be completely honest. I don't have to worry what they'll think of me because the photo shows me at my worst. And they know I curse and don't want to talk bullshit.'

I clapped. 'That is the most impressive online dating activity I've ever seen. I'd say you could be up for an award.'

Ping ping ping.

'Jesus, what have I started?' Marion giggled. 'Who knew men wanted honesty? They're usually a bunch of lying pricks.'

We cracked up laughing.

'Well, that's lovely. Am I included in that?' Harry said, as he walked into the kitchen.

Marion patted his cheek. 'No, you're one of the rare good guys.'

Harry began to faff about with his ridiculously over-the-top coffee machine. It was his Christmas present to himself last year. It was like something you'd see in a very high-end coffee shop. He still didn't know how to use all the accessories and kept scalding himself.

'Glad to hear it. Would you like coffee to go with your brandy?'

Marion grinned. 'Yes, I would. I'm celebrating, Harry. I'm going on a date. With a square of a fella who seems genuine. Julie chose him over the small fella I thought was funnier. She said I need to go for kind over funny.'

'Probably good advice.' Harry swished the milk under the milk-frother thing. It made violent spitting sounds and I saw him wince as boiling milk drops landed on his hand.

'Well, I went for kind and it worked out well.' I smiled at my husband.

'Am I not funny too?'

'Sometimes you can be,' I said.

'To be fair, Harry, you're about as funny as a fucking Mormon, but you are one of the kindest people I know.'

'I don't know whether to be insulted or flattered.' Harry smiled as he handed her a coffee.

Marion showed Harry a photo of her date.

'He looks like a decent bloke. Might I suggest you try not to use every curse word known to man in the first five minutes?'

Marion sighed. 'The whole point of this exercise is that I'm going to be completely myself, no tricks, no fakery, no lies . . . If he likes me, great, if he doesn't, he can fuck right on down the road.'

Harry poured hot milk into his cup. 'I'd consider opening your date with a different line.'

Marion laughed.

'See, I can be funny too.' Harry grinned.

My phone rang. It was Louise. 'I'm on my way. I'll pick you up in ten minutes. Are you nearly ready?'

'Yes,' I lied, still in my pyjamas.

'Right. Be outside in ten.'

I hung up and put down my cup.

'I wish Sophie hadn't organized this.' I groaned.

'It's important that you all support your dad, Julie,' Harry said gently.

'I know. I get that Dolores is in his life, but I don't necessarily want to spend much time with her. It's too early. It feels like we're all saying, "Welcome to the family."'

'Fuck it, Julie, you don't want him lonely, believe me. It sucks. Let him throw the leg over Dolores. What difference does it make? It actually takes pressure off all of you. If she is cooking for him and riding him and playing golf with him and massaging his crusty toes, then he's happy. You don't want him at home alone crying in the dark, do you?'

No, I didn't. After our chat in Italy, I had slowly come around to the fact that Dad was seeing Dolores and she was helping him through the long days. He said they were only friends, but I knew Dolores wanted more. I didn't mind Dad going out with her, but I didn't want her to push him into anything serious. Dad was a lonely widower, and vulnerable to being controlled by determined women like Dolores. Sophie said we should all meet up because he was spending more time with Dolores now and we would lose him if we didn't include her in our lives too. She was right, but it didn't mean I had to like it.

Harry looked at the kitchen clock. 'Julie, go and get ready. You know how irritated Louise gets when you keep her waiting.'

I rushed upstairs. Harry was right: Louise did not react well to my tardiness. Also, she was particularly wound up at the moment with Marco coming over next week to meet Clara. Her nerves were extra frayed.

Sophie and Gavin were in the café when we arrived. Sophie had booked a round table.

'I can only stay an hour. I have to go into work.' Louise sat down and peeled off her coat. 'Zoë sent out the wrong information to a client and I have to clear up her mess. I swear to God, I think she may drive me to murder.'

'Hello to you too,' Gavin said.

'An hour will be plenty,' Sophie assured her.

'Hi, Gavin, how's Lemon?' I asked.

'A little bit better. With her mum right now. Jack's washing-machine trick is helping, although our electricity bills are going to be huge.'

'Whatever gets you through,' Sophie said. 'It's worth it.'

Gavin handed Sophie a bag. 'Jess texted for more supplies of Shania's tan,' he said.

'Thanks, she loves it. But let me pay you.'

'No, don't worry, she's paying us in publicity – she's promised to tell all her mates to buy it and make TikTok videos of it.'

'How are things with Marco?' I asked Louise.

'Good, actually. He's very gentle and careful with Clara. She's warmed to him really quickly. They FaceTime every day now, just for a few minutes, but she seems to connect with him. Still, seeing him face-to-face will be a whole other level for her.'

'That's really positive,' Sophie said. 'The fact that he's so keen to be involved and so respectful of you and gentle with Clara is huge. Pippa is disinterested in Robert and so difficult to handle. It makes co-parenting so much more difficult.'

'So is he, like, a really outdoorsy country bloke?' Gavin asked.

'He owns an olive farm so, yes, obviously he is.'

'Jeez, Louise, no need to be so snappy. I'm just asking, seeing as I wasn't involved in the trip.'

'He is lovely and his mother is a sweetheart. The farm-house is gorgeous and the setting is like something from a movie,' I said.

'Nice. Maybe I can come with Lemon next time, when I've got a better handle on the whole baby thing, although I am getting much better at settling her and she is sleeping for much longer at night. But I'm not gonna lie, it's harder than I thought.'

'Welcome to parenthood,' I said.

'We might not go back to Italy. Clara hates travelling so I'm not sure we'll be going to visit. Marco will have to fly to Dublin to see Clara. For the moment anyway. Actually, he told me on one of our calls that his ex-wife had a late miscarriage and it's one of the reasons they broke up. She refused to try again because she was so traumatized and he was desperate to have a child.'

'Oh, my God, poor Marco and his ex,' I gasped. 'That's awful, but it must make Clara all the more special. She must be like a miracle for him.'

'Yes, he's used the word *miracolo* a few times all right,' Louise said drily.

'Wow, kids . . . Whether you want them, don't want them, have them, don't have them, raise them alone, with an ex or with a partner, it's never straightforward,' Sophie said, shaking her head.

Louise bit her lower lip. 'It sure isn't.'

'Well, I'll give you my honest opinion of Marco when I meet him next week. I'll pin him down and put the hard questions to him, don't you worry,' Gavin said.

Louise snorted. 'What is it with men? Dad acted like some kind of Mafia boss when we were in Italy and now you're puffing out your chest and declaring you're going to put Marco through his paces. Thanks for the support, Tarzan, but, believe me, I've asked Marco all of the hard questions.'

'He seems very patient and chilled out, which is good,' I said.

'He is the yin to Louise's yang,' Sophie added.

'It was his yin yang that got her into trouble,' I said, giggling.

We all cracked up and even Louise laughed. The respite was brief, though, because Louise looked at her watch. 'Where the hell is Dad? We're here for him – he could at least be on time.'

'Why don't we order?' I suggested. Maybe food would help to calm my elder sister.

Louise called the waitress over. She had a way of commanding people so they jumped to attention. We ordered our food just as Dad and Dolores arrived in.

'Well, she certainly got dressed up for us,' I muttered.

'It's a lot.' Sophie's eyes widened as she took in the sight.

Dolores was dressed from head to toe in a bright blue trouser suit *à la* Hillary Clinton. She had a big, puffy, fussy pink shirt underneath. It was an onslaught of colour.

'She looks like a Liquorice Allsort,' Louise grumbled. 'And what the hell is Dad wearing?'

Dad was wearing a bright green jumper with a big golf ball in the middle of it. He looked ridiculous. Mum had always made sure he dressed smartly in navy and dove grey. He looked like he was wearing a novelty jumper.

Sophie stood up and greeted them warmly. 'Hi, Dad, hello, Dolores.'

'Well, hell*oooooo*, Sophie. How kind of you to invite us out to brunch. We were delighted, weren't we, Georgie?'

Georgie? Did she just say Georgie? I felt my stomach flip.

'Nice jumper, Dad. Where did you get it? The joke shop?' Gavin asked.

Dad looked uncomfortable. 'No, ah, Dolores here bought it for me.'

'I think bright colours suit him. He was always in very

sombre colours. Wearing bright colours lifts your mood, I always think.'

'You must be ecstatically happy then,' Louise said, as I stifled a giggle.

'So, Georgie, how have you been? We haven't seen you since we got back from Italy two weeks ago,' I said pointedly.

Dad shuffled about in his chair. 'Oh, busy playing golf and just getting on with things.'

'What things?' Louise asked. 'Clara was asking for you. I want you to come for dinner tomorrow. It's a big week for her, and she needs to see her granddad.'

'Of course I'll be there.' Even Dad was scared of Louise.

'So what has kept you so busy?' I asked.

'Well, ah —'

Dolores put a hand on his arm. 'We have a hectic social life. Golf and bridge and dinners and we're in a theatre club and a cinema club. It's non-stop.'

'Wow, that's a lot. No wonder you can never visit or even take Lemon for a walk,' Gavin said, just as pointedly.

'Keeping busy is important when you get to a certain age,' Dolores said. 'It stops you being lonely.'

'So is checking in with your family and spending time with your grandchildren,' Gavin said. 'Lemon's doing well, in case you're interested.'

Dad stiffened. 'Didn't I text you yesterday to ask after her?'

'Yeah, you did, a one-line text. I thought you might be interested in actually seeing her.'

'I'll call in tomorrow so.'

'Oh, no, you can't tomorrow, Georgie. We have Enda's eightieth-birthday lunch.'

'And then Dad is coming to me for dinner,' Louise said firmly.

'I hope you'll still be at the triplets' quarter-final game on Wednesday, Dad?' I asked.

'I wouldn't miss it. It'll be a great day.'

'Good! It's a big day for them.' I smiled at him.

'I'll be there too, Julie,' Dolores said. 'I love the rugby. My son played, you know. He lives in Canada now, but he was good in his day.'

Bloody hell. I didn't want Dolores at the match. I wanted Dad there alone, even if he was a bit too critical for my liking. I wanted him beside me. Now she'd be there annoying everyone.

'Please don't feel you have to. Dad can be a bit intense when he's watching the boys. You might be better off staying at home,' I urged Dolores.

'Not at all, Sophie –'

'It's Julie.'

'Sorry, Julie. I'm very keen to see your boys. I hear all about them and all the grandchildren. I'm looking forward to getting to know them all. Georgie is a very proud granddad.'

Our food arrived and the waitress asked Dad and Dolores what they would like. Dad ordered a full Irish breakfast.

'Now, Georgie, we've discussed this. You have to watch your cholesterol. He'll just have brown toast with scrambled eggs, please, and the same for me.'

'Wow, Georgie, it looks like things have changed a lot,' I said.

'Don't you worry. I'm looking after his health.'

'And his whole life,' Gavin noted.

Louise pointed her fork at Dad. 'Do not forget, Clara's father is coming here next week and you are all meeting him on Saturday.' Glaring at Dolores, she said sharply, 'Just the immediate family. No one else. I want everyone at my apartment at five p.m. sharp on Saturday. Do not be late and no excuses are good enough. I don't care whose birthday it is or what golf tournament is on. You are to be there, Dad. This is important to me.'

Dolores tutted. 'I'm afraid that's going to be difficult, Louise. We're away next Saturday in Belfast.'

'Well, now, Dolores, I'll head back on Saturday morning, I need to be there for Louise,' Dad said. 'I wouldn't miss this for the world.'

'But we've dinner booked, Georgie.'

Louise cleared her throat.

Uh-oh. Dolores had no idea who she was up against.

'Does she have a death wish?' Gavin muttered.

Sophie dabbed her mouth with her napkin and whispered, 'Here we go.'

Louise leaned across the table, her nose almost in Dolores's face. 'Did I not make myself clear? My father will be in my apartment at five p.m. next Saturday to meet my daughter's biological father. This is a huge deal in her young life. I don't give a flying fuck about your dinner plans. And, by the way, his name is George, not that ridiculously affected name you're spouting.'

Dolores's face was bright red. 'Well I never,' she spluttered. 'I thought I was invited here for a friendly brunch. Not to be attacked.'

'No one attacked you, Dolores. I'm simply making it clear that my father has an important family commitment next Saturday.'

'Georgie?' Dolores looked to Dad for help.

'It's George,' I said.

'Well, *George*, have you nothing to say?' Dolores scowled at him.

Dad looked desperately uncomfortable as he tried to find the right words. 'I know Louise came across strong there, but she's a bit wound up about Marco coming over. Clara meeting her dad for the first time is a very big deal. Clara is a special girl and we all have to support her.'

'Strong? She was extremely rude.' Dolores was not taking it.

I decided to step in before the whole thing blew up. After all, we were supposed to be putting out the hand of friendship to Dolores so we could see more of Dad. 'Dolores, this is an emotional time for all of us, especially Louise and Clara. We all dote on Clara. It is very important to all of us that Dad is there. We also all miss Mum very much, so please understand that this new relationship is difficult for us.'

'Well said, Julie.' Sophie backed me up. 'We're very happy that Dad has a companion, but it'll take a while for us to get used to the idea of another woman in his life. Please be patient.'

Dolores fiddled with the large bow on her shirt. 'I understand that, but I will not tolerate people being rude to me.'

'Louise has a direct manner,' Dad said. 'You need to get used to her.'

'I say it as I see it,' Louise said.

'You could work on your delivery,' Dad said, raising his eyebrows at her.

Thankfully, their food arrived, causing a welcome distraction from the tension. We ate, while Sophie and I kept the conversation light, veering away from any potential minefields. By the time the hour was up we were at least being civil to each other and Dolores was calling Dad 'George', much to our relief.

26. Louise

I sat on the floor beside Clara's bed and waited. She sobbed her heart out, her breathing ragged as she tapped her fingers together over and over again.

I knew saying anything or trying to touch her would only make it worse. I was an expert on meltdowns. The room had to be quiet, the lighting low, and I had to stay still and silent until she'd worn herself out.

I wondered for the millionth time if introducing her to Marco was the right thing to do. When I'd first told her, she'd seemed happy. She'd been fine until now. They'd had a good few short conversations on FaceTime – I'd kept them to five minutes. They'd also texted a bit and Clara seemed to be connecting well with him, but I knew it was too good to be true. It was a big deal and a breakdown had to come. Marco was arriving tomorrow and, suddenly, the reality of it all was overwhelming her.

After about fifteen minutes her sobs began to subside. She hiccuped and her fingers stopped tapping. I stood up and looked down at her red, swollen eyes.

'Will I get you some water?' I asked gently.

She nodded.

I came back with a glass and some Calpol. 'Do you have a bad headache?'

'Really bad, Mummy.'

'Okay, sweetheart, have a spoonful of this. It'll help.'

Clara took the medicine and lay down again, rubbing the corner of her blanket between her fingers. She'd need a long sleep to recuperate from the meltdown. They always left her exhausted, physically and mentally.

'You know that you don't have to meet Marco tomorrow. We can put it off for a while if you want or for ever. You only do what you want to do. Okay?'

She nodded. 'I do want to see him. I just want him to like me. What if he thinks I'm weird or a freak, like the kids in school do?'

I tried not to cry. How dare those little shits make my beautiful angel feel insecure?

'Marco will fall in love with you the way we all have. He already thinks you're wonderful after your chats on FaceTime. I've told him all about you and how amazing you are, and Julie, Sophie and Granddad told him how fantastic you are too.'

My daughter's pale face gazed up at me. 'Do you really think he'll like me?'

'I one hundred million per cent know he will.'

Clara frowned. 'It's one hundred per cent, Mummy, not one hundred million per cent.'

I smiled down at her. 'Yes, you clever girl, it is.'

'I think it's good that we've learned some Italian too.'

'It is, and Marco's English has improved a lot. He's making a huge effort for you.'

'I'm scared he'll meet me and not want to be my daddy.'

I took a risk and held her hand. She didn't pull away.

'Clara, Marco is over the moon to know he has you as a daughter. He will adore you because you are the most incredible girl in the world.'

She began to fidget. I needed to keep her calm and for her to sleep. Knowing exactly what was going to happen always helped calm her down.

'For now, you need to have a big sleep. Tomorrow I'll wake you up at nine. We'll have breakfast. Then we'll go for a short walk to the bakery and buy some scones and be back home by ten thirty. We'll set the table and fill the kettle and switch on the coffee machine. Marco will arrive at eleven and we'll have tea and coffee and scones in the kitchen and then, if you want, you can show him your bedroom and we can have a chat or watch a movie, or you can read your bird book to him, or play music . . . whatever you feel like doing. Okay?'

She nodded. 'Does he like plain scones or fruit ones or the ones with berries in them?'

'Plain,' I lied. I had no idea, but Clara needed firm answers.

'Like me. Then we'll get two plain scones and a berry one for you.'

'Yes, pet.'

'And we can use the white plates and the blue napkins because they're my favourite. And I want Marco to have the orange mug that says "Smile", and I'll have the blue mug that says "Best Daughter" and you'll have the yellow mug that says "World's Best Mum".'

I smiled. 'Yes, darling, that's a good idea.'

Clara's hands relaxed and her eyelids began to droop. She was ready for sleep.

'You go to sleep now. Will I turn the lights down lower or do you want them as they are?'

'Lower, please.'

I leaned over and kissed her forehead. 'I love you, Clara, and I don't want you to worry about anything. We'll only ever do what you want to do. Sleep well, my love.'

She rolled over and closed her eyes. As I gently pulled the door three-quarters closed, the way she liked it, I heard her whisper, 'I love you, Mummy, and I hope I love Marco too.'

Clara stared out of the window as I watched the clock. I'd told Marco he had to be on time. Not one minute late.

At exactly eleven o'clock I heard Clara shout, 'He's here.'

'Are you ready?'

She nodded.

'Okay then. Let's open the door.'

My heart was thumping and I felt as if I might pass out. This was such a huge moment in Clara's life. Please, God, may it go well.

Clara followed me out to the front door, holding Luna to her chest as a shield. As I opened the door, Clara moved behind me.

Marco stood at the door, as I had told him to, not rushing in, not making a fuss and not going directly to Clara.

'Hello, Louisa,' he said calmly, although the flowers in his hands were shaking. Then, without looking at Clara directly, as instructed, he said, 'I am Marco. I am so, so happy to meet you, Clara, and also leetle Luna.'

I took the flowers from his hands and stood back, so he could see his daughter properly. Clara stared down at Luna and petted her.

Silence. Marco looked to me for direction. I indicated that he stay still.

Then, Clara quietly said, '*Buongiorno*, Marco, and Luna says hello too.'

Marco's voice dripped with emotion: '*Buongiorno, bellissima* Clara and *bellissima* Luna.'

Clara turned and said over her shoulder, 'Come into the kitchen. We have scones.'

Marco looked at me. 'Is okay?'

'Yes, you're doing well. Keep really calm and don't reach out. Let her come to you.'

'I want to hold her so much.' His eyes filled with tears.

'I know, but you mustn't. Take a deep breath. You have to be calm.'

He exhaled. 'I understand.'

We followed Clara into the kitchen. She put Luna down and busied herself placing scones on our plates and telling Marco where to sit, which mug to use.

Marco petted Luna and sat down.

'Do you like cats?' Clara asked.

'I love cats. I have four in my farm.'

'On my farm,' Clara corrected him. 'What are their names?'

'Rivera, Rossi, Zoff and Baggio. All Italian football players.'

'Are the cats all boys?'

'No, two boys and two girls.'

'Then why did you give the girl cats boys' names?'

'The names are not the first name. The names are the second name. Like I am Marco Romano. You are Clara Devlin. I call my cat Devlin if a boy or a girl. No?'

'Oh,' Clara said, finally looking at Marco directly. 'I see. They're surnames.'

'Yes, surname.' Marco smiled. 'My English is not so good.'

'*Tuo inglese è buono,*' Clara encouraged him.

'*Grazie.*' Marco beamed. 'You are very clever girl already speaking Italian. You are intelligent like your mother.'

'Yes, Mummy is very clever. Are you clever? Did you get top marks in school?'

Marco laughed. 'Not clever in school. Marco bad in school but good with the nature. I growing beautiful olives.'

'I hate olives,' Clara told him.

Marco shrugged. 'You have not tasted Marco's olives. I think you will like.'

Clara sighed. 'No, I won't. I hate the taste. It makes me want to vomit.'

Thankfully, I had warned Marco about Clara's lack of filter. He was unfazed.

'Do you like dogs?' he asked.

'Only small ones. Only quiet ones. I hate dogs that jump on you or bark loudly.'

There was a pause in conversation. I tried to think of something neutral to say. I didn't get the chance.

'Do you want to be my daddy?' Clara blurted out.

My hand flew up to my mouth.

Marco's eyes welled up. 'I want to be your daddy *verrrrrry* much.'

Clara fiddled with her napkin. 'I'm not like other kids. I'm different.'

'I like different.'

'Some people think I'm weird.'

'What is weird?'

'It's, like, strange.'

'I like strange. Normal is boring. Strange is good. Marco is also strange. Peoples think I am strange because I live with my mother. I love my mother and I love my olives so I am happy. I do what makes me happy.'

'I don't think it's strange that you live with your mother. I live with my mummy and I want to live with her for ever.'

Marco smiled. 'See? We the same.'

'Well, we have one thing in common.' Clara was going to make Marco work for her love and I was proud of her.

I was watching her carefully and she was calm. Marco was handling this first meeting really well. He had kept his emotions in check and allowed Clara to lead the conversation.

'We have the same nose. I can really see it now you're here in front of me. Granny always used to say I had a beautiful nose,' Clara said.

'Your granny was right. It is beautiful nose. Marco has no hair so it's good that Romano nose is beautiful.' He grinned.

'I have Mummy's eyes.'

'Yes, beautiful blue eyes. You are *bella, bella.*' Marco blew her a kiss. 'You will have every Italian boy wanting marry you.'

Clara looked horrified. 'I'm never marrying anyone. I'm staying with Mummy and Luna.'

Marco looked panic-stricken at having said the wrong thing. He needed a bit of help. 'Marco is only trying to say how beautiful you are. You don't have to marry anyone, pet. That's your choice.'

'Marco not marry any more and Louisa not marry anyone so Clara not marry anyone. We all not married and happy. Okay?' He was trying desperately to smooth things over.

Clara's eyes widened. 'I'm glad you're not married. I don't want a stepmother or a stepfather.'

'Just Mummy and also maybe Daddy, yes?'

Clara nodded slowly, and then she stood up. I thought she might leave and take some quiet time out for herself, but then she said, 'Marco, would you like to see my bedroom?'

I had told Marco that if Clara allowed him into her bedroom he had won her over. It was her sacred sanctuary and not many people were allowed in.

Marco's hand went to his chest. 'It would be an honour,' he said, his voice cracking at the significance of this moment.

I laid my hand on his arm. '*Calma,*' I whispered.

He knew what he had to do. To be fair, he was playing a blinder. I watched as my little girl led the way, followed by her father, a man she had only just met. It was a wonderful start, but a small part of me broke. Clara had always been mine, all mine. Now it looked like I was going to have to share her with Marco. I wasn't sure how ready I was to do that. I knew she deserved to have her father in her life, but she was my everything. Was this what parenting was – sacrificing your happiness for theirs?

27. Sophie

Jess sat beside Jack on the couch, scrolling through all the things she wanted for her sixteenth birthday. Jack, as usual, was indulging her.

'You don't need three pairs of cargos, Jess,' I pointed out.

She glared at me. 'I'll wear them loads and they're not even that expensive.'

'Ah, let her get them. It's a big birthday.'

Here we go again with the spoiling and the never saying no. I was not raising a kid who thought she could snap her fingers and get what she wanted.

'Jack,' my voice was firm, 'one pair is plenty.'

'Okay.' Jack winked at Jess, thinking I was stupid or blind. I hated when he did that ignore-Mum-she's-a-pain thing. If I didn't discipline Jess and rein her in, she'd turn into an entitled princess. A bit like I'd been back in the day – a stupid, vacuous (I'd had to look up the word after Louise called me vacuous all those years ago), materialistic, spoiled idiot. Jack had spoiled me and we had lived a lavish lifestyle. I'm not going to pretend I hadn't enjoyed it, but I do think that the crash to earth, in the long run, was a good thing.

Resisting the urge to shout, I asked Jess what she wanted to do on the big day.

'Will I book Nando's for a family dinner? We can bring Robert?' I suggested.

Jess looked appalled. 'OMG, no way. That's so lame. I want a party here.'

This was the first I'd heard of it. 'For how many?'

She didn't even look up from her phone. 'I dunno – like, forty?'

Our house was not big. It was a perfect size for the three, sometimes four of us, but I wasn't sure where forty kids would fit.

'Forty is too many.'

'Well, you're the one who always says include everyone, it's mean to leave people out,' she reminded me.

'Are you inviting boys too?' Jack raised an eyebrow.

'Obviously. I'm not a loser.'

'Will you invite the triplets?' I asked. I knew that if they were coming Sebastian might be too. Maybe it wasn't such a bad thing having the party here. At least I'd get to keep an eye on what was going on and see if she and Sebastian were completely over or if she still had a crush on him, which I prayed she didn't.

'Of course I'm inviting them.'

'And Sebastian?'

'I'm inviting the whole team, so I guess I'll include him.' She scrolled on her phone.

I was afraid to ask any further questions because I knew she'd clam up. It was better for me to see it for myself. I'd agree to the party.

'Okay, let's agree to forty, but not one kid more. The house isn't big enough. Write up a list of names to make sure you've included everyone and that it doesn't go over forty.'

'Oh, my God, what are we? A million years old? I'm not writing a list. I know who's coming and it won't be more than forty.'

'And no alcohol,' I warned her.

'And no canoodling with boys.' Jack grinned.

Jess sighed. 'Forget it. I'm not having a party with you two annoying me.'

Jack wrapped his arm around her and pulled her in for a hug. 'You're so gorgeous. I know tons of boys will be queuing up and it's my job to see them off until you're thirty.'

She swatted him away but was smiling. 'Seriously, though, you can't be there. Go out for dinner or something. No one's parents are at their parties. You have to go out or hide upstairs.'

'I'm not hiding in my own home, thank you.'

'Mum, I'm serious. You cannot come in. It's so embarrassing.'

'Relax, Jess, we were young once. We won't come in. We'll leave you alone. I'll take your mum out to dinner, but we'll be back by midnight to clear everyone out.'

Jess looked relieved. Over my dead body was I going out and leaving a bunch of randy sixteen-year-olds, who would, no doubt, come with backpacks full of alcohol, alone in my house. But I let Jess believe what she wanted. I was determined to get a closer look at Sebastian and her relationship with him. Julie was no help with information. All she kept saying was that the triplets didn't know anything, but that Jess should stay away from Sebastian. I wanted to see for myself that she was, and if having forty teens in the house was one way of doing that, then so be it.

Jack's phone rang. I saw Pippa's name flash up. He tensed.

'Yes? . . . What? . . . I can't understand . . . Jesus, how much have you had? . . . Is Robert okay? . . . I'm on my way.' Jack jumped up from the couch and rushed to the front door.

'What is it?' I asked.

'She's plastered and incoherent. I need to get Robert out of there.'

'I'll come with you.' I grabbed my coat.

'I want to come too.' Jess looked upset.

'No,' Jack said. 'Stay here, put on some pasta for Robert. I doubt he's eaten. We'll be back soon.'

'Dad, I want to help. I can mind him while you deal with Pippa. I can help.'

I was actually glad to see Jess putting someone else first.

'Let her come, Jack. She's right, she can focus on Robert. We don't know what state Pippa will be in.'

'Okay,' Jack reluctantly agreed. 'But come on, quick.'

Jack drove like a lunatic to Pippa's apartment. What would usually take twenty minutes, took ten. I clung to the door handle but kept quiet. Jack's jaw was set and his hands were gripping the steering wheel tightly. Jess sat in the back and chewed her thumbnail.

Jack flung the car at the kerb and we leaped out and ran up the stairs to the second floor.

'Pippa? Robert?' Jack banged on the door.

Nothing.

He banged louder and raised his voice.

'Do you think it's really bad, Mum?' Jess whispered to me. Jack's rising panic was worrying her. I began to regret saying she should come along.

'She's probably just drunk, but we need to get Robert out of there.'

One of the neighbours, a lady in her seventies, popped her head out from behind her front door, disturbed by the commotion.

'Sorry,' I said, 'we're just a bit worried. Pippa seemed unwell on the phone. This is Robert's father.' I pointed to Jack.

'I'm Alice. I have a spare key. Pippa often forgets hers,' the lady said.

'Oh, thank God.' Jack went over to her, and she handed him a key.

'It's none of my business but . . .' she hesitated '. . . Pippa seems to be struggling a bit lately. She stumbles a lot and forgets things. I found Robert locked out yesterday. Pippa had popped out to the shops but didn't come back for hours. I brought him in here.'

Oh, God, things were worse than we had imagined.

I thanked Alice and gave her our phone numbers. 'Please call us if it ever happens again. We'll come and get Robert. Thank you so much.'

Meanwhile, Jack opened and burst through the door. I rushed after him, with Jess behind me.

'Jesus Christ,' Jack cried out.

Pippa was passed out on the floor of the living room. There was an empty bottle of vodka beside her and three lines of cocaine on the coffee-table. I reached down and checked her pulse. She was breathing, passed out, but breathing.

'She's alive,' I said.

'Robert?' Jack roared. 'It's Daddy.'

'*Muuuuum.*' Jess looked at me wild-eyed. In that moment, she looked as young as Robert. She was staring around the room, unable to believe what she was seeing. I could barely believe it myself.

I needed to take control and keep Jess from freaking out.

'It's okay, pet. Pippa's going to be fine. Please go and see if you can find Robert. Jack, I need your help, we need to lift Pippa up.'

Jess went into Robert's bedroom and then came out. She shook her head, then went into Pippa's bedroom and I could hear her calling her brother's name.

We sat Pippa up and Jack slapped her cheeks, calling to her, trying to bring her around. She opened her eyes and closed them again.

I went to help Jess find Robert. My daughter was looking under Pippa's bed when I came in.

'I can't find him anywhere.' Jess was upset.

I saw a light coming from the slatted door of the corner wardrobe. I walked over, opened the door and found Robert inside. He was curled up on Pippa's fur coat. He had his headphones on and was watching cartoons on his iPad.

'Oh, sweetie,' I said.

'Thank God he's okay,' Jess sobbed.

Robert smiled. 'Hi, Sophie, did Mummy wake up? I'm really hungry,' he said, taking off his headphones.

I picked him up and hugged him.

'Hey, Robert.' Jess stroked his hair as she fought back tears. 'It's okay, we're all here now.'

'Tell your dad,' I told her.

'Dad, Robert's in here,' Jess called, through the bedroom door.

Jack raced in and took Robert from me. Holding him tightly, he exhaled. 'Oh, buddy, I was so worried.'

Jess slid her hand into mine and leaned into my shoulder. I kissed the top of her head.

'You're squashing me, Daddy.' Robert squirmed under Jack's tight hold.

'Sorry – I'm just so happy to see you.' Jack's voice shook as he put his son down gently.

Over Robert's head I whispered, 'Should we call an ambulance?'

'No.' Jack told Jess to take Robert into his bedroom and pack a big bag because he was coming to stay with us for a while.

'Come on, we'll pack all your favourite things.' Jess held her little brother's hand.

I continued to try to wake Pippa properly while Jack went

to the kitchen and filled a jug with cold water, which he then poured over Pippa's head.

'*Arghhhhhhh!*' she shrieked, her eyes opening wide. 'What the hell?' She sat up and looked around. 'What are you doing here? How dare you throw water on me? I'm soaked.'

Jack crouched down. 'You are a complete disgrace. This is it, Pippa. This is the end. I will not let my son be raised by an addict. Anything could have happened to him. What kind of a mother downs a bottle of vodka and snorts cocaine in front of her kid?' Jack's voice shook with emotion.

'He didn't see me. I put him in his room. I just needed a little pick-me-up,' Pippa slurred.

'Pick-me-up for what? You barely work. You fleece me for cash and go around shagging married men. What exactly do you need a break from?'

Pippa looked awful, underweight, with bags that looked like purple bruises under bloodshot eyes.

'Vincent dumped me. He promised he'd leave his wife, but the bastard dumped me and I got dropped from the show. They're giving my slot to a younger girl. I just . . .' she waved her arm around '. . . I just never thought my life would be this. Single mum, no career, no man.' She began to sob. 'It's all gone wrong. I . . . What am I going to do? Who am I? I've got nothing, Jack, nothing.'

As much as I disliked her, as much as part of me wanted to say, 'Who you are is a selfish bitch who doesn't care about anyone, even your own son. You made your bed, now lie in it,' I also felt sorry for her. She was crushed. I knew that feeling. I knew what it felt like to have your life fall apart. But I had never put Jess in danger. I had put her first, even when that was the hardest thing in the world to do.

'You have a beautiful son who needs his mother,' Jack hissed at her. 'Get your shit together. Drinking and snorting coke aren't going to solve your problems. Stop sleeping with married men. Turn up for work on time and sober, and maybe your life will turn a corner. But for now, Pippa, I'm taking Robert and you will not be seeing him until you have sorted yourself out.'

'Stop lecturing me. It's all right for you with your happy life. It's not easy for me, Jack. Give me a break. I'm really struggling here. I could do with some support,' she cried.

'A break? I've given you a million chances. Our six-year-old son could have taken the cocaine you left lying around and died,' Jack shouted. 'Stop sitting there feeling sorry for yourself. It's pathetic. And I have supported you financially since the day we met. Grow up and cop on.'

He was yelling at her, and it wouldn't get him anywhere. Jess had come in to see what has happening and she was standing in the doorway, watching Jack lose it with Pippa. She looked at me and I gave her a little smile, to reassure her.

'Jack, go with Jess and check on Robert.' I pushed him out of the room. 'Go on.' I gestured at Jess. 'It's okay. Pippa and I are just going to have a chat.'

'Okay.' Jess turned and left.

Pippa bit her lip. 'All right, then, Sophie, why don't you slate me too? I know, I know, you're a great mum and I'm a loser. You have a successful career and I have none. You're the love of Jack's life and I was just a temporary fill-in. The great Sophie, Jack's soul-mate.'

What? Did she actually believe that? When she was with Jack, I'd been jealous of *her* – she was young, beautiful and successful. My husband was in love with her and my daughter adored her too. I had felt so left out and lonely when Jess went to stay with Jack and Pippa. And here we were, a few years later, and now she felt about me the way I had felt about her. Life was so strange, so full of blind corners. If someone had described this turn of events to me back then, I would have laughed and said it wasn't possible.

I kept my voice low and gentle. We wouldn't get through to her by yelling in her face.

'Pippa, I'm sorry you're struggling. I can see how hard things are for you, but drinking and doing drugs is not going to help anything or anyone, least of all you. Robert adores you and he needs you. He's such a great kid and they grow up so fast. Don't miss out on these precious years. Take some time, get sober, get healthy, and you'll be able to see things in a much clearer light. You're young, you're beautiful – you have so much potential. You can turn your life around, believe me, I know you can, and I'll help you. I'll see if I can get you some work through the agency. It'll be okay. You just need to dig deep and look forward.'

Pippa rubbed her mascara-smudged eyes so she looked even more like a sad panda. 'I just feel like such a failure. My life was supposed to be fun and glamorous. I want to travel and have money, not be stuck in stupid Dublin in a two-bed rental apartment with a kid. This is not the life I want. I hate it. I can't bear that this is it. There has to be more. I'm not a suburban mum. I'm worth more than that. This is Hell.'

Welcome to the real world, Pippa, I was thinking. You have a child who needs to be looked after. You're never going to travel the world on private planes partying with the jet set. That's not your life. It's not your reality.

'A lot of people feel overwhelmed by motherhood and crushed when their careers don't work out as they imagined. I know life can seem a bit boring, especially when you have a kid, but it's what you make of it. You need time to figure out what you want for your future, but you can't sort out your life when you're drunk and high. You need a clear head to find clarity and purpose.'

Pippa bit her lip. She looked broken. 'I'm sorry I was such a bitch to you and to your lovely Jess. I always felt insecure around you because I knew Jack still loved you. And then when Robert was born, I really struggled.' She leaned over and whispered, 'I hated being a mum and I couldn't handle Jess coming over to stay because I was embarrassed at how badly I was handling motherhood. I pushed her away and I'm really sorry. She's a great kid.' Pippa began to cry again. 'I've made such a mess of my life. I thought I'd be famous, rich and successful. I'm drunk, unemployed, and if it wasn't for Jack paying for my apartment, I'd be homeless too.' She sobbed into her hands.

It was so weird – I was suddenly seeing the past in a whole different light. All those weekends of pure loneliness when I'd cried my eyes out because Jess was off with her 'new mother', the one she preferred, and all the while Pippa was struggling and things were falling apart. Mum used to tell me that how you viewed the world changed as you got older – and now I could really see what she meant. I had seen what I thought was there – and been completely unable to see what was actually happening. I had seen only what I had looked for and been blinded by jealousy and heartbreak. Watching Pippa cry, realizing the truth about her situation, I made myself a promise that I wouldn't do that again. Getting older was challenging in so many ways, but the good thing was that you were finally able to cut through all the bullshit – your own and everyone else's.

I rubbed her back. 'Come on now. Everything looks bleak because you've got a booze and cocaine hangover. Get some sleep and things will look different. We'll take Robert for a few weeks to give you some space. I'll check in on you tomorrow. We'll help you get back on your feet.'

'Thanks, Sophie. I always thought you were a bit of a cold bitch, but you're not.'

Ouch. I chose to ignore the backhanded compliment.

She looked at me and her shoulders hunched, the picture of defeat. My heart went out to her.

'The honest truth is,' she said, 'I don't like being a mum. I hate being tied down. I hate the mundane routine. I hate not being able to be spontaneous. I feel like there's a noose around my neck and I'm being strangled with responsibility. I know that makes me a terrible person even to say those words out loud, especially because Robert's so sweet, but I just don't think I'm good at being anyone's mum.' She wept into her hands.

Things were a lot worse than I'd thought. This was a total nightmare. She was a wreck. But how could she make any decisions in this state? We needed to help her sober up, clean up and be a decent mother to Robert. She had to grow up. But in my heart of hearts, I wasn't sure she ever would or could.

I got her a glass of water and covered her with a blanket. Then I went to find the others.

Jack stood back, jaw clenched, as Robert hugged his mum goodbye. Jess stood close to me and watched as Pippa told Robert she loved him but she was a bit tired and needed a few days' rest.

'I know I can be a pain to you, but I'm so glad you're my mum,' Jess whispered.

'Thanks, and I love you even when you're a pain.'

Jess smiled, then held out her hand and walked Robert to the car, chatting to him about his favourite superhero.

I said goodbye to Pippa and she nodded tiredly, almost asleep. I tucked the blanket around her and we walked out.

Jack's breathing was laboured. I took his hand. 'Breathe slowly or you'll have a heart attack and then Robert will be royally screwed.'

Jack grinned and pulled me close to him. 'If I haven't told you lately, let me be clear – I love you, Sophie Devlin, and I thank my lucky bloody stars you took me back.'

'Well, to be fair, the bar is set fairly low with your ex.' I laughed, relieved at easing the tension. 'But thanks, and I love you too.'

'Pippa will never be able to threaten me again about custody. I took photos of her, the table, the cocaine, the drink . . . everything. I will never, ever put my son in danger again. She's going to have to prove to me that she's capable of looking after Robert before I let her take him out of my sight again.'

While I understood and agreed with Jack on the importance of Robert's safety, I really needed Pippa to sort herself out or I'd end up raising Robert full-time. Being honest, it was not something I wanted to do. I had not signed up to be a full-time mum to a child who was not mine. I had very specifically chosen not to have another child after Jess. I did not want more children. I accepted that Jack had a son when we got back together and I was open to him co-parenting, but not full-time.

In two years Jess would be eighteen and, if she did as I hoped, she'd be headed to college. That would open up a whole new life for me and Jack. But it wouldn't happen if we had to raise Robert to adulthood. It had felt so good to have Jess take my hand and look to me to sort Pippa – it had been a long, long time since she'd looked at me like that, like she actually respected me. This had been one hell of a day, but the silver lining was that I felt like things were going to be okay with Jess. All the teenage eye-rolling and insults, all that nonsense would eventually fall away, and my lovely Jess would come back to me. Then we'd be friends for life – just like I'd been with Mum.

It was all looking good for our future. I'd just have to make damn sure Pippa got back on her feet.

28. Julie

Harry fiddled with his tie and exhaled deeply as we walked towards the headmaster's office. To our right were the carefully manicured playing fields of Castle Academy, to our left the 4G rugby pitch that some multi-millionaire past pupil had paid for.

'Did he give you any clue as to what Liam did?' Harry asked, for the third time.

'No, he didn't. He just said we needed to come to the school to talk to him about an incident.'

In the first few years of their time at Castle Academy the triplets had been in trouble a fair bit, nothing serious, but I had been inside the principal's office several times.

In the last few years, however, they had really settled in. Playing rugby had cemented friendships and their place in the school for them. They felt like they belonged and had stopped acting out. Even I had begun to relax and stop feeling like a total imposter at the place.

But now here we were again, called in to see the headmaster. What had Liam done?

'If he's in trouble, it could endanger his place on the team,' Harry said.

Always back to the rugby. 'Jesus, Harry, I'm less worried about the sodding rugby team and more concerned that he might be suspended or expelled. We don't know how bad this is.'

Harry looked appalled. 'You don't think it's that serious, do you?'

'Hopefully not. We'll find out soon enough.' I stopped outside the headmaster's office and knocked.

Mr Henderson greeted us politely and asked us to sit down. His office was large and filled with light. Behind him was a wall of book-lined shelves. It even had one of those ladders you see in libraries, like on *Downton Abbey*, which they're always climbing up to pull down big, dusty books.

Harry and I sat down on the two dark green leather chairs opposite the headmaster.

Mr Henderson took off his glasses, cleared his throat and clasped his hands together.

When people take off their glasses and do the hand-clasping thing it tends to mean trouble, big trouble. I held my breath.

'I've called you here today to discuss a serious incident involving Liam.'

Harry looked at me, panic-stricken. Serious incident was bad news.

'Liam is a really good kid,' I said. 'What exactly happened?'

'This morning, at early-morning training, Liam punched another boy in the face. We don't believe the boy's nose is broken, but there was a lot of blood, and we cannot condone violence.'

'That can't be right. Liam would never do that,' Harry said. 'Are you sure it was him?'

'Positive.'

'Who did he punch?' I wanted to know. Liam was not a kid who went around punching people for no reason.

'Sebastian Carter-Mills.'

Of course it was. No surprise there. This was not unprovoked. Sebastian had clearly wound Liam up.

'What led to the incident?' I asked.

'Apparently there was a quarrel that, unfortunately, ended up with Liam resorting to violence.'

'Did Sebastian hit him first?' I asked.

'No.'

'We will speak to Liam and I can assure you this will never happen again.' Harry was eager to placate the headmaster.

'What was the quarrel about? I know my son. He did not punch Sebastian without serious provocation.'

'We have asked Liam to explain his actions, but he insists he has nothing to say. He made it clear that he would rather not discuss what happened. Besides, the question here is not what the quarrel was about but how your son reacted. Violence towards another boy is unacceptable. Mrs Carter-Mills was extremely distressed to see her son injured and has taken Sebastian to hospital to make sure his nose isn't broken, although the coach, Mr Long, is certain it isn't.'

I could just imagine the scene Victoria had caused. She'd make our lives hell over this.

'We will, of course, cover any medical bills and Liam will apologize to the Carter-Mills family,' Harry said.

Hang on a second, why was he offering them Liam on a plate?

'While I obviously agree that Liam shouldn't have punched Sebastian,' I said, shooting a look at Harry, 'I would first like to talk to my son and find out more about the incident. Liam is not someone who loses his temper easily. We need to find out what led to the punch. Sebastian must have said or done something awful to provoke that reaction from Liam. There's more to this than we know at present.'

'As I said, winding someone up is still no excuse for violence. That is our primary concern here.'

'Generally, I'd agree with you, but we don't know what Sebastian's part in this was and I think that's a key factor in this scenario.'

'We will speak to our son, make sure he apologizes and then we can all move on,' Harry said. 'We have a semi-final to focus on.'

Mr Henderson cleared his throat. 'Regarding the semi-final. Mrs Carter-Mills is asking for Liam to be expelled. While that is far too strong a punishment, considering he has been an excellent student up to this point, we have considered suspending him for a week. However, I have spoken to Mr Long and I feel that the best way for Liam to learn from this lesson is to exclude him from the team for the semi-final. We know how much his rugby means to him and by excluding him we believe that he will truly understand that actions have serious consequences.'

Beside me, Harry made a strangled sound. I knew he was devastated.

I had to say something to try to save Liam. 'I think that's very unfair. We don't know the true circumstances. Liam is one of the captains. He has been a real leader for this team and one of the best players. He has put his heart and soul into training and being part of the squad. This semi-final is the biggest moment in his young life. Please don't take that away from him. Suspend him, by all means, but don't leave him out of the team.'

The headmaster shook his head. 'The decision has been made.'

I stood up. 'I think that's incredibly unfair and I will get to the bottom of this.'

Harry finally found his voice. 'Is there any way you would reconsider this decision?'

'I'm afraid not. Liam will be waiting for you outside the

main reception area. I think it best he goes home immediately.'

'But there must be something we –'

I grabbed Harry's arm before he got down on his knees and offered to donate a kidney if Liam was allowed to play. I dragged my devastated husband out of the office.

We walked down the corridor, me fuming and Harry saying, 'No no no no,' over and over. I stopped just inside the main door and shook him.

'Harry, we know our son. There is a lot more to this than meets the eye. I know you're upset, and so am I. But you need to pull yourself together for Liam's sake. He's waiting for us outside and he needs us to be strong for him. Let's hear his side of the story before we jump to any conclusions.'

'I'm so gutted for him, Julie. I know how much this will hurt him and I'm furious with him for allowing his temper to ruin this huge moment in his life.'

'Harry,' I barked, 'Liam needs our support right now. We have to listen to his side of the story.'

We walked out to where Liam was standing, head bowed, at the entrance. He looked shattered. I could see he'd been crying.

I went over and hugged him. 'It's okay, come on, let's get you home.'

'Jesus, Liam, the semi-final,' Harry muttered.

When he was safely in the car Liam began to sob. 'I can't believe they've dropped me. That prick just . . . just . . .'

I turned in my seat to face him. 'What did Sebastian do, Liam?'

He looked out the window. 'I don't want to talk about it.'

'Liam, I know you wouldn't have punched him unless he said something really shitty. If you tell us, maybe we can talk to the principal and your coach and see if we can sort it all out.'

He shook his head.

'Liam, tell me what happened. I'm trying to help you.' I was exasperated.

'Mum!' Liam shouted. 'I don't want to talk about it. Stop.' He covered his face with his hands.

'Leave him,' Harry whispered.

But there was no way in hell I was leaving it. We drove home in silence. Liam raced through the front door and ran upstairs, muttering about having a shower.

Harry and I went into the kitchen, and as Harry went to put on the kettle, both of our phones buzzed. It was the rugby WhatsApp group.

I wish to inform you that there was a horrific physical assault on Sebastian today by one of the joint captains, Liam. Mr Henderson and Coach Long have decided that Liam is unfit to represent the school at the semi-final. He is a disgrace to this team and to Castle Academy. Clearly he has anger management issues and a violent nature. The good news is that we have just come from A&E where the consultant told us that although Sebastian's nose is badly bruised and he lost an awful lot of blood it is not broken and he will be able to play in the semi-final. I have no doubt he will shine, despite the trauma he endured today. Sebastian is a trooper.

The bitch. The rotten, nasty, gloating bitch. Harry stared at his phone and flung it across the kitchen.

'She is an utter wagon.' His hands were shaking. 'How dare she write that? How dare she say Liam is unfit? How dare she?' He slammed his hand onto the table.

'I'm going to talk to Leo and Luke when they come home.

296

They'll tell us what happened,' I said. I would question them like a KGB operative until I found out the truth.

Ping ping ping . . .

OMG poor Sebastian!

Is he really OK?

Violence is not acceptable.

Teammates are not supposed to turn on each other.

The team will miss Liam, he's such a strong player. What a letdown.

I hope we don't lose now.

On and on the messages went. I turned off my phone and spent the day watching the clock until it was time to pick up the boys. Harry spent the day trying to talk to Liam through his locked bedroom door and getting nowhere.

Luke and Leo flung their bags into the car and slammed the door.

'Fuck Sebastian,' Luke said.

'He's a scumbag,' Leo added.

'I need to know what happened. What did Sebastian do?' I asked.

Leo and Luke looked at each other.

'Boys, your brother is in big trouble and getting blamed for everything. It's not fair, but I can't help him if I don't know what Sebastian did to wind him up. If I know what happened, maybe I can plead his case to the headmaster.'

'It's embarrassing,' Leo said.

'Embarrassing? For Liam?'

'No,' Luke said.

'For Sebastian?'

'No, Mum,' Leo snapped.

'Well, for who, then?' I was so frustrated. 'Spit it out.'

'Fine then. Jess,' Luke told me.

'Jess? What do you mean? Did Sebastian say something about Jess?'

'Kind of.'

'It was worse than that,' Leo muttered.

Jesus! What the hell had gone on in the changing room that morning?

'Guys, I know it's hard for you to tell me, but I need to know everything. It's the only way I can help Liam. I know he'd never punch someone without good reason.'

Leo and Luke looked at one another. I could see they were weighing up how much to say. I stayed quiet, even though I wanted to roar in their faces to tell me.

'He was saying stuff about Jess and . . . he had a photo.'

I felt like my heart had actually stopped in my chest. The air in the car felt dense, like it was pressing against me, suffocating.

'What kind of photo?'

The boys shifted about.

'One of her with no top on,' Leo muttered.

Oh, God, no. 'The bastard,' I hissed.

'And he was saying that she, like, does stuff,' Luke said.

'What stuff?'

'Stuff,' he said, looking mortified.

'Luke, I need the full story.'

'Jesus, Mum, it's . . . it's —'

'Blow-jobs,' Leo blurted out. 'He said she's really good at giving him blow-jobs.'

Oh, my God, she wasn't even sixteen. That lowlife was

showing a photo of my niece topless and saying she was a blow-job queen. I felt a shot of pure rage go through me. I wanted to bash his stupid head in. I could have killed him with my bare hands.

'Did the other boys see the photo?' I said quietly.

'They didn't get a chance. Sebastian just showed it to the three of us, to wind us up. We tried to wrestle the phone out of his hands, but then –'

'Liam punched him?' I interrupted.

'No. Liam punched him when he said Jess was a slut.'

Tears sprang into my eyes. I had never been prouder of Liam. But my poor, lovely Jess.

'Does Jess have any idea he has this photo?' I asked.

'I dunno,' Leo said.

'We tried to get Sebastian's phone, but Coach came in when he heard the shouting, so the prick still has it.'

'Oh, Jesus, poor Jess. We have to delete that photo.'

'Don't worry, Mum. We'll get his phone and destroy it,' Leo said.

'But won't it still be on the cloud or whatever?' I was panicking.

'Not unless it's synced or backed up,' Leo said.

I had no idea what that really meant, but I knew we had to get Sebastian's phone ASAP and delete everything.

'We could go to the guards,' Luke said. 'I mean, couldn't they talk to him and get his phone? Isn't it illegal to have pictures without a girl's consent or whatever?'

I shook my head. 'No. We need to shut this down, boys. We don't want this to get broadcast all over the place. The most important thing here is to keep it quiet so we can protect Jess. I want you to leave it with me. I'll sort it out. But you have to do one thing for me – find out if he forwarded that photo to any of the other lads. And if you find out he did, don't go rogue. We'll handle it. We have to tread carefully. But I promise you this, I'm going to make sure that prick Sebastian pays for what he's done to our Jess and to Liam.'

'Get Louise to sort him out. She's way scary and she can totally legal him,' Luke suggested.

'Yeah, Louise can kick serious arse,' Leo said.

'So can I, boys. Trust me, so can I.'

29. Louise

Everyone, including Julie, was on time. They knew how important today was to me and to Clara. I introduced Marco to my family.

'Nice to see you again.' Dad shook Marco's hand warmly.

'An honour to see the father of Louisa again.' Marco smiled.

'Louisa.' Julie winked at me.

I shrugged. 'I've told him a million times.'

'Clara looks happy,' Sophie noted.

'So far, so good.'

'Hey, Clara, do you want to give Lemon her bottle?' Gavin asked.

'No, but I'll watch.'

'Okay, but I want you to babysit her when you're a bit older.'

'I don't think I'd like to look after a baby.'

'But you so good at looking after Luna,' Marco said.

Clara looked up at him. 'I suppose I am. But Luna is a cat.'

'Animals are like humans,' Marco reminded her.

Gavin looked a bit put out. 'Hang on there, Marco. Lemon needs a bit more attention than a cat.'

Marco laughed. 'Not so much – eating, drinking, sleeping, kissing, caressing. The same.'

'He has a point,' Julie said.

'It sounds like the perfect life,' Harry said.

'I'd fancy a bit of caressing myself.' Jack squeezed Sophie's leg. She swatted him away, laughing.

'I wish Granny was here to meet my new dad,' Clara announced.

Everyone turned to her.

'I do too, darling,' I agreed.

'We all do, pet, but she's smiling down on us from wherever she is and she'd be so proud of the way you're handling all of this newness.' Dad smiled across the table at Clara.

'You know, I think Granny sent Marco,' Julie said to Clara.

'What do you mean, Aunt Julie?'

'Well, I think Granny sent Marco to help look after you and to love you and be in your life. It was a gift she sent to you.'

Clara frowned as she considered this. 'I don't think dead people can send people to you, but I think Granny would like my dad.'

'Yes, darling, I'm sure she would.' I smiled at Clara.

'That make me so happy.' Marco held his hand over his heart.

We sat down to lunch and Harry told Marco the story of meeting Christelle. Marco was hanging on his every word.

'So, I can understand your shock and delight at finding out you have a daughter. Isn't it the best feeling?' Harry beamed.

'The very best in the whole world,' Marco exclaimed.

'Probably even more so for you because you have no children. So now you get to be a father,' Harry said, clapping Marco on the back.

'And without the early baby stage,' Gavin said. 'Which, after a week of zero sleep, sounds kind of great.'

'Oh, boo-hoo, I had no sleep for years. You'll be fine,' Julie said.

'I wish with all of my heart that I was here when Clara was *piccola*,' Marco said.

'I was an angel baby, Mummy said,' Clara said.

'Yes, you were,' I lied. Clara had not been an angel baby, and I had struggled in the early days, but it was a mother's prerogative to rewrite history.

'You were a little dote,' Dad agreed.

'I cannot wait to meet all of your childrens also,' Marco said. 'Clara tells me about her cousins.'

'Well, Marco, if you're around next week, you're welcome to come and watch my three grandsons shine on the rugby pitch,' Dad said.

'Really? I like rugby very much.'

'Well, it's just a match, really,' Julie muttered.

Harry looked at the floor. That was strange. Harry was normally delighted to tell people about the triplets. They seemed out of sorts.

I whispered to Sophie. 'Did one of the boys get dropped?'

'Don't think so,' she replied, under her breath. 'It looks like something's up, though.'

'But,' Marco continued, 'I have to get back to my olives. I cannot leave them for too long. Also, to my mother, Anna. But I am hoping that Clara will come to visit me one day.'

'Maybe in the future, but definitely not now.' Clara was firm.

'Of course, *tesoro mio*, only when you are wanting to.'

The men began to talk about rugby.

Clara asked if she could leave the table and go to her room. 'I'm bored now, Mummy.'

'Of course, darling. I'll check on you in a bit.'

Sophie pulled her chair closer to me. 'You have Marco well briefed. He's doing so well,' she said.

'Yes, he is, but I'll be happy when he goes. It's been stressful. I've been so worried about how Clara would react that I've barely slept. I'm thrilled it's gone well, but I need some down time now.'

Sophie put an arm round me. 'It's been a huge strain for

you and a worry. But, honestly, Louise, I think it's the best thing you could have done. Clara really seems to have taken to him. She's very relaxed around him already.'

'Yes, she really is and that's such a huge relief.'

Julie scooched her chair over as well. 'What are you two whispering about?'

'How it's gone with Marco, and how wrecked Louise is. Can you take a few days off next week to get some rest?' Sophie asked.

'I wish. No, work is nuts and I'm still trying to figure out how to get rid of bloody Zoë, who keeps swanning in late, making mistakes and is completely and utterly wrecking my head. She's really got under my skin. Never spoil your kids. They'll turn out to be entitled arseholes.'

Julie picked at her slice of cake. 'You're right there. But all kids are tricky, and they get trickier as they get older. You have to watch them like a hawk. I think it's good for you to have Clara's father in your life to help you when she enters the teen years.'

'God, yes, Julie's right. You need two of you to manage teens.'

'How is Jess after the whole Pippa fiasco?' I asked.

'She's okay. She's been nicer to me, actually, and she's really sweet with Robert. I think she's realized I'm not so bad after all.'

'Has Pippa started rehab?' Julie asked.

Sophie nodded. 'She went in on Thursday. It's an intensive course, so fingers crossed it works.'

'You're amazing, Sophie, taking on Robert full-time,' I said.

She shrugged. 'What choice do I have? He's an innocent victim in all this. I want him to have as much stability as possible. To be honest, I'm not sure if Pippa's going to get better, and even if she does, whether she's fit for motherhood. I think she saw a baby as a fun accessory, and the reality, as we all know, is hard slog.'

'You've a lot on your plate,' Julie said.

'We all do,' Sophie replied. 'Is everything okay with the boys?'

Julie's face went red and she stared fixedly at her cake. 'Yeah, sure,' she said.

I looked at Sophie and she looked at me, obviously thinking the same thing: Something's up.

'You and Harry both seem a little off today,' I said. 'Is anything wrong?'

'No, no.' Julie shook her head, but still didn't look at us. 'It's grand. Just some . . . you know . . . normal teenage stuff, but it's all fine.'

'Can we help?' Sophie said. 'Is there anything we can do?'

Julie finally looked up at us, and I could tell something was really bothering her. She took a very deep breath and opened her mouth as if to speak, then shut it again. Another deep breath, and she went to speak again, but stopped. I wanted to shake her.

'Jesus, Julie, spit it out,' I urged my sister.

She opened her mouth again, but before she could say anything, Lemon let out a roar and projectile-vomited all over the table. Thank God Clara had gone to her room or she would have freaked out with the mess and the smell.

Everyone helped clear up, and when that was done, it was time for them all to head home. Clara let Marco read her a story before he left for his hotel and I collapsed into bed for an early night. It was only when I was turning off my light that I remembered Julie hadn't told us what was wrong. I'd have to call her and check in.

*

The next morning, Marco stood in our hall, his suitcase at his side. He held out his arms.

'Not yet,' Clara said.

'No problem, *tesoro mio*. A fist pump?'

'*Sì*.' She smiled shyly at him.

He held out his fist and she touched it with hers.

Marco looked at her, his hand on his heart. 'I love you, *amore mio*.'

'*Grazie*,' Clara said.

'Thank you for permitting me to be in your life. I am the happiest man in Italy.'

'I'm glad Mummy found you and that you came over. I like you, Marco. You're kind and funny, and even though you smell a bit funny, I don't hate it.'

Marco's smile widened. 'This makes me so happy.'

Clara smiled. 'Good.'

The taxi tooted outside. Marco picked up his suitcase and turned to go, blowing kisses at Clara. I walked him down the path.

'Thank you, Louisa. Thank you for finding me and giving me this beautiful gift. I am for ever grateful. Clara is wonderful.'

'It's Louise, Marco, and you're very welcome.'

I smiled. All those sleepless nights worrying about how Clara would react to Marco were over. She had taken to him so well. He had been wonderful with her, endlessly patient, following her lead at all times, knowing when to back off, alert to signs of her getting anxious . . . I couldn't have asked for a better result. I felt lighter and hugely relieved.

It had been surprisingly nice to share Clara with him. He adored her and wanted to know every single detail about her. My family loved her and were interested in her life, but Marco was as obsessed with her as I was. He loved her completely.

It was so comforting to have someone who felt the way I did about Clara. Mum had, but she was gone now and the hole was deep. I had enjoyed the visit as much as Clara had, if not more. I'd thought I'd hate sharing her. I'd thought I'd be worried every time I left her alone with him for even a second. But it had been the opposite: I'd known she was in safe hands. I could leave the room and not worry. I could leave them alone and know Clara was going to be okay.

'Thank you for following my instructions and taking it slowly. I can't believe how quickly she warmed to you. It's been lovely for her.'

'I would like very much for Clara to come to Italy to meet my mother and see my farm. Can we think about this possibility?'

'I'll talk to her. If she wants to go, we'll work something out, but to be honest, she's not a very good traveller. She doesn't like change, but we'll see.'

'Thank you. I go now with a big heart full of love. I have the most beautiful daughter. And you are a special and generous woman, Louisa. You didn't have to do this, but I am so grateful that you have. You have changed my life. And please, I will try to bring only good things into Clara's life, yours too. *Grazie*, Louisa.' He kissed me on both cheeks and climbed into the taxi before I could remind him for the millionth time that I hated being called Louisa.

30. Sophie

Julie had arranged for us to meet for a drink. She hadn't been herself at Louise's meet-Marco-in-Dublin event and I was worried something was wrong. I arrived five minutes early and was surprised to see Gavin already sitting at a table, drinking a pint of Guinness.

'Hi.'

'Hi,' he said, his mouth ringed by Guinness froth. 'God, this tastes good.'

'Thirsty?'

'Wrecked and badly in need of a night out and adult conversation. I love Lemon but being on my own with her all day when she's up half the night is beginning to grind me down. Shania's travelling a lot, so it's just me and the baby. The minute she got home tonight I ran out the door.'

The waitress came over to take my order. As I was ordering a glass of red wine, Louise marched in, sat down and barked, 'White wine, Pinot Grigio, not too dry, large glass.'

The waitress scurried off. Sometimes my sister was just a little too curt, but I wasn't going to tackle her on it in the mood she was in.

'Tough day at the office?' Gavin asked.

'It wouldn't have been if Zoë hadn't fucked up yet again by ordering pulled pork sandwiches for a working lunch with my Muslim client.'

'Oh, no!' I gasped.

'Oh, yes,' Louise said. 'I was mortified.'

'To be fair, at her age I probably could have made that mistake.' Gavin held his hand up.

'First of all, I told her he was Muslim and to order the lunch accordingly. She constantly bangs on about being woke and sensitive to sexual preferences, minorities, ethnicities and cultures, but when it comes down to it, the only person she gives a flying fuck about is herself.'

Our drinks arrived and while Louise drank deeply from her glass, I let her cool off as I turned back to Gavin. 'The days with a newborn can be long. You should bring Lemon to those baby-group, happy-clappy things. At least you'd get to interact with other parents.'

'I've tried that, but I'm the only dad and the mums or nannies are all in groups. I end up on my own, like some kind of freak of nature. I've tried chatting to the mums but they either think I'm hitting on them, am a loser or I don't get it because I didn't give birth or breastfeed.'

Louise, who had polished off her wine in about three gulps, snorted. 'Welcome to the real world. When I became the first female partner in my law firm in London, I had to deal with all the male partners thinking I didn't belong, wasn't smart enough, strong enough or ballsy enough to walk among them. I had to fight my corner every single day and prove myself until they finally accepted me and then, when I became more successful than they were, most of them felt threatened by me. It's never easy to be a minority, but you have to tough it out to break down barriers.'

Gavin put down his pint. 'Jesus, Louise, I just want a bit of mindless chat and a coffee with other stay-at-home parents. I'm not looking to change the world. And how thick were the male partners in your firm not to see you were a ball-breaker from the first time they met you?'

'Not thick, just blinded by their own egos.'

Julie hurried across the bar and sat down with us. She ordered a bottle of wine and took off her coat. She seemed distracted.

'How's Lemon?' she asked Gavin. 'Sleeping any better?'

Gavin shook his head. 'Not great. I was up half the night with her. Thank God Shania came back today.'

Julie laughed. 'Get used to it. I survived on three hours' sleep for years.'

'Jeez, Julie, you remind me all the time. I'm doing my best, it's just hard sometimes, that's all. A bit of sympathy wouldn't go amiss.'

Julie looked at me, eyebrows raised.

'He's grumpy because the baby-group mums don't include him and he feels marginalized,' I explained.

'Hashtag leperdad,' Louise said, laughing.

'Welcome to my world,' Julie said. 'And it's not just because you're a man. The other mums sprinted away from me because I had triplets and no one wanted that chaos near their babies. It was bloody lonely for me too. If it wasn't for Marion, I don't know what I would have done.'

'To be fair, Julie, the triplets were kind of wild.' I laughed, trying to lighten the mood. 'If I'd met you in a baby group, I'd probably have run away too.'

Julie flinched, her face flushed with emotion. 'Really, Sophie? Well, you would have been very bloody foolish because my boys are the very people who are putting themselves on the line to defend your daughter right now.'

What? What was she talking about and why was she so angry?

'What do you mean, defend Jess? Defend her from what?'

Julie took a large gulp of wine and exhaled, getting her emotions under control. I looked at Louise and Gavin. Did they know what was going on? No. They were equally shocked at her outburst.

Julie put her glass down. 'I'm sorry for snapping. I asked you to meet me here because we have a problem and I need your help. It involves Jess and my boys too.'

'What problem?' My mind was racing. What had Jess done? Why were the boys involved? Oh, Christ, was it something to do with Sebastian?

Julie rubbed her forehead. 'You know that Jess was seeing Sebastian, right?' she asked me.

'Yes, obviously.'

Twisting her bracelet around her wrist, Julie said, 'Okay, please don't freak out. I didn't tell you this because I didn't want to worry you, you have a lot going on, but at that big party we had for the squad, I found Jess and Sebastian in Tom's bedroom. Jess was drunk and she had her top off. Don't panic, she had her skirt on and he had his jeans on. They didn't have sex.'

My hand flew to my mouth. What? Jess? Topless? Jesus Christ. 'What the hell? How could you not tell me?' I gasped.

'Because she was okay, I promise you I checked. She begged me not to tell you and I didn't want to upset you about it and I knew Jess was mortified and I spoke to her at length and she promised never to do anything stupid like that again. She was so ashamed and upset and I didn't want to make it worse by telling you.'

'Jesus Christ, Julie, I'm her mother! You should have told me straight away.' I felt sick. The wine was curdling in my stomach.

'Technically I should have, but Jess made a silly mistake – we all made mistakes as teenagers. I walked in on them before anything serious could happen. She was so embarrassed and I didn't want to add to her shame by telling you.'

'Well, you bloody well should have.' I was furious. How dare Julie keep this from me? My God, if she hadn't walked in, they could have had sex. Jess could have got pregnant. Did she even know to ask a guy to put on a condom? I hadn't had those conversations with her because she was only fifteen. My head throbbed. I'd have to go home, sit her down and, aside from killing her for being so bloody stupid, talk to her about birth control.

'And what the hell was she doing in Tom's bedroom? You persuaded me to let her stay by promising to look after her. I trusted you to keep an eye on her. I presumed she'd be safe in your house, not drunk and half naked with a guy who was no doubt pushing for sex. Jesus Christ, Julie! What the hell were you doing? Where were your boys? Why weren't they looking out for her?'

'I had nearly a hundred people in my house, Sophie. I was trying to do everything. I didn't think Jess would do something so silly in my house, under my nose.'

'How can you be sure she didn't have sex? Maybe they were half dressed because they'd had sex and were putting their clothes back on. Jess could be pregnant right now, or have an STD!' I was shouting. The people at the table beside us looked over.

'They didn't. Jess told me what happened. She was drunk and they had only been messing about. I talked to her about getting the morning-after pill if she needed it. She swore on Mum's grave that she hadn't had sex.'

I began to shake and cry as rage and shock coursed through my body. 'You spoke to my daughter about the morning-after pill and didn't think it was a good idea to tell me this happened? Oh, my God, I literally cannot believe this!'

Gavin leaned forward. 'To be fair, Sophie, it sounds like Julie was protecting Jess and you. Jess would never swear on

Mum's grave and lie. She's a good kid. They were probably just groping each other.'

I glared at him. 'I do not need to be protected from information about my daughter and her actions, Gavin. How would you feel if this was Lemon?'

He shuddered. 'Lemon isn't going out until she's eighteen.'

'I'm sorry, Sophie. Jess was so distressed and she was desperate for you not to know and think less of her and be furious.'

'I am her mother!' I hissed.

Louise laid a gentle hand on my arm. 'I think Julie's intentions were good. I understand that you wish she had told you, but the bottom line is, Jess is okay and nothing bad happened to her.'

'But he was obviously pushing her to have sex, or at least mess around. I should know that. I know he's a jerk, but I didn't know he was pressuring her to get naked and God knows what else. I bloody well needed to be aware of that so I could protect her. Jesus, I'm so furious I can hardly breathe. I can't stay here. I have to go. I can't believe you did this, Julie. I feel so betrayed.' I stood up and grabbed my bag.

Julie held up her hand. 'Wait, Sophie, there's more.'

'What?' My heart skipped a beat. I couldn't take any more. Julie hesitated.

'What's going on, Julie?' Louise asked.

'Liam got suspended for punching Sebastian in the face. He wouldn't tell me why, but I got it out of the other two. So, it seems that Sebastian was in the locker room boasting about Jess . . . about . . . the . . .'

'Just spit it out, Julie,' Louise said impatiently.

I was frozen to the spot. My heart was pounding in my chest.

'About Jess giving him blow-jobs, and he has a photo of her topless, which he showed the triplets,' Julie blurted out.

'Jesus!' Gavin gasped.

'No no no no no, oh, God, no.' Not Jess. Not photos, not horrible disgusting rumours. Not my beautiful Jess. A girl's reputation was everything. How dare he? How could he hurt and humiliate Jess like that? The room was spinning and I realized tears were sliding silently down my cheeks. Please, no.

Louise put her arm around me and guided me down into my chair. My legs were shaking. 'Breathe,' she instructed.

'So Liam punched him?' Gavin said.

Julie nodded. 'And the triplets tried to wrestle the phone from him, but the coach walked in.'

'So Sebastian still has his phone?'

'Yes.'

'Is the photo on the iCloud?' Gavin asked.

'Oh, God.' I covered my face. This could not be happening.

'I don't know,' Julie admitted.

'How do we find out?' Louise asked Gavin.

'We have to get our hands on the phone. Even if it is on the iCloud, it can be deleted from his photos app.'

'What if he forwarded it to his mates?' Louise asked.

'Well, if it's Snapchat, it's gone. If it's WhatsApp, you'll see it on his phone and we can track down whoever has it,' Gavin said.

I moaned – I actually felt like I was having a heart attack, my chest was so tight. 'I told her to stay away from that arse-hole. I knew he was poison. I'm going to kill her. How could she let him take photos? And give him . . . oh, God . . . oral sex. How could you let this happen, Julie? Why didn't you protect her?' I sobbed.

'I tried, but I had to look after my guests and . . . I know I failed. I'm so sorry. Believe me, no one is sorrier than me.'

'I think you'll find that I am, and that Jess will be when she finds out. Oh, my God, how am I going to tell her? Does everyone in the school know?'

'The kids on the team heard Sebastian boasting about the – the blow-jobs, but he only showed the photo to the triplets. Then Liam punched him and the coach came in and now Liam's been dropped from the team for the semi-final. He's absolutely devastated but he refused to tell the coach he had hit Sebastian to protect Jess. Harry and I were dragged up to school by the headmaster. Harry, the boys and I are doing everything we can to keep this from getting out.'

'Oh, poor Liam, he must be gutted. That's not fair. What a legend protecting his cousin,' Gavin said.

I was in no mood to hear that anyone in Julie's family was a hero – my fifteen-year-old daughter had been left in their care, neglected, and put in a really dangerous predicament by all of them.

'He's barely spoken two words since it happened.' Julie's voice shook. 'He's crushed.'

My rage exploded. 'Not as crushed as I am to hear all of this. Not as devastated as Jess will be when she finds out that she's the laughing-stock of the school and people are talking about her giving blow-jobs and looking at a photo of her breasts!' I began to sob uncontrollably.

'In fairness, Sophie, it's not the boys' fault or Julie's,' Gavin said softly. 'Jess got herself into this situation. And the blow-job story is probably bullshit. Lots of teenage boys boast about things they did with girls that didn't actually happen.'

'I'm so furious with her! I told her to stay away from him and his family. I knew he was trouble,' I spat.

'Don't be too hard on Jess,' Louise said. 'She's a good kid

who fell for the wrong guy, drink was involved and things got out of hand. It could happen to anyone. It happens all the time. What we need to focus on is how to shut down the rumours and get rid of that photo. We need to be strategic about this to protect Jess and give Sebastian his comeuppance.'

'Louise is right,' Gavin said. 'You don't want this story going viral.'

'Oh, Jesus, please, no,' I gasped. The thought of boys and girls looking at Jess's boobs and talking about her in a derogatory and disgusting way made me want to throw up.

'How do we fix this?' Julie asked. 'I'll do anything.'

'Liam needs to play that semi-final. He's a hero,' Gavin added.

'Jess is the priority, not some bloody rugby match.' Jesus, did Gavin not understand this was Jess's reputation on the line? That photo would follow her around for the rest of her life.

Louise sat forward, her face in business mode. 'We do not want to go to the police because you will have no control once they get involved, and who knows what could happen? If we send a legal letter to Victoria about the photo, she'll just come back saying Jess consented to it. It'll be his word against hers. You do not want to get dragged into a legal battle. If we approach the coach and the headmaster, it will be the same kind of thing: Sebastian will deny he said anything and claim that the photo was consensual. Jess will have to come in and say they weren't and it will be pretty humiliating for her. Let me talk to a few colleagues – completely confidentially – and see what their advice is. We need to be very careful with how we approach it. But, don't worry, I'll have a plan in place by tomorrow lunchtime and we'll talk it through. I've got you, Sophie. We'll resolve this mess and protect Jess.'

'Thank you, Louise. At least one of my sisters is going to protect my daughter.'

'Sophie, I'm sorry. I *was* trying to protect Jess.' Julie's voice shook.

'Really? Well, you did a pretty shitty job of it,' I hissed.

I couldn't bear another second of this, or of Julie's face and voice. I got up, grabbed my bag, turned on my heel and stormed out.

I stood outside Jess's bedroom door, trying to get my thoughts straight. Thank God Jack was at the cinema with Robert. I couldn't handle them right now. I needed to clear my head and talk to Jess. I needed the truth, the whole sordid, unvarnished truth, from my daughter.

It was important that I remained calm. Even though my siblings had said *poor Jess* wasn't to blame, I did blame her. I blamed her for getting drunk. I blamed her for going out with such a dickhead. I blamed her for going into a bedroom with him and taking her top off and . . .

I closed my eyes, took four long breaths, and opened the door. As usual, she was sprawled on her bed, face in her phone.

'OMG, can you knock? I could have been naked in here.'

Speaking of naked, I wanted to shout, you don't seem to have a problem with it.

Another deep breath. 'Put down your phone. We need to have a serious chat.'

She rolled her eyes. 'Oh, God, here we go . . . You need to study more, Jess, you need to do better in your exams, Jess, blah blah blah. I've heard it all before, Mum.'

I sat down on the edge of her bed and gripped the duvet. Stay calm.

'Hang up.'

'Fine. Talk to you later, Suzie.' Turning to me, scowling. 'What?'

'Actually, Jess, this isn't about school. This is about something a lot more serious. This is about . . . this is about Sebastian.'

'Oh, my God, I know you don't like him. I told you it's over. We barely speak any more. Let it go.'

I looked at my naïve almost-sixteen-year-old. She was so beautiful and so sure she knew everything there was to know, yet she was completely clueless as to how cruel boys could be. I was about to shatter her illusions.

'Okay, Jess, there's no way to sugar-coat this so I'm just going to tell you what Sebastian is doing and saying.' I paused, then gave it to her straight. 'He has been showing a topless photo of you in the locker room at Castle Academy.'

Jess frowned. I could see her trying to take in the information. She shook her head as if to rid herself of what she'd just heard. 'I . . . What are you talking about?'

I gritted my teeth. 'Apparently, the night I left you at Julie's rugby party, you got drunk, went into Tom's room with Sebastian, took your top off and allowed him to take a photo of you. He is now showing that photo in the rugby dressing room.'

Jess gasped and her hand flew to her mouth. 'No. No way.'

'Yes way.'

'But he said . . . he said . . .'

'What? That it was just for him? That it was private? And you believed him?'

'Yes, and I didn't want him to take the photo but I . . . I was . . . I . . .'

'You were drunk and you made a really bad decision, Jess, which is why I told you not to drink. Which is why I wanted you to come home with me that night, but you begged to stay.

You promised you'd behave, and Julie, my own sister, told me she'd look after you. That didn't work out so well, now did it?'

Tears welled in her beautiful blue eyes. 'But . . . Oh, no . . . He said it was just for fun, that he'd delete it. He said that . . . that I was so . . . beautiful . . . and . . . he was really into me . . . and . . . Oh, my God, did everyone see it?'

'Apparently the triplets tried to wrestle his phone from him before he could show anyone else, and Liam punched him in the face to defend your honour. Liam has now been dropped from the team. Julie and Harry were called up to the school and told that their son is a disgrace.' I laid it on thick. I wanted to drive home how her irresponsible choices had affected everyone. 'To protect you, Liam has refused to say why he punched Sebastian. We need to keep the story quiet. Louise is talking to some lawyer friends tonight so we can figure out how to get the photo and shut Sebastian down.'

'Oh, God, poor Liam, and Louise knows too . . . I'm so ashamed.' Jess began to cry.

Half of me wanted to hug her and half of me wanted to scream at her. I did neither.

'He has also been saying things about you, Jess, and I have to talk to you about it. I'm sorry, but I'm going to be blunt and you have to be honest. I can't help you if you lie. You've lied enough. He said that you've been giving him blow-jobs.'

'*What?*' Jess shrieked.

'Have you?' I asked. We were way beyond awkwardness. We were in survival mode now. I was not beating around the bush.

'No, Mum, I did not.'

'Are you telling me the truth?'

'Yes. I swear to you. He wanted me to, but I said no.'

Thank God.

'Did you have sex with him?'

319

'NO!'

'Jess, if you lie to me, I cannot help or protect you. Your actions have caused havoc already. I cannot ask my family to defend you if you're lying.'

Jess bawled into her hands. 'I never did anything but kiss him and he felt my boobs. That's it, Mum, I swear on my life.'

Looking at her, I knew it was the truth. 'Okay, I believe you, but don't you ever hide something like this from me again. And do not ever ask Julie to keep something like this from me. I am your mother, not Julie. I'm absolutely furious with her for not telling me. I don't know if I can ever forgive her.'

Jess looked at me in horror. 'Don't be cross with Julie, Mum. I begged her not to tell you. She wanted to, but I kept pleading with her.'

'She should have told me.' I was never going to change my mind about that. It was way too serious an incident for Julie not to tell me. Part of me thought she was probably afraid to tell me because it showed she had neglected to look after Jess.

'How could Sebastian do this?' she sobbed.

'I warned you,' I said quietly. 'Now, are there any other photos or videos we need to know about?'

'No.'

'Are you one hundred per cent sure?'

'Yes.' Tears rolled down her face. 'I'm so sorry, Mum,' she whispered. 'I'm so ashamed.'

Good. She should be. I felt sorry for her, but I also wanted her to feel bad so she would never, ever do anything like that again. But she was still a kid, as Louise said, and we do all make mistakes. I had, there was no doubt about that.

I reached over and pulled her in for a hug. 'It's okay, we'll sort it out.'

'How?'

'Louise is going to work out a plan and we'll go over it tomorrow.'

Jess covered her face with her hands. 'They must think I'm such an idiot and a slut.'

'Hey,' I said sharply, 'don't you dare call yourself a slut. You're a fifteen-year-old who made a bad decision. It does not make you a slut. You are a victim. Remember that.'

From behind her hands she asked, 'Does Dad know?'

'Not yet.'

She grabbed my hand. 'Please don't tell him, please, Mum.'

'I don't want to keep secrets from your dad, Jess. I'm seething that Julie kept this from me, so I know exactly how it feels.'

Jess began to hyperventilate. 'No, Mum, please . . . please, I'm begging you, I can't bear him to know. Dad's my absolute hero. I'd hate him to think I'm such a loser.'

The 'Dad's my absolute hero' stung a bit, but I chose to ignore it.

'Dad thinks I'm a princess. I don't want him to know I'm just a stupid slut.'

She was bawling now and struggling to catch her breath. I'd never seen her so upset. I felt completely conflicted, torn between what I wanted to do, which was to tell Jack and share the handling of this horrible situation with him, and not upset her further, which would make things worse. She looked like she'd have a nervous breakdown if I insisted on telling him.

'Calm down.' I rubbed her back. 'We'll keep this between us for now. But I'm not saying I won't tell him in the future. Now, I need you to listen to me carefully.'

'Thank you, Mum. Thank you, thank you, thank you. And thanks for looking after me and trying to fix my mess.'

I kissed her forehead. 'You're the most important person

in my life, Jess. I'd go to the ends of the Earth for you.' And I would. I'd take a bullet for Jess. I'd kill for Jess. I'd lie and steal for Jess.

'I love you, Mum.'

It had been a long time since she'd said that to me. I welled up. 'I love you too.'

We hugged again.

'And, Jess, remember, go for the nice guy next time. Not the overconfident jock, the nice, decent guy.'

'I am never, ever going out with anyone again. In fact, I'm going to be a nun,' she declared dramatically.

I laughed at that.

'Mum?'

'Yes?'

'I know things are stressful with Robert living here full-time and Pippa in rehab, and I'm really sorry I dumped this on you too.'

'Hey, now, hopefully everything will sort itself out when Pippa gets her life back on track.'

'I know it's been stressful for you and Dad. I heard you both fighting the other night and I got scared.'

'Of what, pet?'

'That you're going to break up again, and Dad will move out to live with Robert somewhere else.'

'Oh, Jess, please don't worry. Dad and I argue about things every now and then, but that's normal. All couples argue.'

'But it reminded me of when you broke up and I couldn't bear you to break up again. I love us being a family and I like Robert living here too, even though I know he's not your son and it's different, but I love my little brother so much.'

'Robert may not be my biological son, but I love him too. Sure, he's a little dote. And your dad and I are not going to break up. We're very happy together, and please don't worry if you hear us having little tiffs. It's completely normal. I love your dad and he loves me.'

I had no idea Jess was feeling so fragile about our relationship. I had underestimated how worried she felt about us not being strong enough to last. She had been crushed when we'd separated and ecstatic when we got back together. I realized I needed to be more mindful of her feelings, and that Jack and I had to make sure not to argue when she was around. Poor Jess, she hadn't had an easy childhood and I was hard on her. Probably too hard on her.

'Jess, I'm sorry if I'm tough with you. I know I push you to do well and all that, and if it gets too much, tell me. You've had a lot to deal with in your young life and I'm so proud of you. I don't tell you that enough, but I am.'

'Not much to be proud of today.' Jess smiled sadly. 'I know I've let you down a lot, Mum. I wish I was cleverer. I know I have to work harder and go to university and get a good job and be independent and self-sufficient so that I'm never homeless. And I know I'm never supposed to depend on a man for self-esteem or financial support.'

Yikes! I'd clearly banged on about all of those things far too much. Poor Jess, it was a lot of pressure. It wasn't fair of me to dump all of my insecurities and the mistakes I'd made on her shoulders. I needed to pull back and let the poor girl breathe.

I leaned over and held her hands. 'Jess, you are the light and love of my life. I am crazy proud of you. Please don't ever forget that. It was wrong of me to be so hard on you and put you under so much pressure. It isn't fair and it's my bad. As for the photo, we all make mistakes – God knows I've made a lot – but it's how we handle them that matters. I love you so much. I should tell you that more often too.'

'It's okay, Mum. I know you just want me to have the best

life possible and to be secure. I get it. But if you wanted to pull back a bit on the nagging, I'd be fine with that too.' She grinned.

We heard the front door open and the sound of Jack and Robert's voices. Jess and I wiped our eyes and went down to greet them. I watched Jess swing Robert around as he squealed with delight.

My heart was full. My beautiful family. We were by no means perfect. We had been battered and bruised by life. We had broken up, then Sellotaped ourselves back together. We had learned from our mistakes and we had found each other again. We might not all be biologically related, but we had love in abundance, and we had grit. We had weathered storms before and come out the other side. This storm would pass too and, all going well, Sebastian Carter-Mills would sink without a trace.

31. Julie

The weak early-morning light seeped through the curtains. I chewed on my already bitten thumbnail. It was almost down to the quick. The argument with Sophie had really thrown me.

'Harry!' I said. 'Are you asleep?' I poked him in the back.

'Well, if I was, I bloody well amn't now.'

'Was I wrong not to tell Sophie about Jess?'

Harry groaned. 'Julie, we went over this a million times last night, and my answer is still the same. You were trying to protect both Jess and Sophie. Your intentions were good but, unfortunately, because of the bloody photo, Sophie found out. Should you have told her? Maybe. It was a very tough one to call.'

'You should have seen her face, Harry. She was absolutely devastated. I'm really worried about her. She has so much going on with Pippa and Robert, and now Jess.'

'Sophie is stronger than she looks, you know that.'

'Yes, but –' My phone buzzed.

'Leave it. It's probably another snippy message from Victoria on the rugby WhatsApp.'

Ignoring Harry, I picked up my phone. It was too early for the rugby WhatsApp group. I was right. It was Louise on our Devlin sibling WhatsApp: *Have a plan. Meet for coffee in Fresh and Green 9 sharp. I have a meeting at 9.30.*

Then a text to me from Sophie: *We need to talk. Meet me at 8.30, b4 Louise.*

I quickly typed: *I'll be there.*

I turned to Harry. 'Sophie wants to meet for a chat. Then we're meeting Louise, who has a plan.'

'I hope it involves exonerating Liam and getting him back on the team,' Harry grumbled.

'Me too. If anyone can sort this mess out, Louise can. Okay, I'd better get moving.'

I hopped out of bed and had a long, hot shower, praying that Sophie had cooled down overnight and wasn't going to rip my head off again. I hated falling out with my sisters, or anyone for that matter. I hated confrontation of any kind. I was the peacemaker in the family so this was new territory for me.

I arrived early. There was no way I'd be late for this meeting. I ordered a latte and a skinny oat milk cappuccino for Sophie. She slipped into the café and sat opposite me. She looked almost as exhausted as I did, even with her perfectly applied make-up.

'I got you a coffee – don't worry, it's oat milk.'

'Thanks.'

'Look, Sophie, I'm sorry. I'm sorry you feel let down. I'm sorry you feel I hid something so monumental from you. I honestly thought I was helping Jess and not adding stress to your full plate.'

Sophie pursed her lips. 'But you didn't help me or Jess. If you'd told me, I could have had a proper conversation with Jess and she might have told me about the photo and we could have sorted it out. And I would have been vigilant about Sebastian and whether she was seeing him. Instead, you omitted to tell me and let me think that nothing had happened that night. Now there is a huge mess. I also think you didn't tell me because you knew that you'd messed up by allowing an underage couple to go into a bedroom in your house where anything could have happened. He could have raped her, Julie. They could have had consensual sex and she could be pregnant. He could have filmed her . . . So many horrendous things could have happened on your watch.'

I put my cup down. 'I know I said I'd keep an eye on her, but come on, Sophie, you saw how many guests I had. You knew it was chaos. I fully admit I took my eye off Jess and I feel absolutely terrible about it, but she made those choices herself.'

'I trusted my only child with you. She's all I have, Julie. She's my world. If anything happened to Jess, I would literally die.'

I tried not to get upset. I needed to stay calm. 'I know how much she means to you and all I can say is that I'm sorry. She was so upset and begged so hard for me not to upset you that I caved. I realize now that I shouldn't have. How is she?'

Sophie wiped a tear from her eye. 'She is absolutely devastated, mortified, ashamed and crushed. She feels so betrayed by that little shit. But we had an honest chat, and I think once we can get hold of that photo and control the story, she'll be able to move on. But we have to stop the photo going viral.'

'What did Jack say? I bet he wanted to go straight over and punch Sebastian.'

Sophie hesitated. 'I haven't told him.'

'What?'

'Jess begged me not to.'

Hang on. It was okay for her not to tell her husband because Jess begged her not to, but it wasn't okay for me not to tell Sophie? I bit my tongue. Now was not the time to point it out.

As if reading my mind Sophie said, 'That was why I asked to meet you. When I decided not to tell Jack, I realized it was for all the same reasons you didn't tell me. Because she pleaded with me not to, to protect her from being ashamed in front of her dad, because she couldn't bear him to think less of her, because he's so stressed about Robert and Pippa . . . So I realized I was being hypocritical. I'm still furious you didn't tell me, but I guess I understand your reasoning more now I've spoken to Jess.'

Relief flooded through me. Sophie was not going to hold this against me and she did see my point of view.

'I'm also sorry about Liam. I should have said that yesterday. I really appreciate his loyalty. He put himself on the line for Jess and I'll always be grateful.'

I was glad she'd said it because I'd been annoyed that she'd refused to acknowledge Liam's huge sacrifice. My son was devastated to have been dropped, and if Jess had been more sensible, none of this would have happened. Again, I decided to keep that thought to myself. Sophie and I were on thin ice. Best to keep things cordial. But I wasn't going to sugar-coat Liam's upset either.

'He's a great kid and he's crushed about missing the match. So are the other two. It's just a big mess really.'

'A big mess that I am going to resolve.' Louise came up behind us and sat down. 'I'm in shock that you're here so early, even before me. Have you made up?'

We nodded.

'Don't start without me.' Gavin rushed over with Lemon, thankfully asleep in her buggy.

When she had our attention, Louise told us the plan. She had spoken to fellow lawyers who specialized in criminal cases and they had given her the ammunition, terminology and lawyerly threats to use against Sebastian.

'So what I've decided to do is call in to Victoria today at lunchtime. Julie, you said the triplets mentioned Sebastian goes home on a Wednesday at lunchtime for a private training session in his gym. I'm going to ambush them both at home and catch them on the back foot. I will blind Victoria with legalese and, hopefully, she'll back down when she thinks her son is in danger of going to prison. If we give her time to get legal advice, she could turn on us. We need to act now.'

'Please can I come?' Sophie asked.

'Absolutely not. I'll be going alone, but you can listen in.' She grinned mischievously. 'Gavin?'

'Louise and I spoke last night and I told her she can use Lemon's baby monitor. Shania insisted we get the most high-tech one. Louise can stick the camera onto her briefcase.' He showed it to us: it was the size of a thumbnail and looked like a badge. 'We can watch and listen live while she takes Sebastian down.' He showed us the image on his phone from the camera on Louise's briefcase. It was crystal clear.

'I mightn't be able to angle it perfectly so you see her face, but you'll get the gist of it,' Louise said.

I'd gone from eating humble pie to being in a spy stakeout, and it was only ten past nine.

'Give her hell,' Sophie urged Louise.

'Don't you worry, I won't hold back. Right, I have to dash. I'll call you when I'm on my way to her house so we can connect up.'

Sophie hugged Louise tightly and thanked her.

I kissed her cheek and wished her luck. 'I know the photo is top priority but, if you can, could you try to get Liam back on the team?' I whispered in her ear.

She nodded. 'I'll do my best.'

Gavin high-fived her and made sure the camera was secure.

As she turned to go Louise said, 'Just to be clear, this goes no further. Our methods are not strictly legal and I could

329

lose my job. So, no one, not Dad or any of your spouses, gets to hear about this. This stays between us four. Understood?'

We all nodded. I crossed my fingers and prayed it would go well.

We sat in Gavin's Mini, which was parked around the corner from Victoria's house. We watched Louise get out of a taxi and march purposefully up the wide driveway and climb the steps.

I was holding my breath, and beside me, Sophie was shaking. Gavin was holding his phone screen up so we could see it.

The front door opened and a woman with an accent answered. 'Can I 'elp you?'

'Yes, I'm here to see Victoria Carter-Mills.'

'Does she know you are coming?'

'It's a very urgent matter regarding her son, Sebastian.'

Moving past the housekeeper, Louise entered the hall and closed the door behind her. All we could see through the camera were the housekeeper's knees and the marble tiles in the hallway.

'I told Louise to put the briefcase on her lap or beside her on the chair when she sits down. We'll see better then,' Gavin said.

'Who is it, Carmen?' Victoria's shrill voice rang out.

Her Lycra-clad legs appeared on screen.

'I'm sorry – who are you and what are you doing here?'

'I'm Louise Devlin, senior legal partner at Price Jackson, I'm here about a very serious matter involving your son, Sebastian, and an explicit photo of my client, a minor, that he has on his phone and was showing in the locker room. I'm sure you are aware that taking explicit photos of a minor without their consent with the possible intent of causing

330

harm is a serious criminal offence, which your son has now been accused of.'

'Excuse me?' Victoria's voice rose ten octaves.

'I think we should talk in private. It would be better for you that no one else hears what I have to say.'

Gavin whistled. 'Louise is such a badass.'

I could see Sophie was holding her breath. Her face was white. I nudged her. 'Breathe or you'll pass out.'

She exhaled. 'I didn't know I wasn't.'

We could see more of the hallway, then a door, a plush carpet and a couch. Next, we heard rustling and Louise put her briefcase on the couch beside her so now we had full view of Victoria's face.

'What the hell is going on?' She looked furious.

'What's going on, Mrs Carter-Mills,' Louise's voice dripped with disdain, 'is that your son took a photo of my fifteen-year-old niece Jessica Wells when she was drunk and has been showing it around the locker room. Exposing this private photo to anyone is an offence. A serious one. The law has clamped down in recent years on this kind of morally reprehensible behaviour since several young girls committed suicide after similar incidents.'

'Your niece?'

'Yes. I'm Sophie Devlin's sister. That's why I'm here, making this courtesy call to you before we press charges. This is your one chance to keep Sebastian out of the police station and court, not to mention the press. I'm sure they'd love nothing better than a story about a private-school boy taking photos of a drunk underage girl and showing them off to his teammates.'

'But – but hold on now, if it was consensual, why is Sebastian being blamed?'

'A private consensual photo is not meant for public

consumption, Mrs Carter-Mills. Surely you understand that. Jessica is distraught. We are extremely concerned about her. Sophie had to call in a doctor last night to sedate her. Her mental health is on the edge after finding out about Sebastian's betrayal.'

'Yes! Stick it to her.' I clapped.

'Thank God Jess is a lot more resilient than Louise is making out, but I'm loving this,' Sophie said.

'How do you know Sebastian showed the photo?'

'My three nephews are on the team with him. He showed them the photo of their cousin in the locker room. That was why Liam punched him. He was trying to protect Jess. Your son was also accusing my niece of performing oral sex, which did not happen. So we have the photo and the slander. Those are two very serious accusations against him. I have the paperwork all drawn up here in my briefcase. I have asked my colleague and friend Darina Fitzsimmons to take the case. You may know her name from her recent high-profile case. She got justice for a nineteen-year-old girl who was sexually assaulted by three members of a professional rugby team. No one thought she'd win the case, but she did. She is a very skilled and capable barrister with a particular interest in cases where young women have been wronged.'

'STOP!' Victoria held up her hands. 'I will not hear another word against my son. I want to see what Sebastian has to say about all of these vile accusations.' She left the room.

'If you can hear me,' Louise whispered, 'I think I have her on the back foot, but she's a tough nut.'

'Keep going,' Sophie urged, even though Louise couldn't hear us.

We heard a noise and then Victoria and Sebastian came into view. Sebastian was in training shorts and a T-shirt and was sweating.

'Sebastian denies all of it.' Victoria's chin jutted out. They sat down opposite Louise.

'Really, Sebastian? So you didn't take a topless photo of a very drunk fifteen-year-old Jessica Wells on the night of the twentieth of February in the home of Mr and Mrs Hayes? You didn't then show that photo to the triplets in the locker room last Friday? You didn't also boast about Jessica Wells performing oral sex on you? Because I have a number of witnesses who say that you did all of those things.'

'Yeah, who? Her cousins? They're making it up,' Sebastian said.

'The little shit,' Sophie hissed at the screen.

Louise laughed bitterly. 'Yes, her cousins, but we will be interviewing everyone who was in the locker room that day. There were seventeen boys. I have a list of their names with me. It's amazing how open boys are to telling the truth when they're faced with interviews by the police, testifying in court and being shamed in the press. You see, Sebastian, this is a case against a *minor*. Jessica is fifteen years old. These cases are taken very seriously by the police, the legal system and the public. Jessica is in a very fragile mental state, and we are all very concerned about her.

'As I'm sure you're aware, the police can track phones, download deleted photos and messages and generally track back every move you have made. So you need to think very carefully about how you wish to proceed. As I explained to your mother, I am going straight from here to the police. I have hired the best criminal barrister in the country, and as this case involves my niece, whom I love like a daughter, I will not rest until justice is done. I have come here today to see if we can resolve the matter before all of that happens. We'd all like to avoid a media circus in court, and I'm worried it would push Jessica over the edge. I don't think you'd want the death of a fifteen-year-old girl on your hands, would you, Sebastian?'

Victoria's chin dropped and she gripped Sebastian's arm. 'Sebastian, Daddy and I do not want anything or anyone to tarnish our family's reputation. Have you a photo of this girl?'

'Yeah, but she knew I took it.'

'Do you still have it on your phone?' Louise asked.

'Yeah.'

'Have you forwarded it to anyone via any means?' Louise kept up the questions. 'Think carefully before you answer, because if I suspect you're lying, I'll leave right now and bring the case against you.'

'Sebastian,' Victoria snapped. 'Your father and I can only help you if you tell the truth. What the hell happened? If this woman has her facts wrong, we will make her very sorry she ever darkened our door. But if she's correct here . . .'

'Christ, Mum! I didn't share it! I'm not one of those guys. Jeez, I liked her.'

'But you did show it in the locker room?' Louise reminded him.

Sebastian went red and looked at his mother. 'Well, yeah, but I only did it to wind the triplets up. I kind of knew Liam would lose it. He's got a bit of a temper, and I reckoned if he punched me or whatever, it would get him kicked off the team, and I figured he wouldn't say why he punched me because he'd want to protect his cousin.'

'The bastard! He had it all planned out.' I was shocked at his twisted manipulation. 'What sixteen-year-old boy thinks like that?'

'One with a mother like Victoria,' Sophie said.

There was a silence then, as Louise and Victoria digested what Sebastian had just admitted. I could nearly hear the cogs in Victoria's brain racing as she tried to figure out her next move. Louise let her stew and said nothing.

'Liam should not have hit my son,' Victoria said finally, but her voice was weak. She sounded as if she knew she was beaten.

'Really, Mrs Carter-Mills, you're going to talk about Liam behaving badly after your son has just admitted to using the topless photo of a *minor* to deliberately upset and entrap her cousin?' Louise's voice was cold and icy.

'Well I – I'm –'

'Let's move on.' Louise was in kick-ass lawyer mode. 'Sebastian, I need to see your phone. I need you to delete the photo and show me that the iCloud Photos sync function is turned on. We want the photo deleted from all your devices.'

'Do it,' Victoria barked.

Sebastian's hands shook as we watched him delete the photo, supervised by Louise looking over his shoulder.

'Now to the slander. I have witnesses telling me you spread untrue and vile rumours that Jessica performed oral sex on you.'

Sebastian squirmed beside his mother, who sat rigid, clasping her hands together tightly.

'Jesus, I feel sick.' Sophie covered her face.

'She has to get him to admit it,' Gavin said.

Silence.

'Sebastian,' Louise's voice had a threatening tone, 'answer the question or I'll leave and you can suffer the consequences of your actions.'

'I . . . like . . . I . . . I just said it for a laugh.'

'I see. So you think it's funny to lie about a young girl giving you blow-jobs? You think it's okay to slander a minor?'

Sebastian was sweating now from fear, not exercise. 'No, like, I didn't mean it. It was stupid.'

'Stupid is one word for it. Defamation is another. If you utter another word about my client, I will slap you with a lawsuit so fast your head will spin off. Is that clear?'

He nodded.

Victoria cleared her throat. 'Sebastian will not be mentioning the girl's name again. Have we finished?'

'Not quite. We still have the matter of Liam being dropped from the rugby team because of your son's conniving and underhand behaviour.'

'Well, violence is still unacceptable,' Victoria said quickly.

'I'm quite happy to head up to the school now. We can let the headmaster and coach decide what they want to do when they have the full story laid out in front of them. I believe the headmaster has a fourteen-year-old daughter. I'm sure he'd have a lot to say on the matter.'

'Christ, Sebastian.' Victoria held her head in her hands. 'What have you done?'

Sebastian threw his hands into the air. 'You and Dad keep banging on and on about how much you want me to play and how I should be on the team and not wasting my time on the bench. Dad is always going on about how he was the captain and star player and I need to work harder and get on the pitch and . . . I'm never good enough. Never. You keep pushing and pushing – you put so much bloody pressure on me all the time.' Sebastian burst into tears.

'Pathetic crocodile tears,' Sophie said.

'No sympathy for the little prick,' Gavin agreed.

I felt a little bit sorry for him. He was only a sixteen-year-old kid after all, and his parents clearly did push him all the time. Still, his actions had made my Liam cry, so ultimately my sympathy was short-lived.

Louise was clearly unmoved too. 'Right. In that case I suggest you contact Coach Long, tell him you're injured – you can figure out what injury you have – and that you're not fit to play.'

'Okay, we'll do that.' Victoria actually looked relieved. Louise had really done a number on her.

'Oh, I haven't finished,' Louise said. 'You will also inform Coach Long that you said something to Liam that was truly awful and that you deserved to be punched. You will not divulge what you said, obviously, but you will tell him that Liam deserves to be back on the team and that you, Sebastian, take full responsibility for what happened and are deeply sorry.'

'Fine,' Sebastian said, rubbing his eyes hard with his hands.

'When I receive notice from my sister that Liam has been reinstated in the team, I will shred the legal papers I drew up against you. Until then, they will stay on my desk. I recommend you head up to the school now and sort this out.'

Louise got up to leave, and Sebastian and Victoria's pale, shocked faces left the screen. We were back to looking at their knees.

'One final thing, Sebastian. Not only will Jessica's name never come out of your mouth again, you will never speak to her again or look in her direction. And going forward, I advise you very strongly to think before you act. This could have ended very badly for you.'

'I think you've said enough,' Victoria said, moving to stand in front of her son. 'Sebastian will speak to his coach immediately and this sorry episode will be over.'

We watched as Louise's feet walked back across the tiled hallway. In the background we heard Victoria scream, 'How could you be so stupid? You've ruined everything!' Then Louise's feet walked out through the front door and down the stone steps. We heard the door slammed shut behind her.

Louise came around the corner. Sophie darted out of the car and threw her arms around her. I followed with Gavin.

'Thank you, thank you, thank you, thank you,' Sophie gushed. 'You were magnificent.'

I leaned in for a hug. 'You were incredible, Louise. Honestly, I'm in awe.'

'The baddest badass in town!' Gavin high-fived her.

Louise grinned. 'I need a drink. It's a lot harder when you're emotionally involved. I wanted to do my best by Jess.'

'You did, you so, so did. I am for ever in your debt.' Sophie began to cry.

'Hey, you've all been amazing to me with Clara and Marco. I owe you all.'

'You were awesome, Louise, just . . . Wow.' I struggled to find the words and choked up.

'Ah, come on, no crying. I'll drive you to the pub and then I've to go home to Lemon, Shania has a meeting at three.'

I sat in the back of Gavin's Mini and breathed a huge sigh of relief. Jess was protected, Sophie didn't hate me any more and, hopefully, by the end of the day Liam would be back on the team. And it was all down to our eldest and finest sister.

32. Louise

Sophie bustled around the kitchen making us all coffee and offering us healthy snacks. Clara was in the playroom watching a movie.

Julie wrinkled her nose as she took a bite of one of Sophie's energy balls. 'It tastes like dust and cardboard smushed together with a bit of peanut butter.'

'They're healthy and good for you,' Sophie told her.

'Do you eat these, Jess?' Julie asked.

'No way!' Jess shook her head.

'Any chocolate biccies in the cupboard?' Julie asked.

Jess grinned. 'Yes, actually. Mum has a secret stash of chocolate fingers that Robert and I raid all the time.'

Sophie smiled. 'I noticed they were disappearing at a very fast rate.'

'Thank God for that. I need some sugar. Harry and I were up all night bursting with excitement about the game today. I'm knackered now.'

Jess handed her a packet of biscuits.

'How are you doing, pet?' Julie asked.

Jess blushed. 'I'm okay, thanks to you all having my back. Thanks again, Louise. Mum said you were unreal. I'm sorry that, well –'

'Hey,' I cut across her, 'you have nothing to be sorry for. Nothing. You made a little mistake. We've all made them. Unfortunately yours was with a complete jerk. But he won't be bothering you again.'

Sophie tucked Jess's hair behind her ear. 'Are you sure about going to the match today?'

'Don't do anything you don't feel up to. But if you do come, you know we're all there to protect you,' Julie added.

Jess looked at her mum. 'I want to go. I have to face him sometime and you'll all be around me.'

Sophie gave her a side-hug. 'We'll be a force field around you. I'm very proud of how you're handling this.'

'We all are. You're a fantastic girl,' Julie said.

'Hear hear,' I agreed. My phone pinged: a WhatsApp from Zoë. She only left voice notes because she was too lazy to type. I found them very passive-aggressive. 'This should be good. Listen to the crap I have to deal with every day.' I pressed play.

'Hey, Louise, so I just had a falafel sandwich from Pret and I feel really sick. Like, I'm dying here. So, I'm going to head home. I know you wanted me to finish that PowerPoint presentation for you but, like, I really think I'm going to throw up. I'll do it tomorrow, if I'm feeling better. Have a great day.'

'Wow, she sounds very perky for someone who's dying,' Sophie noted.

'This is the crap I have to put up with all the time. I really can't take much more.'

'Surely you can fire her,' Julie said.

'I told you, she's Walter's goddaughter and he dotes on her. You should see her with him – she plays him like a fiddle. Why are sixty-year-old men so bloody stupid?'

'How long more is she going to be with you?' Julie asked.

'Her internship is up in three months.'

'Don't let her get under your skin so much. Try to block her out. The end is in sight,' Sophie said.

'It's a pain when I have to go over all the work I give her

because she's so useless and unreliable. It makes my job even harder.'

'I'm good with PowerPoint. I could help you,' Jess offered.

'You're so sweet, but I'll figure it out. Thanks, though. Any word from Pippa? Her rehab ends this weekend, right?' I wanted to change the subject. Thinking about Zoë raised my blood pressure.

Sophie nodded. 'Yes. Jack says she seems to be sober on the phone and determined to get her life back on track. I guess we'll have to wait and see. I hope so, for Robert's sake. He misses her.'

'I hope so for your sake. It's not easy for you either,' I noted.

'He's a sweet kid and Jess has been amazing with him, but it does mean I have to do a lot of juggling.'

'I think stepkids are a blessing. Honestly, I love Christelle so much. She just slotted into our family so easily that I couldn't imagine anything different.'

Sophie bristled. 'It's different for me, Julie. Christelle was an adult when you met her, a well-adjusted, self-sufficient, independent young woman. She was amazing with the triplets and Tom. She enhanced your life. Robert is a little boy who is really upset about not seeing his mum and, judging by what we saw that day in the apartment, I'd say Pippa's neglected him. He acts up a fair bit, which is understandable, but he needs a lot of mothering and minding. It's a completely different situation from yours, and if Pippa doesn't stay sober, I could end up raising him full-time. I love him, but it's not always easy.'

'I'll help you more, Mum, I promise,' Jess said.

'You're a huge help already, sweetheart.'

Sophie was right. Her situation was vastly different from Julie's. Robert was a lovely kid, but he was very young and needy. You could see he was affected by having an absent mother.

Julie backed down immediately. She clearly did not want another argument with Sophie. 'You're right, it's not the same. I think Robert is very lucky to have you. I hope Jack appreciates it.'

'Dad thinks Mum's amazing with Robert. He's always saying so to her.' Jess jumped in to defend her dad.

'Good, because she is,' I said.

We heard a baby roaring.

'Gavin's here.' Julie giggled.

Gavin came into the kitchen with a howling Lemon, her little face all scrunched up. 'I need to feed her.' Gavin reached down for his hemp bag, which looked like something you fed horses from, and pulled out an odd-looking bottle.

'What's that?' I asked.

'It's a biodegradable baby bottle from this new company.'

'Is it made of cardboard?' Sophie looked shocked.

'Some kind of cardboard, yeah. Remember my friend Forest?'

We all burst out laughing.

'Who's Forest?' Jess asked.

'Forest, a.k.a. Brendan Smith, was Gavin's friend from our baby brother's brief stint as an eco-warrior. Gavin brought Forest home for dinner one time and he smelt so bad Mum got the air freshener out and sprayed all around his chair.'

We cracked up at the memory of Forest drowned in lavender-scented Glade.

'His smell lives on in our noses.' Julie chuckled.

'I mean, surely eco-warriors are allowed to use soap?' I added.

Gavin began to pour milk from a carton into the cardboardy bottle.

'Ha-ha. Anyway, Forest has started this company that makes really sustainable, biodegradable, climate-friendly stuff.'

We watched as the milk began to seep out of the bottom of the soggy bottle. Lemon roared to be fed.

'Mmm. Forest may need to rethink his new career.' I pointed to the milk dripping all over Sophie's countertop.

'Does he have a plan B?' Julie giggled.

'Gavin!' Sophie got a cloth to wipe the spilled milk.

'For fuck sake,' Gavin hissed as Lemon tried, in vain, to suck the milk down from the soggy teat.

'Jesus, will you give the poor child a proper bottle before she has a complete meltdown?' I ordered him.

'Fine.' He put the bottle down and handed a very cross Lemon to Julie, who cooed at her, while he rummaged around in his hairy bag. He pulled out a regular baby bottle. 'Shania made me pack this, just in case.'

'Shania is the best thing that ever happened to you,' Sophie remarked.

'I know,' Gavin agreed. He poured the remaining milk into the new bottle and held the teat to Lemon's lips. She guzzled it, making happy baby grunting and sucking noises.

We were enjoying the peace when we heard loud thumping on the kitchen door. 'JULIE!'

We all jumped. Harry was standing outside the kitchen door, red-faced. 'We need to go! This is a very big day for our sons.'

'Hi, Harry, how are the nerves?' Sophie opened the door.

'Not good. I've been awake since three a.m.' Harry rubbed his eyes. 'I don't think I've ever been this nervous.'

'Don't worry, Harry. With Liam back on the team they'll be unbeatable,' Jess said.

'That's sweet of you to say, Jess. I hope so, but the

opposition are strong. Their out-half has a ninety per cent kicking success rate.'

'You've lost me now, Harry.' Sophie laughed.

'Harry, the boys have done you and all of us proud, no matter what happens today,' Gavin said. 'And as far as I'm concerned, you're a legend for having raised triplets. I'm struggling with one kid.'

Harry patted Gavin on the back. 'It's not easy, mate, but you're doing a great job. It does get easier.'

'I don't know. I think it gets harder,' Sophie said.

'Me too,' I added.

'Jeez, thanks, sisters, kick a guy while he's down.'

'Oh, for goodness' sake, you have a beautiful, healthy child and a wife who is taking over the global fake-tan market. Stop moaning.' I refused to indulge his whinging.

'No wonder you're having problems with your intern if you talk to her like that.' Gavin held Lemon on his shoulder and burped her.

'Oh, please, I can't look at Zoë sideways without her mental health being affected when really she's as tough as old boots underneath her snowflake bullshit.'

'Much as I'd love to stay and debate how Louise handles her minions at work, I'd like to be on time to see my sons play in the most important match of their lives.' Harry rattled his car keys. 'Julie, will you for the love of God get into the car?'

'Keep your hair on. We're not going to be late.' Julie grabbed her woolly hat and scarf and the cashmere coat Sophie had made her buy. As 'mother of the captains', Sophie had told her, she had to look respectable and her old puffer jacket was not suitable. I agreed completely.

We all left, me to the office with Clara in tow, while the rest of my family piled into Harry's huge seven-seater car and headed off to the big match. To be honest, I was glad of the excuse not to go, I found rugby boring, plus it was cold and windy. Besides, I now had that bloody PowerPoint to add to my never-ending list of things to do.

33. Sophie

Jess and I sat in the very back, leaving the middle seats for Gavin and Lemon. I was happy to be in the back: Lemon was a projectile-vomiter and I didn't want my nice coat covered with baby puke.

'I presume Dad's coming.' Gavin strapped Lemon's car seat in.

'He said he'd meet us there,' I told him.

'Is *she* coming?' Gavin asked.

'I doubt it. I don't see Dolores slumming it on the cold sidelines of a rugby pitch,' I said.

'I bet she comes. She's like superglue to him,' Gavin said, as Lemon burped but thankfully didn't vomit.

'Bloody traffic! I knew we should have left earlier,' Harry huffed.

'Harry,' Julie said, using her calm voice, 'you need to take it easy or you'll crash the car. We're way ahead of kick-off.'

'I want to get my seat on the halfway line. I want to chat to the other dads, hear their thoughts and just soak up the atmosphere of this momentous day.' He swerved to avoid slamming into the car in front of us.

Jess was thrown against me.

'Harry, I know you're wound up, but you're kind of putting Lemon at risk here with the erratic driving,' Gavin called from the middle seat.

'He has a point,' I said, not wanting myself or my own daughter to die.

Harry glanced at us in the rear-view mirror and I watched

346

his hands begin to relax on the steering wheel. 'Sorry, folks,' he said. 'I didn't mean to frighten Lemon, or you two in the back.'

'Or me, I hope,' Julie said.

'I'm just so nervous for the boys. How lucky are we that Sebastian got injured and they're all playing?'

Jess nudged me in the back of the car. I winked at her. No one but Jess and my siblings knew the whole truth. Harry knew most of it, but not all.

'I want them all to play well and be happy with their performances. It's been a long week.'

'Don't worry, Liam will be fine. He's a pro,' Gavin reassured him.

Harry sighed. 'I'd hate for any of the boys to be disappointed with how they played. If the team wins, great, but what matters most to me is that the triplets don't come off beating themselves up about anything they did. I'm so proud of them. I never shone at anything in school. I was Mr Average all the way. It's . . . well, it's quite something.'

Jess whispered to me. 'I never realized Uncle Harry was so insecure.'

It was true: despite all the money he'd inherited and the lovely life they lived, Harry never seemed to feel he had achieved enough. I could see it when he was with Jack, in particular. Jack was privately educated and confident. Even when he'd lost everything, he'd bounced back and his confidence returned. But Harry had never had that inner belief. It made me sad for him and Julie. He was a brilliant husband and an outstanding father – he had raised sons who were loyal, brave and kind. I'd been blown away by how they'd jumped to Jess's defence. Hopefully, some day he'd realize that was enough, more than enough.

Julie patted his arm. 'Harry, the boys are lucky to have you as their father and their chief cheerleader. Let's just get there alive so we can enjoy it.'

Thankfully, Harry took his foot off the accelerator. We still arrived thirty minutes early and he got his perfect seat.

I put Jess between me and Gavin at the end of the row. Out of the corner of my eye I spotted Victoria arriving. She was wearing her fur coat but not strutting like a peacock as she normally did. She sat a few rows in front of us.

'I heard Sebastian's not playing. What happened, Victoria? Is he okay?' a parent asked.

Jess flinched. I reached out and held her gloved hand in mine.

'Oh, he got injured on Wednesday when he was training at the gym.'

'How?' a mum asked.

Victoria shrugged. 'He pulled a muscle doing weights or something.'

'Poor Sebastian. That's just awful for him.'

'These things happen.'

'You're taking it so well, fair play to you.'

'And Liam was reinstated. How do you feel about that after he punched Sebastian?'

I held my breath. What would she say? Jess squeezed my hand harder.

'For goodness' sake,' Victoria was brusque, 'boys have arguments all the time. They were probably all wired up and it just got a bit out of hand. It's over now.'

'Someone wants the conversation shut down,' Gavin said, under his breath.

'Hallelujah,' I whispered.

Jess let out a deep breath.

'It's okay, love. She's never going to say anything. It's over.'

'No, Mum, look.' Jess nodded to the corner of the pitch

where the subs were arriving to take their place. Sebastian was fake-limping. He glanced in our direction. Jess fixed her gaze on her lap.

'Put your head up, Jess,' Gavin said, 'and stare straight at him.'

Jess looked up at Gavin, then at me, and smiled. She raised her head and sat up very straight. She looked right at Sebastian, who had the sense to look down and limp quickly past.

'See?' Gavin said, smiling. 'He's a coward. Knew it.'

Jess nodded, but her hand was shaking in mine. I knew that had taken a lot out of her, but I was so proud of her for facing up to him. The first time was always the worst, but she'd done it and she hadn't flinched.

'Well done.'

She snuggled closer to me and I felt a surge of love for my brave girl.

Fifteen minutes into the match, there was no score.

'Where is Dad?' Julie asked.

'No idea. It's not like him to be late. He was mad keen to watch the match. I hope he's all right. Have you texted?'

'Look, he's here now,' Gavin pointed to the right, 'and *she*'s with him.'

We looked over to see Dad with a face like thunder and Dolores scurrying after him, dressed as if she was on an expedition to the North Pole. They shuffled their way over to us and sat down.

'Nice time-keeping.' Gavin poked the bear.

'Don't mention the bloody war,' Dad huffed. 'What have I missed?'

'No score yet. The triplets are playing really well. Liam had a brilliant kick to the winger for a try, but the winger knocked it forward. Leo put in a brilliant run down the middle, but got tackled before the try line. Luke is tackling everyone who comes near him,' Gavin said, filling Dad in. 'Why are you so late?'

'Because Dolores insisted we stop on the way to buy gloves because she forgot hers and it took her fifteen minutes to choose a pair,' Dad hissed under his breath.

Jess and I tried not to laugh. It sounded as if the shine on Dolores was dimming. Mum (a) would never have forgotten her gloves and (b) if she had, she would have put her hands in her pockets rather than be late for a game. She knew how much it meant for Dad to be on time for one.

'Lord, it's very cold here. It's like being in a wind tunnel.' Dolores pulled her coat closed around her.

'It's a cold day. What did you expect?' Dad sighed.

Gavin grinned at Jess and me.

'My grandson is a very gifted musician, so I'm used to going to indoor recitals.'

'Well, my grandsons are rugby stars and I go to all their matches, hail, rain or shine.' Dad was firm. 'And I will *not* be late again.'

'There is no need to speak to me so curtly, George. I'm just not used to the outdoor sports any more. But I'll get the hang of it, I'm sure. Now, what's going on?'

Dad cursed under his breath. 'I can't be explaining now. Just watch the game.'

'Well I never. Fine. I'll not say another word.'

'Good,' Dad said.

I leaned over. 'Dad gets a big agitated during the matches, Dolores. It's not personal,' I tried to reassure her.

'Will everyone just shush and let me concentrate?' Dad complained.

'You won't hear another peep out of me, I can assure you.' Dolores sniffed and gazed straight ahead.

'TRY!' Harry bellowed, as he and the whole Castle Academy stand stood up and roared.

'That's Liam! That's my grandson!' Dad shouted.

I have to admit I'd missed the try with all the Dolores distractions. But Jess and I jumped and cheered for our brilliant Liam. Luke and Leo rushed over to hug their try-scoring brother.

In the row in front of us, Harry threw his arms around Julie and they jumped up and down, fighting back tears. It was lovely to see. They were such a solid couple. They always had been. Through thick and thin they had supported and loved each other. Jack and I were less solid, but I hoped we'd weather whatever lay ahead.

I leaned over and squeezed Julie's shoulder. 'You must be busting with pride.'

'I am, I so am.' She had tears in her eyes.

Who would have thought that the crazy, hyper, naughty triplets would turn into brilliant, accomplished sports stars?

Freaked out by all the cheering, Lemon began to cry. Gavin tried to soothe her, but she was upset and her howling got louder.

'This is no place for a baby,' Dad said. 'It's too loud for the wee thing. Take her home.'

'She'll settle in a minute. I want to see the boys play.' Gavin tried to hush his daughter but Lemon's howls just got louder.

'For the love of God, give her a bottle or something to quieten her.' Dad was not letting up.

'So my baby's crying is bothering you, but it's okay for you to arrive late and have your girlfriend ask annoying questions at the top her voice?' Gavin hissed.

'Excuse me?' Dolores was apoplectic. 'George!' She glared at Dad, waiting for him to defend her.

'Why don't you take the baby and head off for a coffee?' Dad suggested to Dolores.

'You want me to take your son's baby after he insulted me? What do you think I am? The hired help?'

'You haven't stopped complaining about the cold, you're not interested in the game and the baby needs to be calmed down. Gavin wants to watch his nephews. What's the problem? It's a win-win.'

Dolores's face was now a bright shade of scarlet. 'I will not be ordered about to babysit your grandchild. I have never in my life been so insulted.'

Ignoring her, Dad turned back to the game and roared, 'Good tackle, Luke,' as his grandson thrust a giant on the other team to the ground.

Gavin shoved a normal baby bottle into Lemon's mouth and she stopped crying and began to suck.

Dolores stood up. 'I know when I'm not welcome or appreciated. I will not sit here for another minute.' She glared at Dad, waiting for him to beg her to stay.

'Dolores, this is a huge day for my family. Can you please just sit down and watch the game quietly or head off and I'll see you later?' Dad said, barely looking at her, his eyes glued to the pitch.

'Uh-oh,' Jess whispered. 'She's not going to like that.'

'I'm leaving.' She paused for a second to see if Dad reacted. He studiously ignored her.

Dolores stomped off in a rage.

'Well, at least she has a nice new pair of warm gloves anyway.' Gavin grinned and cheered on the boys.

Gavin and I did a discreet fist pump. Ding dong, Dolores the witch was gone.

34. Louise

Clara put on the top Marco had sent her. It was soft, had no seams and had blue and white Breton stripes. He had completely understood what she liked to wear and she loved it.

'I want to wear it so he can see it arrived in the post and I like it,' Clara said, as I set up my laptop for her Zoom call with Marco.

We dialled the number at the prearranged time of eight p.m. He answered immediately and his smiling face filled the screen.

'*Buonasera, tesoro,*' he said.

'*Buonasera*, Marco.' Clara smiled at the screen.

'Your smile is like the sunshine,' Marco gushed. 'It fills my heart with love.'

Clara giggled. 'How is the farm? How are the cats?'

'The farm is good. I am working very 'ard. I cannot wait for you to come and visit.'

'I want to come but I hate flying. It makes me anxious.'

'I know Claretta, but my mother is too old to come to Dublin, so can you thinking about it?'

'You mean, can I think about it?'

From behind Clara, I shook my head at him. I didn't want Marco putting any pressure on Clara to travel over. I had told him not to push it. I knew his mother was eighty-three and not in good health, but I didn't want Clara to feel any kind of guilt or obligation to have to go.

Catching my cue, Marco said, 'Yes. *Esattamente*. But you only do what is right for you. You only come if you are not frightened. I can come to you and you can talk to Mamma on the Zoom.'

He called his mother and she came shuffling into view.

'Claretta,' she cooed. *'Mia bellissima nipotina.'*

Clara greeted her grandmother in Italian. Anna then began to talk fast as Marco tried to translate.

'You're so beautiful and brave. I love you. I want to hold your face and kiss you before I die,' Marco translated.

Clara gasped. 'Is Anna going to die like Granny did?'

'No!' I jumped in. Jesus, Marco, come on.

'No.' Marco realized his mistake. 'She is healthy woman. She is excited to meet you. This is just her way of saying this.'

Clara's breathing settled and she chatted to Marco and Anna for another ten minutes before saying she was tired.

They blew her kisses and waved as I closed down the call.

Clara was quiet as I tucked her into bed. I knew my daughter like the back of my hand and I knew she was mulling something over in her beautiful, complicated mind.

'Are you all right, sweetheart?' I asked.

'I really, really want to go and see Marco and Anna. I want to see the farm and the olive trees and the animals – except the big dog.'

'I know you do, but if you're worried about the flight and the travel, then wait until you feel calmer about it. There's no rush. They're not going anywhere.'

'But Granny died. I thought she would be by my side for ever, but she's gone now. What if Anna dies too? I need to go over, Mummy. I have to be brave and just go.'

I held out my arms for her to snuggle into. 'Clara, you are only to do what you feel up to. If you decide you want to go, we will organize every detail together and I'll be by your side every step of the way.'

She pulled back and lay down. 'I think I will go. I'll decide for definite tomorrow.'

'Okay, sweetie.'

I turned her lights down low and left her to sleep on this big decision. I was worried it might be too much. But her relationship with Marco was developing so well and she really did seem to be getting closer to her father, so if she wanted to go, I would support her all the way.

The next day, Zoë arrived late, yet again, for our Tuesday meeting. The other four made it in on time, but not Zoë. I'd been awake half the night researching the best, least stressful and calmest way to get Clara to Italy and worrying about it overwhelming her. Marco was brilliant with her and understood her boundaries, but I wasn't sure Anna would. I was concerned that she might smother Clara and bring on a big meltdown.

Zoë swanned in, with a barely mumbled 'Sorry for being late,' sat down and proceeded to drink her take-out coffee. She was, as always, immaculately dressed in a designer trouser suit with a large Cartier watch sparkling on her arm. Clearly Mummy and Daddy had a lot of cash.

I glared at her.

'What?' she asked, as cool as you like.

'I'm confused. If you were running late, why did you stop for a take-out coffee?'

She giggled. 'OMG, Louise, if I don't have my coffee in the morning, I'm a monster.'

'Why are you late?' I could feel the other interns tensing.

'I was awake all night having, like, mini panic attacks, so I slept through my alarm.'

'What were you panicking about? Being late for work? Shoddy work? A bad attitude to authority?'

Zoë's eyes narrowed. She placed her coffee down. 'Actually, Louise, I have some personal issues I'm struggling with right now. My mental health is very fragile.'

'What issues?'

Her eyes widened. 'Personal ones that I have no intention of discussing.'

'What are you doing about it? Are you seeing a therapist? On anti-anxiety medication?'

'That is none of your business.' She looked at her fellow workmates for support, but they were all studying their notes with great intensity.

I stood up. 'Actually, it is my business because your very convenient mental-health issues are affecting my clients, my department and my reputation. So I need to know what you are doing to make sure you begin working to a level that is worthy of my team.'

She stood up and eyeballed me. 'I am working really hard. I was here until seven last night, wasn't I, Josh?'

Josh looked up. 'Uhm, about six thirty, seven.'

I began to clap slowly. 'Congratulations, Zoë. You didn't rush out of the door at five, like you usually do. You deserve a promotion.'

'There's no need to be a bitch.'

I froze. 'Excuse me? What did you call me?'

Zoë reddened. 'You're being totally unfair and kind of a bully right now.'

A red mist descended on me. I was just so tired of looking at that face lying to me and using mental health to do it. It was wrong and cynical, and I had reached my limit.

Leaning across the table towards her, I roared, 'I am so sick of your bullshit, your whining and the way you throw mental health around as if it's a cold. There are people in this office dealing with serious issues, people who have real problems, but who still manage to make it in on time and do their work. You are an overindulged, entitled, pathetic excuse for a young woman. Your attitude stinks. You don't have mental-health issues or anxiety. The only things you have are a shoddy attitude, a complete self-obsession and a pathetic attitude to work. It's disgusting the way you use mental health so casually to excuse being hung-over, lazy or late. You are insulting and demeaning the people, like my own daughter, who truly struggle. You need to take a long, hard look at yourself and figure out if you want to continue going through life being a selfish, self-centred, pathetic excuse for a human being. You will go nowhere and achieve nothing with your attitude. Now get out of my sight and do not come back to this office.'

Zoë's eyes flashed. 'How dare you speak to me like that? I'm going straight to HR and, FYI, I recorded your hate speech.' She waved her phone at me triumphantly.

'Run along, Zoë. Go and tell HR about your mean boss.' I kept my voice calm, but my mind was racing. What was the legal position of filming without my consent? Could the recording cause me trouble?

I got an answer to that question very quickly. At midday my assistant, Jenny, came into my office and shut the door behind her.

'Louise, I've just received a call asking you to report to the HR office immediately.'

I looked at her. 'Okay. I'll just finish this and head over.'

She hesitated. 'Just to let you know, one of the girls over there gave me a heads-up. There's been a serious complaint made against you. I'm just saying that so you're prepared. It sounds like there'll be a few of them waiting to talk to you.'

I sighed. 'Thanks for the info. I appreciate it. I know what it's about. I'm sure you can guess that Zoë's involved.'

Jenny nodded. 'No surprise there, it's been coming for a while, hasn't it?'

'Yes, it has. Right. I'll go and talk to them, see what's happening.'

I got up, smoothed my dress, then walked purposefully down the hallway. I was aware of all eyes on me as I went by – obviously word had got round that there had been a drama between me and Zoë. I held my head high and looked at no one.

Outside the door of HR, I took a deep breath, then rapped smartly.

'Come in.'

I opened the door and stepped inside.

Julie handed me a coffee laced with whiskey. 'So, you were asked to take a day or two off to cool down?'

'HR said the video was "problematic", and as I had no evidence of Zoë calling me a bitch and bully, it looked one-sided. They told me to work from home for a few days while they try to figure it out.'

'That sneaky little bitch.' Julie handed me a brownie.

'I shouldn't have lost my temper. It was unprofessional.'

'You've a lot on your plate. Give yourself a break.'

'Yes, but I still have to be unflappable in work.'

Marion came through the kitchen door holding up her phone. 'Louise, you're trending on Twitter.'

'What?' Julie and I looked at her.

'There's a video of you online losing your shit.'

'Oh, my God, she posted the video,' Julie gasped.

I felt sick – the thought of her doing that hadn't even entered my head.

'You have about fifty per cent support. Pro you is hashtag mentalhealthisreal and the ones against you are hashtag bossbully. They're tearing into each other, one side saying you were bang on, the other saying you can't talk to anyone like that in a work environment.'

I put my face in my hands. This was bad. It was really, really bad.

Julie tutted. 'Don't worry. Marion said lots of people support you.'

I groaned. 'Julie, no one is going to hire a lawyer who is videoed losing her temper with an intern. This is a disaster.'

'I think you come across like a total badass. I'd want you to represent me,' Marion said. 'I've been on happy pills for years, and it pisses me off to think some spoiled cow is faking problems and throwing anxiety around like it's a fucking joke.'

I took off my glasses and put them on the countertop. 'I'll have to get a cease-and-desist, but it's too late. It's out there now. I may be looking for a new job.'

'But is this not a good thing?' Julie said. 'I mean, Zoë has launched a private company matter into the public domain. Is that not against her work contract?'

I shrugged. 'You may be right, but you know how law firms are. They hate adverse publicity of any kind. So, yeah, it's a strike against her, but she only posted a video. I'm the one shouting and roaring. I'm the one who lost control. She'll play the victim card and Walter is so besotted with his precious goddaughter he'll probably believe her.'

'It's a shit show,' Marion said, staring at her phone. 'This video has caught fire. It's all over Instagram now too. That young one has royally screwed you.'

'Okay, let's look at it from a different perspective,' Julie said, desperate, as always, to make things better. 'Why don't you use this incident as a sign that you need to take some time off? You've had a really tough year with Mum and Marco and all of the things that have happened.'

'I have a mortgage to pay and a daughter to raise.'

'I know that, but come on, Louise, you could take a few months off. You have plenty of savings. I think it would be good for you,' Julie insisted.

'I think you should have your own show, like *Judge Judy*, or you could be the new host of *The Apprentice*,' Marion said.

'I don't think so.' I fiddled with my cup. This was bad. A video of me eviscerating a junior on my team was not a good look. Damnit, why hadn't I controlled my temper? She had been niggling me for months and I should have managed her better from the beginning. But I knew I hadn't been firing on all cylinders in work for the last while. I was not the usual Louise, all over everything, putting out fires and dealing with difficult employees. I had let myself down and now Zoë had the upper hand. I was furious with myself. 'Before I go home and think this through, distract me with news. How are the triplets? Are they excited about the final?'

Julie filled Marion's cup with whiskey. 'Not as excited as their father but, yes, they're up to ninety. I can't wait for it to be over. It's consumed our lives. It's wonderful, but I've had enough now. I don't want to hear another word about rugby. And, truth be told, I'm also very glad that I won't have to wear the scratchy hat and scarf ever again and I can leave the WhatsApp group.'

'How about you, Marion? What's new in your life?' I wanted distraction and Marion was usually good at providing it.

'Actually, my car crash of a life is not too bad at the moment. Greg has paid his child support without me having to chase him for the last two months and . . . I have a boyfriend.' She grinned at us. 'And he's nice and kind and lovely to me.'

'That's great.'

'A farmer called Seamus,' Julie said.

'Where did you meet?' I asked.

'He was one of my sex-line callers.'

'Right.' I was lost for words.

'All he ever did was chat about his cows and his sheep, life and nature, and we got to know each other really well. He never seemed to want the dirty talk. Anyway, after six months, he asked me out. So, I met him and he isn't a hunchback, he doesn't have a face like a slapped fish or a deformity or erectile dysfunction. He has all his own teeth and a fairly decent body. He's attractive and seems normal.'

'He's mad about her.' Julie beamed at her friend.

'Good for you.' I meant it. Marion was a lot to take, but she'd been through the mill and she deserved happiness.

'Ah, he'll probably turn out to be a serial killer and you'll find my head in his fridge and my tits in the freezer, but for now, it's nice.'

I fished my phone out of my bag to check the time. I had forty messages, five missed calls from HR and one from Walter. I held it up to show them.

'It looks like the video has made it into the office. I have to go and sort this out, if I can. Thanks for the coffee.'

Leo burst through the kitchen door. 'Mum, Louise is trending on TikTok.' Then he saw me at the counter. He high-fived me, looking very proud, to my surprise.

'This is gold, Auntie Louise.'

'What are people saying?'

Leo stopped scrolling. 'Well ...' he hesitated '... it's mixed.'

'Give it to me straight,' I said.

'It's not good. People don't like that you accused her of faking mental-health issues. It's kind of a trigger word on TikTok. It's a bit of a pile-on.'

Julie hugged me tightly. 'Don't worry, Louise. You did nothing wrong. People will see that. This is just a knee-jerk reaction to the initial post. People will see your side. We're all Team Louise here.'

'I think it's kinda cool. There's a meme!' He laughed and turned his phone to show me.

It was me shouting, 'I am so sick of your bullshit,' with fire coming out of my mouth.

This was not good. Clients could see it. My headache was getting worse, I needed to go home. I stood up and grabbed my handbag.

Julie walked me out. 'It'll be okay. It's a storm in a teacup. It'll blow over. Let me know if I can do anything.'

'Thanks. I will.'

I had a distinct feeling there was nothing anyone could do. I was going to have to weather this storm alone and I had no idea what the fallout would be.

35. Sophie

Jess walked towards the car, beaming. She was holding a piece of paper. She jumped into the front seat and handed it to me. 'I got an A in my English essay, Mum!' she said. 'Mrs Power said it was the best essay she's read in ages. I've never got an A in English before. It feels amazing. It's my birthday gift to myself.'

I was delighted for her. 'Well done, Jess. I'm really proud of you.' And I was: I was ridiculously proud of her. 'But do you still want all the birthday presents I've wrapped, ready to give you on Saturday?'

She laughed. 'Hell, yes, I still want those, all of them!'

'But definitely not a party, even just a few girls over?'

Jess shook her head. 'No. I just want you, me, Dad and Robert.'

'Okay, pet, whatever you say.'

I glanced down at the essay. The title was 'My Patchwork Family'.

'Oh, is this about us?' I asked.

She nodded. 'But don't worry, I didn't say anything about Pippa and rehab and all of that. It's just about how we're a mixture of two families rolled into one. It's about how Robert is my full brother to me, even though he's technically a half-brother, and how having a stepmum wasn't easy for me and being a stepmum isn't easy for you, but how amazing you are with Robert. I said you treat him like your own son and protect him and comfort him the way you always protect and comfort me.'

'Oh, Jess.' I didn't know what to say – I was blown away.

'You do, Mum,' Jess said. 'You've always been great with Robert, but since Pippa went to rehab you've been incredible.'

'Thanks, love. I just feel really sorry for him. He's had a tough time, tougher than we realized.' I'd been love-bombing Robert since his mum went into rehab. The poor kid needed to feel secure, safe and loved. He'd been acting up a lot. His little head was confused and he was upset.

Jess put on her seatbelt and I drove out of the school car park.

'Do you think Pippa will stay sober now?' she asked softly.

Pippa was out of rehab and, so far, every time she had turned up to the house to visit Robert, she had been sober and together. She looked very fragile, though. She'd lost a lot of weight and was very drawn. Jack insisted on being there when she came to see their son and watched her like a hawk. He'd been so upset by what we'd witnessed at Pippa's apartment that he was determined to make sure he protected Robert at all costs.

'I'm praying Pippa stays sober, but I'll be honest with you, I'm not sure she will. She seems very vulnerable, and she's lost her purpose, her confidence and her job. Somehow, she'll have to find a way to build herself up again. We'll help her, of course. I've already asked Quentin to see about getting her some catalogue modelling work. We'll just have to take it a day at a time and see.'

'Mum?'

'Yes, pet.'

'I never said this to you, but I want to say thanks for not falling apart when you broke up with Dad, and for being so brave, going out and getting a job, paying the rent and looking after me. I know it must have been a total nightmare, but you were amazing.'

I pulled the car over, put my head down on the steering wheel and began to bawl my eyes out. For so long I'd wanted Jess to acknowledge what I'd done for her. I'd wondered if she'd ever know how deep I'd had to dig not to fall apart. I'd wondered if she'd noticed how hard I'd worked to keep us afloat. All I wanted was my beautiful daughter to see what I had done and to recognize the courage it had taken. It meant the world to me.

'Jesus, Mum, what's wrong?'

'No . . . no . . . I'm just . . . I'm just so happy that you . . . that you said that.'

'Well, then, why are you crying your eyes out?'

Because I was a middle-aged woman whose life had turned out to be very different from what I'd imagined, but who, after a few really rotten years, was happy with my lot. I had a man I loved, a daughter I adored and a stepson I loved more every day. I had my sisters and Gavin, and I had Dad, who was around a lot more now that he'd broken up with Dolores. I'd had a brilliant mum to show me the way. I was lucky, very, very lucky.

I took a deep breath and hugged Jess. 'Until you have a child of your own, you'll never know how much you can love another human being. You are my everything, Jess. And all the strength you see in me, it's in you. I see it.'

'Stop,' Jess cried out. 'You'll make me cry.'

We hugged, and when I had finally stopped crying, we headed home.

The doorbell rang and I went to answer it. It was Pippa. She wasn't due to visit Robert today. She was dressed nicely, make-up on and hair done. She looked more like her old self.

'Hi,' she said. 'I know it's not my day, but I really needed to see him. Can I come in?'

Jack and his lawyer had been very clear. Pippa was allowed to visit only at allocated times when Jack was in the house. But she was a mother who missed her son. I couldn't turn her away and, besides, I was there in case anything went wrong.

'Please, Sophie.'

'Okay, come on in. He's in the TV room.'

Pippa went in, said hi to Jess and hugged Robert, who was thrilled to see his mother. Jess and I left them alone but kept the door open and hovered outside.

'I didn't know you were coming today. Daddy said you were coming on Sunday when we all go to the zoo, you, me and Daddy together,' Robert said. 'Daddy said we can go and see the new baby elephant.'

'I wanted to see you because I miss you, baby.'

'I miss you too, Mummy. Can I have ice cream on Sunday?'

'About Sunday, sweetie, there's been a slight change of plan.'

What? What did she mean 'a slight change of plan'? Jack would go nuts. Robert had been looking forward to it all week. I'd spent hours the night before looking up all the animals and making a list of the ones he most wanted to see and working out where they were on the zoo map.

'Oh, no. He'll be crushed.' Jess put her hand to her mouth.

'What does that mean, Mummy?' Robert's little voice sounded so young and innocent. How could she let him down again?

'It just means that we'll go to the zoo another day.'

'But I want to go on Sunday. You promised.' Robert's voice began to waver.

'It's okay, darling, we will definitely go to the zoo, just not this Sunday. I have to go away for a few days.'

Go away where? Was she drinking again? Was she going back to rehab? What the hell was going on?

366

'I want to go on Sunday. You said we were going. Why can't we go?'

'Well, you know Mummy has been sick?'

'Yes, but you're all better now.'

'I am, but I'm tired and I need a little holiday. My friend has invited me to go away to the sun for a few days. I think Mummy deserves a little holiday, don't you?'

Oh, my God, how could she? How could she let her son down like this? What friend? What holiday? How dare she make this all about her? He was a six-year-old kid, who needed his bloody mother to show up.

'I suppose so.' Robert's voice quivered.

Jess shook her head and whispered, 'How can she do this to him?'

'Don't look sad. Be happy for Mummy. When I come back from my holiday, I'll be feeling good and we can go to the zoo then.'

'But I want to go this week.'

'I understand, but I can't go. I need a break, Robert. I'm exhausted. Don't make Mummy feel bad.'

'Sorry, Mummy.'

That selfish bitch, crushing his little heart, then making him feel guilty for being disappointed. Enough of this crap.

I walked into the room, Jess hot on my heels, and glared at her. 'Holiday, Pippa?'

'Yes.' She flicked her hair back.

'Who's the friend?'

'None of your business. I have to go now. Bye, my love.' She hugged Robert, whose arms hung limply by his sides.

'Jess, stay with Robert, please. I'll walk Pippa out.' I closed the TV-room door behind us. Turning on her, I hissed, 'How could you do that? He was so looking forward to the day out with you and Jack.'

'He's fine. I'll bring him next week and it's really none of your business.'

'It is my business, Pippa, because I'm the one who'll have to pick up the pieces of his broken heart when you swan off on your holiday.'

She rolled her eyes. 'It's a trip to the zoo, Sophie, not his graduation ceremony.'

'He's a kid who has been through a lot lately,' I reminded her. 'Please don't let him down again. It's just not fair.'

She swung around. 'Do not tell me how to raise my son. I don't tell you what do to with Jess, so back off with Robert.'

'You don't have to deal with the fallout from this. *I do*,' I hissed. 'I'll be the one consoling him because his mother put herself first, again.'

'Oh, please, stop with the Saint Sophie crap.'

'I'm no saint, Pippa, but I try to be a good mother. Just change your plans and go away next weekend.'

'I can't.'

'Why not?'

'Because Vincent can only go this weekend.'

I stared at her in shock. 'You got back with that jerk? I thought you'd left all that behind?'

'He missed me. He begged me to come back to him and he swore he'd leave his wife this time.'

Dear God, was she really that stupid? 'Come on, Pippa, you know that's bullshit.'

'I need this.' She bit her thumbnail. 'I need to feel – to feel like I matter. I need to feel loved. I hate myself. I hate my life. I need some fun.'

I had to make her see. 'Pippa, you'll build your confidence back up by being a good mother. You'll find joy in Robert. He's a brilliant kid. Spend more time with him. He adores you.'

Pippa fished around in her oversized tote for her car keys. 'It's not enough,' she said quietly. 'I know it should be, but it isn't.'

It sounded so cold it took my breath away. I had never heard any woman ever say those words.

I put my hands on her shoulders. 'Pippa, look at me.'

She avoided eye contact.

'Please, please, don't do this. Getting back with Vincent is not good for your recovery. Think of your son. What we saw that day in your apartment was distressing, to say the least. You have a beautiful child. Fight for him, Pippa. Get well for him. Love him, engage with him. He will give you so much joy.'

'I can't do it.' Tears rolled down her cheeks. 'I just can't. I don't want to be tied down. I don't know how to be a mother. I resent him. That's the truth, Sophie. I know I'm evil and heartless for saying that, but I do. I'm a shit mother and I'll only ruin his life. He's better off without me. You're a good mother. He'll be happy and safe with you and Jack. I'm not good enough to be his mother. He deserves a happy life and he'll have that with you guys.'

I stood there in absolute shock. Was she really saying that she was giving up? Was she giving up her son? My brain couldn't even process it.

She turned and walked towards the front door. I called after her, 'What am I supposed to tell Jack?'

She returned, her face streaked with tears. 'Tell him I'm sorry, but I need more. Being a mum isn't enough. I realize that makes me some kind of freak and a monster, but it's the truth.'

'Please, Pippa.' I was crying now too. 'Robert needs his mum. You'll regret this. Please.'

She shook her head. 'I can't, Sophie . . . I just can't. I've made my decision. Jack can have full custody. I'll visit, but I'm not made to be a mum. I'm sorry.'

She walked away from me and from her son. I was now officially going to be a full-time stepmum to a broken-hearted little boy.

36. Julie

The boys stood in their school blazers, arms around each other as I took a photo. They looked so handsome and grown-up. Where had my three tearaways gone? I was looking at three almost-sixteen-year-olds. They were all much taller than me and had developed broad shoulders from training.

'I'm so proud of you.' My voice shook.

'Oh, Mum, don't start crying,' Luke said.

'It's supposed to be a happy day,' Liam reminded me.

'We need to go.' Leo was the most nervous.

Harry came into the hall and handed the boys three Tupperware boxes. 'Your protein snacks.'

'Thanks, Dad.'

'Now remember, Rockford Manor are very strong upfront. Don't let them boss you around in the scrum.'

The triplets grinned. 'It's okay, Dad, we've got this. Coach has told us what we need to do.'

Harry nodded. 'Right, then. Let's get you into school.'

'Wait!' Christelle and Kelly came up from the basement in their pyjamas, still jet-lagged from their South American trip. 'Good luck from us.' They handed the boys bead bracelets. 'They're made with huayruro seeds from our trip to Peru and are believed to bring positive energy, love, happiness, and good fortune to the person who wears them,' Christelle said.

The boys looked at the red and black beads and reluctantly put them on.

Christelle laughed. 'You don't have to wear them, just put them in your kitbags for luck.'

'Okay.' They looked relieved and stuffed them into their bags.

'We'll be there to cheer you on,' Christelle said. 'Good luck.'

They piled into the car, Tom following in their wake, as always, and Harry drove them to school.

We sat together: Harry, me, Marion, Gavin (and Lemon), Dad, Louise, Sophie, Jess, Jack, Robert, Christelle, Kelly and Clara with her headphones on.

Marion pulled off her hat and scratched her head.

'Sorry, but these are the worst fucking hats ever. Did the sheep have nits? They're the itchiest things. I'd take out a loan and pay for Victoria's posh cashmere not to have to suffer these needles on my head.'

'They're made of Irish wool, the same wool that Aran sweaters are made of. Bespoke, hand-knitted by the local community.' Sophie was still defensive about her sourcing of the hats.

'No wonder they're awful, Aran sweaters are itchy as fuck. Only bog-men wear them. I'd say Seamus has a few in his wardrobe.'

Sophie glared at Marion, while Jess giggled.

'Can we please focus on the match?' Dad said.

'How's single life, George?' Marion asked.

'Oh, he's not single,' Gavin said. 'He's already got a new bird. I caught them having coffee yesterday when I called in.'

'Pat is not a new *bird*. She is a friend who called over for a cup of coffee.'

'Pat O'Loughlin from the golf club?' Sophie asked.

'Yes.' Gavin smirked.

'Careful, Dad, you may cause a serious cat-fight up in the

golf club if you keep dating women from the same pool,' I warned him.

'I know of a very good sex line if you just need to, you know, release some tension,' Marion chuckled.

'Christ almighty, will you all put a sock in it? I'm trying to watch my grandsons.'

'Pat's nice. I always liked her,' Sophie said.

Dad stood up and forced me to swap places with him. 'I'm sitting beside the only sensible person here, Harry.'

'Thanks a lot, George,' Jack said.

'You're welcome to come over here too.' Dad acknowledged Jack, who stood to move up beside the men, with Robert.

'I want to stay with Jess and Sophie,' Robert said.

'Okay, buddy.' Jack sat in beside Dad.

Liam caught the ball and passed it to Luke, who ran the length of the pitch and offloaded, at the last minute, to Leo, who dived over the line.

'TRY!' Harry roared. 'Julie! Did you see it?'

I did – I had seen it. For once I hadn't been chatting or distracted. I had seen my three sons score a beautiful try.

We jumped up and down and cheered loudly. I thought my heart would burst with pride.

'Well, now, Anne would have loved to see this,' Dad said.

We all smiled. Mum would have loved to see the boys shine. She'd have told everyone who'd listen about the try.

'She's watching and cheering.' Louise squeezed Dad's hand.

'And telling everyone up there that the boys got their sporting ability from her,' Sophie added.

We all had tears in our eyes.

I reached over and hugged Dad. 'I miss her too,' I said.

Lemon began to bawl and Dad looked like he was going to have a hernia at the noise. Jess offered to give her a bottle. Gavin gratefully handed her over.

Two rows up, Victoria said, 'Who brings a baby to a rugby match, really and truly? The crying is distracting everyone.'

'A devoted father,' Sophie replied.

'A supportive uncle,' Louise said loudly.

'A proud modern man,' Dad said.

Gavin stared at him open-mouthed. 'Did you hear that?' he whispered to me.

'Yep, modern man no less.' I grinned.

'Your gimpy kid isn't even playing, so what are you moaning about?' Marion shouted at Victoria.

I looked at Jess, who giggled. I winked at her.

The match continued at a ferocious pace. We were ahead. Then Rockford Manor scored two tries.

At half-time we were down by three points. Harry was chewing his lip. The teams trooped off the field and we all sat back in our seats, breathing normally again.

'How are things in work now, Louise?' Sophie asked.

'The video trended for only a day, and then it quietened down, thank God. But I've been told I have to go on an unconscious-bias training course.'

'What? That's ridiculous! You called Zoë out on being a lazy, incompetent employee. That's your job as a boss,' Sophie said.

'Believe me, I agree with you, but HR said I have to do this. It's more for optics than anything else, to show I'm willing to grow and learn.' She made a vomit face.

'What happened to Zoë?' Gavin asked.

'She's been reprimanded for videoing me and posting it online, which she denies. Apparently, her "friend" took her phone and posted it. She's been moved to a different department, permanently, but Walter won't get rid of her.'

'That's crazy,' I said. 'But at least you won't have to deal with her.'

'Well, I bumped into her in the kitchen yesterday and she was as cool as you like, "Hi, Louise, how are you enjoying your notoriety?"'

'She didn't?' Sophie was shocked.

'Oh yes she did. I wanted to punch her smug face.'

'I don't know how you controlled yourself. I'd have walloped her,' Marion said.

'Louise, you don't need that stress in your life.' I felt really bad for my sister. Although she was putting on a brave face, I knew she was really shaken by the whole fiasco. Louise had spent her whole career building up a reputation as unflappable, tough and formidable. This video of her had tarnished all of that. The triplets said the pile-on was unreal, threats and everything. I know she was trying to stay off social media, but it had to have had an effect.

Louise sighed. 'It's made me reassess working there. Let's be honest, my position and my reputation have been badly damaged. There are some people who will no longer speak to me. They've sided with Zoë, think I'm a bully and refuse to acknowledge me. Even people I got on well with before. It makes it very difficult. I need to think about my next move.'

'Would you consider leaving?' I was surprised. Louise had worked so hard and was a senior partner at the firm.

'Maybe. And not just the firm, but from securitization.'

I was never totally sure what 'securitization' meant, but I knew Louise was good at it.

'What would you do instead?' Sophie asked.

'I don't know, to be honest.'

'Legal aid?' Christelle suggested. 'You'd be brilliant.'

'Maybe.'

'Or something completely different?' Kelly suggested. 'What would your dream job be?'

'I've only ever wanted to be a lawyer,' Louise said, 'but the shine has gone. I've achieved everything I wanted to achieve. But if I'm not a lawyer, who am I? I also have a daughter who may never be financially independent. It's a lot of responsibility.'

'Marco can help with that now,' I said.

'No. He's not giving Clara one penny. If he does, he can claim rights. No, I'm her financial stability. I just need to figure out what I want to do next.'

'I think you'd be brilliant in academia,' Gavin said. 'You do like to lecture people.'

'I can totally see that,' I said. 'A law lecturer.'

Louise paused. 'That's not the worst idea. Maybe.'

'The hours would be much better and you'd have more time with Clara and great holidays,' Sophie said.

'Speaking of jobs, I'm going to work part-time with Shania,' Gavin announced. 'I'm getting some help with Lemon in the mornings. Shania is out-the-door busy and she needs my input. I'm actually looking forward to it. I love Lemon, but the days are long and I know everyone says things have changed and stay-at-home dads are the norm, but they're not and we're still treated like pariahs.'

'Good for you,' I said.

'Part-time is the perfect solution,' Sophie added.

'Yeah, and Shania misses Lemon, so if I can help her out more in work, she'll get more time with Lemon, so it's a win-win.'

'It's never easy,' Sophie said. 'Whether you stay at home, work part-time or full-time, it's still a constant juggling act, but you guys will work it out.'

'Kids are a fucking drain emotionally and financially,' Marion said.

'Yes, but they're also wonderful and worth it.' Sophie beamed at Jess and Robert.

I was very proud of my sister and how she had embraced Robert. Sophie had a huge heart.

'Okay, silence again, here they come,' Dad said.

The second half got under way.

'*Nooooooo!*' Harry, Dad and Jack shouted.

Rockford had just scored, from their first touch. We watched over the next thirty minutes as the match slowly slipped away from Castle Academy.

Then it was over.

I cried as I watched my three brave sons sobbing their hearts out on the pitch. They hugged each other and their teammates.

Harry was speechless. Dad patted him on the back and said, 'The boys were a credit to you and the school. They couldn't have done more.'

'They gave it everything,' Jack said.

'They were the core of the team,' Gavin added. 'Born leaders, the three of them.'

Marion said, 'Fuck Rockford Manor and every prick who goes there.'

We all burst out laughing and the sting of losing was slightly lessened.

37. Louise

Clara gripped her blanket as the plane took off. 'How long exactly until we land?' she asked, eyes wide.

'It should be three hours and five minutes, but it depends on winds and air traffic.'

'What if we get stuck in the sky?'

'Clara, planes don't get stuck in the sky. There are flights every day from Dublin to Rome. They always land.'

'Planes can crash, Mummy.'

'I know, but they very, very rarely do.'

'I wish Luna was here.' Clara's hands began to flap.

'Christelle and Kelly will look after her so well. She'll get lots of cuddles.'

'She'll miss me.'

'Yes, pet, but we'll be back in three days.'

'Seventy-six-and-a-half hours.'

'Yes, as long as nothing is delayed, which hopefully it won't be.'

'What if the car you hired breaks down?'

'It won't, Clara. I've booked the most reliable, safest car they have.'

'What if . . . what if . . . Anna doesn't love me?'

'Oh, sweetheart, of course she will. She loves you already from your calls.'

'Lots of people in school don't love me or even like me.'

'Well, they're just stupid.'

'No, Mummy. Oliver is very smart. He gets almost as good grades as me.'

'I mean emotionally stupid, immature. They don't see how incredible you are.'

Clara sighed. 'Sometimes I really wish I was like other kids. Life would be much easier. I'd understand games and jokes and I wouldn't feel strange.'

Oh, Clara, my beautiful, precious Clara.

'Darling, no two people are the same. And, yes, I know that having autism makes life more difficult. I understand that it's harder for you to navigate the world than for other people, but that's your superpower. You see the world from a different angle. It's what makes you unique and incredible.'

'That's what Granny used to say.'

'Granny was a very wise woman.' Thank you, Mum, for loving Clara with all of your heart, I thought, for the millionth time.

'What if the pilot gets sick and we have to land somewhere else?' Clara's eyes were wide again.

I knew this could go on for hours. My head was throbbing from lack of sleep. Clara had come to me five times the night before to ask questions and check the travel schedule.

'Will I put on *Casablanca* for you?'

'Okay.'

Yes!

She put on her big headphones and I played the movie. I sank back into my seat and closed my eyes. Hopefully we wouldn't be delayed landing and the queue for car hire would not be long. Clara didn't do well in crowded public places. I was also terrified she'd have a meltdown when she got to Marco's place. I had a knot in my stomach. I still wasn't even sure I was doing the right thing. She said she wanted to go to see her dad and meet her *nonna*, but would she actually be able for it? Were we moving too fast?

*

I stopped the car halfway down the lane to the farmhouse and turned to Clara. 'If you have any doubts, we can turn back. You don't have to do anything you don't want to.'

'I want to do it.'

'Okay.' I started the car.

'But, Mummy?'

'Yes?'

'Will you hold my hand?'

'Of course I will, and I won't let go until you say it's okay.'

Marco was outside waiting for us. I'd texted to say what time we'd be arriving. He waved his arms in the air and ran towards the car. I signalled at him to calm down.

He stood back and let Clara open the door.

'*Amore,*' he said.

'Hi.' She was shy. I got out and went around to her. I felt her hand slip into mine.

Marco resisted hugging her. 'Welcome to my house,' he said.

'It's much bigger than it looks in photos,' Clara said. 'I don't like the colour of your shutters.'

Marco laughed. 'We'll change them and you can choose the colour. Now, will you come in and meet my mother? She is preparing the cake for you.'

Clara hesitated, then tentatively followed Marco inside, still holding my hand.

'Come, come.' Marco opened the door to the kitchen.

I could feel Clara tense. Anna turned around and squealed. She came rushing over with her arms outstretched.

'No, Mamma,' Marco warned her.

She pushed him aside and shuffled straight over to us. Clara squeezed my hand. I tried to put out my arm to stop Anna, but she was not to be deterred. She put her hands up to Clara's face, looked into her eyes and said, '*Mia cara* Claretta.'

Clara was frozen to the spot. None of us moved.

Slowly, Clara let go of my hand and put it on her grand-mother's shoulder. She gently pulled back. 'I am glad to meet you, but please don't touch my face.'

Marco translated. His mother dropped her hands and spoke to him.

'She is very sorry. She is just so excited to meet you at last.' Anna nodded, she turned to the oven and took out a freshly baked cake. '*Torta per* Claretta,' she said.

She cut slices while we sat down and handed one to Clara.

Clara looked at it and pushed it away. 'It's soggy. I can't eat soggy food.'

'Marco, can you please explain to your mother that it's not the cake. Clara just has issues with the texture of food.'

To make up for Anna's disappointment, I ate my slice and Clara's.

Clara looked around the kitchen. 'Everything is very old here.'

Marco laughed. 'Yes, we 'ave lived here for a long time. We like the old things. They 'ave memories.'

'It smells funny.' Clara sniffed the air. 'Everything is different. It's not home . . . it's . . .' I saw her hands flapping. I could see her cheeks were flushed.

I was too late to stop it. She began to rock, then cry, scream and hyperventilate. I had to get her out. I half carried her to the car and sat her in the back seat. I climbed in beside her. I didn't touch her. I knew I had to let this run its course. I handed her her blanket and played 'Fernando' on my phone.

She cried and cried. Marco and his mother stood at the front door with tears streaming down their faces. I left Clara and went over to them.

'I'm sorry,' he said.

'It's okay. It's just a lot for her to take in.'

'Do you want to leave?'

'No. We need to let her calm down. She has her blanket and her music and she needs quiet now. I'm going to sit beside her until she feels better. It could be a while. Why don't you go inside and I'll come and get you?'

Twenty minutes later, Clara stopped rocking and crying. She laid her head against the seat in front. 'I want to go home, Mummy,' she whispered.

'Okay, sweetheart. We'll go. Let me just tell Marco and Anna.'

Marco was crushed. Before we left, he asked if he could show Clara something he had got for her. I wasn't sure, but I felt bad about the whole fiasco, so I said okay.

He came over to the car holding a tiny chocolate Labrador puppy. He had floppy ears and a black button nose.

Marco held the sleeping puppy up to the car window. Clara looked at it.

'Give her a minute,' I whispered.

She rolled down the window and took a closer look.

'This is for you. His name is Miracolo, because you are my miracle.'

I petted the puppy's sweet head. It was like velvet.

Clara tentatively reached over to the puppy. She touched his head with the tip of a finger. She didn't flinch, which was a good sign. It meant that the feel of his fur didn't bother her. She petted him again using three fingers. The puppy opened his eyes and looked up at her.

'Oooh, he's so cute,' she said.

She petted him again.

He licked her hand. Oh, no. I waited for her to pull away.

'His tongue feels just like Luna's, Mummy. It's a bit rough and scratchy.' She wiped it on her trousers.

The puppy began to whine and stretched towards Clara for more petting.

'He likes you, Claretta,' Marco said. 'My arm is getting tired. Can you 'old him for one minute?'

'Okay.'

Marco gently placed the puppy into her lap. He sat looking up at her with his big brown eyes and I watched as my daughter fell in love with him. She petted him while Marco and I watched in silence.

'He's shaking, Mummy.'

'I think he's nervous because you and I are strangers to him. Give him a cuddle,' I suggested.

She held him close and the puppy began to calm down and snuggle into her shoulder.

'Well done,' I whispered to Marco.

'I research and they say Labrador ees the best dog for the autism,' he whispered back. Then he said aloud to Clara, 'Miracolo will be 'ere for you any time you want to come and pet him.'

Clara looked up. 'I don't think I should leave him. He's only just stopped trembling. He needs me to stay and comfort him. He's scared of everything because he's so small and it's all new to him.'

'Do you want to come and give him the food, see the bed I 'ave for his sleeping?'

Clara opened the car door, careful not to disturb Miracolo, and slowly climbed out. She followed Marco back into the house to check her puppy's bed.

I followed them. I knew Clara would be exhausted and need a long sleep. Meltdowns wore her out. But I was so glad the puppy had worked its magic and got her to go back in and feel more at ease.

Anna took my hand as I walked into the kitchen.

'*Va bene*, Louisa, *tutto bene*.' She patted my hand.

I hoped she was right and that everything would be okay.

We heard laughing and peered into the back porch where Clara and Marco were giggling at the puppy, who was running in circles chasing his tail.

'He's just like Luna,' she said to Marco. 'He's like a boy and dog version of her. I love him.'

I smiled at Anna and she rubbed my back. '*Tutto bene.*'

Clara crashed out as soon as we got to the hotel. I knew she'd sleep for at least fourteen or fifteen hours. My phone had been hopping all day. It was time to fill in the family on how things had gone.

I set up a five-way chat with my siblings and Dad. All of their faces came on screen except Dad's.

'Hold your phone up higher, Dad,' Sophie said.

'All we can see are your knees,' Julie told him.

Dad rustled around and eventually got the phone to show the top half of his face. It would do.

'Well?' Julie asked.

I filled them in.

Julie reacted first. 'Poor Clara. But brilliant about the puppy.'

'Marco sounds like he really gets Clara,' Sophie said.

'That was a clever move. Labradors are the best.' Gavin was impressed.

'Will she go back tomorrow, do you think?' Dad asked.

'I think so because she said she wants to feed the puppy. But I won't know until tomorrow morning when she wakes up. Hopefully she will. Any news from home?' I was happy to be distracted with other news.

'Tell her about Pippa,' Julie told Sophie.

'She's signed over full custody of Robert to Jack.'

'Wow, how does Jack feel?'

'He's gutted for Robert that his mum has basically dumped

him, but he's happy that he doesn't have to worry about his boy being with her if she falls off the wagon.'

'Are you okay about it?'

Sophie shrugged. 'I have no choice. What can I do? He's Jack's son and I love him. He's a great kid. Do I want to raise a little boy who is not technically mine? Not really, no, but he's part of our family and we'll muddle through.'

'I hope Jack is giving you all the kudos you deserve,' Julie said.

Sophie smiled. 'He is. In fact . . .' She waved her hand in front of the camera.

'OMG, is that a ring?' Julie gasped.

'Yep. Jack asked me to marry him.'

'Sure, you're already married.' Dad was confused.

'Divorced, Dad, remember. We're going to get remarried.'

'Lord save us, married to the same fellow twice.'

Ignoring Dad, I congratulated my sister.

'Thanks. Jack wants to make us an official family again. He's very emotional about the Robert situation and he wants us to be legally married.'

'What does Jess think?' Gavin asked.

'Actually, she's thrilled. It's been really sweet to see how happy she is. She's currently spending hours looking up websites to find her bridesmaid's dress.'

'Damn, I was hoping to put on a big pouffy dress and be your bridesmaid.' Julie laughed.

'Do I have to make a speech?' Dad asked.

'Just make the same one you did last time.' Gavin chuckled.

'Ha-ha, very funny. No, Dad, no speeches. It'll just be a really small family wedding. Nothing like the circus our first wedding was. We're going to the registry office and then having a family lunch at home. I don't need two hundred guests, some of whom I barely know. I just want you guys. It's kind of a new beginning for us, now we're officially a family of four. Jack really wants to do it, so I'm going with it. It'll be nice and Jess is so thrilled. It's so lovely to see her excited about something again. I think she was always secretly worried that Jack and I might break up again, so I'm happy to show her that we're fully committed to each other.'

'Can we do it abroad, somewhere warm and sunny?' Julie asked.

'Yes! Shania and I could do with a break,' Gavin agreed.

'Poor you. Are you worn out working part-time?' I smirked at him.

'Yes, actually, I am, because it's not part-time. Three weeks in and I'm running the whole production side of the business already and looking after Lemon in the afternoons. I don't want to hear any more crap about men not being able to multitask.'

'Good for you,' Julie said. 'I need a better balance in my life. I'm too invested in the kids. I need something for me.'

'Go for it, Julie. It would be good for you to have your own identity outside the house,' I encouraged her.

'It really helped me,' Sophie admitted. 'Although I was forced back to work due to being broke, I enjoyed earning my own money. It gave me my confidence back. Mind you, I have to admit that the modelling world is losing its shine for me, and with Robert to look after and his school schedule, it's going to be tricky to juggle the long hours. I need to have a chat with Jack and really dig down into how we're going to manage everything going forward.'

'It'll be hard on you, Sophie,' Julie said.

'I know, but it's my new reality.'

'How are you, Dad?' I asked.

'Ah, sure, ticking along.'

'With Pat by his side,' Julie added.

'Really? More dates?' I raised an eyebrow at Dad.

Dad cleared his throat. 'A few.'

'Do you like her?' Sophie asked.

'She's a nice woman. A lot more considerate and kind than Dolores. Less forceful.'

'She always seemed nice,' I said.

'Bring her over for coffee next week,' Julie said.

'Really?' Dad was surprised.

'You deserve to have companionship in your life, and I'd like to have her over.'

'Can I come?' Sophie asked.

'Me too. Can you do afternoon coffee?' Gavin asked.

'Me three. I'll be home on Sunday and I'm still on leave from work.'

'I'd better go, Lemon's kicking off,' Gavin said, as Lemon roared in the background.

'Hold on!' Sophie waved her hands.

'What?' Gavin asked.

'Are you all free the weekend of the 12th?'

'Yes,' we all answered.

'Good, because Jack and I are going to get married on the Saturday, and after the registry office bit we want you to come to a lunch here at the house to celebrate.'

'Amazing!' Julie said.

'Suits me,' I said.

'Deadly!' Gavin grinned. 'I'll let Shania know.'

'Pat is welcome to come too, Dad.' Sophie smiled.

'Ah, hold on a minute now, we're just pals. It's a bit early for family weddings.' Dad was taken aback.

'I just don't want you to be lonely,' Sophie said.

'I'm always lonely, but I'm learning to live with it and getting used to the quiet.'

'Mum would be so happy you and Jack are getting married again, Sophie,' Julie said.

'She loved a wedding,' I added.

'Stop,' Sophie sniffed. 'I wish with all my heart she was coming.'

So did I, and I wished she was there with me right now, helping me and Clara to navigate this new part of her life. And mine.

Italy

Louise looked around to make sure everything was perfect. She wanted today to be a day of pure celebration. It had been the toughest year of her life, yet incredible things had happened too.

'Thanks, Mum,' she whispered at the blue Italian sky. 'Thanks for sending Marco and Anna to me.' Louise saw her mother in Anna. The way she adored Clara, the way she looked at her as if her heart would burst with love. She still tried to touch Clara too much, but Clara was getting used to her and Anna was getting better at holding back and waiting for Clara to hold her hand or hug her.

Louise felt lighter in Italy. Away from all the stress of work and having to drag Clara to school and fast city living. It was only when you removed yourself from your life that you realized how much of a hamster wheel you were on. When she woke up in the morning, her heart wasn't pounding and her mind racing with all the things she had to do. Here, she woke up when Clara came into her room and they did everything slowly and calmly, no rushing, no having to be anywhere by a particular time. It was bliss, and Clara seemed really content. She was even spending time outside with Marco on the farm and had got a little colour on her usually ghostly white face.

Louise counted the chairs again, nineteen plus Lemon. Yes, there was one for everyone who was coming. The villa she had rented was quite small, but it had the most beautiful garden with a view of the rolling hills of Lazio. She had set up the long trestle table under the hanging vines. Today was

going to be a celebration of Clara's tenth birthday and everyone who mattered would be here. Everyone who had come
into their lives, at different stages, for different reasons.
Louise also wanted to celebrate Sophie and Jack's wedding,
the triplets and Jess turning sixteen, Marco and Anna coming
into their family. The only pang, the only sadness was Mum.
If only Mum could have been here . . .

'Mummy, do you think Miracolo will be okay with all the
people coming?' Clara asked.

'Yes, sweetheart. I'm sure he'll be happy to meet Granddad, and your uncles and aunts and cousins.'

'Yes, I suppose he will.'

'Are you looking forward to the party?'

'Kind of. I want to see everyone and show them Miracolo,
but I'm worried it will get super-noisy.'

'Well, whenever you want, you can go to bed. I've closed
the shutters and the windows so the noise won't be loud in
your room.'

She nodded. 'Okay, Mummy. Come on, Miracolo. Let's
go to the gate and see if anyone is coming.' Clara led her
beloved puppy down the lane to the gate. She looked calm
and happy.

Everyone arrived at the same time, with wine, flowers,
gifts for Clara, chatting and laughing, oohing and aahing over
the beautiful garden and sweet villa. They were all introduced
to Anna, and with broken English and Italian, sign language
and hugs, they all connected.

Anna pointed to Clara, then her heart, and said, '*Miracolo.*'

They all nodded, yes, she was, and yes, this whole situation
was a miracle.

Louise, with Marco's help, served everyone drinks. 'Oh.
Louise, it's like being in a movie.' Sophie gasped at the view.

'Spectacular,' Jack agreed, holding her hand.

'Harry, can we buy a place here?' Julie asked. 'I never want to leave.'

'Yes, please,' Christelle and Kelly chimed in

'Hang on, it's nice and all, but we're not staying more than a week.' Leo looked horrified at the prospect of being stuck in a remote village.

'We had a deal, Mum,' Liam reminded her.

'Like, it's a bit dead,' Luke said.

Harry took charge. 'Why don't you go and grab a cold drink and talk to the birthday girl?'

The triplets took Robert to where Clara was introducing Miracolo to Tom.

The puppy was sitting in her lap. 'You have to be extremely gentle. He's still only a puppy and he doesn't like meeting new people, just like I don't.'

Tom reached over and very gently stroked him. 'You're so lucky,' he said. 'I wish we had a dog, but Mum said our house is already like a zoo, so we're not getting one.'

'My daddy says I can have as many animals as I want. He's so nice. Look, Miracolo likes to be scratched behind the ears.' Clara showed her cousin.

'He's so cute,' Liam said.

'My daddy says we can get a dog when I'm a bit older,' Robert said.

Clara nodded. 'I think you need to be at least nine before you can get one, because you need to look after them and take them for walks.'

Jess stood beside her mum, happy to chat to the adults for a while.

'I see you're wearing your gran's necklace again,' Julie said to Jess.

'Yes. It was only on loan to my mum for her wedding.' Jess touched the Tiffany heart necklace that her granny had given her on her thirteenth birthday.

Sophie kissed her daughter's head. 'When Jess said I needed something borrowed for the wedding and gave me her precious necklace, I was so touched. Honestly, if it wasn't for waterproof mascara, I would have arrived at the registry office looking like Alice Cooper.' She laughed. 'It was such a gorgeous thing to do.'

'That's our Jess, thoughtful and kind.' Jack put his arm around her. 'Just like her mum.'

'Oh, God, you're all loved up after the wedding. How long is this mushy stuff going to last?' Julie fake-groaned.

'Hopefully for ever.'

Sophie laughed. 'Okay, Jack, let's be realistic.'

'I am. I've always loved Sophie, but I've been blown away by how incredible she's been about the whole Pippa and Robert situation. She didn't sign up to be a full-time mum to him, but she's been unbelievable, and I'm so grateful. I'm crazy about her.'

'Julie was incredible about Christelle too. These Devlin women are pretty special,' Harry said.

'Agreed. Julie has been the best stepmother ever.' Christelle was effusive.

'Yes, and Louisa is so kind to share Clara with me,' Marco said.

'Yeah, yeah, the women are all amazing. What am I, then?' Gavin demanded.

'You're great too, babe.' Shania patted his back reassuringly. 'You're just outnumbered three to one.' She laughed.

As they sat in the beautiful garden, overlooking the hills, Julie watched her niece playing with Tom and Robert.

'Clara seems so happy,' she said. 'I've never seen her look like that before, to be honest, so relaxed.'

Clara had lost her pallor and the anxious look in her eyes. She had colour in her cheeks, her eyes sparkled and she seemed happy. Genuinely happy.

Louise's face lit up. 'She is. She's spending more time outdoors than ever before. She helps Marco on the farm and he gives her little jobs to do, which she loves. We also spent the week doing up her bedroom in the farmhouse and making it Clara-friendly. We added lamps and soft rugs and I brought over her second-favourite blanket and copies of her favourite books. And we painted the room a pale lilac, so the whole feeling when you enter the bedroom now is of calm. Clara loves it.'

Dad squeezed her shoulder. 'That's fantastic, Louise. You did the right thing finding Marco.' He turned to Marco. 'You're wonderful with Clara and we all appreciate it.'

'Thank you, George. That is making me so 'appy to 'ave the approval of the grandfather.'

'She's as happy as I've ever seen her, the little dote. Anne would be so pleased.'

'Thanks, Dad.' Louise leaned her head on his shoulder.

To her left, Sophie could see Jess and the triplets bending over a phone. She sat back in her chair so she could hear them.

'What about him?' Luke asked.

'Not my type.' Jess shook her head.

'Okay, him?' Liam swiped the screen.

'Maybe,' Jess said.

'He's a really nice bloke, not like Voldemort.'

They all cracked up laughing and Sophie's heart lifted. If Jess was able to laugh with her cousins about Sebastian, it was truly behind her.

'How is Voldemort?' Jess asked.

'Still a total arsehole, but a much less arrogant one. What-ever our mums said or did to him seriously humbled him.'

'Our mums are kind of badass,' Jess said.

'Yeah, Mum will never tell us, but I bet they set Louise on him. I'd be terrified if she came after me,' Leo said.

'Jeez, me too.'

'Me three.'

'Me four,' Jess said.

They all giggled.

'She's a brilliant aunt. Louise will always have your back,' Jess said. 'Just like you guys had mine. Thanks for that.'

The triplets shrugged. 'You're family,' Liam said.

Jess beamed. 'Thanks.'

Luke stood up. 'Right, Jess, boys, let's play a bit of footie. Come on, Robert, Tom, let's see how good you are.'

'Dad? Jack? Marco? Granddad? Gavin? Christelle, Kelly? Football?'

'Sure,' Harry said.

'Yes!' Jack said.

'Bring it on.' Kelly jumped up, followed by Christelle.

'My hip is at me,' Dad said.

'Give me ten minutes.' Gavin was feeding Lemon.

'I can feed her.' Shania held out her hands to take her daughter.

'No, I'm knackered. I want the excuse,' Gavin whispered.

'*Sì*, football.' Marco was straight up and over to the boys.

'I'm striker,' Jess said.

'I goalie,' Marco said.

'Other goalie,' Harry said.

'Defence.' Jack stretched his hamstrings.

Anna went over to sit with Clara, who was playing with Miracolo.

The rest of the family sat at the table, watching the stunning sight as the sun set behind the hills. Louise came out with two bottles of champagne.

'I kept these for a family toast.' She poured the glasses and raised hers. 'Thank you all for being here. It honestly means the world to me that you all came over to see us in Italy, meet Anna and celebrate Clara's birthday, but this is a celebration of so much more. It's a celebration of my family. I honestly could not have got through the last year without your support.'

'Right back at you,' Julie said.

'I feel the same,' Sophie added.

'It's a magical place,' Julie noted. 'Thanks so much for having us all over.'

They watched Clara playing with Miracolo while Anna looked on, beaming at her granddaughter.

'Clara seems to have warmed to Anna,' Julie said.

'Yes, she has. It was a slow start and I really had to be firm with Anna and ban her from touching Clara, but she gets it now and she's taking it slowly. Clara let her hug her for three seconds yesterday, which was a big breakthrough.'

'I'm so glad it all worked out with Marco too. He's fantastic with her,' Julie said.

'He really is. Honestly, Julie, I couldn't have wished for a better dad. He's so gentle and caring with her.'

'Like Dad with us,' Sophie added.

'Ah, now, I wasn't half as hands-on as all you modern dads,' Dad admitted. 'Anne did the heavy lifting.'

'They were different times, Dad, and you were always there when we needed you,' Sophie reassured him.

'I see Gavin there with Lemon and I have to say, son, you're brilliant with her.'

Gavin looked shocked. 'Uhm, thanks.'

'He so is. He's the best daddy in the world. Honestly, he's much better with her than I am. I'd be lost without him by my side,' Shania gushed.

They beamed at each other over Lemon's bald head.

'Here, babe, let me take her and put her down. You enjoy your champagne. I'll be back in a bit.' Shania took Lemon inside.

'I'd say Clara will find it hard to leave this heavenly place, and especially to leave Miracolo,' Sophie said. 'She's devoted to that puppy. Could you bring him back to Dublin?'

Louise paused. Then, smiling at us, she said, 'Actually, we're not going home.'

Every face turned to stare at her. 'What?'

'Clara told me she wanted to stay here. She said she feels safe here and less stressed because it's not noisy and busy like Dublin. I've thought about it long and hard and I'm going to give it a go. I've rented this house for a year. I'll home-school Clara and she can live between me and Marco. Actually, Dad, I'll need you to keep looking after Luna until I can organize for her to be sent over.'

'Oh, my God, that's huge news,' Julie gasped. Louise was not a risk-taker: this was a big decision.

'What about work?' Sophie asked.

'I've handed in my notice. The whole Zoë drama really made me think: what do I want? And, Gavin, what you said about working in academia stuck with me. I contacted the head of the law department at Trinity College, whom I know from days of old, and she said they'd be happy to have me. I start lecturing in September. I can do a lot of it online, so if we do decide to stay here longer term, I can commute to Dublin when I need to.'

'But you're such a city person, won't you get lonely here?' Julie asked.

'I'd go anywhere to see Clara happy. And I'll have to fly home at least once a month to deliver in-person lectures, so I'll have the best of both worlds. Besides, having Marco to share parenting has been a huge relief. It's taken the full burden off my shoulders.'

'I'm going to miss you so much.' Julie sniffed. Louise was her person. She had always been a rock of sense, the person Julie went to when she was overwhelmed or needed to make an important decision. And even though she and Sophie had made up after their argument, there was still a little distance between them. She knew it would pass with time, but she would miss Louise desperately.

'You can come and visit any time,' Louise told her, 'and we'll make a date every month to meet for dinner when I'm back.'

Sophie raised her glass. 'Well, cheers to you, Louise. You're incredible. This is going to be fantastic for Clara, and for you too.'

Gavin nodded. 'It's brilliant. I've never seen Clara so happy. Are you and Marco getting together?'

'God, no.' Louise snorted into her drink.

'He's a great guy.'

'He's not my type.'

'He was once.' Gavin winked at her.

'Once was enough. I have, however, hired a very attractive Italian language teacher.' Louise grinned.

'Sex under the Tuscan sky.' Sophie smirked.

'We're in Lazio.'

'Fine. Love and lust in Lazio,' Sophie replied.

'Maybe.' Louise laughed. 'Honestly, I feel freer and less weighed down than I have in so long. Clara's happy and I have help with her from someone who loves her and is as much invested in her wellbeing as I am. I know now that I can leave Clara with Marco and trust that she will be completely safe, loved and cherished. I'm looking forward to this new adventure. And the best part is, I don't have to deal with or put up with any bullshit office politics.'

'Cheers to that!' Julie clinked her glass.

They could hear Lemon howling inside the house and Shania trying to soothe her.

'Kids are kind of always there, aren't they?' Gavin said. 'Like, always, every minute of every day.'

'And they get needier and more difficult to manage,' Sophie told him.

'And hormonal and moody.' Julie smiled sweetly at her brother.

'And more complicated and more of a worry,' Louise piled on.

'Great, thanks. Any more helpful tips?' Gavin grumbled.

'Yes, you love them more every day, in spite all of that,' Sophie said.

'I've realized that you would do anything for your child's happiness, because it means everything,' Louise added.

'And I can tell you that you become even prouder of your children as you see how they handle life's adversities. I'm very proud of you, Louise,' Dad put in.

Everyone's eyes filled. Louise was a walking example of what a mother's love meant. She had moved Heaven and Earth for Clara but, funnily enough, she had found happiness for herself in the process.

'You know,' Sophie said, 'the whole Robert situation is forcing me to reassess my situation too. Jack travels a lot with work and I can't look after Robert with my current hours. Also, I want to be around more for Jess. I've been thinking about retraining.'

'As what?' Julie asked.

'A special-needs assistant. The course is only ten weeks long and then I get to train in the classroom. I was thinking I could get a job in Robert's school or a school nearby. Then I'd be around for him and Jess in the afternoons.'

'That sounds amazing, Sophie,' Julie said. 'Brilliant idea.'

'It would be a big drop in salary,' Louise, the ever practical sister, observed.

Sophie nodded. 'Don't worry, I've thought about that. I've been able to save a good bit of money since Jack and I got back together and, thanks to your advice, I've invested it wisely. I think I can do this without too much risk, and it'll make a huge difference to our family life.'

'Good girl, Sophie. That's absolutely fantastic. The poor little fellow needs a proper mother in his life. God knows he's had a useless one,' Dad said.

'Yes, but it is a big decision,' Julie said. 'It's a lot of sacrifice from Sophie for Jack's child.'

Sophie agreed with her sister. But she wasn't just doing this for Robert. She was tired of the modelling game, and after finding out that Sebastian had been in their house in the afternoon while she was at work, she realized that Jess had too much unsupervised time after school to get into mischief. She needed to be around more, needed to get on top of things.

'It's a big change but I've made a commitment to be with Jack, and Robert is part of the package. If I've learned anything this year, it's that you can't fight what you can't control. Jack has full custody now, so we're a family of four. I also want to be around to help the transition for Jess too. And, to be honest, the modelling world has lost its shine. It's time to move on.'

Julie was proud of her sister: she had changed so much in the last ten years. She had grown into a selfless, caring, sensible and strong person. Ten years ago she would have thought Sophie as a special-needs assistant was a crazy idea, but it made sense for her sister now and the person she had become.

'Your mother would be very proud of you, Sophie, and of you, Louise, making brave decisions for your children's sake,' Dad said.

'What about me and Julie?' Gavin said.

'He's already praised you,' Julie pointed out. 'And you have the part-time working and parenting thing sorted out. I'm the one who seems to be standing still.'

'You've had a crazy year too,' Louise said.

'Yes, but the triplets will be gone soon, and Tom will be off with his friends, and where does that leave me? I don't have anything but motherhood on my CV.'

'Well, you're in the lucky position of being financially able to do anything you want,' Sophie said.

'I know, but who wants to hire a woman who hasn't worked outside the home in sixteen years?'

'Retrain like Sophie or go back to college.' Louise was blunt.

Julie felt uncomfortable, she didn't know what she wanted to do or was good at or could offer the world. She could make a mean chicken piri-piri and do three batches of laundry a day, but who wanted that?

'What about writing again? You loved doing your blog and your column on parenting,' Gavin suggested.

Louise sat up. 'Yes! You could do an MA in creative writing. It would give you the time and space to figure out your next move. You're brilliant with words – I bet you'd love it.'

Julie hadn't thought about writing in so long. After her column had dried up, she'd kind of got lost in motherhood again. She had loved writing, Gavin was right. She'd forgotten how much. But would she be able for an MA? 'I'm only used to doing a piddly little column, not writing literary prose.'

'You'd be well able. In fact, I'll do it with you,' Dad said. 'I've always wanted to do a writing course. Your mother always said she loved my letters to her. It'd keep me busy and who knows what might come out of it? Sure, we'd have fun anyway and be learning, and we could critique each other's work.'

'That would so fantastic,' Sophie said, laughing. 'Unexpected, I grant you, but fantastic.'

Hang on a minute. Did Julie want to go back to college, and with her dad? Was that going to be fun or a total nightmare? She looked at her father's excited face. This was all a bit mad and quick, but what the hell? At her age, she had nothing to lose. Why not just go for it? And she did love writing, and she did miss it, and with her dad by her side she'd be less nervous.

'Okay.' She smiled at her father. 'Let's see which college will take in two very mature students with very little experience.'

Dad stuck out his hand. 'Deal.'

Julie and her dad shook hands, while the others whooped.

The footballers, sweaty and dusty after their game, came over and plonked themselves down.

'What have you Devlins been chatting about?' Harry asked.

The Devlins laughed.

'We've just been setting the world to rights,' Julie told him.

There was a loud clinking sound. Everyone turned around. It was Dad. He was standing on the steps of the villa, tapping his glass loudly with a fork. 'Before the night is over, I want to say a few words.'

'I'm tired, and Miracolo wants to go to bed. Will you be quick, Granddad?' Clara asked.

'I really need to go and help Shania with Lemon,' Gavin said.

'For the love of God, will you all just listen for a few minutes?' Dad huffed.

'Keep your hair on, Granddad.' Clara giggled.

'Clara made a joke!' Luke high-fived his cousin and everyone cheered.

'The hair you have left.' Tom chuckled.

'The comb-over.' Leo snorted.

'Leave your granddad alone.' Sophie shushed them.

Dad pulled his shoulders back, cleared his throat and began to speak: 'First of all, thank you, Louise, for treating us to this magnificent villa. Life's not been easy since your mother passed. But many wonderful things have happened too. I didn't expect to be giving my youngest daughter away to the same man twice, but they were meant to be and I'm delighted they've committed to each other again. Sophie, I've always been proud of you, but I've never been prouder than to see how you've welcomed Robert into your life, like one of your own. That takes a big heart and you've always had that. You are also a wonderful mother to our beautiful Jess.

'I'm proud of all my children. Julie, I wasn't sure when they were young tearaways, but your triplets have grown into three exceptional young men, who gave us so much joy and pride this year. And, Tom, you're just like your mum, kind, generous and a friend to all. Christelle, you were the loveliest addition to Julie and Harry's brood, and Kelly is the perfect match for you.

'Louise, our smart, tough eldest child, you've probably surprised me the most. The way you've loved and nurtured Clara has been a revelation to us all. Clara is the luckiest girl in the world to have you as her mother, and we welcome Marco and Anna into our family too. You're a wonderful addition to the Devlin clan. Clara, you will always be our little star.

'And now for my youngest and, let's be honest, the slowest burner. Gavin, I know I've given you a hard time, but you've grown up a lot in the last couple of years and I credit Shania for a lot of that. When I see you with Lemon – I'll eventually get used to the name – I see a natural-born father. She's a lucky little girl. I don't tell you enough, but I'm very proud of you, son.

'Every family occasion will always have a little sadness to it now that Anne isn't here. I miss her every day, but when you love someone and have been together for more than fifty years, you know that when they go the loss will be devastating. I know, wherever she is, that Anne is smiling down on us today.

'So here's to you, Anne, and our messy, complicated, brilliant family. I couldn't be prouder of every single person here today. Cheers.'

'Granddad, you didn't include Miracolo.'

'I'm so sorry, Clara. I can't believe I left him out. I'm proud of every single person here today and of our newest family member, Miracolo.'

They raised their glasses and cheered as the sun set behind the hills and an imperfect family's perfect day came to a close.

Acknowledgements

I have loved going back to see what happens to the Devlin sisters after so many years. This book was a joy to write. I had a lot of fun with it. I hope you enjoy it and that it brings laughter as well as tears.

A big thank-you goes to Rachel Pierce, my editor, who, in my opinion, is the best editor in the business.

Thanks to: Patricia Deevy, for her invaluable input and being such a rock. Michael McLoughlin, Cliona Lewis, Carrie Anderson, Laura Dermody and all the team at Sandycove for their continued support and help. To all in the Penguin UK office, especially Tom Weldon, and the fantastic sales, marketing and creative teams.

To my agent Marianne Gunn O'Connor for her encouragement, championing and friendship. To Hazel Orme, for her wonderful copy-editing and for being such a positive force.

To my fellow writers, my tribe, thanks for your support, encouragement and for always knowing when a kind word of encouragement or a coffee is needed.

To my mum, sister, brother and extended family. Thanks for always being there.

To all of my friends – thanks for your love and loyalty and for all the laughs.

To Hugo, Geordy and Amy, my three teenagers, who sometimes drive me nuts yet never, ever, cease to make my heart sing.

To Troy, for everything.